D1590073

Mystery Charle
Charles, Ann, 1971-
Rattling the heat in Deadwood /
$14.99   on1017739780

IN DEADWOOD

"Whip-smart. Hilariously funny. I'm packing my bags and moving to Deadwood."
   ~**Pamela DuMond**, USA Today Bestselling Author

"Fasten your seatbelt and get ready for another Deadwood roller coaster ride! Violet and the gang are back, and the stakes couldn't be higher. I loved it!!"
   ~**Kristy McCaffrey**, Author of the Award-Winning Wings of the West Series

"Hilarious, exciting, suspenseful, a touch creepy, and enough steam to power a sauna … Violet and the Deadwood Crew deliver it all. This book is unputdownable!"
   ~**Elaina Boudreaux**, Deadwood Mystery Series Fan

"*Rattling the Heat in Deadwood* is a galloping, good ride down the ghostly trail through Deadwood. Shine up your boots and polish up your spurs for another unforgettable, exciting adventure with Ann Charles."
   ~**Craig Watts Scott**, Pastor, Liberty Station Cowboy Church

For more on Ann and her books, check out her website, as well as the reader reviews for her books on Amazon, Barnes & Noble, and Goodreads.

WITHDRAWN

Dear Reader,

Before you dig into this eighth book in the Deadwood Mystery series, I want to point out a couple of things.

First, this book happens on the Deadwood series' timeline prior to Tequila & Time, the fourth in my Deadwood Shorts collection. I guess you could say it's sort of a prequel to that short story—a nice, lengthy prequel with one particular subplot or "thread" that leads up to the tale of Natalie and Violet's adventures with tequila at the Purple Door Saloon.

Second, in this story we're going to revisit the case involving Ms. Wolff from An Ex to Grind in Deadwood (the fifth book in the Deadwood Mystery series). Previously, Violet found out the what, how, and when of that mystery, but she still didn't know the who or why. Violet wasn't the only one curious about these last two answers. A couple of Deadwood detectives (aka "the Heat") had a vested interest, too, which led in part to how I came up for the title for this book.

While writing about Violet's latest mishaps in Rattling the Heat in Deadwood, I laughed, flinched, grimaced, and covered my eyes many times. How one woman can take as much as Violet does is beyond me, but I guess being a single mom of twins prepared her for a wagonload of insanity.

Ol' man Harvey sends his love and this bit of advice: "If you climb in the saddle, be ready for the ride."

Enjoy the ride!
Ann

Ann Charles

www.anncharles.com

BATTLING THE
HEAT
IN DEADWOOD

ANN CHARLES

Illustrated by C.S. Kunkle

To Laura
The nicest sister ever!
(shhh ... don't tell Shell)

Rattling the Heat in Deadwood

Copyright © 2017 by Ann Charles

All rights reserved. Except as permitted under the U.S. Copyright Act of 1976, no part of this publication may be reproduced, distributed, or transmitted in any form or by any means now known or hereafter invented, or stored in a database or retrieval system, without the prior written permission of the author, Ann Charles.

This book is a work of fiction. Names, characters, places, and incidents are the product of the author's imagination or are used fictitiously. Any resemblance to actual persons, living or dead, business establishments, events, or locales is coincidental.

Cover Art by C.S. Kunkle
Cover Design by B Biddles
Editing by Eilis Flynn
Formatting by B Biddles

Library of Congress: 2017914210
E-book ISBN-13: 978-1-940364-52-0
Print ISBN-:13: 978-1-940364-53-7

Acknowledgments

Once again, I have many people to thank for their help with this book.

My husband for helping day after day with plotting, editing, formatting, cover design, and so much more.

My kids for understanding why I had to work sometimes instead of gaming with them.

I'd also like to thank the following amazing folks:

My First Draft team: Margo Taylor, Mary Ida Kunkle, Kristy McCaffrey, Jacquie Rogers, Marcia Britton, Paul Franklin, Diane Garland, Vicki Huskey, Lucinda Nelson, Marguerite Phipps, Stephanie Kunkle, and Wendy Gildersleeve. You having my back gives me the courage to keep plowing forward.

My editor, Eilis Flynn, for clarifying blonde vs. blond and making me look good on the page.

My Beta Team for giving me excellent feedback in such a short timeframe.

My brother, C.S. Kunkle, for his awesome illustrations and great original cover art.

My graphic artist, Mr. Biddles, for stepping up to the task and then some.

My readers for your positive words and uplifting comments via email and social media. You are the reason I keep writing many times when I want to bang my head on the desk and succumb to my doubt demons.

Finally, my brother, Clint, for finally trimming his beard. I was tired of singing ZZ Top songs every time I looked at you.

Also by Ann Charles

Deadwood Mystery Series

Nearly Departed in Deadwood (Book 1)
Optical Delusions in Deadwood (Book 2)
Dead Case in Deadwood (Book 3)
Better Off Dead in Deadwood (Book 4)
An Ex to Grind in Deadwood (Book 5)
Meanwhile, Back in Deadwood (Book 6)
Wild Fright in Deadwood (Book 7)
Rattling the Heat in Deadwood (Book 8)
Deadwood Shorts: Seeing Trouble (Book 1.5)
Deadwood Shorts: Boot Points (Book 4.5)
Deadwood Shorts: Cold Flame (Book 6.5)
Deadwood Shorts: Tequila & Time (Book 8.5)

Jackrabbit Junction Mystery Series

Dance of the Winnebagos (Book 1)
Jackrabbit Junction Jitters (Book 2)
The Great Jackalope Stampede (Book 3)
The Rowdy Coyote Rumble (Book 4)
Jackrabbit Junction Short: The Wild Turkey Tango (Book 4.5)

Goldwash Mystery Series (a future series)

The Old Man's Back in Town (Short Story)

Dig Site Mystery Series

Look What the Wind Blew In (Book 1)
Make No Bones About It (Book 2)

Coming Next from Ann Charles

Deadwood Mystery Series

Title TBA (Book 9)

Jackrabbit Junction Mystery Series

Title TBA (Book 5)

Cast

KEY: **Character (Book # in which they appear)—Description**

Violet Lynn Parker (1,2,3,4,5,6,7,8)—Main heroine of the series, Doc's girlfriend, Aunt Zoe's niece

Willis "old man" Harvey (1,2,3,4,5,6,7,8)—Violet's sidekick and so-called bodyguard

Dane "Doc" Nyce (1,2,3,4,5,6,7,8)—Violet's boyfriend, main hero, medium

Detective "Coop" Cooper (1,2,3,4,5,6,7,8)—Deadwood and Lead's detective

Zoe Parker (1,2,3,4,5,6,7,8)—Violet's aunt and mentor in life

Layne Parker (1,2,3,4,5,6,7,8)—Violet's nine-year-old son

Adelynn Parker (1,2,3,4,5,6,7,8)—Violet's nine-year-old daughter

Natalie Beals (1,2,3,4,5,6,7,8)—Violet's best friend since childhood

Jerry Russo (4,5,6,7,8)—Violet's boss, owner of Calamity Jane Realty

Mona Hollister (1,2,3,4,5,6,7,8)—Violet's coworker and mentor in realty

Ray Underhill (1,2,3,4,5,6,7,8)—Violet's coworker and nemesis at work

Benjamin Underhill (1,2,3,4,5,6,7,8)—Violet's coworker

Cornelius Curion (3,4,5,6,7,8)—Violet's client; so-called ghost-whisperer

Reid Martin (2,3,4,5,6,7,8)—Captain of the fire dept., Aunt Zoe's ex-lover

Jeff Wymonds (1,2,3,4,5,6,7,8)—Violet's client; dad of Adelynn's best friend

Prudence (2,3,4,5,6,7,8)—Ghost who resides at the Carhart/Britton house

Zeke and Zelda Britton (2,4,5,6,7,8)—Owners of the Carhart house in Lead

Wanda Carhart (2,3,4,5,6,7)—Previous owner of the Carhart house in Lead

Tiffany Sugarbell (1,2,3,4,5,6,7,8)—Violet's rival Realtor; Doc's ex-girlfriend

Susan Parker (1,2,3,4,5,6,7,8)—Violet's evil sister; aka "the Bitch from Hell"

Quint Parker (1,2,3,4,5,7,8)—Violet's supportive brother; Layne's hero; giver of her famous purple boots

Freesia Tender (5,6,7,8)—Owner of the Galena House

Stone Hawke (5,6,7,8)—Coop's ex-partner; detective called in to solve cases

Rex Conner (3,4,5,6,7,8)—The biological father of Violet's children

Rosy (6,7,8)—Camerawoman from TV series called "Paranormal Realty"

George & Eddie Mudder (3,6,7,8)—Owners of Mudder Bros Funeral Parlor

Dominick Masterson (4,7,8)—Owner of Sugarloaf Bldg.; previous client of Violet's old boss, Jane.

Ms. Wolff (5,8)—Previous resident of Apt. 4 in the Galena House

DEADWOOD

N W E S

Spearfish
Sturgis
85

Jackpot
Gas-N-Go

Lilly Devine's
House

Days of '76
Rodeo Grounds

Burnham

The Old Prospector
Hotel & Casino

Williams St.

Crescent Dr.

Purple Door Saloon

Railroad Ave.

Prairie Dog Palace

Candy Corral

Main St.

Madam Chow's
Restaurant

Forest Ave.

Chuckwagon Charlie's/
Charles' Club

The Wild Pasque

Tin Cup Cafe

Mt Moriah

Lucky Horseshoe
Casino

Library

Adams Museum

Mt. Moriah Dr.

Fire
Station

Main St.

Aunt Zoe's
House

Madison

Jackson

Calamity Jane Realty

Doc's Office

Upper

Old Train
Station /
Info. Center

Sherman St.

Adams

Rec Center

14

Police
Station

Doc's New House

Lead
Center City

Taco John's

Mudder Brothers
Funeral Parlor

Bighorn
Billy's

Adams House
Museum

85

Hessler House

Old Man
Harvey's
& Lead

Hospital

Important Reader Note:

If you have read my story, *Deadwood Shorts: Tequila & Time*, please note that this book, *Rattling the Heat in Deadwood*, takes place before that story begins.

Think of it as a prequel—a whole book's worth.

Enjoy!
Ann

Chapter One

Saturday, December 1st
Deadwood, South Dakota

In my world, police detectives came in two flavors: Acidic Asshole and Bitter Butthead.

On this cold, windy afternoon, I had the molar-grinding task of house hunting with …

"You're speeding again, Parker," Detective Cooper barked from the passenger seat of my Honda Pilot.

Right turn, Clyde, I heard Clint Eastwood's voice in my head. I clenched my right fist and imagined slamming it into Cooper's left cheek. But common sense prevailed before I followed in the steps of the orangutan from *Every Which Way But Loose.*

I took a deep breath, reminding myself that punching an officer of the law would most likely land me in a heap of trouble … if not jail. The probability of being slapped with an assault charge was even higher with this particular detective since I'd "accidentally" broken his nose a few months ago, and he was still clinging to a grudge about that teeny-tiny incident. The big baby.

"Relax, Detective." I spoke through gritted teeth. "I'm only going thirty-five."

"That's ten over the limit for this neighborhood. Slow down."

Detective Cooper and I had a colorful history filled with blackened eyes, blue bruises, and red welts. Months ago, as payback for breaking his nose, the jerk had thrown me in jail. He'd denied that one was related to the other, but since his nose was still bent out of shape and bandaged when he slapped the cuffs on me, leaving my wrists battered along with my reputation, I had my doubts.

Since then, he and I had exchanged plenty of insults and a healthy amount of swearing, but we'd managed to find some common ground, too. For example, besides my acting in his best interest as his Realtor, we shared a partiality for Doc Nyce, my boyfriend and Cooper's current roommate. We'd also bonded over a mutual loathing for Cooper's current crime-solving partner, Detective Stone Hawke.

Unlike Cooper, who was a decent detective except when he was harping on me for something that wasn't my fault, Hawke was a pen-clicking, brown-nosing dipshit who'd most recently mistaken me for a witch. Not the nice, sexy sort of witch either. More like the wart-covered, spell-casting type with knowledge of mind-altering potions and disfiguring hexes. I wasn't sure if this included flying broomsticks, but most days I wouldn't put it past Detective Doofus.

I slowed to thirty miles per hour, but that was as far as I was going to bend for Cooper this afternoon. "Are you telling me that you always do the speed limit?"

"Unless I'm in pursuit."

A guffaw came from the back seat. I looked in the rearview mirror at Cooper's uncle, old man Harvey, who was tagging along today to keep me out of trouble. The buzzard knew me too well when it came to his bristly nephew and my daydreams about jumping on Cooper's back and pummeling him with a rubber chicken.

"That's a whole lotta corral dust, Coop," Harvey said.

Corral dust? That was a new one for me. Harvey had a way of speaking that often left me either scratching my head or fanning my cheeks.

"I've seen you rip-roarin' through town, tearin' up the streets without your cherry lit too many times to recall."

After shooting his uncle a glare, Cooper pointed at my speedometer. "Slow down, Parker, or I'll give you a speeding ticket."

I batted Cooper's hand away. "You can't give me a ticket when you're not on duty. Hell, you're not even wearing a tie or one of those bulky police utility belts." Not to mention his short blond hair looked like he'd been trying to tear it out tuft by tuft.

Surely he'd already clocked out when I'd picked him up at the station a couple of hours ago to find a new place to call home-sweet-home. His house up in Lead was in the process of being sold, thank God. As far as I was concerned, moving Cooper out of my boyfriend's house couldn't happen soon enough. I preferred my morning-after cups of coffee with cream and sugar, not scowls and interrogations from a rigid-jawed, Daniel Craig doppelganger.

"I'm always on duty, Parker. That's something you should remember the next time you plan to break the law at one of my crime scenes."

A snicker came from behind me. "It's hard to belly through the brush when the law is planted in yer front seat, Sparky."

I slowed and pulled as far to the right as possible on the steep hillside located above Main Street while a Chevy pickup rattled past. It continued down Star Street, taking the branch onto Centennial Avenue toward downtown.

"You're one to talk," I told the old man in the mirror.

"What? I shoot straight every day, don't I, boy?" When Cooper didn't answer, Harvey reached forward and flicked his nephew's ear.

The squint Cooper aimed at his uncle would have sizzled the backside of a less ornery rooster, but after years of hanging around his nephew, Harvey had a nonflammable set of tail feathers.

"Keep it up, Uncle Willis, and I'll shoot straight, too—right at your big toe."

I pinched my lips together to keep from grinning when Cooper's focus centered on me for several seconds before returning to the windshield again.

"What's got ya so buggered up this afternoon, boy?" Harvey asked as I hit the gas and steered away from the hillside. "You should be nicer to poor Sparky. She's tryin' to help git ya situated in some new digs."

"Your uncle's right. All I want to do is warm the cockles of your heart. You know, that beating organ in your chest that's coated with glass shards and wrapped in barbed wire?"

Cooper smirked at me. That was the closest he'd come to a smile since he'd crawled into the cab with me and unzipped his leather coat. "When did you start letting Uncle Willis call you 'Sparky'?"

Harvey had taken a shine to the nickname I'd earned from the captain of Deadwood's fire department after numerous multiple-alarm incidents that also weren't my fault.

I shrugged. "I've given up on telling him to stop. You know as well as I do when it comes to your uncle that sometimes it's easier to let him do his thing."

"You can borrow money on that," Harvey agreed.

"You shouldn't encourage my uncle. It only makes him more incorrigible."

"Me?" I frowned at Cooper. "What about those illegal traps out at his ranch that you keep pretending he doesn't have?"

A sputtering sound came from the back seat. "Ain't a man allowed to defend his property anymore in this country?"

"What do you call Bessie?" Cooper asked.

Harvey had named his favorite shotgun after a cow. At least I'd always figured he borrowed the name from a cow. Maybe it came from an old flame. Harvey had enough of those flickering around the Black Hills to keep the fire department hopping.

"Bessie is my peacekeeper," Harvey explained. "But she ain't enough to scare off those damned Slagton whangdoodles on a dark night. I've been shoppin' for a cannon online."

Cooper made a choking sound. "I'd advise against it."

"A cannon?!" I gaped at Harvey in the mirror. "Who do you think you are? Yosemite Sam?"

"I'm a Hessian without no aggression," Harvey said, quoting Sam.

Chuckling, I slowed to a stop in front of one of my coworkers' new listings—a three-bedroom, two-story house built in the early 1900s high in the Forest Hill neighborhood. The roof of one of my listings, the Galena House, was visible through the bare cottonwood branches below us.

The cottage-style house out my window had been renovated recently inside and out, according to Ben Underhill, my male counterpart at Calamity Jane Realty. The updates were clear to see in spite of the growing gloom as dark clouds moved into the gulch. From the black shutters bracketing the windows to the fresh coat of gray paint with white trim on the gables and porch railing, the place looked spiffed up and ready for a new owner. I figured Cooper would like the lack of color on the exterior since his current bungalow was filled with black furniture, white curtains, and plenty of steel-gray firearms.

Cooper stared at the house, his face lined with craggy ridges. I'd seen a similar profile on a PBS show last week showcasing Ansel Adams' monochrome photograph of Manly Beacon in Death Valley National Park.

"What do you think?" I asked, letting my Honda idle. It was too dang cold to make the short hike up to the front door if he wasn't interested in the property. "It sort of looks like a storybook house, don't you think? Especially with that curly design detail at the apex of the gable."

"Curly design?" Cooper raised one eyebrow. "Do I look like the type of guy into curly things?" His gaze moved to my curly blond hair. "You have me confused with Nyce."

I bared my teeth at him. "Don't start with my hair today, Cooper. I won't be held responsible for my retaliation if you do, which may include a windmill maneuver or two."

A smile cracked his expression. The sight of it had me reaching for the door handle in case it was really a precursor to his biting me. "I could use a good laugh, Parker, especially after the bullshit going on at work."

What was going on at the police station? Was that why Cooper was being extra bristly this afternoon? Did it have anything to do with me? Detective Hawke? Both of us? Or had someone else turned up dead? Someone not linked to me for once. Wouldn't that be a treat—not that I wanted someone to die, but a distraction from my trail of suspicious crumbs would be good.

"That rock wall looks purty solid," Harvey interrupted, his nose pressed against the window. "Ya reckon they've fortified it recently? A couple decades ago they had a whoppin' bunch of problems with the walls crumblin' on this here hillside after the snow melted."

Cooper's focus shifted back to the house. "Since we're here, we might as well check it out."

Or … we could return to the police station and I could shove him out the door as I detoured through the parking lot on my way home to Aunt Zoe's kitchen and her cookie jar filled with lemon drop cookies. Personally, the cookies sounded like a better choice to me.

He opened his door, letting the freezing wind inside. "Let's go, Parker."

Unfortunately, the lemon drops would have to wait. I killed the engine, careful not to let the wind catch my door and slam it into the retaining wall Harvey had been admiring. The wind nipped at my long corduroy skirt, hurrying me along. By the time I made it to the porch steps, it had torn some of my curls free from the bobby pins I'd used this morning to keep it from morphing into an eagle's nest. Tiny pellets of ice peppered my cheeks as I climbed the steps. My fingers shook when I fished the key from the lockbox. I'd like to blame the cold for my trembling, but I had a feeling the stress of sitting so close to Detective Cooper this afternoon, putting up with his nit-picking about my speeding and more, was strumming my nerves.

"Hurry up, girl." Harvey pulled his sheepskin coat tight around his neck. "It's colder than Jack Frost's balls out here."

After pausing to wrinkle my nose at him and remind him of my new decree about his refraining from testicle-talk around me, I pushed open the door and led the way inside.

The house smelled like a mixture of old varnish and new paint. The heat had been turned down since the owners lived on the other side of the state, so I kept my red pea coat buttoned—all except for the missing one in the middle that my daughter's stupid pet chicken had undoubtedly stolen again.

Slipping off my boots, I grabbed two pair of booties from the basket on the sideboard and held them out for Cooper and Harvey. Both men looked at the shoe-coverings as if they were slimy and squirming.

"What? If you want to see the place, we have to abide by the rules. You know all about rules, remember, Detective? You were blathering on and on about obeying them all the way here."

With a wrinkled upper lip, he snatched the booties from my hand and slipped them on over his black cowboy boots. When Harvey still bucked me, I pointed at his feet. "Harvey, those shit-kickers look fresh from the pasture. Put the damned booties on or you're waiting outside in the cold."

Cooper pushed past me as I waited for Harvey to take the coverings. The clump of the detective's heels on the hardwood flooring was muffled by the booties as he moved toward what appeared to be the dining room.

As soon as I made sure Harvey had his booties in place, I sought out Cooper. He'd apparently bypassed the dining room with its gorgeous maple crown molding and lace curtains and headed for the kitchen. The modern appliances, wood floor, and can lighting gave it a warm, homey feel. Cooper, however, was too busy opening and closing the doors of the double oven to focus on his inner comforts.

"What do you think?" I asked. "Perfect for Christmas dinner, right?" Did Cooper even bake? I should ask Doc since he'd been sharing kitchen space with Cooper for over a month.

I knew from first-hand experience that Cooper's uncle baked. Harvey could give Betty Crocker a run for her money if she weren't a figment of fiction. His cooking was so delicious that I'd asked him to marry me in an effort to keep him cooking for me and my two kids until death did us part, but the bachelor refused to even consider it, saying I was too much work.

"The oven door creaks." Cooper demonstrated the issue for me.

"I'll come over and oil it once a week for you."

"The counters are low."

"They're standard height. Have you considered that maybe you're too tall in those boots?"

"The can lights are spaced too closely."

I was beginning to think I'd have better luck catching raindrops with a fishnet than finding Cooper a damned house.

"So, we've determined that the kitchen is not up to your standards." Neither were the last two kitchens we'd toured, nor the bathrooms, the bedrooms, or the garages—especially not the garages where he planned to keep his prized Harley Davidson. "Do you want to look at the rest of the house or call it a day?" *Please say call it a day.*

He walked away without answering, heading through an archway into what looked like a living room. I stayed put, not really interested in hearing his list of complaints about the rest of the house. I'd plumb run out of give-a-damn about twenty minutes ago.

Harvey grunted from the doorway. "Somebody must've put a horse chestnut on his chair this mornin'."

Or was hanging around with me making him snarl more than usual this afternoon? Cooper and I rarely spent even ten minutes in each other's company without ramming our horns together. "I vote we throw down our cards and try another hand at this game when he's not so irritable."

"I don't know." Harvey combed his beard with his fingers. "The Rocky Mountains will probably go flat before then. Although we could try gettin' him a fine heifer. Nothin' like a pair of grippin' hips and a full rack to smooth out a man's burrs."

I let his "grippin' hips" comment go without an eye-roll because he'd spurred an idea for a way to make my next house-shopping trip with Cooper less scratchy. I needed a distraction for the detective, and I had just the girl for the job—my best friend since childhood, Natalie Beals.

According to Natalie, Cooper and she had shared a brief but heated history, as in one evening at the Purple Door Saloon where some heavy flirting apparently took place. But then work had interfered and Cooper turned back into the tin man, minus the desire to find a heart. Recently, however, the tables had turned, and now Cooper was often pawing at the ground whenever she was around. Natalie, on the other hand, was in the midst of a sabbatical from men and appeared to be oblivious that the detective's hot-for-her-bod feelings had returned tenfold.

I was in the process of planning how I could trick Natalie into joining us on our next house-hunting trip when Cooper backed into the kitchen and tried to run me over. His boot heel came down on my sock-covered toes, making me howl and shove him away.

"Watch where you're stepping, Cooper." I hopped on one foot while I rubbed my toes.

"Uh, Sparky." Harvey pointed at his nephew. "I reckon his knees are about to turn to puddin'."

Harvey was right. The detective had backed as far as the kitchen counter would allow, his face noticeably pale, eyes wide. "Are you okay, Cooper?"

He stared at the archway leading to the living room. "Do you see that?"

Harvey and I both turned to look, peering into the room filled with long afternoon shadows. "See what?"

"That … that …" He shook out of his trance-like stare and scoured my face, searching for what, I had no idea. I smiled, or at least I tried to, but since my toes were still throbbing it probably came out wrinkled.

Dark red circles bloomed on Cooper's pale cheeks. His eyes narrowed. "Damn you, Parker!" With a litany of cursing, he strode out of the kitchen, slamming the front door in his wake.

I turned to Harvey. "What did I do?"

"For one thing, yer breathin'. That alone pisses off Coop most days. Then there's yer crazy hair …"

"You leave my hair out of this, old man." I frowned toward the archway, wondering what the detective had seen in the living room. I tiptoed over and peeked into the room.

Someone breathed down the back of my neck and then snorted.

"Looks like a plain old livin' room to me," said the heavy breather. "Only thing odd is the TV."

"What TV?" I didn't see one.

"That's what I mean. It's missin'. Who doesn't have a TV these days?"

I sniffed to see if I could smell anything unnatural. Doc had taught me that trick months ago, only he was a mental medium who could sense ghosts at a mere sniff. His abilities were actually much more complicated than just being able to "smell" ghosts, but for a lack of a more thorough paranormal vocabulary, I stuck to the basics.

While my boyfriend had an ability to interact with the ectoplasmic crowd, I normally couldn't even sense a ghost when it was standing inside of my skin, hiding behind my face. A creepy dead prostitute had actually tested that for me one time, and it still gave me goosebumps.

After tossing a shrug back and forth, Harvey and I headed for the front door. I collected his booties and slipped into my boots. Cooper must have stormed out with his booties still on—a parting gift from Ben and his client.

We found the surly detective leaning against the hood of my SUV, not a bootie to be found.

I held my tongue until we'd all climbed inside, escaping the wind. "Care to explain your damning me back there, Detective?"

"I don't want to talk about it."

"What'd ya see in there, boy?" Harvey asked, rubbing his hands together in between blowing on them. "A ghost?"

Cooper squeezed the bridge of his slightly crooked nose. "It was nothing, Uncle Willis. Just shadows messing with my head."

Shadows, huh? Right.

I chewed on my lower lip, wondering if I should play parapsychologist and dig deeper into the truth of what Cooper had seen in the living room. Guilt tied my tongue, though.

Recently, the detective had attended a séance where he was given the job of keeping an eye on me while I was "under." Being the diligent cop that he was, Cooper had trailed me when I left the group and he'd been plowed down by a ghost.

Okay, so maybe it wasn't just any ghost, but a very powerful and twisted one.

And I suppose it could be said that he wasn't merely plowed down, more like blasted clear through by the evil presence.

Also, there was a *slight* chance that I was partly to blame since I had been the one who accidentally conjured this nasty being somehow, but those details were insignificant at the moment.

The main thing was that Cooper was now sort of seeing ghosts, whether he wanted to or not. Judging by his reaction to whatever was floating around inside of the house, he was still in the "not" category.

Doc had prophesized that the detective wouldn't accept this newfound ability without a fight, and Cooper had proved him right to date. Every time Harvey prodded his nephew about catching sight of "wispy folks," Cooper dug in his boot heels and came up with a laundry list of excuses for what he must have seen.

The shock of having this new ghost vision had apparently shifted to denial. How long he could keep pretending ghosts weren't real was a worry that those of us who knew him best debated behind his back. Doc's concern was that Cooper's rigid mind might break instead of bend. My worry was that if he *did* snap, he'd blame me and fill me full of holes for dragging him into my chaotic world.

"So." I decided to change the subject from ghosts. "I take it that's a 'No' on this house."

His wrinkled upper lip was my answer. I pulled out a sheet of listings I had brought along with several circled. "You sure you don't want to move to the country? I have a couple of properties that match your want-list about five miles out of town."

When Cooper had first hired me to sell his place up in Lead, he'd told me he wanted to move to the country, far away from the civilians he protected day and night. But he'd had a change of heart since then.

I had to wonder if it was something to do with his job and all of the overtime he kept putting in; or with his friends who lived in town, including Doc and their other poker buddy, Deadwood's fire captain.

Then again, maybe it had to do with Natalie, who'd recently mentioned an interest in moving closer to Deadwood so she could hang around with me and my kids more. Cooper had been pretending to read the paper when she'd told me that, but I doubted he missed much when Natalie talked, let alone breathed, within the same four walls.

Cooper's phone rang before he could answer me. He pulled it out of his coat pocket and frowned down at the screen. "Shit." He held the phone to his ear. "Detective Cooper speaking."

I scanned my listings sheet again, checking if maybe one of the other agencies in the area had something on there that I'd overlooked.

"She's right here with me," Cooper said to whoever was on the phone.

I frowned at him, wondering who was asking. Was that Doc? If so, why hadn't he called me instead of Cooper? I pulled out my phone to see if I'd missed his call.

Nope, nothing from Doc.

"You've got to be fucking kidding me." Cooper's words were clipped.

I lowered my phone, my chest tightening. Harvey's wide blue eyes in the rearview mirror matched mine.

Cooper rubbed the back of his neck. "No. I need to come see it first."

"See what?" I whispered, twisting my hands together.

He held up his index finger. "You're overreacting, Hawke."

My stomach tanked. Oh, no. What did Detective Hawke want with me now? The Columbo wanna-be had a real hard-on for the idea of seeing me behind bars. He really needed to get a hobby. Maybe I should give him a paint-by-numbers set for Christmas. Then again, numbers were pretty advanced for the blockhead. I should probably stick to something with shapes.

"I'll be there in five minutes." There was a pause, and then Cooper added, "No, I'll be alone. We can discuss your theory after I take a look."

He hung up without waiting for an answer from his partner. His eyes held mine, the lines on his forehead doubling and then tripling before I even got a word out.

"I didn't do it. I swear." I had no idea what I didn't do, but I was sure I could come up with an alibi.

"What has Hawke all lathered up, boy?" When Cooper didn't answer, Harvey leaned between the seats, prodding his nephew with a poke in the shoulder. "Spit it out. Yer scarin' poor Sparky."

"She should be scared."

"Why? What happened? What did he say?" I rattled off, ending with, "I'm innocent."

"I need you to drive me back to work, Parker. Detective Hawke claims to have learned of new evidence on Ms. Wolff's murder case."

Ms. Wolff was a previous resident of the Galena House, the old boarding house turned into apartments down the hill from where we were currently parked that I was trying to sell. She'd lived there for decades, I'd been told, much loved by the other residents from the past and present.

A month ago, however, Ms. Wolff had dialed my number out of the blue, told me I had to come see her immediately, called me something in German that later turned out to be the word for *Executioner*, and then hung up on me. After I'd shaken off my surprise, I'd fetched Harvey to go with me to visit her apartment. We'd shown up a short time later and found her dead and then some—she'd been decapitated.

What was even more bizarre, her head was shriveled up like a raisin and her body looked like a bunch of bones tossed into a wrinkled leather sack. Cooper had been less than thrilled to receive that phone call from us, adding yet another dead body to his stack of unsolved cases.

I shifted into reverse, backed into a nearby drive, and then headed down the hill to the police station.

"What sort of evidence?" I asked as we crossed Main Street. More important, "What's it have to do with me?"

Maybe they'd found the missing picture of my son that had been stuck in Ms. Wolff's mirror at the time we stumbled onto her body. Why my son's picture had been slid in the dead woman's bedroom mirror frame was a spine-chilling mystery that had not been solved yet by Detective Hawke and his clicking pen.

Cooper stared out the window, not making a comment on my speed, which was ten miles over the posted sign again. As we pulled into the police station parking lot, he finally answered, "All I can say for now is that it's police business."

"Dammit, boy! Ya can't drop a bomb like that and then cover up yer mess with a load of horseshit about police business."

"I'm sorry," he said to me more than his uncle. "Until I see what Detective Hawke claims to have found, that's as much as I can tell you."

I idled at the steps leading up to the cop shop's front doors while Cooper climbed out of the SUV. A blast of wind plastered his coat against him, trying to take my door down the road with it.

He frowned at me. "Do me a favor, Parker. Keep this between the three of us and Nyce until I find out for certain what is going on."

"Fine."

"I mean it. Your aunt and Natalie are not on the need-to-know list. Understand?"

I pretended to cross my heart. Keeping tight-lipped that I had a detective potentially trying to pin a crime on me again was not a problem. It was almost quitting time, anyway. I planned to go back to work, check in with my boss, and then head home for supper—which I might drink my way through until I heard back from Cooper.

"How long will it take you to find out if I'm in some kind of trouble for something I didn't do?" I asked him, refraining from adding an "again" to the end of my question since he was kind of on my side this time … so far, anyway.

"I don't know." He rubbed his eyes. "But when I call, you'd better answer your damned phone."

Chapter Two

Calamity Jane Realty's office was located on the bottom floor of a two-story brick building that dated back to the late 1800s. Like many of the old structures throughout Deadwood, the old gal had withstood her fair share of floods and fires, standing tall and sturdy against the rough and rowdy hands of time.

I parked in my designated spot behind the office. "What do you think is going on over at the police station right now?" I asked Harvey, who'd joined me in the front seat after Cooper had left.

His two gold teeth shined back at me. "I reckon Coop is thinkin' about burnin' some powder."

That was a given with Cooper's fetish for firearms. "I mean besides that? What do you think Hawke is trying to pin on me now?"

"I don't know, but at first glance Hawke is purty good at puffin' up the truth enough so you can hardly recognize it. Whatever he's locked his jaws onto this time can't be that big of a deal, or Coop would've dragged you into the station with him."

That was true. I'd been ordered to join Detective Cooper inside of the Deadwood Police Station more times than I had fingers and maybe even toes.

Harvey opened his door. "Might as well get on with livin' until Coop or Hawke are barkin' at your doorstep."

I followed Harvey out into the cold wind, making fast tracks across the parking lot. Harvey veered left, toward Doc's back door.

"Where you going?" I asked, slowing.

"I'm gonna pay a visit to yer biggest fan and let him know which way the wind is blowin' this afternoon."

A gust blew up my skirt just then as if showing me which direction it was heading—right up the old ying-yang. My knees shivered, my feet itching to keep walking and escape the freezing blasts. "Fine. I'll stop by after I wrap up at work."

"Don't dillydally. I want to git a jump on supper."

I licked my chops without even caring what was on the menu for tonight. Knowing Harvey would be cooking supper was enough to put a smile on my face and a skip in my step in spite of Detective Hawke's newest threat. "I'll be quick."

He gave me a thumbs-up and we parted ways.

A lone fluorescent light flickered in Calamity Jane's back hallway. The other three bulbs were dark, along with the bathroom doorway. My boss, Jerry, wasn't in his office, but his desk lamp was on, lighting up a medium-sized box sitting on his desktop. I sniffed, catching a whiff of his sandalwood cologne. He must be working out front again.

Lately, Jerry had taken to sitting out amongst the rest of us desk jockeys in the front office. While he claimed his reasoning was to make us feel more like a five-man team, I knew better. His change of setting was spurred by the ghost of his dead ex-wife, Jane Grimes. Jane was not only the "Jane" in Calamity Jane Realty, but she also used to be my boss before she was murdered back in August.

Now Jane was back in the wispy form, but as far as I knew, her return was not common knowledge. Doc had been the first to pick up her scent several weeks ago. Since then, neither Jerry nor I had actually "seen" Jane around the office, but he periodically found his paperwork and furniture rearranged overnight to her liking, and he claimed to smell a trace of her perfume every now and then. I'd been around enough ghosts in this town to take the evidence presented to me by both men and believe without question that Jane's ghost was haunting Calamity Jane Realty.

Shivering all the way to my desk, I didn't bother taking off my pea coat. There was no way I was going to be able to focus on work until I knew what had Detective Hawke in such a lather. As soon as I checked my email and made sure Jerry didn't need me for anything else, I'd be skedaddling.

Jerry was holding court from Mona's desk this afternoon, his extra-long legs sticking out from under the front. Jerry used to play professional basketball back in his heyday. Decades later, he still had the height, shoulders, and solid build of a ballplayer, but his head was immersed in a totally different game—making Calamity Jane Realty the number one real estate business in western South Dakota.

"Hi, Jerry." I flashed him a smile on the way to my desk, which was one of four that he'd positioned in a loosely spaced huddle formation to encourage teamwo … wait.

I stopped, counting desks to make sure I wasn't seeing things. Make that one of five. I lowered my purse onto my desk and aimed a raised brow at Ben Underhill, my only coworker still in the office this afternoon.

Ben sat at his desk, which was now separated from mine by the newest piece of furniture to join our team huddle. His brown hair looked windblown. His blue tie matched his eyes both in color and the way it sort of drooped. The smile he returned sagged at the corners. From the looks of it, I wasn't the only one who'd had a rotten day.

"Do we have company?" I asked Ben, indicating the additional furniture now sharing the room with us.

"Actually, Violet," Jerry answered before Ben could get a word out, "that's your desk. The one your purse is sitting on is now Mona's."

My desk? I sized it up, wondering why Jerry would situate it in the room so that my back was to the door and the plate-glass windows. Jane would not have approved, what with her being into feng shui. Wild Bill would have rolled over in his grave.

"I told Jerry that Wild Bill wouldn't approve of you sitting with your back to the door," Ben said, as if he'd been reading my thoughts.

Unfortunately, I didn't think the famous gunfighter of old had much sway over Jerry "Thor" Russo. Like the Nordic mythological god, Jerry was supersized with a rock-hewn face, booming voice, and extra-large shoes to fill. He also had a tendency to cause lightning and thunderstorms in my world. One of these days I was going to hide his marketing hammer so he'd quit taking swings at my career.

"Ben tried to get me to change to a zone defense," Jerry said, leaning closer to his computer screen, "and line up the desks the way we used to have them. But I think the huddle formation is better for the team."

I mouthed a "thank you for trying" to Ben, who gave me a thumbs-up before returning to his paperwork.

"So who's working at the fifth desk?" I moved my purse over to my new workstation. I had an idea, but wanted to confirm my fears.

"You're looking at him."

"Is someone using your office?" As in someone who used to own this business when she was still alive and wasn't quite ready to move on now that she was dead?

"I'm loaning it out temporarily."

Loaning out his office? Was that the story he was going with to throw off my coworkers?

I hit the spacebar on my keyboard, waking up my computer, and noticed the blinking light on my desk phone. Stuck on the receiver were two notes. They had names written on them that I'd never heard of before along with phone numbers and the *Call back* box checked.

"Is this my phone or did Mona's get mixed up with mine in the move?"

"It's yours, Violet." Jerry leaned back, crossing his arms over his chest. "Did you see the two messages I left for you?"

I nodded, holding them up. "Any idea what these two gentlemen are looking for?"

The pained expression on Ben's face when I glanced his way made me do a double take. "What?" I asked, turning to Jerry. "What's going on?"

He clapped his large hands together, making me cringe. In the past, when Jerry clapped, thunder and lightning usually followed. "I have good news, Violet."

Oh, no. What now? I fell into my chair, my knees giving out on premonition alone. I waited for his hammer to fall.

"Your new billboard is up."

"My *new* billboard? You mean you replaced my billboard over near Sturgis?"

As in the billboard that showcased me wearing a hideous pink silk suit with my hair spiraling out of control? The one with my lips painted blood red, making me look like the queen of the local vampire cult, that told travelers I would show them a "magical place" they'd love coming home to every night? I was still getting shit about that billboard whenever I stopped up at the Piggly Wiggly in Lead to pick up milk and superglue for my kids.

"No, that baby is still up and capturing westbound travelers' attention. The billboard I'm talking about is brand-new, installed yesterday afternoon." His smile stretched to his ears, showing off his pearly whites. "It's over in Spearfish snagging eastbound drivers on Interstate 90."

"Spearfish?" My ears started to ring loudly, alarms going off throughout my brain. Crap, not Spearfish. Please let me have heard that wrong.

"Yep. We're going to give Tiffany Sugarbell a run for her money and drive the ball into her key."

"We are?" The ringing grew louder after hearing the name of Doc's neurotic ex-girlfriend. My upper lip started to sweat. "What key?"

"You know, the key in basketball. Where her hoop is."

Jerry spoke English as a second language, with Sport-uguese being his native tongue. Some days his accent was so thick with basketball jargon that I had to watch the instant replay video to make sense of what he was saying.

"So, you rented billboard space in Tiffany's backyard?"

"That's another way of putting it."

Crud.

Damn.

Hell's bells.

I was dead meat.

As soon as Tiffany caught wind of that billboard, she was going to come at me with her claws sharpened and fully extended. How could Jerry not see that the redheaded sexpot was born on Crazy Creek just this side of Nutterville's city limits?

Jeez-on-crackers, like I needed to give the ultra-competitive, Jessica Rabbit wannabe another reason to hate me to death. She'd already spit sparks at me for stealing Doc—although for the record he'd left her well before I'd come into the picture. That billboard would make flames shoot from Tiffany's eyes. Jerry might as well have painted a target on my ass and handed her a damned rocket launcher.

I held up the two messages, moving on to another element of this disaster that had my shoulders tense. "These two gentlemen saw my billboard today and called?"

"Yep." Jerry pushed out his chest, proud as a peacock with two tails. "They know a good thing when they see it."

See it? Lordy, please tell me he didn't … "Which particular picture of me did you happen to use on this new billboard?"

"The one with you in the black dress and a pen in your mouth."

I crushed the messages in my fist. "Oh, dear." I tried to smile around my frown.

Jerry winced at my expression. "Are you okay? You're not going to start crying again are you?"

I'd cried once in front of Jerry. One freaking time. Apparently, that was all it took to scar the brute for life.

"No tears." But torturing Jerry on the rack did pass through my thoughts. I placed the crumpled messages next to each other on my desk, smoothing out the crinkles. "Just out of curiosity, what does the new billboard say?"

Jerry pulled out his cell phone. "I'll text you the picture I took earlier when I zipped over there to see it for myself." He tapped his screen a couple of times.

My phone chirped in response. I pulled it out of my coat pocket, my gut churning. With Jerry and Ben both watching, I opened the text and tapped on the picture to enlarge it.

It took several seconds for the woman in my head to stop screaming obscenities. After I'd wrestled her into silence, I reminded myself to breathe before I turned purple and keeled over.

I scanned the words again, praying that I'd read it wrong the first time through.

> *Looking for a high-quality, low-maintenance LTR?*
> *Violet Parker is the professional for you.*
> *She can meet your needs and put a smile on your face!*
> *Contact Calamity Jane Realty.*
> *Violet is waiting for your call.*

"Wow," I croaked. *Shit.*

"I tweaked a singles' ad so that it worked for real estate," Jerry explained his madness with a proud smile.

If I aimed my boot heel at his teeth … "And 'LTR' refers to?"

"Long Term Realtor. Clever, huh?"

As opposed to Long Term Relationship, right. *Double shit.* Call me kooky, but I might have spelled that acronym out for drivers.

"*Clever* is one word for it," I said, trying to laugh like my world wasn't swirling down the toilet. My laugh sounded high and squeaky, like someone had stuck a thermometer in Elvis's butt—Elvis as in my daughter's chicken, not the late, great King of Rock and Roll.

"Now, Violet," Jerry said, his tone pacifying. "I can see by your red cheeks that you're not thrilled with this new billboard, but I promise you it's going to pay off."

My eye twitched. Did he mean it would pay off for my future as a real estate agent or a professional call girl? Because from where I was standing, I could only see stripper poles lining up clear to the horizon.

"I have a new billboard, too." Ben spoke up. "We'll be blazing forth together."

"Where?"

"His is down in Rapid City," Jerry answered.

"What's he wearing?" Please let it be only his underwear so that we were at least on an even playing field.

"That black tuxedo Jerry rented for me."

Dang! That tux had given Ben a sleek, sophisticated appeal that my black dress couldn't touch. "What's your ad say?"

Ben held out his phone to me. I took it, enlarging the picture.

Sure enough, he looked handsome and debonair. I read the words on his billboard aloud. "Looking for your next win in the real estate game?

Score big with Realtor Ben Underhill—your local MVP!"

Well, wasn't that just my luck? Ben's billboard looked and read like a men's magazine cover, turning him into a local sports star. I frowned down at my billboard picture again—and I was the slutty blond cheerleader who gave hand jobs under the bleachers. At this rate, I was going to have to hire me a pimp to screen my clientele.

Jerry's phone rang. "I need to take this."

I turned my back on him while he spoke into the receiver and let my emotions have at it on my face, cursing Jerry seven ways from Sunday under my breath.

Ben joined me, leaning back against my desk. "It's not that bad, Violet."

"Have you read it?"

He nodded.

"More than once? Beginning to end?"

Chuckling, he patted my shoulder. "From a guy's perspective, it's sexy, but not over the top. Tongue in cheek, so to speak."

"Ben, I have a pen in my mouth."

He shrugged. "That's part of the sex appeal. Jerry's right—it's going to bring you a lot of new clients."

"Clients who expect what, though?"

Aunt Zoe was going to come swinging for Jerry when she saw this new ad. Her bra-burning days might be over, but that didn't mean she had stopped carrying a lighter in her pocket. She still cursed up a storm whenever anyone brought up my other billboard.

"Did you notice the phone number Jerry listed?" Ben asked.

No, I'd been too busy ranting about Jerry turning me into Deadwood's newest prostitute. I looked at the picture on my phone again, cringing my way through the ad blurb, and focused on the phone number. "That's not mine." It wasn't my cell number or my desk phone.

"It's Jerry's. He's going to screen each of your clients."

Ah, so Jerry was my new pimp. "Screen them how?"

"He told me that he's going to run them through the hoops on the phone first, and then meet them along with us the first time to make sure they're legit."

"These two passed the phone test?" I pointed at the messages.

He nodded. "Four callers didn't make it past your new bouncer."

I glanced over at Jerry, who had his back to us as he spoke on the phone. The man's shoulders were wider than a refrigerator, his forearms giving Popeye a run for his money. The fire inside of me cooled several degrees.

"I know Jerry's tactics are a bit excessive," Ben continued. "But if you step back and look at it from another angle, he's really good at marketing in new ways that most real estate companies wouldn't even think to try. He has guts."

"And a fair share of gall."

"True, but you and I both know that success doesn't come without a willingness to take a few risks."

I blew out a breath. "Damn it," I whispered, pocketing the two messages. "Fine. I'll call these guys in the morning and see what I can do to help them."

"That's the spirit."

"But don't expect me to put on a cheerleading skirt and do any cartwheels about it."

"What? No cartwheels in a short skirt? Dang." He winked.

"So, have you received any calls because of your new billboard?"

He nodded. "According to Jerry, one potential buyer for a property down in Hot Springs and two who were looking for a fun night on the town."

"You're kidding? Two women called for a date?"

One brown eyebrow lifted. "Who said they were both women?"

I smiled as he returned to his desk, glad to have Ben on the front lines next to me. After checking my email, I hoisted my purse. "Tell Jerry I needed to head home a little early."

"Hey, what did your client think of that house in the Forest Hill neighborhood?"

I didn't want to lie to Ben, but I couldn't come out and say Cooper had possibly seen a ghost in the living room. "Detective Cooper is hard to read," I answered truthfully. "I don't know if anything we looked at today appealed to him. I really liked the place, though. It shows well. You did a great job prepping it."

"Thanks. See you tomorrow, Violet."

I decided to head over to Doc's office via the front door. When I opened the door, I ran into a box being carried by Abraham Lincoln. The collision knocked his black stovepipe hat onto the ground.

"Cornelius!" I bent down and grabbed his hat before the wind carried it away. I held out the hat to my previous client and fellow séance buddy. "What are you doing here?"

Cornelius had recently bought a haunted hotel on Main Street through me. Our Realtor–client relationship had quickly turned into something more paranormal after I agreed to attend one of his séances. One séance had turned into two and then three and so on. Most recently, we'd sat back-to-back while seeking to eradicate a dead little girl who had been terrorizing Cornelius to the point of physical exhaustion with her murderous directives.

"Good morning, Violet." Cornelius shoved the box at me in exchange for his hat.

Morning? Had he recently crawled out of bed? It was possible for Cornelius, whose paranormal work often kept him up all night. I took the box.

He settled the hat back on his head where it blended perfectly with his hair. His goatee looked extra pointy today, his cornflower blue eyes a stark contrast against his pale skin. "You can put that in my office with the other one."

Put what? The box? Cornelius often confused me for his secretary in addition to his real estate agent. I shifted the box, which was growing heavier by the second. "Your office? Are you confused about where you are?"

He stroked his goatee, his head tipping slightly. "That's an interesting question, Violet. Have you taken me to a parallel realm again?"

Not yet, but if he kept talking about me and my clandestine paranormal activities in the vicinity of my boss, I might knock him and his box into another state—an unconscious one.

"Violet," Jerry said, speaking from behind me, holding the door open. "Let Cornelius come on in. He's borrowing my office."

I led the way inside. "He's the one you loaned it to?"

Jerry nodded once and then returned to his phone, picking it up and turning his back on me again.

Crappity crap. How was I going to keep my newfound abilities a secret with Cornelius working under the same roof as me day after day? I was going to have to talk to him in private, make it clear that discussing our extracurricular paranormal activities at the office was a big no-no.

I escorted Cornelius back to Jerry's office, dropping the box on the desk.

"Be careful with that, Violet."

"Sorry." That's what he got for drafting an amateur mover. I opened the box, frowning down at several high tech–looking gadgets that I'd seen before hooked up to the multitude of computers in Cornelius's hotel suite. That's when I noticed the numerous monitors lining the wall behind Jerry's desk.

"What is going on?" I asked Cornelius, who had taken off his long wool overcoat, revealing a black thermal shirt and jeans. He was busy untangling a nest of cords he'd pulled out of the other box.

"I'm moving in."

"To Jerry's office, I know, but why?"

"Isn't it obvious?"

"Maybe to someone who reads minds."

"How much have you experimented with telepathy, Violet? You may be as good at it as you are at channeling."

I shushed him, pointing toward the doorway. "Why don't you save me the mental headache and tell me why you are relocating your equipment to this office." I stepped closer, lowering my voice. "Is it because of the ghost?"

His smile was one-sided, making his goatee crooked. "You are already performing thought-transference. Your powers never cease to amaze me, Violet."

I didn't bother telling the knucklehead that my guess had nothing to do with reading his mind. Last month, Jerry asked me about Cornelius and his ghost-detecting gadgets. It appeared my boss had taken the next step in his attempt to rid himself of his ex-wife's restless spirit and hired the self-proclaimed "ghost whisperer" to come witness Jane's activity in person and convince her to go away.

"So you'll be in here trying to talk to her ghost each day while we're working out front?"

"Not just days." Cornelius lifted a monitor and handed it to me. "Don't drop that."

After the lousy day I'd had, he was lucky that I didn't smash it over his damned hat. I set the monitor down on the desktop.

"You mean you'll spend the night in here, too?"

Was he going to set up a cot? Where would he shower? Would I be forced to look at his skinny, hairy legs each morning and that god-awful robe he liked to wear?

"Your telepathic skills improve by the second, channeler. What am I thinking now?" He stepped over to the row of monitors.

I glared at his back "That I look like I'm considering clobbering you over the head."

He lifted another monitor. "Not even close. Try again."

"I'm too tired for this game, Cornelius."

He set the monitor on Jerry's chair. His gaze focused on me, studying my face. "You do look haggard."

"Gee, thanks." He always knew what to say to make a girl feel good and kicked when she was down.

"And your hair is more messy than usual. Were you recently electrocuted?"

"I wish!" A solid zap to my gray matter might erase an afternoon of detective-filled frustration that had ended with boss-inspired humiliation and angst.

"Have you been dabbling in the darkness again?"

"Nope. There was plenty of light during today's clusterfuck."

One black eyebrow lifted. "How would you feel about my attaching brainwave monitoring detectors to your forehead so that I can see the activity going on in your skull?"

"Touch my head and you will die a painful death."

"That's the exact response I'd expect from a physical medium such as yourself. Do you think your boss got the water turned on in the upstairs bathroom?"

"The upstairs bathroom?" I didn't realize this building had a bathroom up there. What else was upstairs?

He fanned his shirt. "Is it hot in here or am I experiencing contact with a non-living presence?"

I wasn't going to go there right now with the drama king. "What's wrong with the shower in your hotel suite?"

"It's not going to work anymore."

Was he into premonitions now? "Why not?"

"Well, for one thing, it's in the process of being torn out by the men I hired to remodel my hotel."

He was having the Old Prospector Hotel remodeled? Good. That place needed some updating. While the bones of the hotel were still solid, the upper two stories were decorated with relics left over from the 1970s. The antiques weren't the only leave-behinds either, according to Doc, who'd run into a handful of ghosts during one of his previous visits.

"What's the other thing?" I asked.

"It's too far away from my back scrubber."

"Your back scrubber?"

He pointed at the ceiling. "And my robe, which is also upstairs."

I cringed, thinking about that robe and the visual buffet that came with it. "Are you trying to tell me that you're moving in upstairs?"

"Precisely."

"As in Calamity Jane Realty's second floor?"

He handed me what looked like a stud finder, red and green lights and all. "We really should be recording your brain waves right now. I'd wager they're spiking off the charts."

"You're going to be *here* 24/7? Right above me?"

"Indeed."

"For how long?"

He shrugged. "My abilities have not yet developed in the precognition field."

I squeezed my eyes shut. First Cooper playing Goldilocks in each house I showed him, then Detective Hawke biting at my heels, then Jerry plastering me on that damned billboard in enemy territory, and now Cornelius filling my days with supernatural cogitations and aggravations. That was it! I was packing up the kids and signing up for NASA's off-planet exploration program. Terraforming couldn't be as bad as they made it look in the science fiction movies, could it? How hard could it be to assemble oxygen-making machines? My son was super smart. He'd figure it out.

"Violet." Cornelius interrupted my interstellar fantasy. "I'd like my protein shake chilled and ready for me at precisely eight-twenty-seven tomorrow morning."

My eyes flashed open. "You expect me to bring ... Cornelius, you're not even my client anymore."

"I know. We went over this already." He took the gadget from my hand. "I'm your roommate, remember?"

Chapter Three

Old Man Winter had arrived early in the Black Hills, the frigid bastard. Along with his trademark freezing temperatures and periodic snow flurries, he brought deep shadows that turned day into night long before I made it home most evenings. Tonight would be no different, except for the detective who'd probably be darkening my doorstep even more at some point.

I closed the back door of Doc's office behind me and leaned against it, soaking up the silence for a moment. Wallowing in a self-pity party sounded tempting, but the inviting scent of Doc's woodsy cologne persuaded me to lift my chin and keep on moving forward. By forward, I meant toward the soft glow at the other end of the hallway where I knew I would find a pair of strong arms and broad shoulders. I'd need both this afternoon to ward off my chills from Detective Hawke's unnamed threat.

"Doc?" I clomped down the hall, the well-aged wooden floorboards creaking under my weight. Where was Harvey? The bathroom was empty and the back room dark. Normally, he'd be filling the quiet with some anecdote or dirty joke.

Doc sat in his leather chair, his laptop closed on his desk. A single desk lamp lit the room, softening the edges of my vision. His dark brown eyes searched mine for several heartbeats.

"How are you doing, Killer?" he asked, using the nickname he'd given me after finding out about the job I had a genetic obligation to fulfill. His dark hair looked almost black in the low light, adding an extra-sexy edge to him this afternoon.

"I've had better days." I leaned my hip against his desk, taking in his brown flannel shirt hanging loose over a white T-shirt. He was wearing a pair of faded blue jeans instead of dress khakis today. Saturdays were usually laid back for Doc, even though his financial planning business was growing by leaps and bounds thanks to word of mouth.

"Where's the Picklemobile?" Harvey's old green Ford pickup had been recently tuned up and spit-shined under Doc's sure hands, no longer belching smoke or backfiring like it had been when I was driving her earlier this fall. "And where's Harvey? He was supposed to wait here for a ride home."

"The latter took the former to your aunt's place to start his famous lasagna."

"We're having lasagna tonight?" I almost drooled a little at the thought of Harvey's delicious homemade tomato sauce.

"He's making it just for you. Mentioned something about you needing to be cheered up."

"That man knows how to make my stomach happy."

"Too bad he didn't accept your marriage proposal," he teased, his gaze flirting.

"Uh, yeah." Marriage was a topic that made me fidget in front of Doc after learning he'd left Tiffany Sugarbell when she started talking about wedding dresses. I changed the subject. "If Harvey took the Picklemobile, how are you going to get home?"

"I was hoping to hitch a ride with a hot blonde."

I batted my eyelashes at him, flirting back. "What's the magic word, big boy?"

"Violet Parker, would you please meet my needs and put a smile on my face?"

Put a smile on ... I cursed under my breath. "You heard?"

"I saw." He caught my elbow and tugged me onto his lap. "I was in Spearfish at lunch to drop off some paperwork at a client's place. I took the interstate back to the Deadwood exit and nearly drove off the road when I saw you there, bigger than life, looking sexy as hell in that little black dress."

I buried my face in my hands. "I'm so embarrassed."

"You'll cause a pile-up or two with those cherry red lips and your violet eyes."

I lowered my hands. "My eyes aren't violet."

"They are on that billboard."

"I didn't even notice my eye color on the picture Jerry texted me. I was too busy staring at that stupid pen in my mouth."

"Oh, man. That pen ..." He cupped my cheeks. "I've been waiting all afternoon to kiss these lips." His mouth brushed over mine. "I stared at your billboard for so long that a highway patrol officer stopped to see if I needed help."

Well, there was one positive about the new billboard I hadn't expected. I'd sort of figured Doc would be unhappy about it. If he were on a billboard for all of the world to see, I'd probably risk life and limb climbing up there with a can of spray paint to blacken his teeth, maybe even give him an eye patch while I was at it. Then I'd write *Doc LOVES Violet* inside a big heart to make sure all of the females in the land understood he was off limits.

"I missed you today, Boots."

There it was, my favorite flirty nickname that signaled hanky panky was to follow. He kissed me fully, taking his time about it. He tasted sweet and lemony, reminding me of …

I pulled back, my eyes narrowing. "Did you swipe some lemon drop cookies from Aunt Zoe's cookie jar this morning and bring them to work?"

"Guilty as charged," he whispered, his eyes still focused on my mouth. "Come back here. I wasn't done."

This time he moved in hard and fast, inviting my tongue to dance. I moaned and sank into him, letting him make me forget about today's shitstorm for a few heated breaths.

When he pulled back, I blew out a low whistle. "Did they teach you to kiss girls senseless like that in college?"

His smile warmed his eyes. "We spent a whole week studying the art of kissing during Economics 101."

"Really? Economics?"

"Sure. It was a good teaching tool for the two fundamental facts of economics."

"What do these two fundamental facts have to do with kissing?"

"First, humans have unlimited wants." He unbuttoned my pea coat, pushing it partway down my shoulders, trapping my arms at my side. "For example, I want to see you naked, morning, noon, and night every single day. One could say that my want for your body is unlimited."

"Are you sure about mornings when my hair looks like I got caught up in a tornado?"

He nodded, unfastening several buttons on my black knit cardigan sweater. I watched as he trailed the back of his fingers over the upper slopes of my breasts, grazing the lacy edge of my red bra. "Especially the mornings, when your smiles are sleepy and your skin is soft, warm, and deliciously bare."

I tried to wiggle free of my coat, but he grabbed the cuffs and held me prisoner. "What's the second fundamental fact?"

"The means for satisfying these wants are relatively scarce."

"What's that have to do with perfecting the art of kissing?"

The pad of his thumb brushed over the front of my bra. The heat in his eyes when they met mine made my upper lip sweat. "I had to study up before meeting you so I'd be able to keep *your* unlimited wants satisfied."

He was doing a mighty fine job of that as of late, spending several nights a week in my bed, waking me up in the morning with his hands and mouth. So far, I didn't think my kids had figured out that our slumber parties were taking place in my bedroom since Doc was always awake and dressed before both of them in the morning, but one of these days we'd have to purposely stay in bed long enough for them to catch us.

I squirmed on his lap to free my arms, wanting to touch, too. His eyes smoldered while they focused on my bared cleavage.

"On whom did you perfect the art of kissing?" I asked.

"You know me, I did more reading than experimenting."

I stopped trying to free my arms and smiled. "You seriously expect me to believe you didn't practice with anyone?"

He shrugged. "What can I say? When I met you, I finally had the opportunity to perfect my technique."

I laughed. His nutty ex-girlfriend would surely tell a different tale. Tiffany would undoubtedly take great pleasure in giving me play-by-play details of their sex life if given the opportunity.

Speaking of Tiffany and her cattiness, I unloaded part of this afternoon's baggage on Doc. "Jerry has decided to pit me against your ex."

"There's no competition." He let go of my sleeves and helped me out of the coat, tossing it on his desk. "You win, hands down."

"You're delusional. It's a side effect of Harvey's homemade love potion that I've been sneaking into your coffee each morning."

"Not delusional, but I am a little worried."

"About Tiffany?" I was, too. She'd already filled up Doc's voicemail many times in an effort to win him back. Going head to head with her on the career front would surely make the snakes on her head hiss and strike every time we ran into each other.

"About you."

"You think she'll claw my eyes out?"

He smirked. "No, Killer. I've seen you swing a war hammer. I think you can handle Tiffany's claws." He toyed with one of my curls that had sprung free. "I'm concerned that this new ad your boss posted is going to bring you a slew of men all trying to replace me in your bed."

I took his hand in mine, lacing our fingers together. "You're jealous? I don't believe it. You never let the green ogre mess with your head." I, on the other hand, had to repeatedly run my ogre over with a Zamboni machine.

He raised our laced fingers to his mouth, kissing my knuckles. "I'm going to have to up my game if Jerry keeps working this marketing angle. Lo and behold, a van of Mensa members cruises past that billboard, sees your sexy lips, and comes knocking."

I'd once told Doc I had a weakness for smart guys. Apparently, he hadn't forgotten about it.

I looped my arms around his neck. "Mensa, schmensa," I said, running my lips along his jaw. "I'm no longer into those brainiacs."

"Who are you into now?"

"Tall mediums." I used Cornelius's term for Doc. I pursed my lips. "*Embrasse moi, ma chérie,*" I ordered him to kiss me, using one of the French phrases I'd looked up on the Internet and memorized just for him.

He traced the line of my jaw. "Ah, Tish. That's French."

"*Oui,* Gomez."

Pulling down the shoulder of my sweater, he kissed his way along my skin to my neck.

I lifted my chin, my body humming to life as his lips headed toward my cleavage.

"Christ, Violet," he said between kisses. "You smell like butterscotch."

"I ordered a butterscotch latte at lunch and managed to spill part of it down my sweater on the drive back to work." It was a wonder it hadn't left a red mark from where it'd burned a trail down to my bellybutton.

Doc looked up at me, his expression taut with need. "That gives me an idea."

"You want to spill hot coffee on me?" I wasn't really into that sort of sadomasochistic foreplay. It rated up there on my "Hell No" list next to golden showers.

"Not coffee. I saw a jar of butterscotch syrup at the grocery store the other day." He planted a kiss on my lips. "I'm going to buy some and lick it off your chin."

"Won't that be sticky?"

"I hope so." He moved his hips under me and returned to taste-testing my neck and chest, distracting me for several breathy seconds while his hand explored under my skirt. "I'll have to lick you twice as much."

My phone chirped in my coat.

I swore at the ceiling.

He fished the phone out of my coat pocket for me.

"It's Cornelius," I said, glancing at the text. "He wants me to give him a wake-up call at seven-forty-one tomorrow morning."

Doc pulled his hand out from under my skirt. "Speaking of your *Planet of the Apes* buddy, he stopped by earlier and filled me in on his new address."

I sighed, wishing we had time for Doc to finish what he'd started. "You realize what this means, don't you?"

"He's going to listen for Jane's ghost?"

"Well, yes." I straightened my sweater. "But I was referring to his confusion about me being his secretary. He already placed his order for a protein shake tomorrow morning."

Doc's chest vibrated against me. "He's going to keep things interesting. I don't think Jerry realizes who he invited to move into your building."

"I think Jerry's main focus is getting rid of Jane. Wait until he sees Cornelius's favorite robe when he comes down for coffee in the morning."

Doc started removing the bobby pins in my hair, freeing my curls. "He wants me to sneak over there one night after all of you leave and help him reach out to Jane."

"Are you going to?"

"Only if he helps me with my problem."

"What's your problem?"

"For one, my girlfriend is being used to lure eastbound travelers on Interstate 90."

"If it's any consolation, Jerry posted his phone number, not mine."

"I noticed."

"He's acting as my bouncer, fielding calls and screening clients for me."

"Good. He should. Zoe is going to be pissed on your behalf."

I smiled, imagining her breaking one of her glass pieces over Jerry's big head.

Shaking out my hair, I felt my tension lessen. Neither my hair nor I liked being confined all day. "So what's this problem of yours that you need help with?" I repeated my earlier question, collecting the bobby pins from him.

He watched me button up my sweater with a frown. "You mean besides you smelling and tasting like butterscotch when Willis made me promise we wouldn't be late for supper?"

"Next time I spill my latte, I'll call you and make sure you keep your calendar open."

He grinned, but quickly sobered. "There are two problems, actually—

Wilda's and her mother's ghosts. I need to find them both and return them to wherever they were before I let them loose."

"You mean before *I* let them loose. You were just saving my bacon, remember?" I was the one who had screwed up during the séance and given Mrs. Hessler and Wilda what they wanted—freedom. "You think Cornelius can help you with this?"

"He's dabbled more in ghost luring than I have. I usually let them come to me of their own free will."

"Maybe they're gone for good. Maybe they just wanted me to help them find each other again so they could spend eternity together collecting creepy clown crap." Mrs. Hessler had been a fan of clown memorabilia— the weirder the better based on what I'd seen of her collection before I burned her house down.

"I doubt it. Both were bent on blaming you for their unhappiness. With eternity to hang around, I have a feeling they'll want to seek revenge at some point or another. I need to find them before they come for you."

"I don't like you messing with them. I'm afraid Wilda will attach to you like she did Cornelius." *Haunting* was too mellow a word for the hell that little brat had put Cornelius through for weeks until she detached from him.

"That's why I'm consulting with Cornelius before trying anything. Now that we know he's the pied piper of ghosts, we just need to figure out how to send them away after we've gotten their attention."

"It sounds dangerous."

"Said the executioner who hunts monsters on the side."

Doc's cell phone rang. He grabbed it from his desk. "It's Willis."

"You better answer it. With lasagna on the menu, we don't want to upset him."

"Hello?" He paused. "Yes, she's here." Another pause. "Okay, we'll be there shortly."

"Let me guess," I said after he hung up. "My kids are fighting."

He frowned. "No, you have a visitor."

I stood up, pulling on my pea coat. "Who?"

"Coop. According to your bodyguard, he's not in a good mood, either."

"Shit." I'd been hoping whatever Hawke had called him about would turn out to be a waste of Cooper's time. That he'd call me tonight and tell me not to worry about it.

"Harvey told me about the phone call from Detective Hawke while you were showing Coop houses." He stuffed his laptop in his briefcase along with some other paperwork.

Had Harvey also told Doc about Cooper probably seeing a ghost in that last house? That was a discussion for later, though, after we found out what Cooper had to say. "I wonder what wicked witch crime Hawke's going to try to pin on me now. I've been a good little green girl lately and kept my flying monkeys at home."

"We'll find out soon enough." Doc locked up and shut off the lamp, leaving us in the dark. He took my hand and led the way to the back door.

A short time later, we were both shivering in my cold Honda. I'd given Doc the keys, asking him to drive since my thoughts were churning.

The five-minute trip up the hill to Aunt Zoe's house was filled with small talk, first about Doc's day and then my take on Cooper's reactions to the houses I'd shown him. Underlying our exchange was a tension that came with the dust devil of anxiety about what Cooper's presence at Aunt Zoe's meant to my immediate future.

The Picklemobile was parked out front of the late 19th-century house my aunt had called home for decades. Cooper's unmarked police SUV was parked behind the old Ford, but Aunt Zoe's pickup was missing.

Doc pulled in the drive. For several ticks of the engine, Doc and I sat in the dark. The sun had already gone to bed and it wasn't even suppertime. The orange glow of the streetlights down the road didn't quite reach inside the rig.

"You want to do some necking?" I asked, trying to lighten the mood while delaying the inevitable.

Doc laughed. "Always, Boots." His hand found mine, squeezing lightly. "But I think Coop will come out and threaten to fill us both with holes if we make him wait too long. How about a rain check?"

"As cold as it's supposed to get tonight, it'll have to be a snow check."

"They aren't calling for any precipitation until later this week."

"As if the weatherman can predict what's going to happen up here in the hills."

Silence filled the cab again as my weather-filled delay tactic stalled out. I remembered a time when I used to get all sweaty and tongue-tied when I was alone with Doc. Funny how time, several séances, and a passel of ghosts had changed that, not to mention a few miles with him between the sheets. And in the shower. And in his office. And … I let my mind wander for a moment.

"What are you thinking about?" he asked.

Sex, I thought. But that was a distraction I was trying to use in order not to think about the truth. "I don't want to go in there, Doc."

"I'll be there with you the whole time."

"You promise?"

He leaned over and kissed my cheek. "Let's go see the kids."

"And eat lasagna." I led the way, groaning in appreciation of the smell of baked cheese and tomato sauce as we stepped inside Aunt Zoe's front door.

Doc took my coat and hung it on the coat tree along with his. Addy and Layne weren't anywhere to be seen, but Scooby-Doo was on the TV in the living room, so I'd lay bets their hineys were around somewhere.

Harvey stepped through the archway leading to the kitchen. "What took you two so long?" He hit me with a one-eyed squint. "You're not in heat again, are you?"

Doc chuckled.

"You can both zip it." I snapped Harvey's suspenders as I strode by him into the kitchen. "Where's Aunt Zoe?"

"She's still at her store," he explained, following on my heels. "She mentioned something about inventory and told us to start without her."

I shot a quick frown at Cooper, who was standing next to the back door, a beer in his hand. What did his drinking alcohol before supper mean? Was it the same as my downing several shots of tequila to smooth the barbs from a particularly irritating day, or was it his usual choice of drink in the evening?

His steely gaze stayed locked on me as I took the half-empty tequila bottle down from on top of the fridge and grabbed a juice glass from the cupboard. Might as well not even mess with a shot glass tonight.

"Let's get this over with, Detective," I said, pouring a healthy swallow—or five—into the juice glass.

Before he could speak, my daughter came running into the kitchen with Elvis, her chicken, in her arms. "Mom, guess what?" Addy's brown eyes were wide with excitement, her blond hair majorly in need of a brush

I turned so my body blocked the bottle of tequila from my daughter's view and tried to smile around my apprehension. "What, honey?"

"Grammy called tonight. She told me she and Grandpa are going to come visit us next weekend."

Why were my parents coming to Deadwood? They'd just seen the kids at Thanksgiving. "Really? Did she mention why she was coming up here instead of inviting you down to her house?"

She nodded. "She said they wanna meet your new boyfriend."

Doc stopped in the midst of opening a bottle of beer, glancing my way with a raised brow.

"My new boyfriend?" I parroted.

"Mom, are you focusing here?" Addy asked, echoing the words I often used when helping her with her math homework. Her smooth forehead wrinkled. "Why is your eye twitching?"

I touched the back of my hand to the corner of my eye, forcing my smile wider. "I got something in it today." As in a sharp stick or two.

"You should rinse it with that eye wash Aunt Zoe keeps out in her workshop."

Thank you, Florence Nightingale. "Did Grammy say anything else about why she and Grandpa were coming up here?" Like anything to do with my killing a nasty monster or two? Aunt Zoe had told me she whispered a few truths in my father's ear when she was down there with the kids over Thanksgiving weekend. Had Dad shared the truth about my new gig with my mom?

"Not really." Addy shifted Elvis to her other arm. "Oh, she did say that Aunt Susan had told her you have a boyfriend that you're trying to keep a secret from the rest of the family."

That no-good skank!

"I am?" I faked surprise while cursing the Bitch from Hell in my head.

My vile younger sister, Susan, had one mission in life when it came to me—to destroy every single thing that made me happy. Highlights from our past when it came to this diabolical mission of hers included bedding not one of my boyfriends, but two. She'd also gotten me fired from multiple jobs, torched my Barbies, gutted my favorite stuffed animals, landed me in jail more than once, and stole my favorite purple boots. The list of her crimes was long and splattered with my blood.

"Grammy said that she didn't like you keeping secrets from her, so she's going to come up here and meet your boyfriend whether you like it or not."

I glanced at Doc, who took a swig of his beer while watching me with an unreadable expression.

Susan was right. I was trying to keep Doc a secret, but only from that man-stealing bitch, not my parents. I didn't want to risk Satan's concubine going for three strikes when it came to Doc. Call me paranoid, but after catching my sister in the midst of bronco-riding two of my boyfriends, I believed my hesitation to broadcast a new man in my bed was understandable.

Plus, I didn't want to rush Doc when it came to this thing going on between us. Meeting my parents seemed like a precursor to marriage talk and I didn't want to make him skittish. Aunt Zoe had once told me that I needed to keep in mind that what transpired between Doc and Tiffany had no bearing on my future with him, but I preferred to play it safe and avoid anything even remotely related to white lace and gold bands.

"Why are you keeping secrets from your mom?" Addy asked me, brown eyes narrowing. "You always tell me that I'm supposed to be honest and open with you."

A snickering sound came from Harvey's direction. My glare went unnoticed as he pulled the casserole dish of lasagna from the oven.

"This is not the same thing, Adelynn Renee," I said in a tone that meant this discussion was over for now. "Put that chicken in the basement and wash your hands for supper."

My daughter's eyes narrowed. "Fine, Mother." She started to turn away and then stopped. "Oh, Grammy also said that you'd better not be giving out free milk to your boyfriend because you should have learned your lesson about that last time."

My face caught fire.

Harvey snorted so hard he coughed.

Doc turned away, his shoulders shaking.

I didn't even dare look in Cooper's direction. My humiliation was already flooding over the levees as it was.

"Grammy told you *that*?"

"Not really. I heard her say it to Grandpa when she handed the phone to him so he could ask me how school was going." She scratched Elvis at the base of her comb. "What does she mean about free milk? Does she mean the milk we get at school for lunch?"

"Probably," I answered, cursing my mother long and loud in my head. I was going to duct tape her lips closed when she came nosing around to meet Doc.

"Anyway, I'm going to show Grammy my collection of chicken feathers when she comes. Do you think she'll want to hold Elvis this time?"

"I think if she's a good grandmother, she will definitely want to hold Elvis." Two could play at this game. "Now go. Oh, and tell Layne to get out the TV trays. You two are eating in the living room tonight."

Addy raced down the basement stairs howling in happiness about getting to eat in front of the television.

I washed my embarrassment down with a sip of tequila and then shot Doc a frown. "I have a good reason for keeping secrets."

Doc didn't meet my gaze. He lifted dinner plates down from the cupboard. "Your mother sounds interesting."

"She means well." I thought she did, anyway.

Susan on the other hand had much darker intentions, I had no doubt. She knew exactly how to play our mother when it came to delicate subjects. I'd bet my purple boots that she'd made a point of playing up the secret idea in order to manipulate me through Mom into showing my cards.

I took another swallow of tequila, this time two fingers' worth.

"You haven't met Parker's parents yet?" Cooper asked Doc as he made himself at home at the table.

"Nope. Only her brother, Quint." Doc looked at me and then pointed at a chair he'd pulled out for me. "Violet likes to hold her cards and her family close to her chest."

That wasn't exactly true. I just didn't want to scare off the one man I'd like to spend the rest of my years enjoying day and night.

My mom had a way of making people want to tear their hair out. Then there was my father and his ability to see right through me. I feared he'd catch me looking at Doc with hearts floating around my head and ask him what his long-term intentions were for me. Dad hadn't been very good at hiding his disapproval when it came to the men I'd dated in the past. I doubted anything short of a marriage proposal these days would make him happy.

"Actually," I said to Doc, sitting in the chair he'd indicated, "it's more a case of keeping *you* close to my chest."

Harvey placed the casserole dish in the middle of the table. "Close to yer chest, huh?" he asked, peeling off the Betty Boop apron he'd borrowed from Aunt Zoe's stash. "Is that why you two were late tonight?"

"We weren't late," I said, dishing up the kids' plates.

"Almost late," Harvey said, taking a drink of his lemonade.

Doc took the kids' plates after I'd filled them and disappeared into the living room. When he returned, he lowered himself into the chair next to me. "It's my fault we were late, Willis."

I held out my hand for his plate. "Why was it your fault?"

Doc grinned across at Harvey when he took back the plateful of lasagna. "Violet spoke French to me."

Cooper made a gagging sound. "You're a sad man, Nyce."

"Did Sparky meet yer needs like her ad promises?" Harvey asked, laughing when I swatted him.

I waited until we'd all settled into Harvey's lasagna before asking Cooper in a quiet voice, "What's the deal with Detective Hawke?"

"The new evidence on Ms. Wolff's death has him worked up."

I swallowed a mouthful of cheesy-tomato goodness. "What's that have to do with me?"

Cooper forked in another mouthful, his eyes on his plate. "It puts you back at the top of his suspect list."

"But Sparky and I showed up after the woman was dead."

"The four of us know that," Cooper told his uncle, "but Hawke doesn't believe it's the truth."

"Detective Hawke is a 'dipshidiot.' " I borrowed one of Natalie's favorite insults, taking another sip from my tequila glass.

"Does Beals know you're stealing from her stock of slurs?" Cooper asked.

I stuck my tongue out at him. "I'm allowed."

"Anyway," Cooper continued, "this new evidence has me a little worried."

"You think it has the potential to stick?" Doc asked.

He shrugged. "Hawke is dead set on pinning Ms. Wolff's death on your girlfriend. He wanted to drag her in for questioning, but I argued that more evidence was needed first. He didn't back down until I came up with a solution that satisfied him."

"What is it with his hard-on for incarcerating me? What did I ever do to him?"

"Besides stomp on his pen and threaten to do the same to his testicles?" Cooper asked.

I waved Cooper off. "That's kids' play."

"For one thing, you pretended to be a witch when I told you not to. To make matters worse, you keep pretending to talk to ghosts in front of him. He's sure you're trying to make a fool of him and determined to show you who's boss."

"By throwing me in jail?"

He nodded, pushing away his empty plate.

"What's he found that has him so set on Violet?" Doc asked.

Cooper wiped his mouth with his napkin. "I can't tell you yet."

"Damn you, Cooper." I glared at him, dropping my fork on the table.

He scowled back at me. "If it gets out that you know what he has on you, he'll come back at me."

"So what?" I said. "Isn't it about time you stood up to him and told him what an ass-kissing moron he is?"

The tequila seemed to have loosened my tongue. Maybe I needed to rein it in a tad bit.

"Stood up to him?" Cooper's eyes narrowed. "The only thing that saved you from being hauled into the station today, Parker, was me standing up to him and making a promise on your behalf."

Doc leaned back. "What do you mean?"

"Hawke wanted to assign Parker a police escort, day and night."

"That son of a bitch," I said in a harsh whisper, trying not to alert the kids that shit was hitting the fan in the kitchen. "Has he thought about how that would affect my livelihood? There's no way to hide a cop following me all around town from my boss or my clients. I'll lose my job."

"I know," Cooper said.

"And then there are my kids to consider. I can't lie to them about a police car following us day after day."

"I know, Parker."

"It's total bullshit that Hawke can harass me like this. Whatever happened to innocent until proven guilty?"

Cooper finished his beer, setting the bottle down on the table with a solid *clunk*. "I warned you about fucking with him, remember? But did you listen to me? No, you thought it was funny to poke the bear and now you've gotten yourself into a pissing match with him."

"What's the promise you made on Violet's behalf?" Doc pressed.

"The only way I could get Hawke to let your girlfriend go on with her day-to-day life without an obvious police presence was if I promised to be solely responsible for her whereabouts 24/7."

I blinked. "Come again."

"You heard me, Parker. Either you have a cruiser parked outside of your office and house day and night or you deal with me."

"Is there a third door I can look behind?"

"No, there's not a third damned door."

I swirled my tequila. "So, you're going to keep tabs on me every day? Does that mean I need to call you before bed every night and tell you all about my day?"

"No, Parker. It means I'm going to watch you closely 24/7, just as I said I would. My ass is on the line here, same as yours."

My heart pounded in my chest. "Please tell me you went out and bought a big telescope."

Cooper shook his head. "I stopped at your aunt's store before coming here, explained the situation, and cleared my plan with her."

"You did?" I tipped to the side for a moment before righting myself. Between the tequila and Cooper's news, my rudder appeared to be no longer working. "What plan?"

"Starting tonight, we're going to be roommates."

Roommates? Hadn't I already gained one of those with a black stovepipe hat earlier today? "You've gotta be fucking kidding me."

He stood and walked to the fridge, grabbing another beer. "Trust me, Parker." He pointed the bottle at me. "I'm as pissed about this as you are."

Chapter Four

Sunday, December 2nd

I woke up with a throbbing headache at too-fucking-early-o'clock and stumbled downstairs in search of caffeine and pills to stop the train of pain choo-chooing around inside of my skull. When I flicked on the kitchen light, I screeched loud enough to wake the neighbors.

Cooper squinted back at me from where he leaned against the counter, wearing jeans, a holey thermal shirt, and a scowl.

"Damn it, Cooper!" I held my hand over my heart, making sure it hadn't exploded out of my chest and raced for the hills with its tail between its legs. I lowered my voice to a whisper, "What in the hell are you doing here in the dark?"

"Waking up." He held up his coffee cup as I walked over to where he stood policing the coffee maker. His unshaven jaw and shark fin hair made him look extra prickly this morning.

I wrinkled my upper lip at him, grumbling under my breath about having to share my coffee time with a grumpy detective instead of a sexy medium.

With Cooper bedding down on the couch, Doc had decided he'd spend the night in his own house so as not to crowd Aunt Zoe, the kids, and me. I couldn't blame him for wanting to go home. For the first time in over a month, he'd have his house to himself. After living as a bachelor for thirty-nine years, being bombarded with multiple roommates in addition to a girlfriend with two kids probably made Doc's head spin most days.

"Christ, Parker," Cooper said as I opened the cupboard next to his head, grabbing one of Aunt Zoe's soup mugs. "Do you always roll out of bed with your jaws snapping like a rabid dog? I'm amazed Nyce still has all of his digits."

I shouldered Cooper out of my way. I didn't care if he carried multiple firearms and a pair of handcuffs on him most days. No man in his right mind should stand between a woman suffering from post-tequila blues and her caffeine.

"For your information, Cooper," I might have snarled while saying his name, or maybe that was only in my head. "There's something special about you that makes me froth at the mouth most days." I dumped about a third of the coffee pot's contents into the soup mug. No steam rose. I stuck my finger into the black liquid. "It's cold."

I heard a chair slide across the kitchen floor behind me. "Brilliant detective work," he said. "I suppose you'd like me to give you an honorary deputy badge for figuring that out."

Tightening the belt of my robe, I resisted the urge to dump my cold coffee over Cooper's head and marched to the microwave, sticking the mug inside.

"Since we have a few minutes to ourselves," Cooper said, "how about we get something straight here."

I leaned my head against the cupboard door, trying to drudge up the strength to deal with Cooper pre-caffeine. "Maybe I prefer things crooked."

"Stop being purposely combative."

"But combat is what I do best." I was only sort of joking.

One positive aspect of finding out that I was genetically programmed to "execute" was that it helped me to understand why I'd always had such a problem getting along with certain aggressive personalities, especially other alphas like myself … such as Cooper. And Hawke. And Ray Underhill, my nemesis at work since day one. And … well, my point was that introspection had opened my eyes. I had yet to figure out how to temper my hostility when dealing with such traits in others, but Rome wasn't built in a day.

"Your belligerence with Hawke in particular is what has us both stuck here in your aunt's kitchen this morning."

The microwave beeped, indicating the end of Round One. I extracted my soup mug of coffee and set it on the table across from Cooper. I grabbed some milk from the fridge, sloshing it into the mug. "Fine." I capped the milk jug and shoved it back into the fridge. "Let the straightening begin."

He waited for me to settle into the chair. "First, you need to check in with me regularly today."

My blood pressure spiked. I reminded myself that Cooper was the better alternative in this mess. "Define 'regularly.' "

"Once an hour."

"That's absurd." It wasn't going to happen.

"Too bad, get used to it." His gaze dared me to challenge him further. When I lowered my eyes to my coffee, he continued, "Second, do not fight with Detective Hawke."

"What if he starts it?" I lifted the soup mug to my mouth.

"I don't care if he walks up to you and insults your hair point-blank, do not engage with him."

I lowered the mug, swallowing a mouthful of milky coffee. "Why would that asshole insult my hair out of the blue?"

"That's just an example, Parker. Relax."

"I'll relax when you leave my hair out of it."

He cursed. "You're too sensitive about your crazy hair. You ever considered therapy?"

"Call my hair crazy again, and you'll need therapy to rehabilitate your kneecap."

"Kneecaps can't be rehabilitated."

"Just shut up."

"Third—"

"How many freaking rules are there?"

"I didn't say these were rules."

"Don't piss down my back and tell me it's raining."

His gaze narrowed. "Don't try to pull that Clint Eastwood shit on me like you did Hawke."

"Officially, that wasn't an Eastwood line."

"I know who fucking said it," he bit out each word.

"Now who needs to relax?" I took another drink of coffee, meeting his glare head on. "How many rules, Cooper?"

"As many as I need to get us through this debacle without you ending up in jail and me losing my job."

"Well, if you list more than three, I'm going to need a pencil and paper to write them down." I yawned. "What's the third one?"

"The third what?" Aunt Zoe asked as she joined us, her sunshine slippers making a swishing sound on the floor. Her thick, silver-streaked hair was threaded into a braid and draped over the shoulder of her red robe.

She kissed me on the temple and gave Cooper a "Good morning" on her way to the coffee maker.

"The third degree," I answered her question. "Cooper was laying down the law."

"That's what he does best," she said, dumping the last of the old coffee into a cup. "The third degree is better than a third strike. How did you sleep, Cooper?"

"I appreciate you allowing me to invade your privacy, Zoe."

"That didn't answer my question." She placed her coffee cup in the microwave and turned, locking him in her sights. "Were you comfortable on the couch?"

"It was fine. Thanks."

Her dark blue eyes narrowed, but she didn't press him any further. "Violet, did Addy tell you about next weekend?"

"You mean my mother coming up here to inspect Doc?"

"Yep." The microwave beeped. She joined us at the table, taking the chair next to mine. "What do you want to have for dinner when they're here?"

"An excuse not to be here."

"Nice try, kiddo."

I swirled the coffee in my mug. "Did she say if Susan is coming, too?"

She shook her head. "But knowing your sister's history with your boyfriends, I'm guessing she'll tag along."

"Shit. First Hawke, then Tiffany, and now Susan."

Cooper's blond eyebrows crept upward. "What does Tiffany Sugarbell have to do with Ms. Wolff's death or your family?"

"Is she harassing Doc again?" Aunt Zoe asked.

"She never stopped, but it's not that."

Both Aunt Zoe and Cooper waited for me to clarify. As much as I didn't enjoy sharing my personal problems with Cooper, he would probably find out soon enough when Tiffany came at me swinging.

Wincing in anticipation of my aunt's response, I peeked at her from under my eyelids. "Jerry commissioned a new billboard ad over in Spearfish."

She grimaced. "Oh, no."

"Uh, yes." I told her about the black dress, the pen in my mouth, and the singles' ad copy. By the time I finished, profanities slid off her tongue like it was coated in butter.

Cooper, on the other hand, was sporting one of his rare grins. "This is another restraining order in the making."

"What in the hell is that blockhead thinking?" Aunt Zoe asked.

"Cooper? He's just trying to protect me."

The detective guffawed. "You're a riot, Parker."

"You know who I'm talking about, Violet Lynn." She leaned forward, her mouth set. "You need to go into work and tell that boss of yours that you will not be used as a sex object for his company's financial gains."

"I can't. The billboard is already up." It couldn't have been cheap, either. I swirled my coffee again, before taking another swallow.

"Yes, you can. That man thinks he's doing your career a favor, but he's objectifying you. You're more than lips, boobs, and hips, baby girl."

"Don't forget her crazy hair," Cooper said, his grin widening.

I set my mug down. "That's it, Cooper. Prepare to start your day with a solid ass kicking." I pushed back from the table. It was time to unleash some of my frustration and angst about the heat I was taking from Hawke via a series of hard pinches and wild windmill swings with maybe a shin kick or two thrown in the middle.

He leaned back and laughed.

The sound of his laughter was so foreign to me that I froze midway out of my chair. Totally befuddled, I stared at him for several seconds. "Are you ill, Cooper?"

He laughed even harder, his whole face crinkling, softening, looking almost human.

"Cooper is laughing." I frowned at Aunt Zoe, lowering back into my seat. "Should we call 911?"

She eyed the detective, apparently as mesmerized as I was by his sudden attack of funny-bone-itis. "Let's give him a few more seconds to see if this spell passes."

It did soon enough. He sobered quickly, turning back into the stony-faced detective I knew and hissed at on a daily basis.

"What in the hell happened there?" I asked him.

He squeezed the bridge of his nose. "I don't know. That was weird. It hit me out of nowhere and I couldn't stop."

Aunt Zoe and I exchanged knowing glances. Some people cried to relieve stress, others yelled and threw things. Cooper, it turned out, laughed.

This sudden spasm of laughter from him made the butterflies in my stomach flutter like mad. Why was Cooper so stressed? Was it a side effect of trying to find a new home for his collection of firearms? Or was the evidence Detective Hawke had dug up more damning than I'd feared?

"What was the third thing you were going to tell me?" I asked him. "The thing before Aunt Zoe joined us."

"I need you to recount everything you can about your actions and experiences in Ms. Wolff's apartment."

"I already did that multiple times while you wrote it all down in your little notepad, remember?"

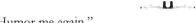

"Humor me again."

I sighed. "Right now?" The last thing I wanted to do with my head still throbbing from tequila was endure one of Cooper's interrogations.

"Yes, Parker."

I looked at Aunt Zoe. She nodded once. I wished Doc were here to back me up and help spur my memory. He'd been there in the apartment with me on multiple occasions.

"Is this on or off the record?" I was going to need more caffeine if what came out of my mouth was going to be used against me in a court of law.

"From now on, you and I will operate *off* the record unless Detective Hawke or any other law enforcement personnel are in the vicinity."

"Okay, if we're off the record, then you need to pinkie swear that you won't threaten to handcuff me or throw me in jail." I held out my pinkie.

He squinted at it as if it were cocked and loaded. "For how long?"

"Until we return to a state of always being *on* the record."

His hesitation wasn't comforting at all. "Fine," he grumbled, but didn't lock his finger with mine.

"Pinkie swear, Cooper."

"Jesus, Parker."

I shook my pinkie at him. He rolled his eyes and leaned forward, locking pinkies with me. "Deal." He pulled free and sat back. "Now, tell me again how it all started."

"You mean with Ms. Wolff's phone call?"

He nodded.

"But I've told you that part so many times."

"Pretend you haven't."

I glanced at the clock, making sure I had time for this trip down memory lane before work. Unfortunately, time was on Cooper's side.

Starting with Ms. Wolff's call, I rehashed how she'd demanded I go to her apartment immediately because she was about to die. In monotone mode, I explained how she called me a *Scharfrichter*, which I later learned was German for *Executioner*, and then how she'd been not only dead when Harvey and I showed up on her doorstep, but decapitated and withered up like a raisin.

"Cut the pissy attitude," Cooper ordered, "and tell me about the clocks."

"The Black Forest cuckoo clocks covering her walls?" Why? Was that what Hawke had on me? Something to do with all of those eerie clocks and the macabre scenes carved onto them?

When he nodded, I asked, "What about them besides how unnerving they are and how they don't seem to need batteries or winding to work?" Although not all of them were working. Some were going off incessantly but only in the world on the other side of her bedroom mirror. Unfortunately, I had no proof of that for Cooper because so far I was the only one who could hear them, which made me feel cuckoo, too.

"Tell me about the unusual experiences you've had in regard to Ms. Wolff's clocks."

I tilted my head to the side, sizing him up from a different angle. "What's this all about Cooper? If Hawke found my fingerprints on the clocks, you were there with me when I was touching them." Although there had been a night when Doc and I had sneaked into Ms. Wolff's apartment and he'd left prints as well. But wouldn't Hawke be picking on Doc, too, if this were only about fingerprints?

"It's about who murdered Ms. Wolff."

"It wasn't me."

Aunt Zoe reached over and squeezed my wrist, her smile offering comfort.

"I know that," Cooper snapped. "But if I'm going to help untangle you from Hawke's web, I need to refresh my memory on all of the details."

"Or are you trying to trip me up?" I leaned forward, searching his face for any signs of deception. "To make me admit to some crime that Hawke thinks I've committed."

Cooper crossed his arms. "You're being paranoid, Parker."

"Can you blame me? How can I be sure you're not a double agent?"

"Do I look like a man who has the patience to play spy games?"

"Right now, you look tired."

"Precisely."

"Pretty worn out, too, like an old boot." I glanced at Aunt Zoe. "I don't think the couch was very comfortable for Cooper's bony ass."

She looked him over, nodding. "The recliner is more cozy. That couch has seen better days. I should probably start shopping for a new one."

"The couch was fine," he grated.

"Your shoulders look stiff, too."

"That's enough. Let's move on."

Oh, I planned to move on—right on past this interrogation, because I was capital D-O-N-E with being pushed around this morning by him. "They're actually a little lopsided," I continued.

His nostrils flared.

"You could use a good massage to relax all of that tension you keep stored between your head and toes."

"Parker—"

"You know who gives a good massage?" I didn't let his glare intimidate me. "Natalie."

Cooper flinched at the sound of her name.

"She does have a lot of strength in her arms and wrists from all of that manual labor," Aunt Zoe added.

"Yeah." I hit Cooper with a knowing look. "Her grip is killer."

Cooper's eyes widened, his cheeks mottling. He pushed his chair back, standing. "I said that's enough, Parker." He grabbed his coffee cup and downed what was left in one gulp.

"Is the interrogation over already, Detective?" I feigned innocence.

"For now."

"You can leave your coffee cup in the sink," Aunt Zoe told him as he left the table.

"Is it okay if I use your shower?" he asked Aunt Zoe.

"Sure."

"Make it quick," I said. "I need to get ready for work, too."

"I'll take as long as I need," he returned with a squint.

"And don't use all of the hot water," I told his rigid backside as he left the kitchen. I turned back to see Aunt Zoe frowning at me. "What?"

"You should be nicer to him, baby girl."

I scoffed. "Me? He's the one who's always making fun of my hair and giving me orders."

"He's trying to save your bacon."

Guilt made my cheeks warm. She was right, of course, but … "Why is he helping me?"

"Maybe because under all of his frustration with his current situation, he respects you."

We both looked up at the ceiling at the sound of the water running in the bathroom overhead.

"Nah. I think he's doing it for Doc. They're like this now." I twisted my fingers together. "Or maybe it's for Natalie, since he knows she'll find a way to end up in jail next to me if Hawke locks me up."

I finished my coffee and started to rise, but she caught my hand and pulled me back down in my seat. "Now that he's out of earshot, we need to talk."

"We do? About what?"

"The book with our family history."

I cringed. "I … uh … I haven't had a chance to read any more of it yet."

She smirked. "And you wonder where Addy gets her procrastination trait."

"I know, I know. I'll get to it. It's just that history isn't my favorite subject."

"This isn't just any old history, Violet Lynn. It's key to your survival."

The book she was talking about was filled with details concerning previous executioners in our family line, including their choice of weapons, tales of executions, and favorite attire for killing. Okay, so that last part wasn't true, but maybe if they'd listed their outfits for each kill I'd be able to picture the scene better and find the stories less dry. Both times I'd tried to really dig into the book, I'd fallen asleep on the open pages.

"I'm going to read it, I swear. I've been a little preoccupied with work and life is all."

"And Doc." Her gaze challenged me to deny it.

I didn't. "And Doc."

She snorted.

"I can't help it, Aunt Zoe. It's been a long time since I've had a man in my life, especially one who likes me in spite of my quirks." And one who could kiss the clothes right off of me.

She lifted my chin, searching my eyes, her forehead wrinkling. "Ah, baby girl. You're in too deep."

"Way over my head." I thought I'd been gaga for Doc before he started spending the night with me regularly, but sleeping next to him had upped the ante. My heart wasn't the only thing in the pot to lose now. If he left, he'd take my soul along as a two-for-one deal.

"I'd tell you to be careful, but it won't do you any good now."

I shook my head. "I'm a runaway freight train. There's no walking away from this if I crash." That's what scared me about Susan trolling my waters again. Why couldn't a twister come to town and carry her away to Munchkinland for good?

"You know I'll be here to pick up the pieces if needed, but I'll be shocked if Doc pulls the shit Reid did." She rose, taking her cup to the sink.

Reid Martin was Deadwood's fire captain—the one who'd come up with my "Sparky" moniker. While he was an ace at putting out fires around town, he had a history of lighting flames in Aunt Zoe's bed. Unfortunately, their relationship had flickered a few years back due to his doubts. Then someone's heart ended up burned—Aunt Zoe's—and the fire got doused. But underneath it all, the coals still smoldered when they were together. I had my fingers crossed the flames would catch hold again, raging into a full-fledged inferno with a little time and help, but Aunt Zoe was being stubborn about adding any fuel to the fire. One burn in a lifetime was plenty for her.

The water shut off overhead.

Wow, that was a quick shower. I probably shouldn't have rushed Cooper. Warm water might have released some of that pent-up frustration that had him snarling at the end of his chain each day.

"Violet, you need to learn about the executioners in our family line." Aunt Zoe pulled a dishrag from the drawer and wet it, picking up Cooper's coffee cup. "You've been lucky so far, but that luck will run dry. Mark my words."

I sighed, knowing when my aunt had her teeth locked onto a bone. "Fine. How about I read a page or two each night?"

"You can't." She washed the cup, rinsed it, and set it in the dish rack to dry.

I joined her at the sink. "I can't?" I didn't understand. Hadn't she just said I needed to read the book?

"Nope." She washed and rinsed her own cup, and then took mine from me. "I put the book in Doc's pickup last night before he left."

"Why?"

"Because I realized that the best way to teach you about the past is through Doc." She rinsed my mug and set it next to the other two, draping the rag over the faucet. "You always were more of an auditory learner anyway."

The sound of the front door opening and closing made us both look toward the dining room archway.

"Hello?" Natalie Beals called, strolling into the kitchen. She shivered, unzipping her black leather coat. The wind had whipped her wavy brown hair into a wild state and kissed her cheeks pink. "Guess what?"

"Chicken butt," I replied, playing one of our childhood games.

She smiled, her eyes lighting up. "Guess why?"

"Chicken thigh."

"Exactly." She shucked her coat. "Woo wee! It's colder than a witch's tit out there this morning."

I leaned against the counter. "You really need to stop feeling up witches."

She finger combed her hair. "Where will I get my kicks then? I'm on sabbatical from cruising for warlocks, remember?"

Natalie had a history of relationship disasters. After the last explosion involving her Mr. Clean–looking boyfriend and a tramp with tasseled nipples, she'd decided to take a sabbatical from men. After a bumpy start, she'd managed to stay on course and was a more confident woman for it. This newfound assuredness was why I was hesitant to bring Cooper's interest to her attention. What if the only reason he was attracted to her again was because she wasn't shopping for a relationship? What if they got together and she fell head over heels like I had with Doc and then Cooper left her crying in the gutter, a bottle of tequila her new best friend? What if …

Damn. As if I didn't have enough worries of my own. There was no need to take on the weight of something that hadn't even happened.

Grinning, I told her, "I've heard tales that one of the older washing machines at Spuds and Suds has an especially pleasurable spin cycle."

She pulled out a chair and fell into it. "Criminy. You know you're at a low point in life when you're hitting laundromats for your next orgasm."

A movement behind her caught my eye. Cooper stood in the entryway, freshly showered and shaven, his hair only spikey where it was supposed to be now. His focus was locked on Natalie, like she'd been singing to him from the rocky shore.

Speaking of low points in life, Cooper represented a current one of mine. "Did you even use soap?" I asked him, amazed at his speed in and out of the shower.

Natalie did a double take at the sight of him, turning back to me with a what-the-hell gape.

"Yes." He leaned against the arch, dragging his gaze off Natalie to better glare at me. "You have a lot of soap options."

I raised my hands. "Guilty, Detective." Doc had a thing for flavored soap, so I'd made it a goal to turn my shower into a buffet line. "Is that illegal in Deadwood?"

His lips thinned. "Why do they smell like different flavors of ice cream?"

He thought they smelled like ice cream? Interesting. That gave me an idea. Something new to torture him with the next time he pissed me off. "Do you like ice cream?"

Aunt Zoe cleared her throat. "I'm making fresh coffee, Natalie. You want some?" She grabbed a coffee filter, filling the coffee pot with water.

"Uh, yeah." Nat glanced from me to Cooper and back. "Zoe, is your front door now an entrance into a parallel dimension?"

"Not that I know of." Aunt Zoe added coffee grounds and hit the brew button. "More coffee for you, Cooper?"

"Thanks. I'll take one for the road, if you don't mind."

Oh, good. That meant he was leaving soon. Early morning interrogations made me jittery.

Natalie stood and walked over to Cooper. "He looks like Coop." She poked him in the chest. "He feels like Coop." Then she went up on her tiptoes and sniffed near his neck. "He even smells like Coop with a dollop of coconut ice cream on the side."

A muscle in Cooper's jaw pulsed as he stared down at her.

"He busts my balls just like Cooper, too," I told her.

Natalie scratched her head. "What did you do with Doc?"

"He's at home."

Aunt Zoe spoke up, answering Natalie's questioning stare. "I've invited Cooper to stay with us for a while."

Natalie searched Zoe's face, then Cooper's, and then mine. "Are you guys playing some kind of practical joke on me?"

"No joke." I wished it was, but it seemed that I'd been blessed with not just one new roommate this week, but two. Unfortunately, neither was the man I wanted in my life day and night.

"Cooper is going to stay here? With Violet?"

"Temporarily," he clarified.

"Did you get in a fight with Doc?" she asked him.

He shook his head. "I figured Nyce could use a break from me."

"You think I was born yesterday, Coop? There's no way in hell you'd leave Doc for Violet. Tell me what's really going on." When he didn't answer, she turned to me. "Spill it, Vi, or I'm going to give you the queen mother of all noogies."

I glared at Cooper. "You better not let it come to that."

"Fine. You can tell her, but that's it. Nobody else."

"Tell me what?"

I filled Natalie in on Detective Hawke's newest attempt to blackmail me, Cooper's promise to keep me in his sights 24/7, and Jerry's latest effort to turn me into a billboard strumpet. The last part had nothing to do with her catching Cooper in my aunt's kitchen first thing in the morning, but while I had the spillway open, I figured I might as well empty the reservoir.

"So you're going to spend every single night here?" At his nod, she asked, "Where are you going to be sleeping?"

That was an interesting question coming from a girl who claimed she wasn't interested in anything the detective had to offer outside of the law.

"He's on the couch for now," Aunt Zoe answered.

I hit her with a raised brow. What was this *for now* business? Did she have plans to add a spare bedroom?

Natalie looked at Cooper. "Sleeping on that couch will make you wake up feeling like you've spent the night in a boxing ring. I'd take the recliner if I were you, old man." Her grin was teasing.

"Old man?" He raised one eyebrow. "I don't have that many years on you, Beals."

Natalie tipped her head to the side. "How do you know my age?"

I scoffed. "He's a cop. He probably has your date of birth, weight, and organ donor status memorized. Hey, that reminds me, what do you want to do for your birthday?" Her big day was coming up soon. "Do you want a wild party or just the two of us?"

She frowned, rubbing her chin. "Let's keep it to you and me at the Purple Door Saloon. We can line up tequila shots."

"I never turn down tequila."

"I'll watch the kids," Aunt Zoe offered, earning an air-kiss from me.

Natalie thumbed in Cooper's direction. "Are you going to introduce him to your parents this weekend?"

"How do you know about that?"

"A little birdy named Addy told me when I called here looking for you yesterday." Her full lips split into a grin. "Then she asked me if I knew whether or not you're giving away free milk to Doc."

I cursed my mother again for opening her big mouth.

"I'll step out while Violet's parents are here," Cooper answered.

"You should stay." Natalie's eyes sparkled with mirth. "I'm sure it would make things more confusing if a man other than her boyfriend is sleeping here with her."

"Cooper is not sleeping with me." I drilled her with a hard stare, wanting to make it clear that this would not be a repeat of the royal fuckup that happened with Doc and her and me after she'd staked a claim on him last summer. While she'd stated multiple times that she wasn't interested in getting to first base again with Cooper, I'd seen her watch his butt when he ran around the infield. There was still a spark there between them, and I was going to stay way up high in the bleachers this time, no matter how the game played out.

"I know that," she said. "But that doesn't need to be public information." When I grabbed a spatula and threatened to throw it at her, she held up her hands, laughing. "Hear me out. If the Bitch from Hell is with your mom and dad, wouldn't you rather sic her on Coop than let her sniff around Doc?"

Cooper frowned. "Are we talking about Tiffany again?"

"Again?" Natalie looked at me. "What's up with Tiff—oh! The billboard." She sucked air through her teeth. "That's gonna go south fast."

"I know, right?"

"We'd better put our heads together and plan a solid defense. Do you still have that stun gun?"

Cooper's eyes got a steely glint in them. "Aren't you in enough trouble already, Parker?"

"You tell me, Cooper."

We exchanged a series of glares until Aunt Zoe interrupted us by handing him a travel cup. "Coffee for the road, Coop."

"Thanks, Zoe." He stretched his back with a slight grimace, focusing on Natalie again. "So what are you up to this morning, Beals, besides trying to row Parker even farther up shit creek?"

She held up a keychain with the number "2" on it. Two keys dangled from it. "I'm moving in to my new digs for the winter."

"New digs?" I blinked in surprise. We'd talked about this last week, but I hadn't expected her to leap so fast. "Where?"

"The Galena House. One of the tenants recently moved out. Freesia is letting me stay there in exchange for playing handywoman."

"Why does she need a handywoman?" Aunt Zoe asked.

"She thinks fixing up the place more will help to sell it quicker."

As Freesia's Realtor, I thought that was a brilliant plan. Plus, now my best friend would live only a hop, skip, and a jump away this winter instead of ten miles out of town on icy roads.

"You're moving into the Galena House?" Cooper asked. Judging from the rigid expression lining his face, he wasn't going to be bouncing for joy along with me.

"Yep, right above Ms. Wolff's old apartment." She shook her new keys at me. "You and Doc should come camp out. We can put our ears to the floor and listen for anything to go bump in the night."

Chapter Five

Mona Hollister's SUV was the only one of my coworkers' vehicles parked behind Calamity Jane Realty when I rolled into the parking lot. I could smell her jasmine perfume as soon as I stepped inside the back door. Unwinding my scarf, I walked past Jerry's open office door only to skid to a stop.

What in the ... I backed up.

"Cornelius?" I called from the threshold to the man sprawled face up on the floor in front of Jerry's desk. Thankfully, he was dressed in a black sweater and pants this morning, which were steps up from the raggedy robe and hairy legs I'd expected to greet me upon arrival.

When he didn't respond, I moved inside the office and stood over him. His chest was rising and lowering under his sweater. "Cornelius?" I said again, nudging his leg.

Still nothing.

I squatted next to him, my knees popping in complaint. "Wake up," I said, shaking his shoulder.

When that didn't work, I touched the side of his neck with my cold fingers.

He jerked upright.

I yipped and fell back onto my butt, my brown suede boots flying up in the air. Good thing I was wearing leggings today under my long wool skirt or I'd have shown him one dandy of a view of London and France along with my damned underpants.

"What day is it?" he asked. His gaze drifted down over my leggings. "Are those cashmere?" His bony fingers reached toward my calf.

"Yes, but no touching." I sat upright and knocked his hand away, pulling my skirt down over my legs. "It's Sunday."

"When did that happen?"

"Just after midnight last night."

"In which time zone?"

There was no way I was starting my day by falling down one of

Cornelius's rabbit holes with him. "I'm done talking about this."

His black eyebrows angled down toward his long nose. His cornflower blue eyes were extra bright this morning without the red lines or sagging lids I'd witnessed last month when he was being haunted by Wilda Hessler and her spooky-ass clown doll. "I'm sensing something here, Violet."

What? Was it Jane's ghost?

He held his hand palm-out in front of my sternum and then lifted it to my forehead. "Your third-eye chakra is blocked, obstructing your intuition and interfering with your ability to focus on the big picture."

"It's not blocked," I told him. "I blindfolded it."

"Why on earth would you cover your third eye?"

"Because what I'm seeing with the other two scares me plenty." I glanced back toward the open door, making sure Mona wasn't witnessing our odd discussion. "What were you doing on the floor?" I asked in a lowered voice to be safe.

"Call it some spiritual housecleaning."

"Fine, but the next time you do some soul ironing while lying on the floor in a haunted office, close the dang door so nobody freaks out and calls 911."

"Ah-ha!" He popped up onto his feet remarkably fast for a skinny stick insect. "You've seen it, too."

"Seen what?" I frowned up at him.

"The apparition."

"Shhhh." I scrambled to my feet, not nearly as quickly or gracefully as he had, stepping on my long skirt and stumbling into Jerry's desk.

"Are you afraid of the entity hearing you?" he asked.

"No, I don't want my coworkers to know."

"So, this is about your ability to communicate with the dead."

"Gahhh!" I rushed over and closed the office door. What part of *shush* didn't he understand? When the door was shut, I strode back to him, still keeping my voice low. "Nobody here at work knows about my side gig and I want to keep it that way, okay?"

He stroked his goatee. "To which side gig do you refer?"

"Which do you think, Cornelius?" I was no jack of all trades. Hell, I was barely a jack of one trade most days.

One black eyebrow inched upward. "My secretary?"

"I'm not your secretary."

"Right. That's a sexist term these days, isn't it? Perhaps we should call you my assistant?"

I balled my fist, fantasizing adding a crooked bend to his nose.

"Cornelius, I am not your assistant either. Or your right-hand woman."

"Of course you're not. I'm ambidextrous."

Sweet and sour pickles! "Let's get this straight here and now—I'm in no way, shape, or form a subordinate of yours."

His forehead pinched. "But you bring me protein shakes."

"I do that because I'm your friend."

"Friend?" He said it as if trying the word on for size. "I only have one of those. He owns a haunted hotel in Nevada."

"Well, now you have two."

"Excellent. The best things come in pairs, like nostrils, pillowcases, and chromosomes." He started to turn away, but stopped, looking back at me. "But you will still bring me protein shakes?"

"So long as you promise to keep the foundation on which our friendship is based a secret from everyone besides Doc."

"What does your doctor have to do with channeling ghosts?"

"Not my *doctor*. I mean Doc." When he continued to give me a blank look, I sighed. "You know, the medium whose office is next door to this one."

"The tall medium with whom you're exchanging bodily fluids?"

I grimaced. Did he have to focus on *that* aspect? "Yeah, him."

He winked at me. "Gotcha."

Did he mean he'd tricked me and really knew who Doc was, or he understood that I meant … fuck it. It didn't matter.

"Did you hear anything last night from our resident ghost?" I asked, looking around the office to see if Jane had been busy relocating furniture and paperwork like she had with Jerry lately.

"The apparition was silent all evening." He moved around behind the desk, bending to look at one of the computer screens. "My video and sound recorders didn't pick up anything other than me."

After how disruptive Wilda's ghost had been for Cornelius, maybe a quiet night was a good thing. He certainly seemed much more rested than he had for a while. Staying at Calamity Jane's could be good for his health.

"When was the last time you saw it?" he asked, his eyes still on his monitor.

"Her," I corrected.

He glanced up. "Who?"

"The apparition you are here to make contact with. It's a her, not an it."

Even though Jane wasn't here in the flesh, reducing her ectoplasmic entity to an "it" grated on me. She had been a wonderful, generous woman full of vitality and spunk until that spikey little bitch had snuffed the life from her. Jane deserved to be called a "her" after pouring so much of her soul into this business that now supported my family.

"Are you sure about that?" he asked.

"Positive."

"Have you reached out to it without me?"

"Reached out to *her*, you mean."

His gaze held mine. He closed one eye and then the other, tilting his head slightly. "Have you made contact with *her*?"

I shook my head. "Doc ... I mean the tall medium was the first to detect a presence here. He confirmed it was a 'her'—my old boss, to be exact."

"I shall speak with the tall medium further about this entity, see what other information he can offer on your ghost boss."

Someone knocked on Jerry's office door.

Cornelius frowned at the door. "Violet, did you hear a knocking sound just now, or have you brought something over from the other side again?"

I rolled my eyes and walked to the door, pulling it open.

Mona stood there with a smile on her glossy pink lips and a curious glint in her eyes. She looked as dazzling as ever, reminding me of Grace Kelly, all decked out for an evening on the town. Her cream-colored mohair shawl made her auburn hair look even more red than usual. A single strand of pearls graced her long neck.

"I thought I heard you come in," she said to me, glancing over my shoulder.

"Mona, you've met Cornelius, right?"

"Yes." Her expertly tweezed, auburn brows lifted. "You were on the floor when I came in earlier and didn't rouse when I called your name. Are you feeling okay?"

"I was recharging."

The corner of Mona's mouth twitched. "Are you back to one hundred percent now?"

"I will be after I finish the protein drink Violet left for me in the refrigerator."

I frowned at him. "What drink?"

I'd been running late this morning after trying to help Layne look for his late library book. For once, he wasn't reading about ghosts. This one focused on weapons from the Middle Ages. My son's interests ran eclectic at best, jumping from history to anatomy to the paranormal. Luckily, we'd found it in the basement behind Elvis the chicken's cage. After dusting off the feathers, it'd looked almost as good as new—a few pecks on the spine notwithstanding.

"Doc stopped by this morning and left the drink for you." Mona solved the case of the appearing protein drink. "He got you a six-pack, actually."

My heart danced a jig of joy. Sweet and considerate Doc. While saying "Good night" to him on the front porch, I'd grumbled again about needing to get a protein drink for Cornelius, my *other* roommate, first thing this morning. He must have paid a visit to the Piggly Wiggly up in Lead and picked up the protein shakes, swinging back by the office before heading south to see his client in Hill City. How could I pay him back for his help? I know, I'd pour some butterscotch syrup down my shirt.

"Violet," Mona said, interrupting my sticky, X-rated head trip. "There's someone here for you."

There was a hesitant undertone in her voice that made me pause. "Who is it?" Please don't let it be Tiffany. I hadn't had enough tequila yet today to handle her sharp talons.

She moved closer, speaking in my ear. "Dominick Masterson."

I pulled back in surprise. "Here? In our office? Right now?"

"Yes, yes, and yes. He's waiting at your desk." She winked. "And looking smoking hot to boot."

"I'll talk to you more later, Cornelius." Shedding my coat and scarf, I hung it by the back door before heading out front to see what Lead's man of mystery wanted.

Dominick sat on the corner of my desk, looking cologne-ad suave in his charcoal suit and half-buttoned wool topcoat. His Italian leather dress shoes probably cost more than my yearly car insurance bill. With his square jaw smooth-shaven and his dark hair slicked back, he looked doubly dangerous to the population—especially those equipped with a uterus. For me personally, he was positively deadly, and standing too close reminded me of that fact every time we shared breathing space.

"Hello, Violet," he said, his voice whiskey-smooth. "That color of blue really suits you."

"Thank you." I swallowed the bout of nausea that came with his nearness and forced a smile to my lips, keeping the desk between us. "What brings you to Calamity Jane Realty this morning, Mr. Masterson?"

"Please, call me Dominick."

"Dominick it is. How's Ginny doing these days?"

His wife's whereabouts were something I'd wondered about since Harvey recently mentioned a juicy bit of gossip speculating that she'd up and left town for another man.

"Didn't you hear? She's left me for another."

He said it like a man who'd lost a free-range cow in the hills, not a beautiful, young, blond wife. "I'm sorry to hear that."

He shrugged. "Her happiness must come first." His eyes drifted down to my mouth. "Besides, there are other fish in the sea."

I knew better than to take his flirting seriously. For one thing, according to Aunt Zoe, I was the sort of poisonous fish his "kind" avoided hooking. For another, we were mortal enemies in normal times, and cautious adversaries at best during dark days like those that were supposedly upon us.

"Good luck with your fishing." The sound of clacking coming from Mona's keyboard made me hold my tongue to only modest salutations. My coworkers knew nothing of the short but bizarre history Dominick and I shared and I wanted to keep it that way. "What can I do for you, Dominick?"

"I'm in need of your services."

"You have some properties in mind?"

My ex-boss and the building's current ghost, Jane, had been acting as Dominick's Realtor up until she'd been murdered. He'd once hinted that he could use another agent to take her place. Had the time come when he planned on following through on that remark?

"A few. I would like you to help me."

There was something about the way he was watching me that made the hairs on the back of my neck rise. "Maybe we should discuss your needs in more detail to make sure I'm the right agent for what you need."

"Oh, you're definitely the right one for the job."

Mona's finger-clacking stopped. I didn't need to look over at her to know she was now all ears on this conversation. She recently had to take over a client of mine who was harassing me when my boss wasn't looking. A client who also happened to be the sperm donor for my children. She was probably wondering if Dominick would be another client from whom I'd need rescuing.

"You'd mentioned a couple of months ago that you'd be looking for a replacement for Jane," I said, trying to smooth things over so Mona would return to her key-clacking. "I'm happy to do what I can to help, although I'm not as knowledgeable as Jane."

"But you have a lot of potential."

For what? Burning down buildings? Getting blamed for an old woman's murder? Killing troublemakers?

Mona returned to clacking.

"How about you follow me out, Violet, and I'll give you the list of potential properties my secretary has put together."

Good idea. Once we were outside he could tell me what in the hell he was really doing here. "Are you out front or in back?"

"Front. Just down the street in the lot next to the police station."

I cringed at the idea of going near the cop shop, but curiosity trumped my aversion to police badges. "Let me grab my coat."

I told Mona I'd be right back on my way past her, coat in hand. She gave me a raised-brow look and I smiled back, letting her know this was all hunky-dory.

Dominick held the door for me. We headed down the sidewalk, passing in front of Doc's dark office, strolling toward Deadwood's Rec Center. I maintained enough distance between us for me to keep the nausea at bay that his presence inspired.

After we'd crossed the street and reached the parking lot next to the station, I stopped. A cold wind blasted my cheeks. I burrowed down into my scarf. "What are you really doing here, Dominick?"

He watched a dirty old pickup with ice-crusted fenders pass on the street. "I want to hire you."

"You were serious about needing an agent?"

"Yes." He looked at me, his eyes so dark that I couldn't distinguish his pupils from his corneas. "But I also want to hire you for your other services."

"What other services?" If that damned new billboard made him think I was some kind of call girl, I was going to find Jerry and pop him in the nose.

"Those you were born to do, *Scharfrichter*."

I took a step back at the sound of my other title. "You have something you want executed?"

"Captured, not executed."

My gaze narrowed, but I said nothing. I was a killer, not a dogcatcher.

"You see, before you executed her, Calypso freed something very valuable to me. Something that can wreak havoc amongst the wrong sort."

Caly had wreaked plenty of havoc on her own, murdering with glee on a whim. Hearing her name again made my molars grind.

"You want me to catch the *lidérc*?" I asked. Just thinking about the other shadowy "being" Dominick wanted me to snare in a net gave me goosebumps.

He nodded.

I'd tried to catch the Hungarian devil before and it'd slipped my grasp with ease. "Why me? Don't you know someone in your 'other' circle who can do the job?"

"It's complicated."

"What's complicated?"

"The capture. It's not for the faint of heart."

I scoffed. "What makes you think my heart isn't faint?"

He laughed, loud enough to turn the heads of a pair of cops rushing through the cold into the station's side door.

"Oh, Violet. You are as funny as you are deadly."

He should see me and my hair first thing in the morning. I'd tickle the living hell right out of him ... if that was even possible for a man I suspected to be a native of the fiery realm.

Dominick sobered in a flash. "Think about my offer."

"What's in it for me?" Besides the possibility of having the *lidérc* attach itself to me and make my life even more hellish than getting stuck on the Tilt-a-Whirl ride at the county fair with Cooper and Hawke for hours on end.

"What would you like, *Scharfrichter*?"

Guaranteed safety for my family, college tuition fully paid for my kids, a certain blowhard detective to be shipped off to the Antarctic to measure the sea ice for a season or two ...

Movement over by the side door of the station caught my eye.

Detective Stone Hawke stared across the lot at me. Make that more like glared with his thick unibrow looking like a single fat caterpillar glued to his forehead.

Shitballs! Hadn't Cooper's rubber glove treatment this morning been enough punishment for one day?

"Same Hell, different devil," I muttered as Hawke headed my way. "Dominick, you should probably leave now."

"Is that Detective Cooper's partner coming our way?"

"Yes, unfortunately, and I don't think he's happy about me talking to you."

Dominick held out a business card. "Call me when you've had time to think about my offer."

What offer? We hadn't made it through the what's-in-it-for-me part yet.

After a nod good-bye, Dominick strode over to a black, shiny Land Rover, leaving me to face off with Detective Hawke on my own on the count of three, two ...

"Parker, what in the hell are you doing talking to a key witness in my murder case?" Hawke's bluster matched Mother Nature's this morning.

As usual, the big buttinski stepped over the invisible line I'd toed on the asphalt and right into my comfort zone. His cheeks looked extra ruddy up close, almost clownish. I scowled at him, taking in his baggy pants, his puffy brown polyester jacket, and scruffy sideburns, which blended into the earflaps of the winter trapper hat he had pushed down on his overinflated noggin.

"Dominick Masterson is hiring me as his real estate agent, Detective. Not that it's any of your business."

His beady eyes narrowed. He leaned down, shoving his index finger in my face. The coffee on his breath smelled acidic, just like his personality. "Every single move you make these days is my business, Parker."

I will not bite his finger.

I will not bite his finger.

I will not bite his fucking finger!

Barely keeping my choppers behind my lips, I stepped back and put some much needed space between us.

"I won't put up with your police harassment, Detective. While I am allowing Detective Cooper to keep tabs on me for the time being, I'd advise you not to push your luck and piss me off."

"Why? What are you going to do, Witch Woman? Put a spell on me?"

I wasn't sure a spell could do the trick he direly needed. Detective Hawke had a problem—his ego was two sizes too big for his bumbling body. Besides that, he had this misconception that he was a great detective, but the only thing he was actually good at being was an ass.

As much as I'd like to stomp on Hawke's toe and ram my knee into his groin, I'd told Cooper I'd play nice. "I'll file a police harassment report on you."

His laugh was downright mean. "Oh, you do that, Parker. I'll make sure personally that it gets filed … right down the toilet with your reputation."

Another cold blast made me pull my coat tighter around me. "Can we have this pissing match some other day, Detective? It's cold out here."

"Sure, as soon as you tell me what you did with the clocks."

"What clocks?"

"The ones stolen off the walls in Ms. Wolff's apartment last night."

"Why would I steal her clocks?"

"That's what I'm asking."

"Do you have any proof that it was me? Cooper was in the same house as me all night, remember?"

"You could have had one of your minions do it while you distracted Cooper."

Oh, right. Hawke believed I was the Queen of Minion-land.

"As for my proof, don't worry that frizzy blond head about it."

A streak of red shot across my vision at his hair insult. It took me a couple of blinks to clear the fireworks it left behind from my sight. "I don't know anything about missing clocks, Detective."

"I don't believe you."

"Believe what you want, but I have alibis besides Cooper."

"Who?"

"My aunt Zoe, for one."

He guffawed, a billow of steam coming from his mouth. "Your aunt is about as trustworthy as you are."

Something tightened in my spine, making me stand up straighter. "My aunt is a well-respected woman in this community. She's been here all her life and many of those who are on the city council and part of the Deadwood Chamber of Commerce will vouch for her."

"That's because she has them under her spell. If she's your flesh and blood, then she undoubtedly has her fingers mixed up in all of your schemes and crimes. I'm keeping an eye on her, too. First the bedroom mirror somehow got shattered and now more clocks are missing. Something smells fishy, and your aunt handles glass for a living."

I hid my wince. The bedroom mirror was sort of my fault, but there was no way I was owning up to that one. "I repeat. My aunt is innocent of all of these so-called crimes you're trying to pin on me."

The leer on his face made me clench my fists. "According to what I've heard from several of the locals, she's far from innocent."

My ears started to steam. The wind was no match for the furnace he'd lit inside of me. "What is that supposed to mean?"

His smug grin was begging for my fist. "She's been around, burning plenty of sheets in town."

That was it. It was one thing to insult me, but nobody disrespected my aunt to my face.

I closed one eye and cackled loud and long. An old man walking his dog on the sidewalk stopped and looked my way. Wiggling my fingers at Hawke's wide eyes, I donned a creaky voice and chanted, "Eye of newt, leg of klutz, wither his pecker and shrink his nuts. Shazam!"

When I pretended to zap Hawke with my fake spell, he stumbled backward in surprise, tripped over a concrete parking curb, and fell flat on his rump on the asphalt.

I stepped over the parking curb and leaned down, pointing at his third-eye chakra so he'd clearly see the big picture I was about to paint. "You say one more derogatory thing about my aunt, you egotistical snot-bucket, and I'll make your twig and berries fall right off." I pretended to throw invisible fairy dust at him and added for good measure, "Poof!"

He snarled, sputtering before regaining control of his tongue. "Are you threatening an officer of the law, Parker?"

"Nope. I'm warning a piece of shit civilian who thinks wearing a badge on his crummy 1970s blazers gives him the freedom to insult upstanding citizens in this community."

After one more threatening wiggle of my fingers, I strode toward Calamity Jane's.

"You're going down, Parker!" he yelled at my back. "Mark my words."

"Don't get cold water on your weenie, Detective," I said over my shoulder. "It'll shrivel up twice as fast."

After a smile and a wave at the old guy on the sidewalk still gaping at me, I crossed the street, escaped to the warmth inside Calamity Jane's, and parked my ass at my desk.

Now to wait for the shit-storm sure to blow my way.

Chapter Six

It turned out that pretending to put a hex on Detective Hawke was not one of my brighter moves, a detail that Cooper cursed at me about via text messages repeatedly throughout my day until I put my cell phone in silent mode.

Unfortunately, with Doc working down near Hill City all day, I couldn't scamper over and hide in his office. I couldn't even call and whine in his ear because his client lived in the boonies out of cell phone reach. So I was on my own, but with the influx of potential buyers and sellers thanks to Jerry's new billboard pimping me, I kept busy enough to stay out of trouble for the rest of the day. After a couple of brief afternoon meetings with Jerry and the two new prospective male clients who'd made it through his screening process the day before, I was beginning to think Jerry might be onto something with that damned billboard ... but I wasn't hoisting any victory flags until I made a sale or two.

When I pulled into the drive that evening, Aunt Zoe's pickup was the only one parked there. Harvey had a hot date tonight, according to the message he'd left me. We weren't supposed to expect him for supper or breakfast tomorrow morning—if he was lucky. I tried not to think about Harvey and his hot dates any more than I had to, in spite of the details he always insisted on sharing.

Christmas lights hung crooked in the front window, twinkling, inviting me in out of the cold. It appeared Aunt Zoe's plan to have the kids help her decorate for Christmas worked. I looked forward to seeing the results of their work and soaking up some holiday cheer. Cornelius meditated to recharge his aura. Snuggling with my kids healed my soul and brought me back to life.

Collecting my bag, I skirted Aunt Zoe's truck and climbed the front porch steps. I was reaching for the front door when I heard a familiar engine coming up the street. I waited as Doc parked the Picklemobile behind my Honda.

He didn't waste time in the cold air, his long legs making fast work of the front sidewalk. "Hey, Boots, how was your day?"

I blew a raspberry for an answer.

Chuckling, he joined me on the porch. Our breath steamed in the frigid air. "I finally got your texts after I made it back to the highway. Has Cooper stopped chewing you out yet?"

"Well, he hasn't texted me in the last two hours, so maybe he ran out of hot air."

"This too shall pass." Doc gave me a hug and kissed my forehead, his lips warm.

"You missed," I said, puckering up.

"Damn, I'll have to try again. Let's see if I can nail it this time."

He hit the bull's-eye, molding me against him. His cologne enveloped me, enticing me to explore more of his skin under his layers of clothing. His mouth made my head float, wiping out all thoughts about my crappy-ass day for a few blissful moments … until the front door creaked open.

"Mom," Layne, my son, interrupted us. "Addy says she gets to frost more Christmas cookies than me because I was bad at school last month. Is that true?"

I crashed back to earth, extracting myself from Doc's arms. "Layne, after all these years of making sure everything is equal down to the last Tic Tac, do you really think I'd let your sister frost more cookies than you?"

"Probably not."

"There's no probably about it." I'd learned early on that even-steven was the only way to go with my twins if I wanted to keep my sanity. Although they had found plenty of other ways to encourage bouts of temporary madness in me.

Layne looked around me. "Hey, Doc, did Mom tell you that my grandparents are coming to check you out this weekend?"

I winced on Doc's behalf. "Go tell your sister that she is not the head elf in charge of cookies this year. I'll determine who frosts how many and when."

"Can I tell her that you're going to yell at her for trying to be the boss of me?"

I leaned down. "Absolutely not." After planting a kiss on his forehead, I shooed him out of the doorway.

Layne raced up the stairs, hollering his sister's name.

I slipped off my coat as Doc closed the door behind us. "I can try to delay my parents' visit." I hung up my coat and then took his.

"Why?"

"So you don't have to meet them." I avoided his gaze while hanging up his coat, my stomach full of butterflies about his reaction to this whole meet-the-parents deal. If he took me up on avoiding them, what would that mean?

"Violet, is there something you're not telling me about your parents?"

Besides my mother being a pod person from the peace-love-and-happiness era and my father possibly browbeating Doc into a marriage proposal? "No."

"Then why wouldn't I want to meet them?"

Because that was sort of a precursor to a more serious relationship than we currently had, and there was a squirmy chance that my mother would scare him off with unfiltered stories about my past calamities on the dating front.

I shrugged, feigning nonchalance. "Because—"

The front door banged open behind Doc.

Cooper burst in with a gust of wind, both giving off arctic blasts. "Jesus, Parker! Could you have fucked this up any more?" He slammed the door behind him.

My cheeks spontaneously caught fire with indignity. "That asshole shouldn't have insulted my aunt."

He rushed me, his steely eyes even more hard and flinty close up. "That's just sticks-and-stones bullshit. Did I or did I not explicitly tell you this morning not to fight with Hawke?"

I jammed my hands on my hips, not backing down an inch. "You said not to take the bait if he made fun of my hair, which he did and I didn't."

"I wasn't only talking about your damned—"

"Coop!" Doc gripped the detective's shoulder, pulling him back a step before we bumped noses. When Cooper scowled at him, Doc nudged his head toward the top of the stairs where Addy stood watching us with wide eyes and an open mouth.

Cooper pinched his lips together. His nostrils were still flaring when he turned back to me. "I'm sorry, Violet."

I did a double take at his instant change of face. "Um … apology accepted," I said, and then pasted on a bright smile for Addy, who was easing down the steps. Her wrinkled brow told me she wasn't fully buying our sudden niceties. "Hi, sweetie. Did you have fun hanging Christmas lights today with Aunt Zoe?"

"Yeah." Addy paused when she was eye level with Doc. "She made us caramel apples for a treat when we were done." Her narrowed gaze bounced from me to Doc, then held steady on Cooper. "Why are you mad at my mom, Coop?"

Cooper's cheeks darkened slightly. He smiled, his whole face softening along with his mouth. His transformation from stormy to sunny always made me gawk, like catching sight of a double rainbow. "I'm not mad at your mom, Addy. I'm just upset about some stuff that happened at work."

"Then why were you yelling at her?"

"Because she was there when everything went to hel … heck."

In other words, I was to blame by association. Guilt twisted in my chest. Okay, so I had been the one who'd uttered the spell, but only because Hawke pushed me too far.

"Are you going to take her to jail?" Addy asked, her frown edged with worry.

I looked at Cooper with raised brows. Great question. Inquiring minds would like to hear his answer.

His steely gaze slid my way. "No. But she and I do need to have a serious talk later about why she needs to keep her nose out of trouble. Does your brother ever stick his nose in your business and make you mad?"

She nodded so hard her chin bobbled. "All the time. He likes to boss me around. It drives me crazy."

"Hear! Hear!" I said, baring my teeth at Cooper.

He cocked his head sideways, his hardened jaw and matching glare issuing a warning.

"Are you staying for supper again, Coop?" Addy leaned her hip against the stair rail.

"Well, here's the thing, Addy. You're sort of stuck with me for a while."

"Like overnight again?"

"Even longer."

I growled under my breath.

"Hear! Hear!" he shot back at me before returning his focus to Addy. "You see, my house is being sold and Doc needs his spare room back, so I don't have anywhere to sleep each night and it's too cold outside to camp."

"Oh, that's sad. You can have my bed, Coop. I'll sleep with Mom. Her bed is huge."

Dammit. I crossed my arms. There went any more slumber parties with Doc for a while.

"That's very sweet of you, Addy, but I can sleep on your couch if that's okay."

"No!" She put her foot down on the stair step for emphasis.

Cooper and I exchanged raised eyebrows.

"Why not?" I asked.

"Because that's where Doc sleeps when he stays over. We need to leave it open for him." That answered my question if the kids realized Doc had been sleeping in my bed when he stayed during the last week. Addy crossed her arms, mimicking my stance. "You sleep in my room, Coop. Mom always says that we're supposed to be giving, especially at Christmas. I'd like to give you my bed until you find a new house to live in."

"Addy," Aunt Zoe hollered from the kitchen. "Come set the table."

"What about Layne?" Addy yelled back.

"He's part of the clean-up crew tonight."

"Oh, yeah." With a smile at Doc, she leaned over the stair railing and whispered something in his ear. At his nod, she skipped down the stairs and around us into the kitchen.

I started to ask Doc what she'd said, but then bit my tongue. That was his and Addy's business. I turned to Cooper. "How do you feel about pink polka-dotted bedspreads?"

"I'm not taking your kid's bed."

"I don't think you understand how Addy works," I said. "She will badger you until you give in."

Doc chuckled. "She comes by her willfulness genetically." He dodged my swat, his smile fading as he looked back at Cooper. "What's this business about more clocks being stolen from Ms. Wolff's apartment?"

Cooper took off his coat and draped it over the stair rail. "There are four more clocks gone as of this morning. Unfortunately, nobody saw anyone suspicious hanging around—not Freesia, or any of the officers we've had patrolling, or any of the other Galena House residents."

"Why did Hawke automatically start sniffing around me? I don't know anything about those kooky clocks." An idea hit me. "Does this have anything to do with the new evidence he has?"

Cooper shook his head. "Don't you get it, Parker? Hawke is so set on finding you guilty of *something* that every single crime that occurs now ties back to you somehow in his head." He squeezed the back of his neck. "Then you go and pull this hocus-pocus shit out of your ass and it reinforces his nutty beliefs about you being a witch even more."

"What 'hocus-pocus shit'?" Doc asked.

I winced. I'd purposely omitted that tidbit from my long-winded texts, wanting to lay out the whole scene for Doc before letting him know where I'd fallen short in the maturity department.

"Your girlfriend pretended to put a hex on Hawke today."

Doc's dark eyes widened. "A hex?"

"It wasn't really a hex," I said.

Cooper scoffed. "How was that not a hex?"

"A true hex is something passed down through a book of spells. I made it all up on the fly."

His gaze narrowed at my explanation. "Christ, Parker. You're really something, you know it?"

"Thank you. I'll take that as a compliment, Cooper."

"What did you say, Killer?" Doc asked.

I repeated my spell for him, acting it out with the one-eyed squint, croaky voice, and wiggly fingers.

While Doc leaned back against the stair rail and laughed, Cooper glared at me, confirming my suspicion that the detective's funny bone had been removed at some point in his bullet-filled past and jammed up his anal cavity for safe-keeping.

"I told you not to interact with Hawke," Cooper grumbled. "What in the hell were you even doing in the police parking lot?"

"I was walking Dominick Masterson to his Land Rover."

That sobered Doc in a flash. "Masterson? What did he want?"

"He wants to hire me."

"As his Realtor?" Cooper asked.

"Partly."

Doc crossed his arms, bristling like Cooper. "Hire you to do what?"

"Find the *lidérc*."

"And kill it?" Doc pressed.

"No, bring it to him alive."

Cooper cursed under his breath.

Doc's jaw visibly tightened. "Does Masterson think you're some kind of bounty hunter?"

"I don't know what he thinks." That was the truth. Dominick was a total mystery to me, from the extent of his non-humanness to why he had returned to my world. He'd claimed he was sent back to help, but something in his black eyes told me that trusting him would be hazardous to my health.

"What was your answer?" Doc asked.

"I said I'd think about it."

He swore. "He's trouble, Violet. He's not here to make sure you live happily ever after."

"I know," I whispered, glancing toward the kitchen to make sure we didn't have an audience. Well, I didn't really know anything for certain, but Doc and I were on the same page when it came to Dominick. "Think about it, though. If I don't catch it, that thing is out there roaming free. It's only a matter of time until it attaches to some poor victim."

"You're a killer," he whispered back, "not a catcher."

"And I told him that, but he seems to think I can capture it without sending it back to whatever hell it came from."

"Please tell me you're not falling for his fake charm and pretty-boy looks."

Did I detect a hint of jealousy there? Doc must know by now that I was smitten to pieces with him. "For your information, I'm not fooled by his charm or good looks because he makes me sick to my stomach."

"Right." Cooper snickered. "Let me guess, you start to swoon in his presence?"

"Don't snicker at me." I pinched his arm. "There's something about Dominick that sets off my warning radar."

"What radar?" the detective asked, rubbing his arm.

"The one that makes me nauseated whenever an enemy gets too close."

"Is that true?" he asked Doc.

"Hello," I said. "I'm the one with the radar, not Doc."

Doc sighed, plowing his fingers through his hair. "Violet, you don't even know how to kill it yet, let alone catch it."

"I have an idea how to solve that." When he continued to frown at me, I explained, "Prudence."

Cooper shook his head. "That's a bad idea."

He said that only because the last time he visited Prudence, the ex-executioner ghost, she wrestled him for control of his body and won. Unfortunately, her victory left me with a nasty bruise on my leg that took almost two weeks to fade.

"Does anyone else have a bright idea on how to catch a *lidérc*?" I asked.

"I do," said a high-pitched voice from the top of the steps.

We all looked up at where Layne stood, his hands in his jeans pockets.

"Hey, honey." I pasted on a fake smile. "Did you wash your hands for supper?"

He nodded, coming down to join us. "I know how to catch a *lidérc*, Mom."

I licked my lips, wincing inwardly at letting him overhear me talk about my other job. The last thing I wanted my kids to know was that their mother was a killer, even if I only executed those who were causing harm to the innocent.

"How do you know what a *lidérc* is, Layne?" Doc asked.

"I read about it."

I worried my lower lip. "You mean in one of those books you got from the library about ghosts?"

Layne shook his head. "It was in that old book I found in your bedroom when you were sick."

My eyes met Doc's. *Shit!* Layne had read the family history book. I should have known that if it had words on the page, Layne would be all over it.

"What's the book about?" Cooper asked Layne, slipping into cop mode.

"It's like a graphic novel with all sorts of pictures of different warriors and their weapons and kills. It's really cool."

"And in this book that you borrowed from your mother," Cooper continued his interrogation, "it tells about one of the warriors killing a *lidérc?*"

He nodded. "But there was one weird thing about the book."

Only one? A voice inside my head started laughing hysterically until I slapped it into silence.

"What's that?" Doc asked, his eyes on me instead of Layne.

"All of the warriors were women." Layne smiled at me. "A couple of them reminded me of you, Mom."

* * *

Monday, December 3rd

I woke up the next morning with a bruised shin and sore rib.

"How did you sleep?" Aunt Zoe asked me when I joined her at the coffee maker while the kids got dressed for school.

"Addy should try out for soccer this spring."

"That girl does like to kick in her sleep. She must have been a mule in her past life."

"She's a mule in this life, too."

Aunt Zoe harrumphed. "Reminds me of her mother," she teased, dodging my rib-poke with a laugh.

I was going to have to put a pillow between Addy and me tonight. While I loved my daughter with my whole heart and then some, I liked sleeping with Doc more. Silly me, I preferred being kissed to kicked all night long.

"Where's Cooper?" I asked, grabbing a cup from the cupboard. Addy's door had been open when I limped past on the way to the bathroom, her bed empty and made.

"He's already left for work." She set my phone down on the counter in front of me. "He said to tell you he put something on your phone that will track you 24/7, so you don't need to check in each hour today."

He did what? I gaped at her, my face burning. "That son of a bitch."

"Now, Violet, I know you probably feel like this is a violation of your privacy and you're right."

I sputtered, eventually spitting out. "You're damned right I'm right!"

"However, consider this—you have to deal with Coop or Detective Hawke. There is no other option until Coop figures out who killed Ms. Wolff."

"Or I do."

Oops. I hadn't meant to say that out loud.

It was something that I'd decided in the middle of the night while my shin throbbed. A way to return my world to its cockeyed version of normal and evict my newest roommate—Cooper, not Cornelius.

Aunt Zoe's dark blue eyes locked onto me. "What does that mean, Violet Lynn?"

"Nothing," I said, pouring coffee into the cup, avoiding her. "What should we have for dinner when my parents come? Roast beef and Yorkshire pudding?" That was one of my father's favorite meals.

"What does that mean?" she repeated slowly, as if I were having trouble comprehending English.

I blew out a breath and turned to face the music. "I'm going to figure out who killed Ms. Wolff."

"What makes you think you can find the answer?"

I tapped my temple. "I have a bigger brain than Hawke."

"What about Cooper?"

"My feminine instincts are better than his bossy male ones." That may or may not be true, but I was going to run with it for now.

Aunt Zoe shook her head. "This is a bad idea, Violet."

"No, it's not." I walked over to the fridge. "Besides, I'm going to have help."

"Oh, really? Who?"

"Doc, for one. And Harvey. Maybe Prudence and Cornelius. Probably Natalie." I grabbed milk from the fridge and smiled at her with a mouthful of my teeth showing like I used to when I was a kid. "And you."

She snorted. "You need to include Cooper."

"Bzzzt. Wrong answer." I unscrewed the milk cap. "Why are you on his side on this? Just because he owns a gun ... or ten?"

"It has nothing to do with his arsenal."

"Then what?"

"You need him."

My laugh had a sharp ring to it. "Yeah, I need him like I need a throbbing, swollen hemorrhoid."

"I'm serious, Violet."

I poured milk into my coffee. "So am I. He is a pessimistic disbeliever who fights me at every turn."

"But he believes you're innocent."

I placed the milk back in the fridge. "Sure, until the wind shifts in the other direction."

"I don't believe that's true and neither do you in your heart."

"My heart doesn't know shit about Cooper. It gets distracted by his guns and handcuffs whenever it thinks about the overbearing detective." I shut the fridge, returning to the counter. "I'm not telling Cooper my plan. Period. And you'd better not say anything about it either, or ..."

"Or what?"

"I don't know. I'll think of something threatening later." I lifted my chin. "Something to do with Reid."

She took me by the chin, leaning in so that we were almost nose to nose. "I'd strongly advise against it, child."

"Okay, fine. Just please don't tell Cooper yet."

She kissed my forehead and then released my chin, stepping back. "Do you realize how hard it will be to hide this from him when he's living under our roof and tracking your phone?"

Swallowing a sip of coffee, I frowned. "There will be sticky moments, but I'm a slippery fish."

She smiled. "That you are. So, what's your first move?"

"Me walking out the front door this morning without falling flat on my face on the icy porch steps. After that, I'll wing it."

"Oh, dear. This has the potential to go nuclear."

I shrugged. "Maybe, but not doing anything and ending up in prison for a murder I didn't commit is a worse fate." A glance at the clock made me squeak. "I need to get dressed. I forgot Jerry wants me in a little early this morning to discuss a strategy for the potential influx of new customers. You sure you don't mind taking the kids to school?"

"Positive." She pointed toward the dining room. "Now get out of here."

"Thanks, Aunt Zoe." I gave her a quick hug.

"Tell that male chauvinist pig your aunt is going to kick his ass for using her darling niece as man bait."

Bait ... that reminded me of my last run-in with the *lidérc*. Something else flitted through my mind about that Hungarian devil, but I didn't have the time to catch it.

"Sure," I told her. "I'll do that very thing as soon as I sell a couple of million-dollar properties and don't need a paycheck anymore."

I raced up the stairs, throwing on a god-awful pink mohair sweater dress that Jerry had made a point of telling me was a game-winner at the office. While I didn't play basketball with him at the Rec Center like Ben, and I couldn't talk smack with him about professional ball players like Ray, I could mimic Mona and dress for success ... at least Jerry's version of success.

After kissing the kids good-bye, I hit the road, shivering and scratching my nose all of the way down the hill to the parking lot behind Calamity Jane's. This dress might be soft to the touch, but it tickled my nose and filled my throat with pink fuzzies. After a day of wearing it, I half expected to hack up a pink hairball.

The Picklemobile was parked in Doc's usual spot. I thought about swinging by his place before going into work and broaching the idea of finding Ms. Wolff's killer, but Ray Underhill, my coworker, pulled up next to me and proceeded to hate me loud and clear through his window.

I rolled my eyes at the overtanned, slick-haired buffoon who had despised me since the first day I'd set foot in Calamity Jane Realty. Poor Ray had issues. Besides the fact that I'd seen him naked and hadn't been impressed, I'd saved his bacon from being fried one night at Mudder Brothers Funeral Parlor. My playing heroine had irritated his overinflated ego and made his old-boys' mentality break into hives. On top of that, while he was currently the top seller at work, his knees quaked at the idea of a woman besting him at the job—namely me.

Due to these issues and a few others, Ray and I suffered from an instantaneous allergic reaction to each other when placed in the same room for too long—he would start sneering and jeering uncontrollably, which triggered me to threaten to repeatedly cram my boot in his stupid pie-hole. We'd agreed to play nice while in the company of clients and our boss, but outside of the ring, there were no rules.

This morning, however, I didn't feel like exchanging blows with the ass-clown. For one thing, I'd promised Cooper last night that I wouldn't inflict bodily harm on anyone else until I was cleared of this Ms. Wolff mess. For another, it was cold enough to freeze my shadow to the pavement.

I'd made it halfway across the parking lot before Ray caught up with me.

"Hey, Blondie." His voice alone made my hackles rise up and start swinging.

"I'm not talking to you, Ray," I said without looking back.

"Good, that's how I prefer blond bimbos." His fancy Tony Lama cowboy boots clomped behind me.

"Go fuck yourself, Underhill."

"Better myself than that public glory hole you call a vagina."

I stopped and whirled on him. "Really, Ray? Jeez, man. You seriously need to pick up a thesaurus and come up with more educated and entertaining insults if we're going to keep up this relentless hatred through the winter."

He frowned. " 'Glory hole' is a perfectly good insult."

"Sure it is … if we were thirteen and you followed it with snapping my bra, you pompous, patronizing prick."

His cheeks reddened. "Oh, like that's any better."

"It's like one thousand times better because it's a funny use of alliteration."

When his forehead wrinkled even more, I exhaled in disgust. "You know, alliteration, as in using the same letter or sound at the beginning of several connecting words. Like mewling meddlesome monkey-butt or puny repugnant pignut."

His whole face scrunched. "Whatever, Blondie. If you don't like my insults, maybe you should find another job."

I tipped my head to the side. "How many times do I have to flush before you go away?"

Before he could reply, I left him standing there.

"Toilet humor is immature, Blondie," he called after me.

"Keep talking, Ray. Someday you'll say something intelligent, I just know it."

"Oh, yeah, how about this? I ran into Tiffany last night over in Spearfish. She knows you're out to steal her clients and she's going to tear you a new asshole."

I didn't look back. I didn't dare, because I wasn't sure I could keep my face schooled enough to hide the ripples of panic coursing over it at the confirmation that Doc's super competitive ex was now out for blood—

mine.

"That's great news, Ray," I lied through my chattering teeth. "I was getting tired of putting up with my current 'asshole,' along with his fake tan, lousy insults, and Tony Lama cowboy boots."

Before he could take another stab at my self-confidence, I slipped inside and walked straight to the safety of my desk, flashing Jerry a thumbs-up as I passed. Mona had taken the day off, and Ben was out with a client according to the note he'd left on the whiteboard behind his desk. Lucky me, it was just the coach and the jackass hanging out at the office today. That sounded like the makings for an old Disney movie.

Ray came in behind me, slicing me to pieces with his eyes when Jerry wasn't looking. I winked back and buried my head in the stack of messages on my desk.

A half hour later, I looked up, literally. I stared at the ceiling for several seconds, listening for the sound of Cornelius walking around overhead, but heard nothing. Where was he this morning? Jerry's office had been dark when I'd raced by on the way to my desk. Maybe he was sleeping in this morning. Did that mean Jane had kept him up all night?

My phone chirped.

I cursed under my breath. What did Cooper want now? I thought the tracking deal was supposed to relieve me of his hourly harassment today. I lifted my phone, my breath catching.

Tiffany Sugarbell had sent me a text. It was short and sweet:

Game on, bitch!

Lowering the phone, I glanced at Ray. The jerk was leaning back in his chair while fiddling with his pen, talking to some client on the phone about a ranch in the western hills near the Wyoming border.

What were the chances of Ray just happening upon Tiffany a day after my billboard went up? I clenched my fists under my desk. Call me paranoid, but I'd bet Cornelius's lucky cannon that Ray "Dickwad" Underhill had made a point of telling Tiffany about Jerry's plan to pit me against her in the billboard strumpet contest.

I needed to talk to Doc before my head exploded and I leapt over Ray's desk and pummeled him to a stinky rotten pulp.

Grabbing my purse, I told Jerry that I needed to run out for a bit to check on a potential property for Cooper and beelined out the back door. Without breaking stride, I made a right turn and opened Doc's back door, scurrying inside.

"Doc?" I called, my voice quivering with a mixture of fury and worry. I marched out front. "You know what Ray …"

The sight of my sister, Susan, lounging in the chair across from Doc's desk made me and my tongue stumble to a stop.

The evil bitch wore an impossibly tight sweater. It would take a hydraulic shoehorn to extract her from it. My gaze moved lower. Where in the hell had she bought that black miniskirt? Whores-R-Us? Criminy, if she shifted just right, her hoo-hah could play peekaboo. Hell, if it were another half-inch shorter, patty-cake would be an option. Thigh-high "pleather" boots with spike heels finished off her pole-dancing attire. Or should I say man-stealing outfit?

Oh, hell. Here we go again.

"Hello, big sister." She emphasized the word *big* as usual, poking fun at my much curvier frame. Her smile had a feral bite to it, meant to shred my hide and leave it in tatters. "Look who I found." She tossed her long, straight brown hair over her shoulder, like she was trying out for a part in a shampoo commercial. "Your new boyfriend."

In my head, my neck creaked as I slowly turned toward Doc's chair, my heart rat-a-tat-tatting like one of Al Capone's tommy guns in my ears.

The man sitting behind the desk gave me a crooked smile.

"Good morning, my fair-haired Juliet," Cornelius said, stroking his goatee. His cornflower blue eyes returned to Satan's concubine. "Wasn't it kind of your genetically diverse littermate to visit me on this winter morning wearing such tiny clothes under her long coat?"

Chapter Seven

"What in the hell are you doing here, Susan?" I didn't waste breath on playing nice. I'd learned from past experience with Satan's concubine that it was best just to drive the stake straight through her heart and call it a day.

"I came to invite Doc to our family dinner this Saturday."

Liar, liar, hot pants on fire. "How did you know this was Doc's office?" Someone had leaked information.

"Addy told me Doc works next door to you."

Dang Addy and her innocent-but-blabbing mouth.

Susan inspected her talons, faking nonchalance. "It didn't take a genius to find his office. When I peeked in the front window, here he sat, working away."

The sound of long bony fingers tapping on keys made me frown at Cornelius. He was typing on Doc's laptop, his black brows drawn as he focused on whatever was on the screen. Apparently, he was finished with us boring mortals.

Where in the hell was Doc? I could smell his cologne in the air, and the Picklemobile was still parked out back, but contrary to what Susan thought, Doc was not here.

"Well, then." I turned back to Susan, my eyes narrowing again at the sight of her overly made-up face. I couldn't help it. Instant loathing was a side effect of brushing too close to her. "You've stated your invitation, now you can leave."

"But your boyfriend hasn't agreed to join us yet," she said in that whiny voice she thought sounded sexy. Pig squeals were less cringe-inducing.

"Cornelius," I said, and then flinched, realizing my mistake three syllables too late. When he didn't look up, I cleared my throat. "Hey, Doc?" I knocked on the desk twice, gaining his attention.

"Why do you go by 'Doc' if your name is Cornelius?" Susan twirled a strand of hair around her finger.

I stared at his forehead, trying to put words in his brain via a telepathic sledgehammer.

"What kind of a question is that?" he asked her.

"I don't understand." She stopped twirling.

"Is it meant as a convergent question or divergent question?"

"Uhhh, divergent?"

"Excellent. My favorite." He leaned back, steepling his fingers. "In that case, we could theorize many different answers. Violet, you go first."

"Isn't it obvious?" I said to Susan, who shook her head slowly. "I can't believe you don't remember Dr. Cornelius the archaeologist from *Planet of the Apes*."

"That was one of Quint's favorite movies," she said, saying our brother's name with a wrinkled upper lip. "Not mine."

What had Quint done to piss her off lately? Susan had always fawned over him when she wasn't gutting my teddy bears or hiding spiders in my bed sheets.

I shrugged. "Your loss."

"So your kids call Cornelius 'Doc' because of some stupid archaeologist monkey on a movie?"

"Chimpanzee," Cornelius corrected her. "He was also a renowned historian."

"Same difference."

He leaned way over the desk, studying her long bare legs for several seconds. "Tell me something, Violet's sister," he said, "are those your real knees?"

Susan blinked several times and then turned to me. "Is your boyfriend always this weird?"

I had yet to have a completely rational conversation with Cornelius, but that was my business, not hers. I kept a straight face and took a card from Cornelius's deck. "Is that also a divergent question?"

She rolled her eyes. "No, it's a convergent."

"Then I refuse to answer based on my extreme dislike for convergent questions." I pointed at the door. "You can leave now."

She pushed to her feet, making a spectacle of pulling down her mini-skirt to non–peep show level. "Fine, *big* sister. I'll go for now." She leaned over Doc's desk, giving Cornelius an eyeful of cleavage. "Will I see you again this weekend at our family dinner?" she said in a husky voice.

Unfortunately for Susan, Doc's laptop once again held more appeal for my pseudo-boyfriend.

I grabbed the man-stealing bitch by the elbow and scooped up her coat. Using my "bulk," I lugged her toward the door, which magically opened right as I reached for it.

The sight of Doc standing in the doorway set off a series of alarms in my head.

He must have read the panic on my face. "What's going on?" he asked, holding a small stack of mail. That answered where he'd been when Susan had showed up. His gaze moved to Susan, his forehead pinching as he glanced over her skimpy attire.

"Hello, Mr. Ahhh…" Shit. *Abort! Abort! Abort!* I glanced at Cornelius. "Romeo, you have a customer." Back to my sister, I said, "You hear that?"

"Hear what?"

"That barking. It sounds like Satan has released his Hellhounds to drag you home."

Susan looked up at Doc, really taking him in for the first time. Her eyes widened. "Oh, my, who are you?"

"He's a customer."

"A sexy customer."

"Off you go, Jezebel." I shoved her out the door, throwing her coat at her face. "The Prince of Darkness awaits."

"I'll see you Saturday, Doc," she called to Cornelius.

At the sound of his name, the real Doc started to open his mouth.

Before anyone could get another word out, I shut the door, locked it, turned the sign to Closed, and twisted the blinds shut. I saw a shadow move toward the front window and grabbed Doc, hauling him close to me and out of her sight.

"Is she looking in?" I asked Cornelius from my hiding spot against Doc's chest.

"Are you referring to someone living or dead?"

"Cornelius!" I growled.

After a couple of seconds, he said, "Your weather-resistant relative is no longer in view."

I blew out a breath of relief and sagged back against the door, squishing the blinds. "What are you doing here, Cornelius? I thought you were working from Jerry's office."

"He needed to borrow my laptop."

"What's wrong with your bank of computers?"

"The power cables have gone missing. I suspect it's the handiwork of your boss."

"Jerry?"

"The other, who no longer requires oxygen."

"What makes you think Jane is the one who hid your cables?"

"Ghosts often have an aversion to electronic devices."

I had an aversion to electronic devices, too. When they didn't work like I wanted them to, they tended to break into tiny pieces, especially when I used my old softball bat.

"I've been thinking about your problem," Cornelius said.

Doc took off his coat. "Which of her problems?"

"The one involving a dead woman."

"That doesn't narrow it down enough," Doc said, hanging up his leather coat. His dark blue shirt topped khaki pants. Business casual was the name of the game today, which may or may not include clients in his line of work.

"I called Cornelius this morning on my way into work and asked him to help me figure out who killed Ms. Wolff."

Doc's eyes narrowed. "Isn't that Coop's job?"

"I'm not going to wait around on the sidelines for Cooper to play Sherlock Holmes while Hawke keeps trying to pin everything he can on me."

"So you enlisted Cornelius?"

"I asked him to help me, and before you say another word, let me add that one of the reasons I came over here this morning was to ask you to help, too."

"You know I'll help you and Cooper."

"Uh, yeah. About that—it's just me."

Doc raised one eyebrow. "So you're not telling Cooper what you're up to?" When I shook my head, he asked, "Don't you think this could end in disaster?"

"You're the second person this morning to doubt my abilities."

"I don't doubt your abilities, Killer, but Coop will have a coronary when he finds out what you're up to."

"Blah blah blah, Cooper likes to yell, blah." I looked at Cornelius. "You said you've been thinking. Does that mean you have an idea for me about how to find Ms. Wolff's murderer?"

"More of an observation. The bedroom mirror," he began, stroking his pointy goatee. "You say it broke when you used transference to share your power with the detective, correct?"

"Sure, yeah, that's what happened."

He stood so fast that I flinched. "I need to go. Don't summon anyone without me, Violet." He departed in a few long strides via the back door, leaving me with my mouth agape. What the hell? What was his observation? I turned to Doc with my jaw still unhinged.

"So, that was Susan." It wasn't a question.

Skirrrrchhhhh. It took my brain a few grinding moments to shift gears. "Unfortunately."

"She appears to have confused Cornelius with me."

"She's a confused girl. Take her outfit—that was definitely an ensemble from her summer street-corner-ho collection, and clearly we're in the throes of winter."

His head tilted to the side as he stared at me, the usual sign that he wasn't buying my snake oil sales pitch. "Care to explain the real reason behind that particular confusion?"

"Susan has always been two tacos short of a combo plate."

"Violet," he warned.

I sighed, hopping up on his desk. "You remember how I told you Cornelius was in my office a few days before Thanksgiving and my ex and Susan showed up?"

"I remember, in spite of the expletive-laden recount." He walked over, tossing his mail on the desk behind me.

I smirked. I'd been especially prolific at the time, experimenting with new combinations of insults. "That day, Rex accused me of sleeping with Cornelius and to protect you I played along."

He nodded. "I remember that, too. Cornelius pretended to be your lover in order to get you to agree on a séance, a slick chess move on his part."

Excellent, we were on the same page. "I also let Susan think that due to a date with Cornelius, I couldn't go to Thanksgiving."

He crossed his arms. "So, she still thinks you're dating Cornelius?"

I cringed, unsure how my real boyfriend would feel about that part of the ongoing deception. "Most likely, yes."

His expression gave nothing away. "You haven't bothered to straighten her out?"

"Not yet." And for good reason. I knew how Susan acted while she was on the hunt. Today was a prologue to the sordid soap opera she probably had scripted in her evil fantasies. The longer I could shield Doc from her, the better.

A shadow in the front window made me cringe. Was she back? No, it was just a passerby.

Doc glanced at the window and then back at me. "If Susan thinks you're dating Cornelius, why was she in *my* office?"

"Because Addy mentioned that my boyfriend works next door to me."

"Ah. What did your sister want with me?"

"She came under the pretense of inviting you to our family dinner this weekend." Another person passed by on the sidewalk, catching my eye. I breathed a sigh of relief at another stranger.

"And her real reason for coming here?"

"To seduce you, or rather Cornelius, who she thinks is you."

Doc rubbed his jaw. "And was Cornelius seduced?"

"I couldn't tell." I got up and went to the window, searching the vicinity to make sure Susan wasn't waiting across the street, watching us with binoculars or a high-powered telescope. "I don't think Cornelius is interested in normal human females."

"That makes two of us." Doc grabbed my wrist and tugged me down the hall to the storage room. Once inside, he turned on the lights and shut the door, blocking out the rest of the world.

"What are we doing?" I asked, frowning.

"Having a private conversation." He jammed his hands in his pockets. "When are you going to trust me?"

"I do trust you." At his steady stare, I lowered my eyes. "Okay, I mostly trust you."

"Violet." He moved closer, tipping up my chin. "I'm not going to hurt you."

"I know," I said quickly. Too quickly, judging from the slight narrowing of his eyes.

"You say that, but your actions speak differently. If you give me the chance, Boots, I'll prove it to you."

"I am giving you a chance."

"How is using Cornelius as a shield giving me a chance?"

I pulled away and walked over to the bookshelves lining one wall, scanning the spines without really reading them. "You don't understand, Doc."

"Then explain it to me."

"My history is filled with Susan stealing things from me and destroying them or what they represent." I wrung my hands together. "I'm afraid of letting her near you."

"Violet."

I scowled. "You saw her. Physically, she's everything I'm not—long legs, straight hair, a slender body with boobs up to her chin. While I was trying to learn what X plus Y equals in school, she was studying boys and figuring out what made them lose their common sense and come running."

"Violet," he started again.

But I wasn't done. "She honed her skills so well that she stole two men out from under me—not one, Doc. Two, including one who fathered my children. And that was before I bore two kids who took one hell of a toll on my body and mind."

"Vi—"

"And before you try to pick up my self-esteem and dust it off with some compliments, keep in mind that both of the boyfriends she slept with swore to me they weren't interested in her. Rex in particular I believed because he was so into his research at the time." I hugged my arms close. "Silly me for letting my guard down."

He came over, taking me by the shoulders. "What will it take to convince you I'm not going to end up in bed with your sister?"

I chewed on my lower lip, digging deep in my heart for an answer. The only thing I could find down there was, "Time."

"Time to show you I'm not an asshole like those other two?"

"Time to let me feel more secure before telling her Cornelius is not the one sharing my bed."

His dark gaze searched mine. "Okay, but I draw the line at you kissing him in front of her. Your lips are mine."

I chuckled. "I think Cornelius would run away screaming if I even puckered up close to him."

"His loss." He lowered his mouth, his hands traveling up my neck, cupping my head. "I've missed you the last two nights, Tiger."

I lined up my lips with his. "Maybe we should do something about that."

"Like what?"

"Run away to Mexico together."

He brushed his mouth over mine. "What about Addy and Layne?"

"We'll send for them after a week or two." I wrapped my arms around his waist, going up on my toes for a second kiss, this one with more heat.

He backed me against the bookshelf. "I shouldn't have taken the bean bag out of here," he said between kisses.

"What were you thinking?" I pulled his shirt free from his pants, wanting to touch skin.

He groaned when my fingernails raked down his back, his hips pressing into mine. "Your dress is so soft." His mouth trailed down my neck. "Reminds me of the skin underneath it."

"Doc."

"What?" He spoke from my cleavage.

"I'm sorry."

"For what?" His lips skimmed along my collarbone.

I looked up at the ceiling, drowning in the sensations he was awakening from head to toe. "Me."

He lifted his head, his eyes dark with need. "You?"

I nodded. "And my messed-up past, present, and future."

His hands spanned the sides of my face, his thumbs tracing my cheekbones. "No apologizing."

"But—"

"I mean it, Violet. No more."

"Okay."

"I don't want to change you."

"Why not? I can list ten things I'd like to tweak without even trying."

He chuckled. "Because I adore you just as you are."

I blinked away a rush of tears, not wanting to ruin the moment by blubbering all over him. "I'll try harder, Doc."

"Try harder at what?"

"Trusting you."

"Good." He kissed me again, filling up my heart two times over.

The sound of the back door closing made us both curse.

"Doc?" Ol' man Harvey's voice was muffled by the closed door. "Sparky?"

Doc stepped back, tucking in his shirt as I pulled down the hem of my dress and adjusted topside so that everything was back in place and pointing the right way.

"I really like that dress," he said, ogling my chest.

"You and Jerry. Pink is his favorite color, I swear."

He grinned. "Pink is my favorite today, too." His gaze skimmed down to my toes. "Damn, Boots. I'm going to need to see more of your skin soon."

A knock sounded on the door. "I can hear ya two lovebirds foolin' around in there."

"Give us a few minutes, Willis," Doc called, reaching for me.

I dodged his hand, laughing, and beat him to the door. Harvey was frowning when I pulled it open.

"What's wrong?" I asked him, sobering right away.

"I need to see a man about a mule."

"We're plumb out of mules, but the bathroom is thataway." I pointed down the hall.

"Before I let my pipe drip," he started, making me grimace. Why did he have to be so pictorial in speech? "I'm here to play Pony Express."

Doc came up behind me, his hand resting on my lower back. "You brought mail?"

"Not mail, a message."

From whom? "That would be more like playing pigeon, wouldn't it?" I asked.

"Do ya wanna hear the damned message, girl, or stand here and argue about metaphors?"

"Fine, what's your message?"

"You need to try to return the call." Harvey looped his thumbs in his suspenders, leaning back on his heels as if he'd just told me the meaning of life.

What call? "What does that mean?"

"Well, accordin' to Abe Jr. next door, you need to use Ms. Wolff's phone to reach out again and see who's listenin' on the other side."

* * *

Natalie was waiting for me on the front porch of the Galena House. Yellow paint splattered her torn jeans, faded Lead Golddiggers sweatshirt, and rosy cheekbones. I'd texted her from Doc's office, making sure she was at her new apartment so that I'd have a legitimate excuse for showing up at the old boarding house and not get carted off to jail for suspicious activity.

"Hurry up and get inside." She leaned against the large wooden door that opened into a long foyer with two apartment doors on opposite walls—one up front on the left and the other at the far end on the right. A wide, polished stairway led to the other two apartments upstairs where Freesia, the owner, and now Natalie lived. "The cops will be back again in forty-three minutes."

I paused, frowning at her crooked ponytail as she shut the front door behind us. "You have it down to an exact time?" Or was she channeling Cornelius? "I thought they just cruised by periodically through the day."

"They did until yesterday. Now a Deadwood cop car stops by every hour. One of the officers usually walks around the house and peeks in the window of Ms. Wolff's old apartment, while the other comes inside to make sure the police tape is still in the same place."

"It's those missing clocks," I said. I'd filled Natalie in on Hawke's clock-napping accusation last night on the phone before going to bed. "Hawke's tighty-whities must be extra bunched over their disappearance."

"He's certainly upping his game." She led the way along the polished wooden floor and semi-recently painted walls to the police tape in front of Ms. Wolff's apartment door. "Where's Doc?"

"He had a customer stopping by." He'd kissed me good-bye at the back door and made me promise not to end up in jail today.

"So, Cornelius really thinks someone will answer when you talk on Ms. Wolff's phone?"

"Yep."

"What about you?"

Me? My knees were trembling about who might be listening when I spoke into the receiver. "It's worth a try."

"You really think you have a better chance at finding Ms. Wolff's killer than Hawke and Cooper?"

"Cooper, maybe. But definitely when it comes to Hawke."

I took a moment to catch her up with all of the crap going down in my life since I'd chatted with her last.

Freesia came down the wide staircase and joined us in the hall as I was wrapping up, ending with Cornelius's idea on my reaching out through the old phone in Ms. Wolff's apartment that wasn't plugged into any wall jack. Her jeans and sweatshirt were splattered with yellow paint, too, as well as her prominent cheekbones and smooth forehead.

Freesia reminded me of a younger Halle Berry, only more curvy with longer hair. For the life of me, I couldn't understand her instant crush on Cornelius, nor could I fathom why he wasn't drooling after her. His lack of interest in Freesia was partly why I didn't think he was interested in normal human women. The other had to do with his firm belief that batteries—not bras—came in double-D sizes.

"You want to go inside Ms. Wolff's apartment again?" Freesia asked, frowning at the door's little brass clock knocker. "It's a bad day for that. The cops are all fired up about more missing clocks."

"I know. Detective Hawke thinks I might have something to do with their disappearance, but I can't prove him wrong unless I figure out who really is responsible for the missing clocks." And Ms. Wolff's death.

The front door opened, making Freesia jump.

Harvey rushed in, closing out the cold air behind him. He'd dropped me off out front and then parked his pickup down the road at a buddy's house so the cops wouldn't come looking for us.

When he saw all three of us looking at him, his gold teeth made an appearance. "You three look as guilty as pot-bellied coyotes with chicken-feather grins."

"Quit your yammering, ol' man, and get your suspenders over here. We're about to go inside." I glanced at Freesia. "If it's okay with you."

She shrugged. "You're my Realtor. As far as I'm concerned, there's no place off-limits to you. It's the cops who are in a toot over this apartment."

Natalie pulled a key ring loaded with keys from her pocket and held it in front of Freesia. It was the same key ring I'd seen Freesia toting around in the past. She must have given it to Natalie, since she was now her official handywoman. Freesia pointed at one of the keys.

"In we go," Natalie said and opened the door.

I led the way inside, slowing as we approached the dining room with its walls full of Black Forest clocks—minus a few here and there. I frowned at them and then toward the open bedroom doorway off the living room.

"Holy shit," Natalie whispered, gaping at all of the clocks. "She really had an obsession with clocks."

This was Natalie's first time in Ms. Wolff's apartment. I'd grown so accustomed to all of the macabre clocks that I was no longer sidetracked by them. However, the lack of sound coming from the bedroom was a different matter.

"What's got yer face all puckered up like that?" Harvey asked, joining me.

"It's quiet."

"What were ya expecting? A brass band?"

"The last time I came in here there were two clocks chiming on the other side of the bedroom mirror. Now, I hear nothing."

"But that mirror is gone now," Freesia reminded me.

Oh, yeah. I walked to the bedroom doorway. The glass shards from the broken mirror were cleaned up, leaving an empty wooden frame attached to the dresser. The two clocks on the bedroom wall that had been going off during that last visit were missing. Had Detective Hawke taken those clocks to the station to be examined, or were they two of the four recently taken? The ones he'd accused me of stealing? I'd like to ask Cooper about the clocks, but then he'd know I'd been in Ms. Wolff's apartment again and probably handcuff me to his side day and night, which would make going to the bathroom a series of awkward moments for both of us.

"Damn, they're all over in here, too?" Natalie said, following me into the bedroom.

"I told you she had them in her bedroom," I reminded her.

"I know, but I figured that you meant she had a few in here, not another wall full of them."

"Are we gonna stand around chewin' the cud in here all day?" Harvey asked from the doorway with Freesia peeking over his shoulder. "Or are you gonna play Chatty Cathy on the party line so we can get outta here before the law shows up?"

Nudging the old bugger aside, I headed back into the living room. The antique phone sat on an end table, a rocking chair next to it. Harvey and I had found Ms. Wolff's body under that chair, her skin shriveled up. Her head had lain next to one of the rocker legs. I tried not to think about the funky smell that had been in her apartment the day we'd found her as I picked up the phone receiver.

Natalie and Freesia bracketed me while Harvey leaned against the bedroom doorway, his thumbs in his suspenders as he watched me listen to the earpiece for a moment. "Well, whadya hear? The sea?"

I'd rather have had my ear to a conch shell at that moment. Besides my pulse making a racket in my ears, all was silent. "Nothing."

"So start yappin'. It's hard to have a conversation when nobody talks."

I turned away from the bossy buzzard and closed my eyes, picturing a candle in a dark room, the flame flickering. This was my usual triggering device for shifting into the paranormal world. After several deep breaths with the flickering candle front and center in my thoughts, I whispered into the receiver, "Hello?"

Wincing, I waited for someone on the other end of the line to breathe, respond ... or yell at me like before.

Nothing.

Frowning, I tried harder, really trying to focus on that flame, watching it dance in the darkness. This time, I used a louder voice. "Hello? Is there anyone listening?"

"What in the fuck are you doing?" Cooper asked.

I screeched and hung up the phone, looking at Natalie. "I heard Cooper on the line." How in the ...

"Christ, Parker! I'm standing right behind you."

Oh, shit. Grimacing, I slowly swiveled, running headfirst into his menacing scowl. "Oh, hi, Cooper. We were just ... ah ... checking to make sure everything was cleaned up in here ... you know, after the ... ah ... the mess with the broken mirror and the ... ah ..."

Natalie covered my mouth, thank God. Somebody needed to shut it before I managed to wedge both feet between my lips.

"Coop," she said, pushing me behind her, facing off with the detective's rigid jaw and squinty eyes. "This isn't what it looks like."

A muscle in his jaw ticked. "So, you three musketeers didn't convince Freesia to let you into this apartment so you could play telephone operator with anyone listening on the other end of Parker's paranormal line?"

Dammit, it *was* what it looked like.

"Not entirely." Natalie didn't wilt under his glare. "I came down to check on a possible leak in the plumbing. Violet happened to stop by along with Harvey, so I invited them to come with me and keep me company." When his eyes narrowed even further, Natalie pulled a small pipe wrench out of her back pocket and a roll of plumber's tape from somewhere else, holding both up as evidence. "Leaks can be expensive if left unfixed."

"And is there a leak?"

Apparently so, since he was standing in here with us.

"False alarm." Natalie held his stare for several beats longer than I could have. Then again, she was related to the Morgan sisters, my childhood neighbors, and facing off with the law was what they did best. Well, second best after fighting. I'd long held the notion that several notorious desperados had hung from the branches of their family tree back when outlaws ruled the West.

The silence grew heavy, so I stepped forward to lighten things up. "Good news, Cooper. It appears that when the mirror broke, so did the connection to the other side." I wasn't sure that was true, but until I could take another shot at reaching out through the receiver, it was the case.

He broke eye contact with Natalie, focusing on me. "You're not hearing any chiming clocks or ringing phones today?"

"No."

"How did ya know Sparky was here?" Harvey asked, scratching his beard.

Yeah, how did he … oh, hell. "You tracked my phone." Sheesh, I was a doofus. Then again, being kept on a short leash was new for me.

"He tracked your phone?" Freesia frowned. "Is that legal?"

"She's lucky I did," Cooper said, crossing his arms. "Detective Hawke has a unit on its way to confirm the current clock count. We have about five minutes before they pull up, so I suggest we—"

His gaze shifted to the bedroom doorway where Harvey still leaned, doing a double take. His face paled.

"What're ya gawkin' at me like that fer, boy?"

Cooper took a step back. "We need to leave now."

"Do you hear the other cops?" Natalie asked, moving over to peek out the window toward the road.

"Do you hear a clock chiming or the phone ringing?" Freesia asked, trying to see past Harvey into the bedroom.

I'd seen that expression before on Cooper. He wasn't hearing anything. He was seeing something that didn't fit in his black and white picture frame. I looked toward Harvey, trying to see if I could pick up a blurry movement of anything else in here with us, someone no longer breathing oxygen. But when it came to most ghosts, I was the mayor of Dud-ville. Today was no different.

"What do you see, Cooper?" I pressed, moving closer to him.

His gaze shifted, moving along the wall to where Natalie stood next to the window.

"Hey," I said, waving a hand in front of his face. He blinked down at me, as if suddenly realizing I was there with him. "What do you see?"

His eyes were filled with uncertainty, something I'd not seen on Cooper before. I grabbed his arm. "What?"

"I ..." In a blink, the shutters closed and shut me out. He grabbed my wrist, lifting my hand from his arm. "I don't see a damned thing, Parker. Now get your ass out of this apartment before you get us both in deeper shit."

Herding us out of the apartment, he locked the door and rushed us up the stairs. We made it out of the line of sight seconds before two policemen pushed open the front door. Mimicking zipped lips at us, Cooper grabbed Natalie's hand and dragged her back to the top stair.

"Detective Cooper," I heard one of them say. "I thought that was your vehicle."

"Did Detective Hawke tell you to meet us here?" another voice asked.

From my post off to the side of the stairwell, I could see Cooper and Natalie's profiles.

"No," Cooper answered, his tone brusque. "I stopped by to talk to Ms. Beals."

"Hey, Nat," one of the cops said. "I heard you moved to town for the winter."

"No keeping secrets around here," Natalie replied, sending a quick frown in Cooper's direction, then down at her hand that he still held in his.

"Since you're staying in town," one of the cops said, "do you feel like meeting me for a beer later at the Purple Door Saloon?"

"Miss Beals is busy tonight." Cooper's tone was edged with liquid nitrogen. "If you two don't mind, I'll finish up my business with her while you count clocks." He looked down at Natalie, saying loud and clear for all to hear, "I'll stop by tonight after I'm off work."

Natalie pulled her hand free and slid her arms around his neck, pressing against him. "You sure you can't come inside for a little bit?"

Cooper's frown mirrored mine. What in the hell was she doing? Had I missed a page?

When Cooper didn't reply, Natalie went up on her toes and kissed him on the mouth. It was more of a quick smooch, but lip contact, nonetheless. "Maybe that will change your mind."

The sound of low chuckling came up the stairs, followed by, "Now you know what she'll be busy doing tonight."

The door to Ms. Wolff's apartment clicked shut.

Cooper stood frozen as Natalie stepped back. "What was that about, Beals?"

"I thought we were role playing to distract them."

"Role playing?"

"Yeah, you know, you said you'd stop by after work, so I kissed you to show them why you're coming back by."

"I meant I would stop by to take care of the reason you'd supposedly called me over today."

"So I didn't call you over to screw around?"

He took an extra-long pause to answer that, his Adam's apple bobbing. "No."

"Well, next time you need to be a little more clear of your plans before flirting with me in front of your work buddies."

"I wasn't flirting."

"You held my hand."

"I led you by the hand."

Natalie looked over at me. "What did it look like to you?"

Cooper squinted at me, warning me to keep my big mouth shut. I shrugged at Natalie. "My eyesight is rotten in this light."

"It looked to me like he was showin' 'em the lay of land," Harvey said, grinning.

"She didn't ask you, Uncle Willis."

"I think it could go either way," Freesia weighed in. "Although you probably should have taken her by the arm instead of hand. Handholding implies intimacy."

"See." Natalie poked Cooper on the chest. "Flirting, handholding, and saying you'd come back after work. I don't know what planet you're from, Coop, but here on Earth, that means you and I are playing footsie under the table."

The low rumble of voices came from downstairs again.

Cooper focused downstairs again. "I'll see you two back at the station in ten."

"Make that twenty, boys," Natalie said and smacked Cooper on the butt. "He's not quite done interrogating me."

A roll of laughter followed, along with, "See you later, Nat."

Natalie smiled, waving them off, while Cooper rubbed his jaw and stared at Natalie. *Flummoxed* was a good description for the expression on his face.

When the front door closed below, he said, "You do realize that they'll go back and tell Detective Hawke that I was here with you, right?"

Natalie shrugged. "A little competition will ruffle Hawke's feathers. Did you really track Violet here by her phone?"

He nodded, starting downstairs. "And I just saved her ass from a shitload of trouble. If I hadn't caught you four in that apartment, they would have."

I joined them on the steps along with my saved ass. More important than whether we'd been caught or not was what—or who—was in that apartment with us. "What did you see down in Ms. Wolff's bedroom, Coop?"

He paused halfway to the first floor, his eyes frosting over when he looked up at me. "I told you, I saw nothing."

Right. "Did 'nothing' happen to have slicked-back greasy hair and a broken neck?" Like the guy I'd witnessed being thrown across the room months ago when I'd stepped back in time and dodged blows from an ax-wielding juggernaut?

Cooper's chin jutted. "We're done here, Parker. Get your ass back to work before you fuck things up even more."

Chapter Eight

Harvey drove me back to work with Cooper tailing us most of the way, damn him. We pulled in behind Calamity Jane Realty and stopped at the back door. Harvey let the pickup idle, turning my way. "Me and you need to head for the wagon yard."

"Is that a metaphor for something?" I asked, reaching for the door handle. With Harvey, I never knew for sure.

"It means it's time to put the chairs in the wagon."

When I continued to stare at him, he motioned for me to open the door. "Get your buns inside, tell yer bossman we're gonna go see a place out-a-ways in the country, and then get back out here quick as a hiccup."

I blinked. Twice. "You want to do this *now*?"

"I reckon so since I've told ya twice already. You need me to draw ya a picture?"

"Maybe, smartass. Where's the house?"

"I'll show ya when we git there." When I opened the door, he added, "And leave yer cell phone in yer desk."

"What? Why?"

"Yer just overflowin' with questions today."

"I need my phone."

"I've got mine. Leave yers."

"What do you have against my phone?"

"It's buggy. I don't want Coop followin' us."

Why not? Where in the heck was he taking me?

"Light a shuck, girl. We need to roll." He scowled out the windshield at the sky. "I don't wanna be there after dark."

Even though my gut told me Harvey was leading me into more trouble, I did as told, hurrying into the office.

Jerry was on the phone, so I wrote him a note saying I'd be gone for most of the afternoon. He gave me a thumbs-up in response. After putting my phone on silent mode and stuffing it in my desk drawer, I returned to Harvey's pickup. The ol' buzzard didn't even wait for me to shut the door before hitting the gas.

We headed left out of the parking lot toward Lead. "Where are we going?" Had he arranged a visit with Prudence the ghost at the old Carhart house with Zelda Britton, the home's new owner?

"Take this." He handed me his cell phone. "Get Nat on the horn."

"You're being extra peculiar today." Without knowing why I was calling, I punched in Natalie's phone number.

She answered on the second ring. "Is it done?"

"No, he's still alive," I answered, playing along. "But we buried him in an unmarked grave for now."

There was a pause from the other end of the line. Then, "Vi?"

"Who else besides Harvey would be calling you on this phone?" I glanced at ol' man Harvey. "Why did I call Natalie?"

"Tell her it's done," was his reply.

"Harvey said to tell you—"

"I heard. Where did you leave it?"

"Where did I leave it?" I asked Harvey.

"I told ya to put it in yer desk."

"Are we talking about my cell phone?"

"Darn tootin'." He turned left on US Highway 385, heading up Strawberry Hill.

"I'll go over to your office in a while and disarm it," Natalie said.

"What do you mean, 'disarm it'? It's a cell phone, not a car bomb."

"I think I know how to get Coop off your back."

Ah, the tracking dealio. "And you chose Harvey as your co-conspirator over me?" Natalie and I had been partners in crime for decades.

"Why not? He lies face-to-face better than you."

"That's not true. I'm a great liar."

Harvey blew a raspberry, for which he received a suspender snapping.

"Please. Your twitching nose gives you away every time. Besides, we only had a few seconds to hatch a plan, and you were busy at the time arguing with Cooper on the front porch about your right to be inside of the Galena House since you're Freesia's Realtor."

Ah, so that's what had been taking Harvey so long to join me outside. I'd figured he was just staying out of the ring, waiting to see how long before Cooper and I came to blows.

"Shit. I gotta go, Vi. I'll let you two know when it's done." She hung up on me.

I set Harvey's phone on the bench seat between us and stared out the windshield at the passing pine trees. "She'll be in touch. Where are we going?"

"I got a call this morning at the crack of dawn."

"From whom?" Probably his ornery nephew. Cooper had woken me up to chew my ass many a morning before the sun popped up.

"I didn't ask."

"Why not?"

"Because it was Coop's home phone and I didn't want to get too nosy."

I guffawed. That was rich. Harvey had his ear tuned in to the Northern Black Hill's main gossip line via his stool at the Golden Sluice bar up in Lead. "Since when?"

"Since Coop threatened to kick me out of his house and make me live with his momma."

"His mom? You mean your sister?" Harvey nodded, grimacing. "What's wrong with moving in with her?"

"For starters, she makes me eat my vegetables every darn night." I laughed, earning a flick on the arm from him. "Anywho, the caller told me about a package waitin' fer pickup."

"A package for Cooper?"

"I didn't ask, just listened."

"Then what?"

"Then he hung up."

"So, Cooper wants you to go get the package for him?"

He aimed a wrinkled brow in my direction. "In a manner of speakin', sure."

I searched his profile. Harvey made a point of focusing out the windshield. "Harvey, did you tell Cooper about the package?"

"I'm gettin' 'round to it."

"Damn it." I reached for the door handle. "Stop the truck and let me out."

"Don't be hollow-headed. I ain't stoppin'."

I glared at him. "First, Natalie is disarming his tracking device on my phone, and now you're dragging me Lord knows where to pick up some suspicious package meant for him. Your nephew is going to tar me up one side and down the other. He won't even bother with a feather coating, probably just stick Elvis to my hide."

"We're only gonna pick up a package for him, nothin' more."

"Then why did you make me ditch my phone?"

"Because we don't need him hornin' in on this."

"I don't understand why you are so bent on getting this package meant for Cooper."

"I'll fill ya in when we get there."

We rode in silence for a few miles. While Harvey hummed along with Merle Haggard on the radio about his mama trying to keep him out of prison, I fidgeted. If Cooper caught wind that I was part of this package retrieval heist, he would probably sew me to my mattress. I could easily envision him pacing at the end of my bed with his Colt .45 drawn, using an apple balanced on my forehead for target practice.

When Harvey turned onto the gravel road that passed by his ranch, I glanced his way. "We're going to your place?" If so, that would make sense why Harvey wanted to see what was in this mysterious package before Cooper squirreled it away.

Harvey had closed his house up for the winter before moving into Cooper's place in Lead. I hadn't been out to Harvey's ranch in a couple of weeks. While it was one of my listed properties, I had put it on the back burner for now, waiting for that lucky day when someone came to me looking for a haunted old house, barn, and graveyard to buy. As a bonus, there was a derelict mine up on the hillside behind the ranch.

Last summer, the sheriff's deputies had discovered a "nest" of sorts inside the mine filled with a creepy collection of human castoffs, including a pair of broken glasses, an old boot, dirty underwear, and human teeth. Oh, and most recently, Cooper had found a faceless dead man up there whose body had been stolen from the morgue at Mudder Brothers Funeral Parlor. I didn't even want to think about the decapitated body that Harvey's yellow lab, Ol' Red, had dug up in the family cemetery out back. Finding a buyer for such a disaster-ridden residence was nearing the needle-in-a-haystack realm.

"Nope, not my place. Not today anyway." His gravel driveway came and went. "I drove out a couple days ago to check on 'er and everything is still locked up tighter than a duck's ass."

That gave me a mental image that distracted me from my troubles for a moment.

"Where to, then?" I pressed, putting dead bodies and duck butts behind me for now.

"Take a tater and wait."

I'd learned from Harvey previously that "tater waiting" meant the same thing as the phrase *Don't get your bloomers in a bunch*. But this trip inspired bunched-bloomers out of the gate, especially since he didn't want Cooper involved. However, I waited as instructed, watching, sweating, fidgeting more and more with each passing milepost. The road went from smooth gravel to washboard dirt with gravel patches, then just packed dirt. Lots of bumpy twists and turns later, we bounced by a sign so rusted and peppered with bullet holes that it was almost illegible.

Almost.

"Did that say 'Slagton'?" I asked, my gut clenching.

Harvey hit the automatic door lock. "Could be."

Oh, sweet baby dills. "What kind of a pickle are you getting me into, old man?"

"No pickles. Only a package. We'll be in and out before any whangdoodles can grab their shotguns and get a bead on us."

"If you're trying to comfort me, you missed the mark by a mile."

Whangdoodles was Harvey's term for the population back in Slagton, a mostly abandoned mining town where rumor had it they'd dug too deep into the earth years back and found something that made them wacky. The more rational folks in Deadwood explained that the mining company that had been operating at the edge of Slagton contaminated the water supply with mine tailings, which led the government to post skull and crossbones signs all over and forced the mining company to offer relocation deals. While most of the population left for cleaner water, many old-timers stayed behind, cursing the government for interfering with a good thing.

These days, there was only a sprinkling of people remaining, clinging to their homes, land, and mining claims. I'd not been to Slagton myself, too spooked by stories of bloodthirsty mutants reminiscent of the movie *The Hills Have Eyes* to drive into and explore this cobweb-filled corner of the Black Hills. However, it appeared that Harvey was about to give me the grand tour.

"Trust me," he said. "Have I ever led you into troubled waters?"

"Yep," I said without even a moment's hesitation.

He snorted. "Maybe once or twice, if yer splittin' hairs."

"Plenty more than that without any hair-splitting involved."

"Name one time."

"How about when you dragged me into the Opera House and I ended up in jail."

"You walked in on yer own two feet."

"True, but technically you were leading the way and those waters were shark-filled." Cooper had been in the building that day, talking to Dominick Masterson, digging for information on the death of my old boss, Jane. I'd had the bad luck of getting caught talking to one of his suspects after she'd dragged me into a cleaning closet to hide me from trouble way bigger than the law. In the end, it turned out hiding me that day didn't save either of us from facing off with the grim reaper.

"Now is not the time to turn over all of the cow chips," Harvey said, interrupting me before I could give him more examples. "I need ya to keep an eye out for alligators."

"Alligators?"

He pointed at the first structure we'd come to since passing the Slagton town sign. "We're hip deep in 'em back here."

A ramshackle house weathered gray lurked under the pine trees. Any paint had long peeled away. The side porch was in the process of collapsing under the weight of what looked like a foot of moss and tree detritus piled on the roof. Dead weeds crowded the yard in front of the house with rusted pieces of metal sticking up here and there. A fence made of razor wire surrounded the place, adding a homey curb appeal for a fellow chainsaw massacre enthusiast.

Faded green fabric hung crookedly behind four-pane windows—one of the panes secured with duct tape. As I watched, one corner of the fabric moved. Or at least I thought it did. I sunk lower into the pickup seat, my hands growing clammy.

"When was the last time you were back here?" I asked Harvey, watching the eerie house disappear in my side mirror.

"A year or two ago, but the folks around here probably remember my pickup. They don't get visitors much … nor cotton to 'em."

We passed another rundown shack, this one even further back from the road with torn white curtains behind the panes of glass. An old ripped-up sofa sat in the front yard, a large wooden wire spool made do as an end table. I frowned at the ax blade buried in the middle of the spool. Holy crap. Who *were* these people?

"I sure hope they remember you. I wouldn't want them to think we were with the government."

He grunted in agreement. "Rememberin' me doesn't mean they won't shoot out my tires, drag us out of the truck, and toss us down a mine shaft for trespassin' if they're feelin' ornery enough."

I grimaced at him. "Are you serious?"

He wheezed with laughter. "Yer so easy." When I threatened him with my fist, he quieted. "Okay, okay."

"That wasn't funny, you old goat."

"Was too." He sobered. "But I wasn't all-in foolin' with ya."

Chills crawled up my arms. "What?"

He shrugged. "It's true what they say about the water back here. It turns plain folks into kooky whangdoodles." He pointed out the windshield. "Take that shack ahead on the left."

I'd rather run from it. It looked like the sort of place a serial killer would call home sweet home. Rusted oil drums lined the front porch, the perfect size for sawed-off body parts. Shotguns laid across the barrels pointed toward the road. I counted six before looking up at the doorway.

A pale face stared back at me through the crooked screen.

With a squeak of surprise, I slinked down even lower in my seat, crossing my fingers and toes that yet another shotgun wouldn't poke out through the huge tear in the screen door below the face.

"They know we're here," I whispered to Harvey, peeking out the window to see if we were clear of the oil drum house yet. In the side mirror, I couldn't see the face in the doorway anymore, only a slanting chimney that looked one heavy snowfall away from keeling over.

"Sure as a dead man stinks."

I frowned up at him. "Could you refrain from using the word 'dead' until we are back in *Dead*wood?"

His bushy brow rose. "What's wrong, Executioner? Feelin' puny without yer war hammer?"

"Poke fun, but Slagton feels like the first town this side of Hell."

He did a double take. "Where'd ya hear that one?"

"I watched some old western the other night with Aunt Zoe."

"Which one?"

"I don't remember." I pointed out the windshield at a two-story crumbling building up ahead on our right. "What's that?"

"It used to be the company store back before things went south." He slowed to a crawl as we drew up in front of it. Broken windows downstairs and up showed a lack of love, along with the words spray-painted on the bullet hole–peppered wall next to the front door: *Trespassers will be gutted and hung!*

"No mincing words there," I said aloud, cringing.

"It's all hot air."

"You think so?"

"Nah, they mean it."

"What? Really?"

He shrugged. "They strung up a stranger back in my younger days. A hunter, I believe, who thought he'd found new stompin' grounds."

"Did they gut him?"

"Nope. They just cut off his hands."

I tucked my two sweaty mitts in my armpits.

"The coroner figured they'd taken his hands before stringin' him up. I don't think the law dogs ever did find those hands. My pa reckoned they fed 'em to a pack of rabid dogs one of the whangdoodles kept penned out behind his barn."

"Oh my God."

"But don't ya fret. Those dogs are long gone."

Sure, the dogs were history, but crazy rarely got cured on its own, especially in a tiny town like Slagton where inbreeding probably ran hand-in-hand with lead poisoning.

We rounded another bend in the road, bumped through several potholes, and went from a dirt-packed road to two muddy tracks.

"It's up 'round this next corner, if memory serves me right."

"What's up there?" I sat up in the seat, staring out the windshield. I prayed it wasn't another weathered shack with moving curtains.

"The old '41 Plymouth Fastback." He looked out his window, hitting the brakes hard. "There it is, back behind that old woodshed."

I leaned his way, peering out through his side window. Around the side of the shed, I could see an old, rusted two-door car.

Harvey shut off the pickup and pushed open his door. "Come on. Let's have a look-see."

A strangled, creaky sound came from my throat.

"Did ya swallow yer tongue?"

"Maybe." My gaze darted from tree to tree, searching for signs of a waiting lynch mob or chainsaw-wielding freak of nature. "Why don't I stay here and hold down the fort?"

Harvey grabbed my wrist in a rock-solid grip and tugged me out of his pickup through the driver's-side door. "Move yer tail feathers, Chicken Little. The sky ain't gonna fall today, ya have my promise."

I was more concerned about him having my back.

We waded through the tall, dry grass, stepping carefully around pieces of lumber and firewood. There was a fetid smell underlying the pine-scented air, or maybe that was my imagination playing tricks on me. I peered warily through a big hole in the side of the shed as we walked past, cringing in anticipation of finding torsos hanging from meat hooks. Instead, a large, shiny saw blade stuck up through a metal bench. Someone was taking care of this place, keeping the saw oiled from the looks of things. Several chains hung from nails on the wall, along with three long, two-man handsaws. While there were no body pieces or blood to be seen, the setting was ripe for a group of stupid teenagers to show up and end up the victims in a gruesome horror film.

A poke in my ribs made me yip and jump back.

"We don't have time for gawkin' this trip. Dark comes lickety split this deep in the hills and ya don't want to be here when the wolves start trollin'."

"We don't have wolves in the Black Hills."

"I wasn't talkin' about the four-legged version."

He led the way over to the old car, keeping a hold of my wrist as if he didn't trust me not to run if spooked.

"What's so special about this car?" I whispered.

"It's not the car." He let go of me, leaning inside the broken passenger-side window. Then he reached in his coat pocket and pulled out a screwdriver.

"Never know when yer gonna need to screw," he muttered, jamming the screwdriver in the key-slot on the door of the glove box.

"Yeah, yeah, yeah," I whispered, my focus darting from tree to tree, searching the shadows. I'd heard that line from him more times than I had fingers. "Quit screwing around and grab whatever it is you dragged me back here to get."

With a twist of his wrist, the glove box popped open. "Well, we know one thing."

"What's that?"

He held up a wrinkled manila envelope. "We weren't led on a wild goose chase."

"We came all of the way back here for *that?*"

"What's with yer clown frown? Ya don't know what's inside this here envelope."

I shivered at the mention of clowns. Thanks to Wilda Hessler's demented ghost, I now had a phobia of the painted-face fools. "Let's get the hell out of here. We can see what's inside once we hit civilization again."

Harvey didn't buck. He shut the glove box door and followed on my heels back to his rig.

I breathed a sigh of relief when the engine turned over without hesitation. I had little doubt that we were watched all of the way out of town. A second sigh came when we passed the hole-filled Slagton sign without a flat tire or shotgun blast.

"We're clear," Harvey said, watching through the rearview mirror. "Open that there envelope."

"You sure we should? It's supposed to be for Cooper."

He stared at me as if I'd grown a second head. "What's wrong with you, girl? Ya lost yer huntin' nerve?"

"Maybe. Or maybe I don't want to end up dangling from a noose down at the cop shop."

"Just open the damned envelope."

"Why are you so hell bent on seeing what's in this?" What would make him want to drive out to that hair-raising place to play courier for Cooper?

"Because Slagton is next door to my ranch. If some crazed bessy bug in Slagton has a secret to share with the police, then I need to be in on the knowin' part before another dead man shows up in my barn or my family boneyard." He sniffed. "I'm gettin' plum tired of findin' body parts all over my ranch, and Coop has too much grit in his gizzard to spill the beans when I prod him."

I was getting tired of Harvey finding body parts, too, especially since his discoveries kept adding papers to *my* police file. I took care breaking the envelope's seal, and then pulled it apart and peered inside. "It looks like a picture."

"It would look even more like one if you'd pull 'er out."

Wiping my sweaty palms on my pants, I reached inside and pulled out a picture, the instant camera kind, frowning at it.

"What the hell?"

"What is it?"

It was hard to tell for sure in the fading daylight. I grabbed his cell phone. "How do you turn on the flashlight on this sucker?"

He took the phone and punched on the light, handing it back to me. I stared down at the picture in the bright light, trying to make sense of the thing half hidden behind a pine tree in the picture. "What the …?"

"What is it?" he asked, speeding along the gravel road.

It reminded me of those blurry camera shots on the Internet of Bigfoot. The thing in the picture wasn't brown and furry, but it was walking upright. Whatever it was, it appeared to have horns, like a bighorn sheep. Or maybe that was something in the background that made it look like … no, those had to be horns on an elongated pale-colored head. The lighting was shitty in the picture. The shot seemed to have been taken from high up, like the photographer had been perched in a tree. It was hard to tell the thing's height from the angle.

I rubbed my chin, trying to make sense of what I was looking at. Whatever it was, it didn't look quite human. I shivered in spite of the heat blowing out of Harvey's vents.

"I'm not sure what it is," I finally answered him.

He pulled into his own driveway, putting the pickup in park. "Let me have a look."

I handed him the picture, happy to be free of it. While he squinted at it, I checked the envelope again. A small piece of paper was tucked into the corner. I pulled it out, holding it up.

"It's back," I said.

"What's that?" Harvey looked over at the paper I held out for him to read.

"It's back," I repeated, reading aloud the words, frowning at the picture. "What's this mean?" I gestured at the picture and the slip of paper.

Harvey stared out the windshield at the dark clouds stacking up in the sky. "I reckon it means ya got a whole new set of problems, *Scharfrichter.*"

Chapter Nine

After debating if, how, and when we should tell Cooper about the envelope with the picture, Harvey and I didn't talk much on the way back down to Deadwood.

Harvey was of the opinion that we should send the picture anonymously to Cooper at work. I worried that no matter how mysterious we tried to be, the detective would dust for fingerprints and I'd be up shit creek with handcuffs locked firmly in place. However, telling the truth about where and when we got the envelope meant Cooper would figure out I'd slipped my leash, aka cell phone tracker, which opened the door for further distrust issues and hoosegow repercussions.

In short, from where I stood on this slippery ledge, we were damned if we didn't and pretty much screwed seven ways from Sunday if we did.

I stared out the window at the twilight sky, the pine trees a dark blur. I slid my Cooper problem under the rug so I could brood about who had captured that shot of the creature. Since the voice on the phone had been male, I assumed the photographer was male, too, saying as much to Harvey. He refused to pick a gender, instead settling on the idea that the photo was taken by a hunter out checking traps and snares. Since one pine tree pretty much looked like all of the others, it would be hard to tell where. Was the creature hiding deeper in the hills? Back near the old mine? Or somewhere close to Harvey's own ranch? Hell, we'd found two bodies there so far. Were those just the warmup for the fun and games to come?

Man or woman photographer aside, why would they give the picture to Cooper? Had the detective posted his phone number on the old telephone poles back in Slagton? Or did the caller know Cooper personally? Maybe they'd connected on another investigation or a previous murder?

Harvey dropped me off at work, where I found a message on my desk in Natalie's writing explaining that she'd left my cell phone at Doc's office for safekeeping. A second message—this one filled with Cornelius's slanted scrawls—said that he needed me to come in early in the morning to witness an amazing feat. He included a list of groceries at the end of the message.

I sighed at the list. An amazing feat would be Cornelius remembering that I wasn't his damned personal assistant. I supposed this was the price I had to pay for his playing the part of my boyfriend in front of the devil's concubine. Sheesh, the things I did for love—or rather in order to not lose Doc to a man-stealing skank. I drew the line at doing Abe Jr.'s laundry though, at least until I had some guarantee of long-term commitment from Doc.

The Picklemobile wasn't in the parking lot at quitting time, so I didn't bother with trying Doc's back door before heading home.

I still wasn't feeling chatty later that evening while making grilled cheese sandwiches in Aunt Zoe's kitchen. The weight of the day's shit-storms raining down on my happy place made my shoulders heavy, something Aunt Zoe picked up on when she came in from her glass workshop to help me set the table.

"What's going on?" she asked, washing up in the kitchen sink.

I flipped one of the sandwiches, frowning at the blackened slice of bread. Oops, that was my third extra-crispy grilled cheese in a row.

"You're burning supper." She took the spatula from me and hip bumped me aside. "What's with your gloomy Gus mask? Did you have a fight with Cooper?"

"No." I leaned against the counter next to her, debating on whether to tell her about Harvey and my trip to Slagton. I frowned at the plates rounding the table. There was an extra one by my count. I pointed at the additional plate she'd set out. "You added wrong."

"No, I didn't." She grabbed several more pieces of bread, dipping a knife into the butter. "Reid's coming."

Come again? "That's funny. I could swear I heard you say that Reid Martin is going to join us for supper tonight."

"You heard me right, Violet Lynn."

I stared at her profile, speculating what her invitation to Reid meant in the grand scheme of their on-again/off-for-good past. "I hope you're not planning on pouring hemlock in his lemonade tonight. I'm already in enough trouble with Detective Hawke for several other murders I didn't commit."

She elbowed me in the side playfully. "Give me some credit. I'm not going to kill him." Her eyes crinkled at the corners. "Not tonight, anyway."

"What gives, then?" Normally, she'd sooner fill Reid's backside with buckshot than let him cross the threshold.

"I invited him."

What? "Is there a world-ending meteor heading for Earth?"

"Not as far as I know." She spread butter on one piece of bread and then another.

I touched the back of my hand to her forehead. "You don't feel feverish." I took her by the shoulders, inspecting her face. "Your pupils appear normal and your skin isn't flushed, which leads me to one conclusion. Who are you really, and what have you done with my aunt?"

Wrinkling her nose at me, she pulled free and returned to buttering bread. "We need to talk to Reid."

"By 'we' are you referring to your id, ego, and superego? Or is this more of a royal 'we'?"

"The latter. I was listening to the scanner out in my workshop earlier and something came across the airwaves that concerns me."

Since my childhood days, Aunt Zoe had kept a scanner in her workshop. Most of the time, the classic rock-n-roll blasting from her stereo overshadowed the periodic static bursts mixed with cryptic code words, but it was always fun to eavesdrop when the fire whistle echoed through the hills.

"What did you hear?" I asked.

Before she could answer my question, Addy slid into the kitchen in her socks. "Hey, Mom, can Kelly spend the night with me this weekend? Her dad said it was okay with him."

Of course Jeff Wymonds, Kelly's dad, would be okay with his daughter sleeping elsewhere. Rumor had it he was still having kitchen-counter sex with his nipple-ringed girlfriend. Actually, it hadn't been a rumor, more like a gloating declaration directly from the horse's big fat mouth when I'd run into him at the grocery store last Saturday. Judging from the volume he'd used, he wanted the whole dang store to know about his sex-capades. My cheeks were still singed from the outraged gawk sent our way by a fellow cereal aisle visitor.

Last month, I'd had the unfortunate experience of walking in on Jeff and his girlfriend doing the wild thing in his kitchen. Driving in for a touchdown had been their X-rated theme. The red thong underwear I'd witnessed flossing Jeff's southern cheeks would forever haunt me. Now, whenever he saw me, Jeff liked to update me on his most recent "score," and no amount of ear plugging seemed to derail the oversexed monkey.

"Where will Kelly sleep?" I asked Addy. "Cooper is in your room and you're in with me."

Addy chewed on her lower lip. "I know. You could sleep with Aunt Zoe. She's got a big bed."

So did Doc. Too bad sharing his wouldn't work since Cooper practically tucked me in at night with whispered threats about what would result if I were thick-skulled enough to try running away.

"Let me think about it," I said, putting Addy off for now. Sleeping arrangements were low on my totem pole of anxieties tonight. Hell, as soon as Cooper found out Harvey and I had picked up a package for him (and taken a peek at its contents while at it), he'd probably throw me in jail. Caging me at the police station would open up my bed for both kids and remove Cooper's need to keep me on a leash.

The doorbell rang.

Aunt Zoe and I exchanged frowns. That would probably be Reid. She motioned for me to answer the door.

The porch was dark and empty. I was wrong about it being Reid, unless Aunt Zoe had previously filled him with lead unbeknownst to me and invited his ghost to supper.

I turned on the porch light, pulling my cardigan sweater tighter around me as I stepped out into the chilly night air. There were no cars parked in the drive or out front. No signs of life anywhere. A freezing gust whistled past, rattling the wind chimes hanging at the end of the porch. Either someone was playing doorbell-ringing games with us or the wiring was on the fritz.

I turned to head back into the warm house and noticed a box leaning against the wall in the corner. Another glance at the street to double-check for a mail or delivery truck came up empty. Maybe one of Aunt Zoe's neighbors had dropped it off. I kneeled to get a better look, making out my name in the dim porch light. It was handwritten with no address below it. The box was big enough to hold a violin and sealed shut with a line of clear tape. Not a single dent or dinged-up corner marked the brown cardboard.

Grimacing, I shivered in the cold. I hesitated to take the box inside. The last time a box had come for me personally with no address, it'd contained a war hammer that looked to have been popular sometime during the Middle Ages. I'd grown wary of gift horses after my adventures with that damned hammer.

The growl of a diesel engine cut through the quiet night. I looked over my shoulder as Reid parked his red dually pickup at the curb. His door slammed, echoing through Deadwood's Presidential District.

"Hey, Sparky," he said as he crested the porch steps. "What are you doing down there?"

In his thick flannel shirt, stocking cap, and blue jeans, Reid Martin looked like he should be carrying a wood ax over his shoulder. I knew of a spare one out in Slagton just waiting for the right psychopath to stop by and gear up for a killing spree.

Reid would make a fine serial killer, since he was a middle-aged version of Sam Elliott with a deep voice to match. He'd probably have no trouble luring a woman, young or old, back to a remote cabin in the hills. Lucky for me and Aunt Zoe, he'd decided long ago to focus on fighting and investigating fires instead of murdering innocent townsfolk.

"Someone left me a box," I told him, beginning to shiver. I crossed my arms, trying to hold onto my warmth as another gust blew my curls in my face.

"You need help carrying it inside?"

"No, I got it." I didn't move, though, still kneeling next to it. "Aunt Zoe's waiting for you. I'll be right in."

He cocked his head to the side. "You okay?"

I hadn't been "okay" since I'd met Wolfgang Hessler back in July and my world had flipped upside down. "I'm fine, I just need a minute to clear my head."

He started to open the door, then pulled it shut again, leaning closer. "Is Zo doing okay?"

"I think so."

"She's not on her deathbed or anything like that?"

"Uh, no."

"Did she recently hit her head really hard?"

"Not that I know of."

His eyes narrowed. "You would tell me if she's waiting in there for me with both barrels of her damned shotgun loaded, right?"

"Sure." I grinned. "Unless she made me pinkie swear to secrecy."

With a growl, he muttered, "You Parker women are hard on men."

"Maybe." I patted his pant leg. "But we soften up with the right liquor."

"Thank God for that." He left me alone, closing the front door behind him.

No sooner had I focused back on the package, the Picklemobile pulled into the drive. I waited while Doc closed the door and made his way up the porch steps.

"What are you doing down there, beautiful?" His gaze moved from me to the package. "What's in the box?"

"Your guess is as good as mine." I stood, moving closer to touch him because I could. After my cold lips brushed his much warmer ones, he took off his coat and draped it over my shoulders. I pulled the warm leather around me, soaking up Doc's scent.

Doc pointed his thumb at Reid's dually. "That's Reid, right?"

I nodded. "Aunt Zoe invited him."

"I hope he borrowed a bulletproof vest from Coop on the way over." Doc drew something out of his pocket and held it out to me.

"He did inquire about her shotgun before stepping inside." I looked down at my cell phone, taking it from him as Cooper's police Durango pulled in behind Reid's truck.

"Natalie told me to tell you she fixed the problem," Doc said, "whatever that means."

"She didn't explain what she was up to?"

"I told her I didn't want to know."

I frowned at the stony-faced detective stepping out of the Durango, sliding the phone into the front of my yoga pants. "She didn't fix my problem from where I'm standing."

"Coop's just trying to help you."

"Tracking me like a wild bear via my phone is taking things a little far." Next he'd want to stick a tag through my ear.

"Maybe, but would you rather it be Hawke?"

I growled in response to Doc's question as Cooper climbed the steps. "What's going on?" he asked, his cop glare scanning my face and then Doc's.

"I'm enjoying a moment alone with Doc," I said. "I'm surprised your phone tracker didn't report how many times I've kissed him so far today."

"That reminds me, what were you doing this afternoon at the Old Prospector Hotel?"

I opened my mouth to inform him that his tracker had my location wrong, but suddenly realized that whatever Natalie had done to my phone had showed its location in the Old Prospector Hotel instead of Doc's office, where she'd left it. "I was looking for something."

"What?"

"Cornelius."

"You'd better be careful, Parker. The last time you looked for Mr. Curion, you ended up in jail."

"He has a good point," Doc said, chuckling.

After jabbing Doc in the ribs, I glared at the man who had put me behind bars. "Bite me, Cooper."

"I wouldn't want to risk rabies."

"Lower your weapons, you two." Doc pulled me back against him, his hands spanning my hips. "Ay yi yi, Tish. Are you wearing yoga pants again?"

An exasperated snort came from Cooper. "You two are like rabbits. Don't you dare start speaking French, Parker. After the shit I've dealt with today, I don't think I can watch Nyce revert to a lovesick fool."

"I was about to beg Violet to offer up a *oui* or *deux* when you drove up," Doc said, wrapping his arms around me. "But your timing sucks, as usual, Coop."

Cooper rubbed the back of his neck. "Hell, I'd sooner be down at the Purple Door drinking whiskey than babysitting Parker."

Babysitting? Like I wanted a freaking watchdog nipping at my heels day and night. I snarled at Cooper, retaliating with, "Don't you mean you'd rather be pining away at the Galena House?" As in where a certain brunette lived these days.

His eyes narrowed. "Why? Are you planning on breaking and entering again?" He sidestepped my jab, delivering one of his own.

"We used a key."

"Next time, use better discretion instead and don't go in that damned apartment at all." Cooper looked back toward the street. "How long has Martin been here?"

"A few minutes," I said, stepping away from Doc's warmth.

"No gunplay yet?"

"Aunt Zoe invited him," I explained.

"You don't say?" Cooper turned back to us. "Did she skip her meds today?"

Doc picked up the box. "Let's go inside before Zoe comes to her senses and loads her shotgun."

Cooper held the door open, closing out the cold behind us.

"You want this box in the kitchen?" Doc asked.

I shook my head, shooting a worried glance at Cooper's back as he hung up his coat. "Leave it by the stairs for now. I'll open it later." As in when a certain detective wasn't standing within hearing distance.

We filed into the kitchen. Reid was at the stove flipping grilled cheese sandwiches while Aunt Zoe poured lemonade. I looked from one to the other, my brow tightening at the Norman Rockwell scene. Something smelled too cheesy about this hunky-dory scene and it wasn't what was for supper.

"What's going on?" I asked Aunt Zoe.

"I'm pouring lemonade." She picked up an empty glass and demonstrated. "What's going on with you? Reid says you got a package."

"Yeah, I did." I changed the subject before Cooper sunk his teeth into the subject of that darn box. "Should I get the kids ready for supper?"

"I already did." Aunt Zoe pointed at the table where bowls of tomato soup sat steaming. "Sit."

I did, joined by Doc and Cooper after they washed their hands. Addy and Layne came shortly after, scooting up to the table as Reid carried over the plate of grilled cheese sandwiches. His and Aunt Zoe's bread was a lovely golden color compared to my charred versions now piled next to the stove, likely headed for the trashcan. While the kids chattered about school and the upcoming holiday program all the classes were performing, I picked at my sandwich and stirred my soup repeatedly.

Doc's knee nudged mine under the table, his brow wrinkled.

I gave him a crooked smile. I wished I could spill about the lack of response at Ms. Wolff's apartment and the trip to Slagton, along with that hair-raising picture, but instead I shook my head. Cooper appeared to be listening to the kids, but I knew better. His glances my way told me he'd picked up on my lack of appetite, too. The damned detective saw too much.

"Hey, Mom," Layne said around a mouthful of cheese and bread. "Have you ever heard of a white demon?"

"Layne, you know better than to talk with your mouth full," Aunt Zoe said.

I stirred my soup some more, wondering where Layne came up with some of his notions. Last week he'd asked me if I would rather be a purple dragon or a red lizard if I lived on a planet named something I couldn't remember. "Is that a character in one of your video games, sweetie?"

He shook his head, swallowing and chasing it with a drink of lemonade. "I read about it in that book I borrowed from you. The one that told stories about the *lidérc* and all of those women gladiators."

Otherwise known as our family history book. "Gladiators" was a much nicer name than "Executioners." It sounded more badass, too, not so creepy.

The other night, when Doc and I had asked Layne more about the family book and what he knew about capturing a *lidérc*, he'd told us that one of the "gladiators" had allowed it to attach to her. At least that was what he thought it described. He'd described it like a tick, stuck on her skin. I didn't correct him to explain that the attachment was more like a mental tethering, not really physical.

When Doc asked how the "gladiator" had removed this so-called tick, Layne explained that according to the book, she'd jumped off a cliff into the rocky ocean below. Doc, Aunt Zoe, and I had discussed his answer later alone in the cold on the back porch while Cooper was in the shower, all three of us wondering what the executioner had been thinking by taking her own life. Was she only focused on freeing herself from the Hungarian devil, or had she truly managed to take the *lidérc* with her to the next plane of existence? Doc and I had no definite answers, of course, but Aunt Zoe believed the *lidérc* had probably lived through the ordeal, found another host, and was still out there ruining people's lives. The disappointment in her voice had been as clear as the star-filled night sky.

I hoped I didn't inspire such feelings from her the next time I crossed paths with a supernatural troublemaker, but like the previous executioners in my family line, I was only human. At least part-human, anyway, according to one of my most recent execution-ees.

Now Layne was talking about a white demon. I probably needed to flip through that family history book, but truth be known I sort of didn't want to know what I might be up against. Ignorance was bliss, especially when trying to stay alive in a world where monsters roamed. My nightmares were bad enough without fodder from those pages.

I shared a worried glance with Aunt Zoe. "No, Layne, I don't think I've heard of a white demon." I'd only seen a black pustule-covered demon with orange eyes that supposedly went by the name of Kyrkozz. "Why do you ask?"

He wiped his fingers on his napkin, my years of badgering him to not use his pants that way finally paying off. "At recess today, I was sitting on a bench looking at the trees on the hill behind the school and I thought I saw one standing up there."

Skirrrchhhh!

"You actually saw a … a white d … demon?" I sputtered.

He shrugged. "It might have been just a really tall, super white-haired guy. Do we have any albinos living around here?"

Mr. Black!

My pulse redlined, my breath rushing from my lungs.

The juggernaut's twin had returned! But why was he watching my son instead of me? Was it something to do with the picture of Layne that had been in Ms. Wolff's apartment when Harvey and I had stumbled upon her withered body? The photo that had gone missing after Mr. Black had paid a visit to the Galena House?

Shit! What should I do? Keep Layne home from school? I'd need to come up with a damned good excuse if I did, since Layne had already missed a week of school due to the fights he'd gotten into at recess last month. I could hire a tutor maybe to homeschool him, but …

Doc squeezed my thigh hard enough for me to wince. "Breathe," he whispered, then took a drink of lemonade.

"Could you describe this white demon to me, Layne?" Cooper asked, interrogation being his second language, of course.

For once, I was grateful to have Cooper sitting at the table with me, allowing me to focus on calming the hysterical broad ranting in my head.

"He sort of reminded me of a bird," Layne said.

"Did he have white feathers like Elvis?" Addy asked, dipping the last bit of her grilled cheese sandwich into her soup.

"Not that I could see."

"An orange beak?" she pressed.

"No beak."

"Tail feathers?" Addy took a bite of the tomato-soaked bread.

Layne sighed, annoyed. "Not like a *bird* bird, Addy. More like an eagle or a duck if it was turned into a human."

Cooper and I shared a frown-filled moment. I'd often referred to the juggernauts as Donald Duck's nephews.

"What's a *lidérc*?" Addy asked, her thoughts random, as usual.

"It's a Hungarian devil," Aunt Zoe answered. When I gave her a what-the-hell look, she shrugged. "That's what she'd find if she looked it up online."

"A hungry devil," Addy said, confusing the reference to the country for an empty stomach. "How cool would that be to see?" She stuffed the last of her tomato-soaked grilled cheese sandwich into her mouth.

Not cool at all.

Silence followed, filled with clanging spoons on bowls and lemonade glasses clinking on the wooden table.

My spoon trembled as I tried to scoop up some soup, spilling half of it back in the bowl. Why Layne, dammit? Was Addy being followed, too, but so busy eating candy and giggling with her friends that she hadn't noticed yet? Prudence the ghost, my executing predecessor, had lost her son to the enemy before they slit her throat. According to her, the idea had been to end her line, which meant my kids were targets along with me. While this wasn't news to me, I wasn't sure what level of paranoia was required in order to raise them to adulthood now that I bore the executioner yoke. Hell, keeping normal kids alive in today's danger-filled world inspired a headful of gray hairs. How was I supposed to keep sane when fighting off monsters?

"Reid." Addy broke the silence, her brow lined. "Do firemen wear underwear under their yellow fire pants?"

My cheeks warmed at my child's personal question. "Adelynn Renee!"

A snort of laughter came from Aunt Zoe's direction.

Reid's grin filled his face from ear to ear. "Most of us do, Addy."

Addy grinned back. "Is your underwear yellow, too, Reid? Or red like your hat?"

Dear Lord, child! I heard Doc laugh under his breath and bumped him with my knee under the table.

Reid's face reddened under Addy's steadfast gaze.

Cooper snickered. "I believe we have an amateur detective in-training here, Martin. Answer the girl's question."

"Well." Reid's blue eyes crinkled around the edges. "I like to wear my lucky underwear to a fire. They've kept me safe time and again."

"You didn't answer her question," Cooper said, setting his empty soup bowl on his clean plate.

Reid slanted a glare at Cooper. "They're black with red stripes."

Addy frowned. "Why are they lucky?"

Aunt Zoe cleared her throat. Her cheeks were now turning an interesting shade of red.

"Did you win them in a card game?" Layne asked.

"Reid," Aunt Zoe warned, shaking her head.

Reid hit her with raised brows. "What, Zo? Coop insists that I answer Addy's questions. I'm on the stand here, woman."

She squinted. "Yes, you are."

"Addy," he said, returning to my daughter's inquiring gaze. "My favorite girl gave them to me years ago and told me that if I wore them to fires, they'd keep me out of harm's way."

Layne's grilled cheese sandwich lowered along with his jaw. "Your girlfriend gave you lucky underwear?"

"She gave me underwear." Reid's eyes twinkled when he looked over at Aunt Zoe. "And then she made them lucky."

"How did she make them lucky?" Layne asked.

"And we're done here." Aunt Zoe started collecting plates, piling them on top of each other without trying to be quiet.

"Do you two still like each other?" Addy asked, not heeding Aunt Zoe's scowl.

Before Reid could answer, Aunt Zoe scooted her chair back. "Who wants dessert?"

"I do! I do!" Addy and Layne both yelled.

Well-played, I thought with a smile at my aunt. She knew exactly how to derail young, curious minds. At least those sharing blood with me, a sugar aficionado.

"Bring your plates to the sink," she told them, "and I'll dish you up some ice cream."

"On a week night?" Layne asked, knowing I was trying to limit sweets during school nights over the holiday season.

Aunt Zoe looked at me for approval. I nodded with a smirk. She'd owe me one for bending the rules.

Twenty minutes later, the table was cleared, ice cream had been served, and the kids were in the living room distracted by a PBS show on the buffalo in Yellowstone National Park.

I stood at the sink, washing dishes while Doc dried them. He flirted with me as we worked, tenderly brushing my hair out of my face while my hands were wrist-deep in dishwater, or running his palm over my hip when he needed me to move to one side or the other to make room for him to put a glass or dish away.

Aunt Zoe leaned against the counter near the stove, her bowl of ice cream in hand. "Reid, I need to ask you about something I heard come over the scanner earlier today."

That made Cooper's ears perk up, judging from his sudden stillness. The detective had opted out of ice cream even though I'd suggested some sugar in his blood might do him some good, sweetening up his disposition. That had earned me a sour scowl.

Reid nodded. "I wondered when you'd get around to it."

"To what?"

"Explaining the reason you invited me over for supper."

"Maybe I missed your charm," Aunt Zoe said with a smirk.

His laugh was low and velvety. "Or maybe you missed something else."

Aunt Zoe's lips flat-lined.

"Like your lucky underwear," Cooper cut in.

I paused mid-scrub to gape at the detective. "Did you just make a joke?" I turned to Doc. "Someone must have extracted Cooper's funny bone from his anal cavity."

"Zip it, Parker." Cooper focused on Aunt Zoe. "What did you hear?"

"There was a report that a cross-country skier on the Mickelson Trail came across a smoking, partially burned crate with human remains in it."

Reid lowered his spoon. "You heard about that, huh?"

"Yeah. It made me curious."

"Why didn't I hear about it?" Cooper asked Reid, his face hardening.

"Hawke took the call. You were apparently busy elsewhere. The report came in just after lunch."

Cooper nailed me with a glare. "I was busy dealing with trouble at the Galena House."

Oops! I hid behind Doc until Cooper focused back on Reid.

"What are you wondering about it, Zo?" Reid asked.

"Were there cloven hoofprints in the area again?"

"What do you mean *again*?" Doc asked.

Aunt Zoe pointed her spoon at Reid. "He's seen this before, haven't you, Reid?"

Reid nodded slowly. "Yeah, unfortunately."

"Cloven hoofprints?" I said, draining the sink. I borrowed the towel from Doc, drying my hands. "Like a pig?"

"Yes." She scraped her spoon over her ice cream, frowning at Reid. "Tell me about the human remains."

"We just ate, Zo."

"Please, Reid. None of us here are squeamish." She scooped a bite of ice cream on her spoon. "Were they partially eaten?"

"It's hard to tell for certain due to the degree of burns."

"But?" she prompted after swallowing the spoonful.

"I think so."

"Damn. I was hoping it was merely a case of plain old murder."

I scoffed. " 'Plain old' murder?"

Doc leaned against the counter. "Who do you think did it, Zoe?" He grabbed me by the waist and settled me back against him, resting his hands on my hip bones. "Or is it a *what* again?"

"The latter." She set her bowl on the counter. "I wonder if we have a *Nachzehrer* on our hands."

"What's that?" Cooper asked.

"It's a creature that feeds off the living to survive."

"Is it parasitic?" Reid asked. "Like a *lidérc*?"

"No, I mean it literally eats human flesh. Folklore lists it more like a German version of a vampire, but it's not a blood drinker. Well, not blood alone."

"This is insane," Cooper muttered.

"So is the creature," Aunt Zoe told him. "It was once human, but after death it reanimates for a reason that nobody knows for certain."

"It reanimates," I said. "So it can be killed again?"

"According to legend, yes. But remember, this all comes from stories that have been passed down one generation to the next. *Nachzehrer* were prominent in the northern regions of Germany according to legend, but I've read similar accounts from other cultures' mythology."

Cooper sighed. "How do we know we don't have just some crazy bastard on our hands who thinks he's a cannibal and then left the burned evidence in plain sight to draw attention?"

Aunt Zoe shrugged. "Time will tell. A *Nachzehrer* will feed on the living after consuming its own death shroud and flesh. If anyone else turns up partially eaten or any graves appear to have been disturbed around—"

"Mom!" Addy cried, running into the room. "Look what I found!"

She held out a clock for me to see.

A German clock from the Black Forest region.

I frowned. "Where did you get that, Adelynn Renee?"

"It was in a box by the stairs."

A box that was addressed to me, dammit. I glared at her for opening something that she had no business touching.

Cooper held out his hand. "Let me take a look at that, Addy."

She handed it to him, pointing at the face. "Look at that. It looks like a big dog mixed with a werewolf."

Aunt Zoe joined them, staring down at it. "A Hellhound, maybe."

I stepped closer, checking for myself, and flinched. Ah, shit.

"It needs winding," Aunt Zoe said.

Or maybe not, I thought, my gut tightening at who might have left me the freaking clock.

"Addy," I said, "go get the box and bring it in here."

Cooper set the clock carefully on the table. There was no misinterpreting the fury lining his face when he looked over at me. "Damn it, Parker. It's one of the missing clocks."

"No shit, Sherlock. The question is, who left it on my doorstep?" I fell into a chair, burying my face in my palms.

And why?

Chapter Ten

Tuesday, December 4th

I woke up fretting about that damned clock.

Cooper had wound it last night in the kitchen, cursing about my being a magnet for trouble under his breath as he pulled on the chains. But even after being wound, the clock sat on the table ... dead ... while we all frowned at it.

Reid and Doc had headed home a short time later, leaving me with a grumpy detective and a bottle of tequila. It didn't take long for me to pick which of the two I would rather spend the rest of the evening with, taking the bottle to my room. In between sips, I'd put away clean clothes, tidied up my closet, and kept my mind from getting stuck on the who and why behind the clock's appearance on my doorstep.

After my morning shower, I tiptoed down the stairs, wary of Cooper's sharp teeth. I doubted a night in Addy's pink room had dulled his temper. Cute kitten posters and stuffed unicorns were no match for a pissed-off detective.

The clock was on the sideboard in the dining room. Its hands were still frozen in time—or rather without time. Not even a few nudges would make them move on their own. I stared at the carvings in the morning light, getting chills all over again at the sight of the large beast with a long snout and pointy ears. Its jaws were spread in mid-howl or roar, its long claws reaching up toward the closed cuckoo door.

"It's still not working," Aunt Zoe said from the kitchen archway, making me jerk in surprise.

"I see that." I walked past her into the kitchen, rubbing away my goosebumps. "Where's Cooper?" I grabbed a coffee mug from the cupboard and filled it full of caffeinated happiness.

"He's already up and gone." She settled into her usual chair, picking at her breakfast muffin on the plate in front of her. "He told me to tell you that he'll be watching you with his phone."

I grumbled something not very nice about Cooper's phone and a certain location on his person where I'd like to shove it. I stuffed two pieces of bread into the toaster, planning to use them to soak up some of the acid in my gut caused by Cooper and Hawke.

Aunt Zoe chuckled. "What are you up to today besides selling houses and complaining about your favorite detective duo?"

"Cornelius wants to talk to me about Jane's ghost, but I have to pick up some groceries for him before I head in to work."

"Want me to take the kids to school?"

I shook my head. "Natalie texted me this morning. She's heading down to Rapid City first thing to pick up some supplies for the Galena House and offered to swing by and take them to school before heading out of town."

"How's she liking living in town?"

The front door creaked. "Honey, I'm home," Natalie called out.

"You can ask her yourself," I told Aunt Zoe, grabbing a slice from the toaster and spreading on a dab of butter.

Natalie breezed into the room, literally, ruffling the December page of the calendar hanging on the wall. "Is that the creepy clock you were telling me about on the sideboard?"

"One and the same," I said, raising one eyebrow at her pigtails, bib overalls, and hiking boots. "Look who's here, Aunt Zoe. It's Daisy Mae. How's Li'l Abner doing these days?"

"He's as simpleminded as always. Reminds me of you." Natalie stole the piece of toast I'd buttered and sat at the table. "What in the heck did you mean by that last text you sent?"

"What did I write?" I buttered the other piece of toast, replaying our texts in my head.

She pulled her phone out of her front bib pocket. "I asked you what Coop said about the clock and you replied: *He sewed me a new asshat.*"

"What!" I dropped the knife in the sink. "I did not type that."

"Yes, you did." She held her phone out for me. I moved closer, taking a bite of my toast as I leaned down to read the text. "That's weird. I swear I wrote: *He chewed me a new asshole.*"

She turned the phone back toward her, staring down at the screen. "Hmmm. Let me look at your phone."

"It's up by my bed." I grabbed my coffee from the counter. "That's what happens when I text while in a pre-caffeinated state with only one eye open."

Aunt Zoe stood up from her chair, carrying her empty plate over to the sink. "How do you like living in town, Natalie?"

"Besides the ghosts banging around in the halls at the Galena House, it's a nice change."

"What ghosts?"

"Freesia says it's her great-great uncle, Big Jake Tender, swearing he'd never hurt anyone. But between you and me, I think there's someone else thumping around, especially the thing up in the attic."

"Are you serious?" I asked, waiting for her to crack a smile.

She didn't. "Yep. I also hear the stairs creak, especially after midnight, but nobody is there when I check."

Another round of goosebumps rippled down my arms. "That's spooky."

She shrugged. "So far nothing has happened in my apartment, and Freesia claims the previous tenant never complained about ghosts, so I just turn up the ocean sounds on the fancy alarm clock you got me last Christmas and go back to sleep."

It would take more than ocean waves to make me forget about the sound of something moving around in the night. Then again, Natalie hadn't faced off with some of the monsters I had over the last few months.

"Have you told anyone else about the noises?" Aunt Zoe asked.

"Like who?"

"Cooper," I offered.

"Why would I tell him? Ever since that mess at the Hessler house at Thanksgiving, he gets his tighty-whities bunched up when anyone talks about ghosts. Plus, the last I checked, he can't arrest ghosts for disturbing the peace."

"I know, but maybe it would soften him up to the idea of letting us back in Ms. Wolff's apartment."

"First of all," Natalie said, a grin spreading across her lips. "Who wants Cooper soft?"

Aunt Zoe laughed from the sink where she was rinsing off her plate. "I'm sure most of the female population in Deadwood and Lead prefer him extra rigid."

I faked sticking my finger down my throat. "Can we not talk about Cooper in the carnal sense while I'm eating breakfast?" I'd sooner focus on sweet things, like honey. Or Doc. Or licking honey off of Doc.

"Second," Natalie continued, "why do you want to go back in that apartment again? You tried the phone and it doesn't work. What's next? Another séance?"

"I want to take stock of the remaining clocks."

"I'm sure the cops have done that already."

I crossed my arms. "Are you new here? Have you not heard about my reputation with the Deadwood police? Do you think I can just walk in the front doors and ask Rudolph the Red-Nosed Rookie behind the desk for a copy of their notes on the clocks in that apartment?"

"I don't think the cop that usually holds down the front desk is a rookie," Natalie said.

"I know that, noodle-head, but *rookie* goes better with *Rudolph* than anything else I could think of when I'm only three sips into my coffee."

"Don't call me noodle-head, you lily-livered pickle-puss."

"When you go back in that apartment," Aunt Zoe said, draping the towel over the faucet, "make sure you wear the charm necklace I gave you just in case anyone non-human shows up for the party."

Aunt Zoe made charm totems that acted as warning devices, triggering a reaction in others who weren't like the rest of us. I'd been wearing one of her charm necklaces once while standing in front of the Galena House when Mr. Black walked past me on his way out. All it took was a single look in my direction for his eyes to morph into snake-like slits, showing his true self to me. That was the day Layne's picture had gone missing from Ms. Wolff's apartment. I'd always suspected Mr. Black was behind taking that picture from her dresser, which was what had me tossing and turning about him possibly being the one Layne had noticed at recess.

Aunt Zoe dropped a kiss on my temple as she walked past. "I'll go get the kids moving."

"Thanks." I turned back to Natalie. "I'd ask you to go in and take stock of what clocks are still there, but I sort of need to see them for myself to make them stick in my memory."

"I thought you were more of an auditory learner."

"When it comes to textbooks, sure." And family history books. "But these clocks each have unique designs. Something tells me that I need to make a few notes about each. That the details may come in handy later."

"Let me see if the cop visits slow down over the next day or two," she said. "I'll figure out a way to get you inside, but it may need to be in the middle of the night."

"I don't love that idea, but I'm desperate at this point."

"I know you are. I saw your new billboard. You stink to high heaven of desperation." She laughed when I grabbed the damp dishtowel and whipped it at her.

Addy came stumbling into the kitchen. Layne followed, and then the chatter turned to what holiday specials were on television later tonight. Before I headed out the door to the Piggly Wiggly to collect the items on Cornelius's list, Natalie had agreed to bring pizza for supper and stay for the old cartoon version of *How the Grinch Stole Christmas*, which Aunt Zoe said was scheduled for this evening according to the commercials.

I hoped that having Natalie around would make our own Mr. Grinch, aka Deadwood's crabbiest detective, smile for once. Maybe Cooper's heart would even grow three sizes too big.

I laughed. And reindeer might really fly, too.

After kisses good-bye from my kids and a raspberry from my best friend, I drove up the hill toward Lead. The grocery store parking lot had only a scattering of cars and pickups. I was in and out before my SUV had time to get cold. Unfortunately, a familiar pickup with a WISH YOU WERE BEER bumper sticker idled next to my Honda.

Jeff Wymonds, the oversexed monkey who liked to wear a red thong during kitchen-counter sex rolled down his driver's-side window as I approached. "Morning, Violet Parker."

I sighed. One would think that after months of being Jeff's real estate agent, as well as the mom of his daughter's best friend, he'd drop the Parker bit and stick with plain old Violet. However, Jeff was a bit thick-headed on some ideas.

"Hey, Jeff. How are you doing?" *Please don't talk about your sex life.*

"Great, especially after last night."

I groaned while stuffing the bag of groceries into my back seat. Maybe I could derail him from the nitty-gritty icky on his nearly naked romps with his girlfriend with a reminder of his soon-to-be ex-wife. "Oh, yeah? Is your divorce finally finished?"

Jeff's wife had left him last summer, taking their baby son with her while leaving poor depressed Kelly behind for her father to nurse back to happiness. While I could understand his wife's motivation for leaving what sounded like a miserable marriage for both of them, leaving Kelly while the girl was in the thick of emotional turmoil over losing her friend the year before seemed a bit odd to the mother in me. I'd rush Hell with a bucket to save my kids from suffering like Kelly had.

"Nah, we're still fighting over custody rights," he said. "What has me whistling with the birds this morning is what happened last night."

I shut the back door. "Listen, Jeff. I'm not really in the mood to hear about your latest sexual encounter with your girlfriend."

"That's good, because last night had nothing to do with my girlfriend."

I pulled my keys from my purse. "What then?" Was it something to do with Kelly?

"I had a little reunion last night at the Purple Door Saloon."

Don't take the bait, a voice in my head warned.

"With whom?" I asked

You're an idiot, the voice in my head answered.

"A friend of yours." Jeff was a lot nicer than my inner demon.

Natalie? No, she would have mentioned hooking up with Jeff.

When I stared at him with raised eyebrows, waiting, he grinned. "You'll never guess who."

"You're right, and I need to get to work, so how about we save this mystery for another day." I opened my door, hoping to end our interaction there and then.

"Tiffany Sugarbell," he said.

I stopped with one leg raised, lowering my boot back to terra firma. "You know Tiffany?"

"Sure, who doesn't? I thought about trying to get into her underwear plenty of times, but I was married, so I kept Vlad the Impaler in my pants."

Vlad the Impaler? Oh dear. A giggle escaped my lips before I could catch it. Jeff had named his penis after the brutal 15th-century Prince of Wallachia whose name was said to be the inspiration for Bram Stoker's *Dracula*? I wasn't going to touch that one without rubber gloves and a ten-foot pole.

"Well, good for you on remaining faithful to your wife."

"But now that I'm almost free of that two-timing bitch, there's no reason to keep Vlad from—"

"Is this story going somewhere, Jeff?" I interrupted, pulling my gloves from my coat pockets. "I don't mean to be rude, but it's cold and I'm sure Tiffany wouldn't appreciate you telling locker room stories with one of her competitors."

"You're wrong about that, Violet Parker. Tiffany told me to make sure you knew about what we were up to last night." He leaned out his window and said in a stage whisper, "And we weren't just playing footsie under the table, if you know what I mean."

I frowned at his wiggling eyebrows for several reasons, only one of them having to do with Tiffany. "Don't wiggle your eyebrows like that, Jeff. It makes you look like you're about to pull out a chainsaw and start chasing me around the parking lot."

He touched his eyebrows. "Sorry."

"I thought you were with that girl with the …" *Don't say nipple rings*, the voice in my head spoke up again. "With the round," I made a circling motion in front of me while I tried to come up with another descriptor that had nothing to do with that damned image of Jeff's bare-breasted girlfriend on the counter shouting out cheers for him as he drove in for a touchdown. "The round … uh, face."

Whew, that was close.

Stupid nipple rings.

"Oh, we're still together," Jeff said.

"But you insinuated something happened with Tiffany."

"It did."

"But your girlfriend …"

"We're not married, Violet Parker." His gaze traveled down over my red pea coat. "Neither are you, for that matter."

"I never claimed to be." Especially in front of Doc. "Quit messing around, Jeff. I'm freezing my ass off out here."

His eyes met mine, serious for once. "Tiffany offered to sell my house for a lower commission percentage if I'd leave you for her."

My mouth fell open. "You're kidding?" She wasn't pulling any punches.

He shook his head. "And she gave one hell of a sales pitch last night, if you know what I mean." He demonstrated with a crude gesture that made me recoil.

The idea that Tiffany was so determined to one-up me on the career front that she'd mess around with Jeff Wymonds knocked the breath out of me. This was a new level for her. Not that Jeff was ugly or anything like that. He cleaned up well and had a quarterback's build with broad shoulders and narrow hips, but when he opened his mouth, caveman gibberish about keeping "the little woman" barefoot and pregnant usually came out.

"I'm sure she did," I said, trying to remain professional in spite of the urge to make a voodoo doll of Tiffany and poke the shit out of it with a thousand porcupine quills. "And what was your decision, Jeff? Do you want to switch Realtors?"

"My decision was to talk to you."

"Talk to me about what?" Lowering my commission percentage to match hers? I wasn't sure how Jerry would feel about that.

"How far you're willing to go to keep me. Tiffany seems to think she's better than you at selling houses." His focus centered on my mouth. "And taking care of her clients with a hands-on approach. So, what do you say, Violet Parker?"

"What do I say about what?" I was going to make him spell this out.

* * *

It turned out I didn't like the way Jeff spelled one bit.

Nor did I like the new game Tiffany was playing with one of my clients.

Sleeping with clients was not my thing, which I'd firmly reminded Jeff. Nor was playing Tiffany's new game and fooling around under the table in a bar, which I'd also had to pound into his thick skull before leaving the Piggly Wiggly parking lot. Whether or not he took Tiffany up on her offer was his choice.

Doc was a client once, the voice in my head reminded me.

"And you can shut the hell up, too, while we're at it," I told the face staring back at me in the rearview mirror when I stopped at the light on the way out of the Piggly Wiggly. I'd had enough of that stupid voice.

While I waited for the light, I pulled up Doc's name and typed him a text: *Where r u?*

The light turned green. I rolled through, heading toward Lead's main drag.

My phone chirped while I waited behind several cars at the stop sign for Main Street at the bottom of the hill. Traffic coming out of Lead was thick this morning, probably due to my timing coinciding with the high school's start time.

Doc had written back: *At a cemetery.*

At seven-ish in the morning? What did he plan for an encore? The morgue? *Why?* I texted. *Digging up a new girlfriend?*

Prefer my current living girlfriend. Nude is even better.

Nude? I pondered him in the buff for a few seconds as the cars in front of me moved forward and then stopped again. Maybe Doc and I could sneak out into Aunt Zoe's workshop at night and enjoy a little time alone on the couch she sometimes slept on out there.

My phone chirped again.

Looking for a grave, Doc wrote.

Good, I'm going to need to bury someone soon.

As in Doc's damned ex-girlfriend.

Intriguing as always, Boots. Where are you?

Leaving Piggly Wiggly.

You're close. Come here.

Where?

The car in front of me rolled right through the Stop sign, cutting off a pickup turning up South Main Street. A blare of the horn followed. I waited for the pickup driver to finish shaking his fist at the other car and then make his turn.

West Lead Cemetery, Doc typed. *Across from the high school.*

Hitting my right blinker, I turned up South Main Street, following the pickup. Minutes later, I inched through the slushy layer of snow in the cemetery's gravel drive. The Picklemobile was parked up ahead on the right.

The sound of my door closing echoed through the trees.

"Over here," Doc called from several rows of headstones up the hill.

Pulling my collar tight to keep out the chill, I stepped with care through the slushy mud. Luckily, I'd worn a calf-length wool skirt today over cashmere leggings, so unless I fell on my ass, the caramel-colored fabric wouldn't get dirty. My black knee-high boots, on the other hand, were going to need a wipe down when I was done here.

Doc waited for me near a small fenced-in set of grave markers under the tall trees, his dark hair and leather coat standing out in sharp contrast against the smattering of shaded snow behind him. He picked up a long stick when I drew near.

"You going to stab me with that?" I asked, pausing at the base of a small slope to figure out how to climb it without landing facedown in the snow.

"I should. You said you'd call me later last night and whisper sweet nothings in my ear." He took a few steps toward me, holding out his hand to help me up the slope. "And then you didn't."

"You were rubbing your eyes when you left."

"That was frustration, not because I was tired. Was it too much to ask for a note with that damned clock?"

I went up on my toes and kissed his cold cheek, keeping hold of his hand. He smelled fresh, like he'd been rolling around in a meadow. I'd rather he'd rolled around in my bed and smelled like my sheets. "I also had a little girl in my room."

"Addy is a hard sleeper. What's your next excuse?"

"I had a bottle of tequila in there, too."

He frowned. "That's it. We need to come up with a new solution for Cooper and you. We can't have you drinking away your troubles all alone."

"I have an idea. You and I sneak out to Aunt Zoe's workshop and play out some of your nude fantasies on her couch."

"The ones involving you or …"

I narrowed my eyes, fake punching him in the shoulder. "Me and only me. Unless you'd rather be nude while I watch."

One of his dark eyebrows inched up. "Is that your word of the day? Nude?"

"What do you mean? You're the one who brought it up."

"You wrote it in your text." He pulled out his phone and scrolled through my texts, and then held his phone out for me to read. Sure enough, there was my text, but it said, *Digging up a nude girlfriend?*

Hmmm. "I could swear I'd written 'new' on my phone."

I pulled it out. Nope, "nude" it was.

Doc chuckled, putting his arm around me as he led me carefully along the edge of the wrought iron fence. "Harvey told me you wouldn't be able to last more than a few days without me before you got randy, what with you being in heat more often than not."

What was with that old man and me being in heat? Criminy. Next, he'd be putting an article in the *Black Hills Trailblazer* about the state of my estrous cycle.

"So who are you going to need a grave for now?" Doc asked.

Several huffs of steam in the cold morning air later, I'd filled him in on Tiffany's latest scam.

His frown lines made an appearance. "And Wymonds thought you might be desperate enough for a sale that you'd sleep with him to keep him on as a client?"

I shrugged. "He'd probably have settled for letting him shove his tongue down my throat again, but I'm not playing that game. I don't fool around with …" I looked up at his grin, knowing what he was thinking. "*You* are an exception, Mr. Nyce."

"And you, Ms. Parker, are exceptional." He squeezed me into his side. "What are you going to do about Tiffany?"

"There isn't much I can do if she's going to throw herself at male clients. No sale is worth my dignity."

"Glad to hear it. Is Wymonds going to stay with you or switch?"

I shrugged. "It's up to him. I told him that I was doing the best I could and I'd be sorry to see him go, but I wasn't that kind of a saleswoman."

"Good. Maybe I need to remind Wymonds that I don't like to share." He turned me toward him, his brown eyes serious when he stared down at me. "Don't let Tiffany get to you. You're a better Realtor."

"You're biased."

"Definitely, especially when you're wearing a skirt and boots." He kissed me, warming my lips for a few seconds. "Did the clock start up yet?"

I shook my head, turning back to the fenced-in gravestones. "What grave are you looking for?"

"It's unmarked."

"Are you acting out the ending of *The Good, the Bad, and the Ugly*?"

"Something like that." He pointed at the largest gravestone inside the fence.

"Hessler," I read aloud, frowning. "Is this Wolfgang's family?"

"Yes. That's Wolfgang's maternal grandfather, the one who started the jewelry store." Doc pointed at the smaller headstone beside it. "That's his wife. She died giving birth to Wolfgang's mother, whose grave is on the other side of the big one. Next to Wolfgang's mother's stone is Wilda's marker." He indicated a smaller gravestone with a little chubby angel carved into the corner.

I stuffed my hands in my pockets to warm them, staring at Wilda's gravestone. The little girl who had terrorized Cornelius was no angel. Not with those freaky black empty eyes and that half-burned clown doll she kept shoving in my face.

On the other side of Wilda's marker was Wolfgang's plot, his grave still a fresh scar on the earth. "I didn't realize they'd buried him here," I told Doc, leaning into him.

"Neither did I until I started looking into his family's history."

"Where's Wolfgang's father buried? There's no headstone for him."

"He was buried with his family up in the South Lead Cemetery. It's the one up near Cooper's place."

Wolfgang's mother had never taken her husband's name. Instead, he'd adopted her family name. Apparently, money trumped tradition in the Hessler family.

Something in his sure tone made me realize he'd already been up to that cemetery to confirm it. "So why are you here? I'd think a cemetery is a tough place for you to hang out."

Normally, the dead were attracted to Doc and tended to rush him like a swarm of killer bees.

"Rarely do I ever come across a ghost in a cemetery. I have a theory that none of them want to be here, where they are reminded that they are dead day after day." He took me by the hand and pulled me along the fence to where Wilda and Wolfgang were buried. "I came to see if I'm right about something."

"About what?"

He took the stick he'd been holding and reached over the fence, tapping the ground behind Wolfgang's grave, and then behind Wilda's.

"What are you doing, Doc? Is that Morse code for 'Wake up, sleepyhead'?"

"Sexy legs and slick wit this morning. Lucky me." He moved behind Mrs. Hessler's stone and tapped the ground around it. I heard the sound of stick hitting stone. Doc let go of my hand so he could lean farther over the fence. He poked the stick around something in the ground, clearing away the snow, leaves, grass, and other debris. The stick scratched over the surface of what appeared to be a small rectangular stone.

Doc grunted. "It appears the Hessler family had something to hide, just as I suspected after that picture."

"What picture?"

"I found a picture in an old newspaper article. It was taken in front of the Hessler jewelry store. Wolfgang's father was holding a little girl who I figured was Wilda. Next to him, his wife had a baby in her arms, which had to have been Wolfgang based on the date of the newspaper. But between them was a third child."

"A third? I thought there were just the two kids."

"So did most, but there was a third. From what I can tell by the birth records, Wilda had a twin sister."

"What happened to her?"

"I'm not sure yet. I need to research some more."

"And you think this rectangular marker is the twin's grave?"

He nodded.

"Why wouldn't they have put a name on it? Or a year of birth and death?"

He rubbed his jaw. "I don't know that yet either."

"What did she look like? Were they identical?" The thought of two little ghostly versions of Wilda running around made me shudder.

"It was hard to tell in the picture."

"Why? Was it blurry?"

"No, it was clear enough."

"Then why couldn't you tell?"

"Because in the picture," he said, "the child in the middle was wearing a costume."

"A costume?"

He nodded. The troubled frown on his face made me want to go back home and hide under my bed. "A clown costume."

Chapter Eleven

Cornelius wasn't "home" when I made it to work with his bag of groceries. "Well!" I huffed at the locked door leading to the upstairs apartment. "So much for our early meeting about Jane's ghost."

I took the bag of groceries I'd picked up for him into Calamity Jane's, storing the eggs in the little fridge under the coffee maker until he returned.

Mona was the only one in the office, apparently getting an early start on her day. Her sweet jasmine perfume mixed with the smell of fresh coffee. The aroma of both, along with her warm greeting, put a smile on my face when I settled in behind my desk. Tiffany Sugarbell and the Hessler clown be damned.

"Did Jerry ask you to come in early?" she asked, pouring herself a cup of coffee.

"No. Cornelius wanted to talk to me about …" I rolled up my tongue before it spilled Jane's name. "Uh, about a property he might be interested in."

"Really? He can afford to invest in another property while he's remodeling the hotel?"

I shrugged. "His grandfather died a short while ago. From what I can garner, he comes from a family with very deep pockets." I did my best to remain vague so as not to complicate my lie in case it came back to haunt me like several other Deadwood ghosts.

"Lucky him. I'll be right back," Mona said, heading toward the restroom.

The door shut as my cell phone rang. I looked down at the number and grunted, taking the call. "Good morning, Cornelius."

"Where are you?" he whispered.

Oh dear, we were starting with absurdity right out of the gate. "I'm sitting at my desk at work with your groceries next to me. Where are you?"

"Are you referring to my mental or physical state?"

I didn't want to go near his mental stomping grounds this early in the day. "Let's start with physical."

"Underground."

"Underground where?" In the Black Hills, that could mean a multitude of places, like the science lab down in the old Homestake mine, Deadwood's Chinese tunnels, the basement of the opera house up in Lead, or a root cellar in the backyard of a murderer's burned-down house, to name a few.

"Under your feet," he whispered. "You need to join me."

Or not.

I looked down at my boots, stomping my heel three times.

Cornelius gasped. "Did you hear that?"

As tempted as I was to mess with him and pretend it was Jane, I played it straight. "That was me, Cornelius. I didn't know Calamity Jane's had a basement."

"It's more like an oversized crawlspace."

I wrinkled my nose. That elicited thoughts of spiders, centipedes, and mice, all of which gave me the heebie-jeebies times three.

"The door is in the floor of the closet. Hurry up, Violet."

The line went dead, leaving me frowning at my phone.

Jiminy Cricket! Hiking around a graveyard was one thing, but I wasn't dressed to scamper around underground this morning. On top of that, I'd left my hair loose. I was sure to end up with a headful of spiders that confused my curls for their webs if I went crawling around down there.

Grumbling, I stomped down the hall, hoping I gave Cornelius a little scare as a pre-payback for what I was about to do per his demand. Mona stepped out of the restroom as I approached Jerry's closed office door.

"Cornelius needs my help for a bit," I told her, reaching for the doorknob.

She nodded. "He's been quiet this morning. I didn't think he was in there."

"He was probably recharging his battery again," I said with a wink. I waited until she was back out front and then slipped inside the dark office, closing the door behind me and flipping the lock.

Across the room, the closet door stood ajar. Upon closer inspection, I found several oak floorboards stacked to the side, bent nails sticking out here and there. Next to them leaned a square piece of steel. Inside the narrow closet, a matching square hole took up most of the underlying wooden floor. Musty air seeped out from darkness. Rickety-looking steps led down, down, down.

I gulped, leaning back, my palms sweaty. There were lots and lots of reasons that I shouldn't climb down those stairs. For starters, everyone knew that dangerous things came from holes. Snakes, for one. Badgers, for another. Sometimes even dead things in my line of work.

I lifted my phone, pulling up Cornelius's name. After the fifth ring, the call went to voicemail.

Damn that long-legged chimpanzee!

Blowing out several quick breaths like a swimmer about to go underwater for a lungful of time, I placed my boot on the top step and inched into the cool, earthy-smelling blackness.

Cornelius hit me with the beam from the flashlight as I landed on the cobblestone floor below. "Did you bring the tall medium?" he asked.

"Sure, I have him here in my pocket." At least I wished I did.

One of his black eyebrows crept up. "I once carried a tree frog in my pocket for a month."

Slimy. Ick. "Why would you do that?"

"Why not?" he replied.

My thoughts sputtered. I blamed the cramped quarters, the bright light he was shining in my face, and my fear of crawly things for my sudden lack of brainpower.

"We'll have to make do without your tall medium for now," he said, clearly disappointed I hadn't thought to bring Doc along on this underground adventure. "Do you have any fig bars?"

Squinting in the light, I jammed my hands on my hips. "Do I look like the Fig Bar Fairy to you?"

He moved the flashlight beam down to my boots and back up. "Where do you find all of your wool?"

"I know a few sheep."

"Foreign or domestic?"

"Cornelius, did you ask me down here to talk about wool?"

"You're right. The debate on sheep captivity needs to be held over a fresh pint." He turned and walked away, ducking to avoid the cobweb-laden, overhead beams.

Or we could just drink and not think, which was my preferred method of intoxication. I should have thought to grab a flask of tequila along with my tall medium before coming down here.

I hit the flashlight mode on my cell phone and followed him, ducking down as well even though I could stand upright. Getting cobwebs in my hair would send me running for the steps. I tiptoed from one cobblestone to another like I was crossing a stream. The walls were composed of a mixture of concrete and the same stones used for the floor. The corners were dark, the shadows seeming to move whenever my light roved near. The musty smell intensified with each step. I skirted a low-hanging pipe, joining Cornelius, who had dropped to his knees on the floor.

"Did you find something to do with Jane down here?" I asked quietly. This place was a little too reminiscent of a tomb for my taste. I dodged a floating cobweb and shuddered.

"Maybe." He shifted aside to give me a clearer view of a round steel grate in the floor edged by cobblestones. "But I have to wonder if this leads to something more troublesome than your deceased boss."

Speaking of holes in the ground … I shined my light on the thick bars of the grate. Jeez, that thing had to weigh a ton.

A centipede as long as my little finger crawled up through the grate opening, scuttling off toward the wall.

I grimaced, stepping back. "Is that some kind of sewer vent? Shouldn't it stink?"

"It would appear so upon first glance," Cornelius said, grabbing a couple of the bars and tugging to no avail.

"But …"

"Your boss implied otherwise."

"Jerry told you about this?"

He dusted off his hands, rising to his feet. "Your other boss. The dead one."

"You talked to Jane?"

"Not exactly."

Oh, right. Cornelius couldn't talk to ghosts usually, only summon them like the Pied Piper. "She showed you something down here?"

"Not exactly," he repeated.

I huffed, crossing my arms. "Explain yourself, Cornelius."

He started kicking at the packed dirt at the edge of the grate with his pointy-toed shoes. "I had a dream last night."

"About this hole?"

"No, about a childhood neighbor." He pulled out a paintbrush from somewhere in his coat and bent down, sweeping the loose dirt away from the edge. "A little girl who liked to bounce around on her pogo stick." He grabbed a hammer lying next to the hole and dug out more dirt at the edge of the grate.

"What happened to her? Did she fall down in a well and die?"

He looked up, frowning. "Has anyone ever told you that you have very dark thoughts, Violet?"

He didn't know the half of it. "It comes with the job," I answered.

"What happened to the girl?"

"She grew up and went to college to be a dentist, I believe. I have never understood the lure of touching other people's teeth."

"What did the dream have to do with this hole?"

"Nothing at all."

I cursed him under my breath.

"When I woke," he continued, brushing away more dirt, "I remembered something I'd seen on the blueprints for my hotel."

"Your hotel? Do you have a hole like this under the hotel?"

"No, but according to the blueprints for the original building, there was an underground stable of sorts where horses and a small wagon or two could be housed during the snowstorms."

That had to smell ripe after a few days. "So neither your dream nor the blueprints gave you any reason to have knowledge or concerns about this hole?"

He shook his head.

But … "You said my boss told you it's not a sewer vent."

"There was no speaking involved."

"Insinuated, then."

He cocked his head to the side. "More like hinted."

"Cornelius," I warned, threatening him with my closed fist.

"Your patience this morning appears to be on the wane, Violet."

"If you don't start making sense I'm going to cram you down between the bars of that grate."

He returned to brushing at the dirt, reminding me of a paleontologist dusting around a fossil. "I was searching the closet in the office for my power cords that your deceased boss hid yesterday. A creaky board led me to believe she may have hid them in a compartment under the floor. I realized the false floor hid more than just cords when I found the door to this crawlspace."

"You mean *tomb.*"

His crooked smile appeared. "Your fondness for histrionics reminds me of a renowned figure from the past."

"Shakespeare and his pen?"

"Lizzie Borden and her ax."

"If you're trying to keep me from hurting you, I'd suggest a different tack."

He returned to digging in the dirt. "I grabbed my lucky hammer and ripped up the flooring. That's when I found the crawlspace door."

And now here we stood—him with his lucky hammer and me with a strong urge to flee topside. "Okay, so how does your finding the crawlspace door jibe with you saying my boss hinted that this is not a sewer grate?"

"She slammed the metal trapdoor on my fingers the first time I tried to open it." He held up his right hand, shining his flashlight at a blood bruise on three of his knuckles.

I winced. "*Jane* did that? You're sure the trapdoor didn't just slip out of your grip?"

"Violet." His tone was droll. "You of all people should understand the difference between gravity and applied ectoplasmic force."

Uhhhh, sure. I learned all about *that* in high school right before figuring out how to tie a cherry stem with my tongue in health class and shortly after mastering how to flip my eyelids inside out during government.

"Okay," I said, moving on before he could continue with more paranormal mumbo-jumbo that would make my eyes glaze over. "So, you believe that Jane didn't want you coming down here? That she was trying to protect you by smashing your fingers?"

"I suspect it was more of a diversion."

"To divert you from what?"

"This." He pointed his light at where he'd been digging and brushing. "And whatever is down in that hole."

I squatted next to the grate, touching the bar of steel he'd uncovered. "What is this?"

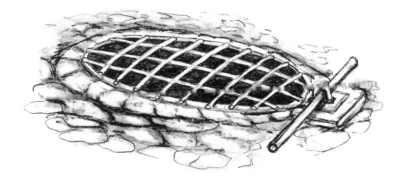

"A rudimentary lock. Someone went through a lot of work to keep this grate closed." Cornelius brushed more dirt away, exposing a bent rod of steel secured in a block of cement, through which another thick iron rod had been jammed, firmly holding the gate closed from anyone trying to come up through the floor.

"If this were a mere sewer vent," he said, "there would be a way to open it from the inside."

"You'd need TNT to blow that sucker open."

He tugged on the rod jammed through the loop of steel. It didn't budge. "This was meant to keep someone locked out."

Or something.

I took his flashlight and leaned close to the grate, peering with one eye between the bars. I could smell the steel of the grate along with an earthy smell drifting up through the slots. The ground appeared to be only eight to ten feet down. A square box with what looked like a dish attached to it sat on the dirt floor.

"What's that?" I asked, angling the light toward it.

Cornelius leaned over the grate, his shoulder bumping mine. "It looks like an old carbide lamp."

"Carbide?"

"A miner's lamp from the early twentieth century."

I angled the light further, focusing on the wall directly under us. "Is that a hole?"

"Or a tunnel," he said.

My stomach knotted. "Where does it go?"

The flashlight went dark.

"Shit." I shook it, and then banged it against the grate several times. "Where did you get this stupid light?"

"Your desk drawer."

I clicked it on and off several times, knocking it against the grate again. The clang of metal on metal echoed through the hole.

A hand grabbed my arm, stopping me. "Violet," Cornelius whispered in the darkness. "Do you hear that?"

I listened, hearing nothing but our breathing. "What? Is it Jane?"

Cornelius was silent for several seconds. I was about to ask him again if Jane was whispering in his ear when a whoosh of air blew up through the grate. Mixed in with the cool, musty air was a whiff of curdled milk with a hint of eau-de-roadkill.

"Do you smell that?" I gagged.

"That's not your dead boss." Cornelius yanked me to my feet. "Let's get out of here."

* * *

After piecing the closet floor mostly back together and barring the door with a chair under the handle "just because," Cornelius headed off to his hotel to deal with a remodeling situation requiring his attention.

I returned to my desk with mere floorboards and an old barred grate between me and whatever might have been in that hole in the floor. I tried to settle into my normal real estate mode, but I kept catching myself listening for the sound of something moving around under my feet.

After dinking around with my Day-Timer for a while, I dissected my wallet in between pacing back and forth to the coffee maker. When Mona asked if I was feeling okay, a weird croaking sound came from my throat, reminding me of Cornelius's pocket frog. Covering my mouth, I escaped to the bathroom and ordered the wide-eyed woman in the mirror to calm her silly ass down. By the time I returned to my desk, Ben and Ray were back from a breakfast meeting with a client. I smiled reassuringly at Mona and shook the tension from my hands, trying to focus on my computer screen.

Something thumped twice on the floor.

I squawked in surprise and leapt clear out of my chair, scanning the floor while panting. "What was that?"

Ray smirked. "Relax, Blondie. I'm polishing my boots."

Looking over, I took in his socks and the two boots lying on the floor next to his desk. The two thumps had been the sound of his boots hitting the floorboards.

Holy shit-inski! I was losing it.

I sank into my chair, my hands trembling when I lifted my coffee cup to my lips.

"Are you feeling all right?" Ben asked, his forehead lined with concern.

I nodded quickly. "Yeah, I'm great." A high-pitched giggle slipped out between my lips, drawing a frown from Mona.

She lowered her rhinestone-studded reading glasses. "Maybe you should take this afternoon off, Vi. You've been pale since your meeting with Cornelius."

"That's no surprise," Ray said with plenty of sarcasm. "Just the sight of that crazy kook and his freaky eyes would put me off my feed for a couple of days."

"Shut up, Ray," was all I could manage at that moment. I'd taken too many world-jarring hits already this morning to be on my game when it came to defending Cornelius from the horse's ass.

I turned to Mona. As tempted as I was to run home and cling to Aunt Zoe's Betty Boop cookie jar for crumb-covered comfort, I decided to run some errands instead and maybe check out some potential properties for Cooper. "I'll be fine. I just need some fresh air." A little space and time away from this building would fix me right up … I hoped.

I pulled my purse from my desk drawer. "I'm going to go take a look at some potential properties for Detective Cooper and grab lunch while I'm out. Let Jerry know I'll be back later this afternoon."

She nodded, still watching me closely as I passed by her on the way out the back door.

The cold air was a welcome relief. Since Doc was busy with clients down in Spearfish for the rest of the day, I didn't bother trying to call him and share my newest source of anxiety. Instead, I ran my errands, relishing in the mundane. After a stop at the bank, I remembered Layne's comment about seeing a white demon while out at recess and checked my watch.

Twenty minutes later it was recess time. I let my Honda idle in the Deadwood library parking lot while eating pretzels and string cheese in the warm cab. Layne sat on a bench in the recess yard, reading a book. So much for my kid burning off excess energy.

I kept my eyes peeled for Mr. Black or any new pale buddies of his, not sure what I'd do if the boogeyman showed up on the scene.

My phone rang, making me drop the cheese between the seat and console, darn it.

The number on the screen wasn't familiar.

I swallowed the bite of cheese in my mouth. "Hello?"

"*Guten Tag, Scharfrichter,*" a wheezy voice greeted me in German. "Did you receive the clock?"

"Who is this?" I couldn't tell if the caller was male or female, thanks to what sounded like a ten-pack-a-day smoking habit.

"Who I am is of no importance." The German accent was almost non-existent when speaking English.

"Is this Mr. Black?" I pressed.

A hissing sound came from the other end of the line. "You should be careful when and where you speak that name, *Scharfrichter.*"

Maybe it was the string cheese, or it could have been the shitty morning I'd already had, but I wasn't in the mood to deal with whispered threats from anonymous callers. "Why? Is he like Darth Vader? Can he choke me with his mind powers if I say his name over and over?"

"There are worse things than dying, *Scharfrichter.*"

"Like what?"

"You do not want to find out."

Prudence and her family's brutal murder came to mind, making me hold in my smartass retort. "Why are you calling me? And don't tell me it's only to confirm that I received your little gift."

"The gift was not from me."

Then who … "You know what, I don't care about that right now." Using my third-eye chakra, I focused on the bigger picture. "Who's taking the clocks from Ms. Wolff's apartment? Is it you?"

"*Nein.*"

"But you know who it is?"

"*Ja.*"

"Who?"

"That is not for me to tell."

The caller must have taken "police business" mantra lessons from Cooper. "Why are they taking the clocks?"

"The death of a timekeeper does not stop the flow of *der Wanderer.*" The caller's breath rattled. "Nor will it stop *der Jäger.*"

I scribbled down the two German words, spelling them out how they sounded. "So, someone is taking the clocks to keep time for these 'vonderers' and 'yeagers'?"

"A timekeeper does not work for anyone, only keeps the balance."

"The clocks are being taken to keep the balance then?"

"*Ja.*"

"The balance between who or what?"

"Not who or what. The balance between here and there."

Jeez on crackers! This was about as clear as a jar of sludge. "What does that mean?"

"Seek your answers elsewhere. My job is finished."

"Your job was to deliver the clock to me?"

"*Ja.*"

"You screwed up. It's broken."

"Is it, *Scharfrichter?*"

Before I could answer, the line went dead. I stared down at my phone for several seconds, waiting to see if the call time would start up again miraculously.

The screen went dark.

I tapped the screen and hit redial. The phone rang and rang and rang. I hung up at the count of ten and stared blindly out the window, replaying the call in my head. By the time I shook out of my reverie, I realized the recess yard was empty.

Fishing out the cheese from between the seat and console, I blew it off, tossed it in my mouth, and then pulled out of the library parking lot.

There was one place I could think of where I might find more answers to this damned clock business.

I dialed Zelda Britton's phone number as I waited for pedestrians to cross the street at the stoplight in front of the Franklin Hotel.

"Hello, Violet." Zelda's sweet voice was a welcome sound after the German clock genie. "It's great to hear from you."

I didn't waste time with formalities. "Zelda, I need to talk to Prudence right away. Is there any way I can swing by in about ten minutes?"

"I'm sure Prudence would enjoy hearing from you, but I'm not home right now."

Dang it. "How about later this afternoon?"

"I'm actually visiting my mother in Nebraska this week. She's not been feeling well and needed a little help around the house."

"I'm sorry." I turned right on Main Street, heading toward Central City. "I hope she gets well soon."

"Oh, she's on the mend already." There was a muffled sound from her end and then she continued. "I'll tell you what, how about I let you know where we hide the spare key and you stop in and have your chat with Prudence without me there."

Alone with Prudence? My heart tried to pummel its way out of my chest at just the thought. I slowed, pulling into a street-side parking spot. "I don't think that's a good idea, Zelda."

"Why not?"

Because I needed someone there to act as a microphone for Prudence, or she might climb into my head and mess me up for good. "I wouldn't feel right being in your house without you."

"Nonsense. You've been in there many times without me."

"But that was back when the Carharts owned the place."

"So what. It was Prudence's house then as it still is now. We mortals are temporary renters in her world."

"I don't think—"

"The spare key is hidden under the sitting room window that faces the Open Cut. You make the call."

"Okay. Thanks, Zelda."

"You're welcome. Stop by sometime when I'm home for cider and cookies, Violet. I miss seeing your gorgeous blond curls."

I smiled. If only she didn't share an abode with a haughty ghost who liked to insult my family lineage when she wasn't creeping the hell out of me. "Take care of your mom."

I hung up, staring out at the gray sky.

Should I go to see Prudence on my own? What would happen without someone there to act as a middleman for me? Would she climb into my head and scramble my brains? Or would she appear in front of me like she had last month in my car and mime her responses to my questions.

Maybe I should wait.

My phone rang again. Damn, I was popular this afternoon. Hoping it was Doc, I looked down at the screen.

It wasn't Doc.

I snarled at a number I'd grown to loathe. Detective Stone Hawke was calling, undoubtedly to accuse me of another crime I hadn't committed. I was about to hit the *Send to Voicemail* button when a light bulb burned bright in my head.

My finger hovered over the screen as two more rings came through. Before I could change my mind, I answered. "This is Violet."

"I'm surprised you answered your phone, Parker."

"It's been an interesting day so far, Detective Hawke," I said, playing nice. "I might as well hear what you have to add to it."

"You're not going to put another fake hex on me, are you?"

"I'm not in the mood for foolery this afternoon."

"You mean Coop told you to keep your claws retracted."

"Detective Cooper may have mentioned maintaining good behavior." More like threatened what he'd do if I caused more ripples for him at work. "Do you have a question for me, Detective?" God, it was making my tongue burn being so nice to the jerk.

"I need you to come to the station and take a look at some photos."

Not the picture game again. "I'm in the middle of a walk-through of a potential property right now, and I have an appointment right after this." The lies slipped out with ease. "How about you meet me here? We can go through your questions while I take care of what I need to in this house."

There was a long pause on his end. "Since you're being civil," he finally said, "I guess I can, too. Where should I meet you?"

I rattled off an address I knew too well.

"You're up in Lead?" he asked.

I shifted into drive and pulled out on the road again, wanting a moment alone to gather my wits before he showed up. "Yep."

"Why does this address sound familiar?"

"Detective Cooper may have mentioned it before."

"Why's that?"

"It was the site of one of my past ... uh ... adventures."

His snort made me grit my teeth. "You mean past crimes."

I let that one slide since he'd unknowingly agreed to come play in a haunted house with me. "I'll see you in ten minutes at the Carhart house, Detective Hawke."

Before he could get another insult in, I hung up my phone.

It was time for Detective Stone Hawke to meet Prudence.

Chapter Twelve

The Carhart-Britton house stood high above the rocky bottom of the Open Cut, a huge hole in the ground left over from Lead's golden days of mining glory. A Gothic Revival style, two-story home painted butter cream with chocolate trim, the historic house was a treat for the eyes. Hansel and Gretel would have stopped to lick the siding if it had been hidden in the trees.

I rolled to a stop in the gravel drive, shutting off the engine. My stomach knotted as I stared up at the white lace curtains in the attic window. Prudence preferred to stay tucked away up there with a dusty old crib, rocking chair, and little cupboard that held her stash of trophy teeth. My last trip up to her attic had been with Doc, who'd been knocked out cold by Prudence while she rode roughshod over him, using him as her personal ventriloquist doll. I still shuddered at the memory of that hair-raising moment.

The curtains in the attic window swayed, as if a breeze had caught them in passing.

But it was no breeze. Prudence knew I was here.

I stepped outside, taking my time walking around the side of the house in spite of the freezing wind. The key was right where Zelda had said it would be.

Key in hand, I slowly climbed the front porch steps. I needed a moment alone with Prudence, but the thought of going inside the house made my knees wobbly. Teeth chattering from nerves and cold, I checked my cell phone for the time. If Hawke had left right after I'd talked to him, he should be here in a couple of minutes.

No more delaying. It was time to enter Prudence's lair. I lifted the key. Before I could even slide it into the lock, the door creaked open.

"Yikes." Chills raced up my arm. I stared into the dark crack, my breath coming in steamy puffs.

I should be used to Prudence's games by now, dang it. But she was the only ghost I'd actually seen while fully conscious. Not to mention that she was unpredictable as hell, seeming to take pleasure in catching me off guard. Interactions with her always came with a jolt of fear that made me want to turn tail and run.

Like Cooper.

Oh!

A flood of empathy for Cooper made me frown. It was no wonder he was struggling with his newfound ability to see the dead in their wispy form. His pale-faced state followed by his dash to the nearest exit made complete sense. How long would it take for him to get used to seeing ghosts?

How long would it take me?

Drawing a deep breath, I pushed inside the house. The door clicked shut behind me.

I stood in the foyer, listening in the shadow-filled room for a sound. A ticking clock kept time in the stillness. A smiling image of Wanda Carhart in her blue gingham dress fluttered through my thoughts, followed by a pang of sadness. These walls had seen too much death.

My gaze darted around the narrow hallway. Zelda had left much of the house exactly as it'd been when the Carharts had lived here. Since Wanda had sold the furniture along with the house, it was no surprise, but Zelda later informed me that she left the previous furnishings in place because Prudence preferred it this way.

The furnace kicked on, rattling the vents. The aroma of cinnamon and apples wafted around me on a warm draft. The smell reminded me of my last visit to the house with Harvey and Cooper when Zelda had been busy baking an apple pie, only too happy to share with company.

Prudence, on the other hand, wasn't nearly as giving as Wanda or Zelda. I'd need to make sure I kept my distance from Hawke once he arrived. The dead executioner had a mean streak that often left me bruised. A thought occurred to me. Could her grumpiness be spurred by professional jealousy, since I was alive and fighting and she could only coach from the sidelines? Maybe, but I knew better than to ask Prudence about the source of her crankiness. A sweet and kind fairy godmother she was not.

I unbuttoned my coat. For the first time ever, I wished Detective Hawke would hurry up and join me. This was the first time Prudence and I had been alone in the house since I had "met" her. She usually had someone else to use as her karaoke machine.

What would happen if she tried to muscle her way into my head? Did it hurt when she made her victim's eyes roll back until the whites showed?

Cooper and Doc were both big, strong guys, and she'd left them weary and battle-bruised with seemingly little effort. Would I remember what transpired between us when she finished with me? Only Harvey had made it through her exploitation while remaining conscious, and I had no doubt that she'd made sure he was "awake" through it all.

Something shifted in the narrow room. Nothing I could see, smell, hear, or touch, but it was here. Or I should say, SHE was here.

"Hello, Prudence." In need of her help, I spoke in a humble tone, my head lowered. While my executioner lineage had outlasted hers, it was mutually understood that I was a bumbling amateur by comparison. Had the police and other humans not betrayed her over a century ago, she might have taken care of the "other" problem with which I was now forced to deal.

The Tiffany-style stained glass wall sconces flickered and then went dark again.

My heart thumped hard enough for the seismograph monitors over in Yellowstone to register. Criminy, I wished Doc were here to hide behind. He was so much better at handling this ectoplasmic crap.

I backed against the door, leaning on it for support. "We have only a few minutes before Detective Hawke from the Deadwood police force shows up on your doorstep, so I need you to listen." With shaking hands, I took off my gloves and stuffed them in my coat pockets. "Detective Hawke believes that I'm a witch who can work spells and hexes, which you and I both know is absolutely ludicrous. The imbecile also believes I murdered Ms. Wolff, the timekeeper I found dead back in October."

I licked my lips, looking around for something to focus on while I spoke. The inability to make eye contact while chatting made me fidgety. Not that I wanted Prudence to show her unnaturally luminous face or those chilling black holes where her eyes were supposed to be.

"You're probably wondering why I've invited the detective to your house, especially since I know how much you loathe lawmen." A creaking sound came from somewhere overhead in the old house. "I came to talk to you about the timekeeper's clocks, but I don't want you to crawl inside my head and scramble my brain, so I was hoping you could use the detective's big fat mouth to answer my questions."

The silence seemed to thicken, broken only by the whistling of the wind through the seams around the door.

"Of course you want to know what's in this for you, right?" Prudence's help usually came at a cost. Once, she'd even taken her payment in teeth. "For one thing, this lawman is usually a rude asshole to me. So, if you feel the need to insult my professional incompetence, Detective Hawke is an excellent mouthpiece for—"

The sound of a car door shutting outside interrupted me.

"Shit, he's here." I stepped away from the door, twisting my hands together. "Okay, I'll lure him inside and then you can work your freaky magic. Just, please, don't take any of his teeth while you're playing puppeteer. I'm already in plenty of trouble with this jerk, and if he loses a tooth while here with me, he'll probably arrest me for assaulting a police officer."

Footsteps thudded outside on the porch, followed by three heavy knocks on the door.

"You can do this," I whispered, coaching myself. "Remember, no fighting with the doofus. Play nice, even if he insults your hair and your aunt. You need to keep him inside long enough for Prudence to try to get into his thick skull."

I pulled open the door.

Hawke's shoulders filled the doorway.

Looking up, I pasted a wide, toothy smile on my face. "Hello, Detect..." My focus landed on his eyes, which were all white.

I screeched, stumbling backward.

Hawke stepped inside the foyer, his legs stiff. Throw in a couple of bolts and he'd make the perfect Frankenstein's monster. His mouth opened and shut a couple of times before words began to come out. "I will remove the lawman's teeth if I so desire, Executioner."

It was Hawke's voice, but Prudence's Katharine Hepburn–like accent was there under his low tones.

I tried to unglue my tongue from the back of my throat.

The door slammed behind Hawke, making the sconces rattle. "I cannot fathom how you would allow such a buffoon to intimidate you. He is a mere human, apparently inept at that."

"He … he's a cop," I stammered, backing into the living room as she moved Hawke toward me. I hit the arm of the couch and fell onto the cushions, my boots in the air.

Hawke loomed over me, his lower jaw shifting side to side in jerky motions as if Prudence were practicing her technique. "Unlike the lawman you accompanied to my home prior, this one is all bark."

She had that right. "How can you tell that already?"

"Subjugating his will required minimal effort." She moved his left arm up and down, then his right, demonstrating her puppet on a string control.

"Can you tweak his mind a little while you're in there? Maybe convince him that I had nothing to do with Ms. Wolff's murder."

Hawke's right arm dropped to his side. "We are executioners, not enchantresses. Small wonder he confuses you for a sorceress."

I doubted my pretending to put hexes on him helped my cause either, but we could save chitchat about my vocational blunders for another day.

"The timekeeper is not the only death for which he blames you," Prudence said through Hawke's stiff jaw.

No shit. "Is it easy to read his thoughts?"

"No. His thoughts are filled with nonsense. It is difficult to find anything of quality."

I wiggled upright, my boot heels sinking into the plush white rug underfoot. "What sort of nonsense?"

Nonsense about work? Women? His mother issues? This was my opportunity to find out more about Hawke's weaknesses. Potential weapons to use in a future battle. For a second, guilt nagged at me for cheating via a mind-reading ghost. Then I shoved that guilty feeling in a closet, locked the door, and waited for Prudence to give me the goods. War was not pretty.

"He has heady aspirations, including fame and fortune. This lawman is dangerous. He is a snollyguster."

"A snolly-what?"

"A snollyguster."

"What's that?"

"I should not be surprised by your ignorance, considering your lineage."

I resisted the urge to tell her to kiss my ignorant ass.

"A snollyguster," she continued, "is an individual guided by personal advantage rather than morals."

I smirked. The first time I had met him I'd figured that out about Hawke without having to crawl into his head, so she could stuff that in her snooty-patooty.

"Who else does he think I killed?" I asked, scooting to the opposite end of the couch. I wanted to be well out of Hawke's reach in case Prudence turned into Mr. Hyde again and decided to punish me with a bruised leg like she did with her last puppet.

She was silent for several beats. "Who is Jane?"

"My ex-boss."

"Why did you kill her?"

"I didn't." What on earth made him think I had anything to do with Jane's death? I thought I was well cleared of that one.

"He deems otherwise." Hawke's body shuddered for a few seconds. "He also believes you murdered Lila Beaumont."

"What? That's bullshit! She fell on a glass shard." In this very room, as a matter of fact.

"Must you resort to profanity in my house?"

"Yes, damn it." I shoved to my feet, pointing at Hawke. "Especially when it comes to this jackass."

His jaw unhinged, doing the side-to-side trick again for a couple of seconds. I'd have been more wigged out by it if I weren't so pissed about the accusation about Jane and Lila.

"You did not slay Lila," Prudence said.

"I know I didn't."

"I dispatched her."

"What makes this bonehead think that I ..." Her words caught up with me. "Come again?"

"I drove the glass into her throat."

"You ... But ... Lila fell on the shard."

"Do you not find that somewhat convenient?"

"I hadn't before now."

I replayed the scene of Lila's death in my head, reliving the struggles to escape her slashing arm. Lila had been coming for me with a shard of broken glass when she fell. Then she'd gone still. I'd rolled her over to find the piece of glass jammed into her throat, blood everywhere.

I'd thought it was an accident.

"You stabbed her to protect me?" I asked, blinking back to the present.

"I stabbed her to prevent your blood from being used to summon a demon to our plane. Do you have any idea of the frenzy an executioner's blood can rouse in demons?"

My blood? A demon frenzy? "Uh, no."

She moved Hawke's mouth in that weird way again. "Who is George Mudder?"

"Who?" I was still shaking off the nightmare of what a demon frenzy set off by my blood might look like. "Oh, George. He co-owned the funeral parlor down in Deadwood."

"Why did you behead the owner of a funeral parlor?"

"What! I didn't touch George!"

Hawke's head tipped to the side and back. "You should have informed me that you have interacted with a guardian."

"What's a guardian?"

"Did it put on airs?"

"Who's a guardian?"

"They try to behave so formally now that they have learned to blend in with the humans, but they are still contemptible fiends."

Did she mean Kyrkozz? He'd hidden behind Wolfgang's face in my dream before tearing his way out. I still cringed at that memory.

"Oh, dear," she said, turning those empty white eyes my way again. "What have you done?"

"I don't know. What have I done?"

"You gave the timekeeper a lock of hair?"

"I did?" I shook off my stupor. "I mean, I did not."

"The lawman is convinced a lock of your hair was found clutched in the hand of the dead timekeeper."

This time it was my jaw that opened and closed several times. "My hair?"

"Do you realize what that means?" Hawke's head fell forward as if Prudence had been holding it up for him all of this time and suddenly let go.

"It couldn't be my hair." I crossed to the window overlooking the Open Cut and gripped the curtains. The urge to crash through the glass and run away, escaping the weight of so many false allegations washed over me.

"The timekeeper was tying you to another," Prudence said from behind me.

I shook my head at the Open Cut. "How could she have gotten my hair?"

"Being tied is extremely precarious."

"I hadn't even met Ms. Wolff before the day I found her dead."

"If death comes the one to whom you are tied, your life will be forfeited as well," she said.

"That must be the evidence Hawke thinks he has that pins me as a prime suspect in her murder."

"It was very risky even to try to tie you."

"Someone must have planted that lock of hair in her hand."

Hawke made a gurgling sound behind me. "It is no wonder the timekeeper was eliminated."

"Cooper must have convinced Hawke to wait until the DNA results come back on the hair to bring me in."

"Timekeepers should not dabble in such dark practices."

I squeezed the back of my neck. How long did it take for DNA results to come back? On television shows, it was sometimes a matter of hours, but there was no way they could map DNA that fast, could they? Surely that was Hollywood magic.

"Was the timekeeper tying you to another to protect you?" Prudence's voice cut through my worries. "Or compromise you?"

A thought flittered through my head that knocked the wind out of me. Had Cooper snipped a piece of my hair to send in for comparison? Was that part of his ploy for moving into Aunt Zoe's? He could have easily gotten out the scissors and sneaked into my room in the middle of the night.

Checking my hair for short strands, I turned around. Hawke's head still hung low, his shoulders drooping. He reminded me of a robot that had powered down.

"Who was the one to be tied to you?" Prudence asked.

"That's not important right now." I strode over to Hawke. "I need to talk to Cooper."

His head jerked upward, the empty white eyes staring down at me. "You are in grave danger, Executioner." His mouth moved almost perfectly in tune with the words.

Me? Grave danger? I cackled with mad laughter.

Detective Hawke slapped me across the face.

"Damn it, Prudence!" I stepped back, holding my stinging cheek. "What the hell was that for?"

"You have muddled the situation with the timekeeper."

"Wait a second. All I did was answer her call and find her dead."

"Are you certain? Time can be a tricky devil."

"Yes, I'm sure." I rubbed my cheek, the skin hot under my palm. "I need to find the other timekeeper."

"Why? So you can wreak more folly?"

"Because someone is stealing the clocks from Ms. Wolff's apartment and one of those clocks ended up on my doorstep."

"You received a clock?"

"Yes."

Hawke's head tipped to the side, resting at an awkward angle. "Is it running?"

I had to wonder if he'd have a cramp in his neck when Prudence freed him. "We wound it, but it's not working. Earlier today I got a phone call from someone who wanted to confirm that I'd received the clock."

"How can this be?"

"How can *what* be? The phone call?" I'd wondered that, too. My billboards didn't have my cell number on them.

"You have been chosen."

"I have?" Ah, hell. I'd bet Harvey's favorite testicle that being chosen was not a good thing. "For what?"

"You are in grave danger."

"You already said that." And then she'd smacked me, dammit. My cheek still burned.

"It is important that you listen to me carefully."

"I'm all ears, Prudence."

"Do not move the hands of the clock."

Oops! "Why not?"

"You must wait for it to start on its own."

"What if it doesn't?"

"That would be most fortunate."

So the clock starting was bad juju. Great. "And what about the lock of hair? And Detective Hawke's determination to pin every murder he can on me?"

"Snollyguster."

"Snollyguster?" We'd already established Hawke was a selfish, egotistical bastard bent on conquering the world for his own good, the rest of us be damned. "What about it?"

"Use it when you need a distraction."

"Use what?"

Hawke reached up and awkwardly jammed his meaty fingers in his mouth, stretching his lips wide.

I cringed at the wet sounds he was making. "What are you doing, Prudence?"

"I want a tooth."

"No!" I grabbed Hawke's hand, tugging on it, but Prudence was much stronger, and Hawke's slobber made my grip slip. "You promised you wouldn't take his teeth."

"I promised no such thing."

"No, Prudence!" I wrapped both hands around his forearm and pulled harder, using my weight to draw down his arm.

She let me win the tug-of-war with a huff. "Fine. I will leave his teeth be for now."

"Thank you."

"But the next time you come, Executioner, you must bring me a tooth for my collection."

Grimacing, I wiped Hawke's slobber off on his corduroy coat. "Or what?"

"Or I will take one of your teeth instead."

I had little doubt that she meant that, too. I didn't waste time with good-byes but headed for the door, waiting for the detective out in the cold, ghost-free air.

Prudence released Hawke as soon as he crossed the threshold, which made him stumble on his way out the door. Before I could catch him, he tripped over his own feet and fell down the porch steps, landing in a jumbled heap on the sidewalk below.

I smiled, applauding her exit from the bumbling gumshoe.

When I tried to help Hawke to his feet, he shied away, scuttling across the wet, snow-splotched grass like an Alaskan King crab. He gained his feet, unsteady for several seconds, and then finally got his balance and faculties back north and south of his neck.

"What in the hell did you do to me, Parker?" he snapped, his beady eyes accusing.

"I don't know what you mean, Detective." I kept my tone light and friendly, holding my hands wide. A picture of innocence, I was.

He rubbed his eyes. "You put some kind of hex on me in there, didn't you?"

"Come on, Hawke. How many times do I have to tell you I'm not a witch?"

"How come I can't remember anything after leaving the car?"

"Maybe you hit your head getting out."

"I didn't hit my damned head."

I held my hand to my mouth, pretending to think while covering my smile. "You know, I've heard that this mile-high altitude can cause periodic blackouts due to lower levels of oxygen. Maybe you had a little blackout moment."

He glared at me. "I've never blacked out before."

"But you've been under a lot of stress. Have you been sleeping well?"

"That's none of your damned business."

"I can't help you when you're being so hard-headed."

His eyes narrowed. "Why is your cheek red?"

Because I'd let my guard down around Prudence.

"I scratched it." I took a step toward him, testing.

He backed up three more steps, warding me off with his index fingers crossed. "Stay back!"

He was confusing his witches with vampires now. "Detective, calm down. I didn't do anything to you."

"You lying bitch!"

I took another step just to watch him stumble in fear. The power was quite heady. No wonder Prudence liked to play her games.

"You knocked on the door, Hawke, and I opened it."

He scratched his head. "I sort of remember knocking."

Interesting. Prudence must have still been in the process of taking control at that point. "You came inside, asked me a bunch of questions, and then said you needed to go. When you walked out onto the porch, you tripped over your own feet and fell down the steps."

His forehead wrinkled. "I don't remember asking questions."

I changed course. "What do you remember?"

He stared toward the mine, creases rippling over his face like clouds on the prairie. "It was so dark. Something was pressing down on my chest, making it hard to breathe. There was this claustrophobic feeling that I couldn't shake."

Cooper had mentioned a similar feeling after his one-on-one with Prudence. "Stress can do weird things to the body and mind. Maybe you should go see a doctor."

His gaze held mine for several seconds, then his upper lip curled. "Fuck you, witch."

He stalked over to his cruiser without another word. The slam of his door echoed out over the Open Cut.

I should have let Prudence take the idiot's tooth.

Gravel flew when he reversed onto the road, followed by the squeal of his tires.

I flipped off his taillights, cackling away.

When I quieted, I looked up at the attic window.

The white lace curtains swayed.

* * *

I managed to keep my wits about me the rest of the afternoon.

Barely.

As soon as I'd returned to my desk, I'd expected a phone call from Hawke, accusing me of more witchcraft, but my phone lay dark on my desk. I imagined Hawke tattling to Cooper then, and waited for an angry text message from my roommate, chastising me for taking his partner up to see Prudence. But that didn't come either.

I sent Doc a couple of texts, really needing to talk to him about the lock of hair, Prudence, and all I'd learned about Hawke. Fifteen minutes passed with no reply, which meant he was busy with a client. Crappity crap!

The afternoon dragged on, my frustration steaming and billowing. I pretended to research listings for Cooper and a few of my new clients that Jerry's sexpot billboard had hooked. But truth be told, I was focused on listening for sounds underfoot in between spinning wild theories about that damned lock of hair. Theories ranging from being set up by someone from that demon-worshipping group with the goat-pig tattoo, to Mr. Black, Ray, Tiffany, Cooper, and even Detective Hawke himself.

By the time five o'clock finally rolled around, I'd made an executive decision about the Ms. Wolff situation.

I called Aunt Zoe, telling her I needed to push supper back an hour while I took care of something. She took it in stride, confirming only that I was okay and not headed to jail for another crime I hadn't committed.

Then I sent a text to both Cooper and Doc, telling them to meet me at the Purple Door Saloon in a half hour.

A group-reply text from Cooper came through ten minutes later as I crawled into my Honda.

The Purple People Eater?

I frowned and typed: *What are you talking about?*

Where in the hell is the Purple People Eater? Is that some kind of stupid joke?

You're a stupid joke.

Real mature, Parker.

Doc entered the texting conversation: *She means the Purple Door Saloon.*

Then why didn't she just say that? Cooper wrote.

I did!

No, you didn't.

I scrolled up my screen. Damn it, he was right. For some reason, my phone had changed the words to *Purple People Eater.*

Whatever, Cooper! Just get your ass to the bar, pronto.

When I hit the Send key, the word *ass* turned to *cat.* "Stupid phone," I muttered, shaking it.

I'm busy, Parker. Some of us don't have cats. We're too busy solving murders to live the good life.

I rolled my eyes, texting back: *I know your big secret, Cooper. We need to talk now!*

That should get his "busy" cat-ass moving in my direction.

Twenty minutes and half a shot of tequila later, Cooper stormed into the Purple Door Saloon. His steely eyes searched the bar one table at a time, finally finding me tucked into a corner by the pool table.

I nodded once.

He shook his head and walked over to the bar.

While he waited for his drink, Doc came in. His gaze homed in on me immediately, as if I were strapped to a homing beacon. He said something to Cooper on his way past the bar. His dark hair glistened under the bar lights. The weatherman must have gotten the sleet prediction right this time.

"Hey, Killer." Doc's hand was cool when he took mine, but his lips were warm on my cheek, which I knew from a mirror check no longer bore Prudence's red mark. "How was your day?"

"Disturbing." I pulled him down for a second kiss, this time on the lips, showing him how much I'd missed him. I didn't care who was watching tonight.

"Damn, Boots. Do that again and I'll drag you upstairs for more." He grinned, slipping off his coat. "Why was your day disturbing? Did you see Ray in the buff again?"

That surprised a laugh out of me.

Cooper slammed his glass of whiskey down on the table, silencing all sounds of happiness. "All right, Parker. You have us here. Now spill. What's this so-called secret of mine you think you've figured out?"

"I paid a visit to Prudence this afternoon."

His forehead pinched. "I thought we'd decided that was a bad idea."

"We never pinkie swore to anything."

His jaw tightened.

"How are Zelda and Prudence getting along?" Doc asked, pulling out the chair next to me.

"Zelda wasn't there."

Doc stilled. "Then who acted as the medium?"

I swirled the tequila in the bottom of my glass before tossing back the last of it. "Detective Hawke."

Cooper's eyes widened. "Jesus, Parker. Are you insane?"

"Only on Tuesday afternoons in December. Tell me something, Mr. Know-it-all Detective." I crossed my arms, preparing to lock horns. "Who the hell is trying to set me up for murder?"

Chapter Thirteen

In the history of epic battles of will, my stare-off with Cooper didn't quite reach the magnitude of the long, bloody standoff between the German and French in the Battle of Verdun, but it did dry out my eyes.

He blinked first, uttering a defeated "Christ, Parker." He grabbed his whiskey and drained the glass. The ice clinked when he set it down. "You're a real pain in the ass, you know that?"

"I believe you've said something along those lines before."

Doc hailed a passing waitress, ordering refills for Cooper and me, and a beer for himself. After she left, he drilled me with his dark eyes. "Start at the beginning and don't leave anything out."

I hesitated. "But if I tell all …" I thumbed in Cooper's direction, and whispered, "He's a cop, remember?"

"He's here to listen only, aren't you?" Doc challenged Cooper.

Cooper looked back and forth between us, finally giving a nod.

It was a begrudging nod, if you asked me. I shot Cooper a one-eyed squint. "You solemnly swear not to repeat anything I tell you here today?"

"Sure."

"Or use it against me?"

"Yeah."

"In or out of a court of law?"

"Parker!"

"Swear it, Cooper."

A muscle ticked in his jaw. I thought we were going to go for Round Two of our battles of will, but then he held out his hand, pinkie raised.

I locked mine with it.

"Would you look at that?" Doc chuckled. "You two are so cute when you're not at each other's throats."

"Kiss my ass, Nyce." Cooper pulled his pinkie free.

"You'll have to speak French to me first," Doc shot back.

A grin cracked the detective's granite face. "I'll leave the French to Tish here. She has a way with words, just ask Hawke."

I stuck my tongue out at Cooper. "Before we get rolling, I need to use the restroom."

After a short, tequila-sponsored pep talk in front of the mirror, reminding myself not to say the wrong thing in front of Cooper, I returned. The waitress was dropping off our drinks as I parked my caboose next to Doc's again at the tall bar table. Somebody had pumped change into the jukebox, lighting it up with Creedence Clearwater Revival warning me to run through the jungle because the devil was on the loose. I couldn't agree more with them. Looking back was way too scary these days.

I waited for the waitress to move out of earshot before recapping my visit with Prudence, starting with the phone call I'd received that inspired my visit.

As I relayed the caller's words, Doc stared at his beer, the lines on his forehead carving deeper, multiplying.

"But you never got a name?" Cooper asked, interrupting me.

"You mean of the caller?"

"Any of the players involved."

"Nope." Well, besides Mr. Black, but the mystery caller had never confirmed he was involved. I'd purposely left out the whole bit about saying his name during the call, along with my Darth Vader comparison, when replaying what was said to Doc and Cooper. If the cops learned about that name, I didn't want it to be traced back to me. Rumor was that Mr. Black had a fetish for body parts. What that fetish was exactly, I had no desire to find out, especially not first-hand just because I'd run my big mouth.

"Tell me again what was said about the death of a timekeeper," Doc ordered.

I pulled out the note I'd scribbled during the call. "Something about the death of a timekeeper doesn't stop the …" I paused to check my notes. "The 'vonderer' and 'yeager' was what it sounded like."

"Vonderer," Doc repeated, scratching at something on the table.

"Yeager?" Cooper asked, typing on his cell phone. "Like the beer?"

Doc looked across at him. "Jägermeister."

"That too."

"That's what it sounded like," I told them both. "Only there was a 'dare' in front of it."

Doc stopped scratching. "It sounded like *dare vonderer* and *dare yeager*?"

"Bingo." I sipped the tequila he'd ordered for me, taking it slow since I hadn't eaten in a while and wanted to keep my head vertical tonight.

"If I remember correctly," Doc said, "*der Jäger* means 'the hunter' in German."

"*Vonderer* is 'wanderer' according to this." Cooper pointed at his phone.

Doc rested his elbows on the table. "So, per your caller, the death of a timekeeper doesn't stop the wanderer or the hunter."

"There you go," I slapped my palm down, sarcasm pouring out through my lips. "That sure clears everything up, doesn't it?"

"I miss the good ol' days," Cooper muttered, taking a drink.

"You mean when murder was just plain old homicide?" I asked.

"Yeah, as in life before you came to town."

"Uh, correct me if I'm wrong, but when I came to town you already had a serial killer on the loose."

"At least he was human and didn't magically disappear in smoke when stabbed."

"It's more like a superheated flash, not smoke."

"Shut up, Parker."

"Violet," Doc tapped on my arm, disrupting our bickering. "The caller said something about timekeepers not working for anyone, only maintaining the balance between here and there, right?"

"I think that was the gist of it."

"Give me that piece of paper you scribbled on."

I gave him both the paper and a pen from my purse.

While he was writing, Cooper asked me, "What in the hell prompted you to invite Hawke up to see Prudence?"

I shrugged. "I called Zelda and learned she was out of town. She offered her spare key. I was in the midst of deciding whether or not to face Prudence on my own when Hawke called and said he wanted to ask me questions about some pictures."

"What were his questions? Which pictures?"

I thought about the whole scene and scoffed. "You know, he never got around to asking me anything or showing me any pictures. Prudence pulled the rug out from under him."

"Did you tell Prudence about the clock?" Doc asked.

"Yep." I closed my eyes, trying to remember all she said. "She mentioned something about me being a chosen one."

"Chosen for what?" Cooper asked.

"She never said exactly, only that I was in grave danger."

Doc cursed under his breath, taking a swallow of beer.

"What happened then?" Cooper asked.

"She smacked me. I mean Hawke did with her help."

"What?" Doc's drink hit the table hard enough to spill some beer over the rim. "That son of a bitch hit you? Where?"

"Prudence hit me," I corrected. "I don't think there are any bruises."

"Where, Violet?" he pressed.

I pointed at my cheek. He took me by the chin, turning that side of my face toward the stained-glass light over the pool table.

"Wait," I said, thinking about the conversation. "Prudence didn't smack me after telling me I was a chosen one. She smacked me the first time she told me I was in grave danger."

Doc let go of my chin, capturing my fingers in a soft squeeze. "What prompted her to lay a hand on you?"

"I laughed."

"To clarify," Cooper said, slipping into detective mode. "Prudence used Hawke to smack you because you laughed?"

"I may have been a little hysterical at that point in our conversation."

Doc lifted my hand, kissing my knuckles. "Sweetheart, you need to start at the beginning, before Prudence smacked you."

I resisted the urge to hold out my other hand for him to kiss, followed by other body parts of mine in dire need of attention from his lips. Instead, I backtracked, telling him about my pre-Hawke moment in the foyer with Prudence, and then how I opened the door to find that she'd already turned him into her puppet.

Cooper grunted at that point, mumbling something indistinguishable, and then took a gulp of whiskey.

I continued with Prudence's comment about Hawke's mind being full of nonsense.

"She actually used the word *nonsense*?" Doc asked, a hint of a grin on his cheeks.

I nodded, skipping the part of our conversation about the word *snollyguster* and my ignorance of its definition. "She said that Hawke thinks I killed Jane and Lila Beaumont."

"What!?" Doc sounded as outraged as I'd been at the allegation. "You're clearly innocent of both."

"Not crystal clear," Cooper said. "There are some foggy spots."

I nailed Cooper with a glare before returning to Doc. "Get this, Prudence claims Lila's death was no accident."

"According to your and Wanda Carhart's statements," Cooper said, "Lila fell on a glass shard."

"I remember what I said, Cooper." He'd only made me repeat my story three damned times that night while he wrote in that stupid notebook of his. "But truth be told, I didn't actually see the glass jam into Lila's throat. She fell with her back to me. When I rolled her over, the glass was there. Today, Prudence informed me that she stuck the glass shard in Lila's neck."

Cooper shook his head slowly.

"She killed Lila to help you?" Doc asked, distracting me from trying to figure out if Cooper believed me or not.

"That's what I initially thought, but of course Prudence had a more logical reason than saving my ass. She said something about preventing my blood from being used to summon a demon to our plane. According to her, an executioner's blood can cause a demon frenzy."

"This is insane," Cooper said.

"A demon frenzy?" Doc took another swallow of beer. "Christ. What else did Prudence the Wise have to say?"

"That Hawke thinks I beheaded George Mudder."

"Yeah," Cooper said with a smirk. "Hawke hasn't been able to let that one go since the first day he read your report on the events that took place that night at Mudder Brothers."

"I didn't kill George," I told him, just as I had Prudence.

"Too bad you had to execute the one who did."

"It was an accident."

A bark of laughter escaped from Cooper's lips. "Parker, slicing your finger with a kitchen knife is an accident. Driving a giant pair of scissors into a criminal's back isn't on the same level."

"He was going to kill Doc." I defended now as I had then. "Besides, I didn't know he would disappear like that."

Doc patted my shoulder. "Let's get back to Prudence."

I sent another frown in Cooper's direction before continuing. "After the bit about George Mudder, she said something about me interacting with a guardian."

"George was a guardian?" Cooper asked.

"I don't know," I told him. I thought about that part of our conversation. "Wait. No. I don't think she meant George, because she said something about how guardians blend in with humans now, but that they're still really nasty."

Cooper took a drink. "So who is the guardian then?"

"She got distracted before we got to that part."

"Distracted by what?" Doc asked.

"Distracted by the knowledge that there was a lock of what Hawke believes is my hair in Ms. Wolff's hand when they found her body."

Doc eyes widened. "What?" He frowned across the table at Cooper. "Is this true?"

Cooper held his stare. "Unfortunately."

"Was it planted?" I asked.

His steely gaze turned my way. "Not by me."

"That doesn't answer my question."

"Honestly, Parker, I don't know. I wasn't in charge of tagging and bagging on that run, just investigating the crime scene."

My stomach bucked, either not liking his answer or the tequila I was dumping into its mostly empty hold. "Could someone have planted my hair in her hand before they shipped the body off for an autopsy?"

"Possibly."

Doc picked up his glass, worry lining his face. "Maybe your hair really was in Ms. Wolff's hand at the time of her death."

Cooper and I both looked at him as if he'd sprouted thick, curling horns and started bleating. I beat Cooper to the punch. "How in the hell would my hair get in her hand?"

"Ms. Wolff called you, remember? Maybe she'd received a lock of your hair, along with Layne's picture. One or both could have instigated the phone call."

Crud. I hadn't thought of that during my afternoon of what-ifs. "Do you think the murderer gave her my hair and then … ?" I mimed slicing my neck.

Doc shrugged. "Or someone else gave Ms. Wolff your hair. Then the killer showed up and took her out of the game."

Cooper sat back, arms crossed. "Jesus, the shit just keeps getting deeper."

"Did Prudence have anything to say about your hair and the timekeeper?" Doc asked.

I had to ponder that for a moment or two. I'd been a little distracted by the news about the lock of hair when Prudence was talking about the timekeeper. "I remember something about the hair being tied to someone. Or was it me being tied to them? No, wait, it was the timekeeper who was using my hair to tie me to someone."

"What about it?" Doc pressed.

I chewed on my lower lip. "This is why I like to take friends along to Prudence's house."

"Think, Parker."

"I'm thinking, I'm thinking." I closed my eyes, trying to remember details. I'd been standing by the window, looking out at the Open Cut. She was talking behind me through Hawke's limp lips. "There was something about being tied to someone, that it was a bad thing."

Doc squeezed his forehead. "Why?"

"It's a no-no for the timekeeper to mess with tying. Prudence wondered if that's why the timekeeper was killed." Then I remembered why being tied was bad. "If I'm tied to someone, and either of us dies, then the other dies, too."

A mouthful of curses rolled off Doc's tongue.

I gripped his arm. "Listen, Doc. Prudence wasn't sure if it was actually a done deal. Ms. Wolff may have been killed before tying me to another."

"Who was the other?" he asked.

"I don't know. Prudence also wasn't sure if the timekeeper was tying me to another to protect or cause harm." I touched my cheek. "It was after this part of our conversation that she slapped me."

Cooper smirked. "You were laughing hysterically?"

"Well, she told me I was in grave danger."

"I can see now why you laughed," Doc said.

"Did Prudence have any ideas about who might be taking the clocks?" Cooper asked.

"No, but when I told her about the one I received, she warned me not to move the hands of the clock."

"You haven't, have you?" Doc asked, his brow creasing.

I cringed in response.

Doc scowled and growled out another round of curses.

Cooper's gaze bounced back and forth between us. "What happens if you move the hands?"

"She didn't say," I told him. "But she did tell me that the clock may start up on its own, and when it does, it's not exactly a good thing."

"Did she explain why?" Cooper asked.

I shook my head.

"Figures," Doc said. "Prudence is a pain in the ass that way."

Cooper harrumphed. "It must come with the Executioner title."

I flipped him off.

"I'm surprised she didn't take one of Hawke's teeth," Doc said.

"She tried, but I got her to stop …" I hesitated before adding, "in exchange for something."

"What?" they asked in unison.

"The next time I go see her, either I take her a trophy tooth or she'll pull one of mine."

"Where are you going to find a tooth?" Cooper asked.

I gave him a toothy grin. "How about another drink, Cooper? Or five?"

"Touch me and you'll regret it, Parker."

"I'll be your huckleberry," Doc said with a wink.

"No way. I like your mouth too much," I closed the distance between us, my eyes on his lips. "Especially when you—"

Cooper's hand slid between us, risking my bite. "Save it for later when you're alone. We aren't done here."

I sat back with a sigh. "There is no such thing as *alone*, not with you parasitically attached to my side every waking moment."

"So cruel." He mocked a knife to his heart. "My heart bleeds for you. Really. Now tell me how it ended."

"How what ended?"

"Prudence and Hawke. What did he say when she released her hold on him?"

I snorted. "He called me a witch. You'd have been proud of me for keeping my feathers unruffled."

"I'd prefer you do one of your windmill maneuvers on him," Doc said. "Teach the son of a bitch not to lay a hand on you."

"That smack was one hundred percent Prudence. Hawke told me he couldn't remember anything after arriving at the house except being in a dark claustrophobic place."

Doc tipped his head slightly, his gaze focused above my head. "So, Hawke doesn't remember telling you about the lock of hair."

I shook my head. "Unless his memory has returned since leaving."

"At least we have that working in our favor."

"How does Detective Hawke being even more convinced that Parker is a witch do us any good?"

"I'm not talking about the witch part. Hawke not remembering what he told Violet gives us a window of opportunity to return to Ms. Wolff's.

Return? Why? "You want me to try to make contact through the telephone again?"

He finished his beer, focusing on Cooper. "I had something else in mind."

Cooper's eyes narrowed as he held Doc's gaze. "Why are you looking at me like that, Nyce?"

"I need to pay another visit to Jake Tender."

I groaned. "No, Doc." Last time we'd held a séance and he'd gone under, he'd almost not made it back to the surface.

"Violet, the mirror is gone."

"That doesn't mean the juggernaut isn't still waiting there for an opportunity to come through some other way. Besides, doesn't Hawke have police going in there every hour now?"

"What can we do about that, Coop?"

"Shit." Cooper leaned forward, covering his face with his hands.

Doc watched him with a gunslinger squint.

"I don't want you to take that risk," I said, touching Doc's arm. "We can figure out how that lock of hair got there another way. Hell, I'm still not convinced it's my hair."

"How many curly-haired blondes do you think Ms. Wolff knew, Violet?" His frown stayed on Cooper even though he was talking to me. "Blondes whose son's picture had been stuck in Ms. Wolff's bedroom mirror?"

"Right," I sighed. "Okay, maybe tomorrow I can—"

"Stop." Cooper interrupted me. He lowered his hands. Tension mixed with tiredness added more jagged ridges to his face.

I ignored him, continuing with, "What about if I—"

"It won't work," Coop said. "Her apartment is too hot."

"Maybe Natalie—"

"Don't drag Beals into this."

"Damn it, Cooper. Quit interrupting me."

"Hawke told me that he thinks you put Natalie up to living in the same building. He's keeping a close eye on her, too, because of you."

"That's going to really piss her off," I said.

"You need to put more effort into not dragging her down with you on this one." he said.

There was an edge to his comment, one that sliced a little too deep. I leaned forward. "Listen, *Detective*, I don't like this situation any more than you do, and I certainly don't want to hurt Natalie in any way, shape, or form. That includes adding to her police record. However, I'm not sure if you know this, but Nat's even more allergic to the cops than I am. She comes by it genetically. Brushes with the law make her itch to wreak large-scale havoc." I poked him in the arm. "That's something you need to remember, Johnny Law, if you ever scrounge up enough gumption to play Romeo."

His steely eyes grew frosty. "I have plenty of gumption in that department, Parker."

"Oh, yeah? From here, it looks more like you're too gun-shy to do more than stand below her window and stammer."

"What are you doing, Violet?" Doc asked.

He and I had discussed the topic of Cooper and Natalie becoming an item several times, and each time I'd concurred that it was probably best if I stayed back and kept my mouth shut. But something was shifting in Natalie's head. I had seen it after her last few brushes with Cooper. His mixed messages were starting to erode the wall she'd built after he'd blown her off last time. It was my job as her best friend to spell something out to him before she started drawing hearts around his name in the snow, and there was no time like the present.

"I'm issuing a warning," I told Doc while holding Cooper's glare. "You see, Cooper here keeps playing games, like holding Nat's hand and saying things that make it sound like he's interested in something more than friendship. If this is all a game to him, then he needs to back off and find someone else to fuck with."

"My private life is none of your business, Parker," he shot back through gritted teeth.

"It is when it begins to affect the woman who's been my best friend for over three decades." I tapped on the table with my index finger. "That's thirty-plus years of love and laughter, tears and joy. When it's all said and done, it's my job to pick up the pieces after the next bastard breaks her heart. Keep that in mind if you like your teeth, Romeo."

After several more tense seconds, he nodded. "I overstepped, Parker." His tone was repentant. "I'm sorry."

I scowled. "Damn it, Cooper. Quit trying to make me like you."

"If you two are done with your pissing match," Doc said, "how about we get back to the situation with Ms. Wolff's apartment?"

"As of this afternoon," Cooper told him, "Hawke stationed an around-the-clock patrol outside of Ms. Wolff's door."

"He did?" I massaged the back of my neck, trying to ease the tension that kept cinching my shoulders tighter.

Cooper continued, "He came back from lunch all wild-eyed and told the chief that he wanted to have the apartment watched continuously because he'd received information that someone was going to be breaking in soon to take more clocks."

"Crap." Maybe Hawke had been conscious on some level when Prudence was digging around in his head, sharing his secrets.

"There has to be another way," Doc said. There was something about the manner in which Doc was watching Cooper that had me scratching my head. "It's time to stop playing games, Coop. We need your help."

Cooper toyed with his glass, spinning it on the table. He smirked at

Doc. "I'd rather keep pretending nothing's changed."

"What's going on?" I felt like I'd skipped a page of the script. It took me a moment to understand what Cooper's fidgeting meant and grasp what was really going on under the surface between Doc and him.

"You can only keep your head in the sand for so long." Doc took a swallow of beer, his smile bitter when he lowered his glass. "Trust me. I know from years of experience. Like I told you the other day, bargaining with the devil won't make it go away. It'll only get you closer to Hell."

Cooper shoved his glass away. "This is so messed up."

"You'll get used to it in time."

"If only Parker hadn't—"

"Placing blame won't change anything," Doc said. "It was there all along. It was only a matter of time until it surfaced."

I leaned in, lowering my voice. "We are talking about seeing ghosts, right?"

"I don't care what your boyfriend says," Cooper said to me. "I'm still blaming you for fucking up my world."

I blew a raspberry. "If I had a dollar for every time a guy had told me that."

Doc glanced at me with a raised brow. "How many dollars would you have, Boots?"

"That's not important," I said, waving him off, focusing on Cooper. "When we were in Ms. Wolff's place the last time, you saw someone, didn't you?"

At Cooper's nod, I clapped quietly. "I knew it! The way you paled and rushed me out of that apartment. Who was it? Who did you see? Was it Ms. Wolff?"

My heart raced. If there was some way to find out the truth from her about her killer, it could keep my bacon from getting sizzled.

"I saw Jake Tender," Cooper admitted. "At least I'm pretty sure it was Freesia's great-great uncle."

"There was more to it than just that, wasn't there?" Doc's voice was smooth, encouraging. It was no wonder he was able to get people to trust him with their money to make his living. "What happened when he noticed you noticing him?"

Cooper looked down. "He stared at me with his dead eyes."

"What else?" Doc pressed.

"I think he was trying to tell me something. His mouth moved like this." Cooper mimicked exaggerated talking.

I recoiled. It was too much like Prudence's puppet show.

"But when his mouth moved, no sound came out."

I turned to Doc. "What does that mean?"

"It means Coop needs to work on developing his sixth sense."

"I'm not going to go out and start talking to every fucking ghost I see," Cooper snarled.

"*Every* ghost," I repeated. "Cooper, how many ghosts have you seen since the séance?"

He scowled at me. "They're everywhere."

Chapter Fourteen

Wednesday, December 5th

I woke to the sound of somebody screaming bloody murder.

"Parker!" Cooper's voice cut through the commotion.

I sat up with a gasp, holding my throat. "She got me," I cried, panting. I pulled my hand away from my throat, expecting it to be covered with blood. My palm was wet, but with sweat.

"Oh, fuck." I fell back onto my pillow, blinking in the bright ceiling light over my bed.

That's when I realized I had company.

Cooper stood next to my bed with bloodshot eyes, his head covered with blond shark fins. "What the hell, Parker?"

I yanked the covers up to my neck, covering my pajama top. "What are you doing in here?"

Movement behind him drew my gaze down over his bare chest. Multiple scars were spread across his upper body. Sheesh, he was a regular war zone under his shirt.

Addy poked her head around from behind his black sweatpants. "Are you okay, Mom? You were screaming."

Oh. It all clicked into place. Another nightmare. I must have been the one screaming. Addy had gone for backup.

"I'm fine." Especially now that Lila Beaumont and her sideboard full of knives, barbed hooks, and other rusted, pointy objects were nothing more than fading vapors in my head. I sat up, holding my arms wide for Addy. She rushed to me, squeezing me hard. "I'm sorry I scared you, baby."

"You screamed so loud," she said against my chest.

I petted her hair, my hands still trembling with adrenaline. "Is that why you went to get Cooper?"

She nodded, looking up at me. "I couldn't get you to wake up and Doc wasn't here."

Yet another reason to figure out who'd killed Ms. Wolff ASAP. I hadn't had a single nightmare the whole time Doc was in my bed. He kept me too busy in fantasyland to have any bad dreams.

"Were you having a scary dream?"

"Yeah, baby. It was just a nightmare." I kissed the top of her head, breathing in the sweet scent of her strawberry shampoo. I glanced up, meeting Cooper's raised brow. "Sorry about that. Usually the kids aren't close enough to hear me."

"Usually?" he repeated. "Do you have nightmares often?"

"That depends."

Addy's weight shifted as she relaxed.

"On what?"

"Several factors," I said, keeping things vague since I had little ears listening. I pointed at Addy and then held my index finger to my lips.

With a nod, he backed out of the room and closed the door behind him.

I hummed under my breath for a few minutes while stroking Addy's back. When I felt her sag against me, I put her under the covers and eased out. I tied my long, black knit sweater over my pajama top and slipped into a pair of flannel bottoms. After I shut off the lights, I listened for a moment to make sure Addy's breathing was slow and even before stepping into the hall.

The smell of fresh coffee hit me halfway down the stairs.

I peeked into the living room. Natalie lay curled up on the couch, snoring lightly under the thick quilt Aunt Zoe had given her last night before going to bed. It appeared our evening with Dr. Seuss's residents of Whoville had worn her out, but I had an inkling the exhaustion lining her face last night had more to do with working her ass off at the Galena House. Or maybe she wasn't sleeping well over there due to the nighttime visitors she'd mentioned hearing.

Cooper had his back to me when I stepped into the kitchen. He hadn't bothered with a shirt or socks yet. I frowned at the abundance of scars on his back. "Jeez, Cooper," I said, joining him at the counter. "Did you roll around in a ball of barbed wire when you were a kid?"

He glanced sideways at me, the rough edges on his face looking like he was the one who'd been dueling with Lila and her collection of sharp objects all night instead of me. "The scars come with the job."

"I hope you got paid a bonus for each one." I grabbed a mug from the cupboard and set it on the counter, second in line for caffeine.

He focused back on the coffee maker.

The hiss and sigh as the coffee brewed filled the room as we waited.

"Aren't you cold?" I asked, snuggling into my sweater.

He shook his head. "I keep my house in the low 60s."

Of course he did. My hazy morning brain had forgotten he was half-machine.

The coffee maker hissed and sighed some more.

"What was the nightmare about?" he asked.

I shrugged. "Lila."

"You screamed because?"

"Two men wearing potato sacks with cutout eyes held me down while Lila sliced my neck." The nightmare was a real-life blend of Prudence's death scene and my experiences in the Carhart house months ago.

"Damn. You have these sort of dreams often?"

"Often enough ever since Wolfgang Hessler's tea party. I think waking up in that room with those poor girls cracked my brain."

"You mean cracked it wider."

"Careful, Cooper. Word on the street is that you're seeing ghosts. That's not exactly sane behavior."

He snorted.

Hiss. Sigh.

I stared out the kitchen window into the dark backyard. The weatherman was calling for snow flurries this afternoon. I wondered if Cooper would be going to Doc's tonight for their weekly poker game, leaving me alone.

"I don't know how Nyce does it," Cooper said.

"Does what?"

"Puts up with you and that crazy hair." He dodged my jab, a rare grin making an appearance for a split second. "I meant how can he talk about finances and retirement portfolios one minute and fend off ghosts another?"

Last night, after Cooper made me promise to stay home with Natalie and keep my ass out of trouble, Doc had driven him up to the Golden Sluice bar in Lead. The idea was to give Cooper an opportunity to drown his ghost-spurred frustrations in whiskey at a location Doc was relatively certain was free of the wispy folks.

"For one thing," I told him, "Doc's been dealing with this shit since he was a kid, whereas you're only a week or so into it."

He smirked. "True."

"For another, I'm not sure if you've caught on yet during the séances you've witnessed, but the man is a master of ceremonies when it comes to supernatural phenomena." I didn't bother adding my accolades for his mastery between the sheets, but paused for a few seconds to smile about it. "Doc has spent his life studying the paranormal world as well as living within it."

"It's fucked up."

"I know." I rubbed my eyes. "Without him around to explain what in the hell is going on, I'd be in a padded cell pulling my crazy hair out." Cornelius wasn't helping the matter either, which reminded me that I needed to tell Doc about that hole in the floor under Calamity Jane's.

"I felt like I was steering in that direction until I blew off some steam last night."

Hiss. Sigh. A gurgle followed, the brewing process wrapping up.

I crossed my arms, leaning my hip against the counter. "How late were you two out?"

"Nyce dropped me off after midnight."

I looked at Aunt Zoe's Betty Boop clock. No wonder Cooper's eyes were red-rimmed. It wasn't quite five.

"Did Doc help?" I hope he planned on mentoring Cooper. The idea of Cooper with a screw loose and a house full of guns made me cringe.

"He fed me drinks until I couldn't see straight and then drove me back here."

That was one of my favorite ways of taking off an edge. "You should go back to bed."

"So should you."

I looked down at my hands. "I'm afraid I'll dream again."

"Maybe you should pull that tequila bottle down from above the refrigerator and try Nyce's remedy."

"I'd rather spend several hours alone in his company, but I doubt you'll allow that until Ms. Wolff's killer is found."

The coffee maker beeped.

Cooper filled my cup and then his. I moved to the table, dropping into a chair. "So, what's next?" I nodded when he held out the milk with raised brows.

"You go to work and find me a house while I go to work and find us a killer." He poured milk in my cup and then his, returning the jug to the fridge.

I circled the rim of my coffee mug with my finger, my lips pursed as I debated my situation. I could search on my own for Ms. Wolff's killer and risk getting caught by Hawke, or I could do what I know Doc would want me to do and come clean here and now.

Doc won.

"Yeah," I said, "about that." I looked up to where he still stood at the counter.

He stared at me over his coffee cup, his eyes narrowing at whatever he saw on my face.

"I'm going to try to find Ms. Wolff's killer," I said.

"No."

"I'm not asking for your permission."

He lowered his cup. "Don't be an idiot."

I didn't say anything.

"You're going to get yourself in even deeper shit."

I circled the rim of my cup again with my finger.

"Christ, Parker. You don't know the first thing about detective work."

"Then teach me."

"I'm not a teacher."

I lifted my mug. "With or without your help, Cooper."

"Don't make me throw you in jail again."

"You gave me your word you wouldn't threaten me with that."

He cursed, crossing over to the table. He took the seat next to me for some reason, probably planning to intimidate me with his big shoulders and multitude of scars. I sat up straighter, bracing myself for battle.

"Don't you get it, Parker? If you start messing around with Ms. Wolff's apartment, you're going to look even more guilty, like you're trying to hide something from the police."

"I'm not going to sit here and wait for those test results to come back. If it is my hair, it was planted there by one of your officer buddies. I need to figure out who is behind this. I need to know if the reason Ms. Wolff was killed was only to set me up for a fall, or if there is something bigger going on that I need to prepare for up here." I pointed at my temple.

"Jesus. I don't know who's worse—Nyce or you."

"What did Doc do?"

"He offered me a deal—he'll teach me how to block out ghosts in exchange for my help."

"Your help with what?"

"Getting him inside that apartment again so that he can try to save your ass."

I grimaced, even though it warmed the cockles of my heart that Doc was trying to save me. "We can't let Doc go under again in there. Cornelius was sure we'd lost him the last time. There's something in that apartment that's the equivalent of a revolving door. Sometimes the door stops revolving, leaving you stuck on the wrong side."

"I don't want either of you back in that place. Like I said before, it's too hot. If either of you are caught in there, Hawke will press charges and probably keep you under lock and key for as long as he can. The same goes for Natalie now."

"What about Natalie?" a voice said from the dining room.

The woman in question shuffled into the room, her eyes half-closed with sleep. Massaging her lower back, she went straight to the coffee maker. "Why are you two up so damned early?"

"I had a nightmare."

"Oh, man. You didn't pull your wake-up-screaming routine again, did you?" She poured herself a cup of coffee, spilling a little in her sleepy state.

"Guilty. Addy got Cooper to come and give me hell because I wouldn't wake up."

I glanced over at Cooper. He was too engrossed in the sight of Natalie's butt in yoga pants to participate in the conversation, let alone lower his cup back to the table. When she turned around, coffee in hand, Cooper's eyes widened. His flinch made me look over at Nat again.

Ohhhhhh. No wonder Cooper had checked out of the conversation. In her half-asleep state, Natalie hadn't remembered to throw on a bra under her pink thermal shirt. She walked over to the fridge, still blinking awake, and leaned over to grab the milk.

Poor Cooper was a goner. If he wasn't careful, he was going to be caught with his tongue hanging out.

I nudged his arm, trying to get him to come back from whatever wet dream was probably playing in his head.

Milk in hand, Natalie walked over to the counter. She set the jug down and paused to rub her back. It must be bothering her after a night on the couch. Her profile shot included a slice of bare midriff when she raised her arms to the ceiling and arched her back for a deeper stretch.

Cooper sucked air between his teeth.

I poked him in the ribs hard enough to make him spill his coffee onto his hand.

"Damn it, Parker." He growled at me, wiping his hand off on his sweatpants as Natalie dumped milk into her cup.

"Oops," I lied when he glared at me.

Nat returned to the fridge, giving me a few seconds to scowl at Cooper, point at Natalie and then him, and then mimic slicing my throat. That gesture reminded me of my nightmare and made me scowl even more.

"What's with that face?" Natalie asked, dropping onto the chair next to me.

"I was thinking about what Cooper said before you joined us."

She glanced over at Cooper, and then did a double take. Her eyes lingered south of his stubble-covered chin. "Damn, Coop. Did someone use you for target practice?"

"Scars come with his job," I told her.

"I hope the chief at least offered to kiss them better."

Cooper stood and left the room, returning seconds later wearing the red flannel jacket Doc kept here. "Sorry about that," he said, lowering back into his chair. "I'm not used to sleeping with women."

Natalie's eyebrows rose. A grin played at the corners of her mouth. "And here I'd figured you for a regular playboy with a different woman hanging on your arm each night."

He shrugged off her teasing. "Women don't usually like cops. We keep shitty hours."

"True, but you probably make them feel safe when they're in your bed."

"Safe?" He leaned forward, resting his arms on the table, his steely eyes locking onto hers. "*Safe* is the last thing I want a woman to feel when she's in my bed."

Wow! That was a good one. I would have clapped had I not been stuck playing monkey in the middle.

The tension in the room cranked up several notches.

I glanced at Natalie to see if he'd hit the mark. From her slightly parted lips and flushed face, I'd say it was a bull's-eye. She shook her head slightly, then chuckled and made a show of fanning herself. "Whew, Coop! You need to take it easy on us poor local girls. We can only swoon so much before we keel over from a broken heart."

He took a swallow of coffee, his eyes still eating her up. "Have you looked in a mirror this morning, Beals?"

"No, why? Do I have something on my face?"

I looked back and forth between them. This was the shit I was talking about when I'd warned him last night. Here was his opportunity. He clearly had her attention. Now all he had to do was make his move.

He lowered his gaze, focusing on his coffee cup. I could practically feel the big chicken retreating.

"Yeah," I answered her in his place, grinning. "A big fat nose."

She flicked me on the shoulder.

"How did you sleep?" Cooper asked her, back to boring old questions now that the heat of the moment had cooled.

She rubbed her back again. "The couch is not my favorite place to crash in this house. I should have moved to the recliner, but I was too sleepy."

"Next time you stay," he said, "take Addy's bed. I can sleep on the couch."

Yawning, she shook her head. "I'll just crawl in with Vi and make an Addy sandwich."

"Better yet," I said, "you two can have my bed and I'll take the couch." Maybe I could convince Doc to spend the night on the torture device with me if I offered to rub away his aches throughout the night.

A high-pitched, choking laugh came from Natalie. "I'm sure Coop doesn't want to share a bed with me, Violet. I snore, remember?"

Cooper and her? She'd misunderstood what I was saying.

"Not to mention," she continued, challenging Cooper with a glare. "He doesn't sleep with local girls."

Cooper stared right back. If she'd made a dent in his armor with that jab, he didn't show it. "I believe Parker meant you and Addy could share *her* bed."

"Oh." Her face turned bright red. "Of course." She hid behind her coffee cup.

Dear Lord, if this conversation grew any more squirmy, I'd slip right out of my chair. I scrambled for something to fill the awkward silence that had joined the three of us. "Hey, Nat. Cooper and I thought it might be a good idea for you to join us on our next house hunting trip."

Both of them looked at me as if I'd sprouted a daisy from the middle of my forehead.

"Me?" Natalie asked. "I'm not looking for a house."

"But you're as good as having a home inspector with us. You can assess the structure and let Cooper know if it has any potential problems."

Her gaze swung from me to Cooper. "What's in it for me?"

I followed suit. "What's in it for Natalie?"

Cooper's forehead wrinkled. "What would you like, Beals?"

She sipped on her coffee, pondering his question. "How about a guided trip inside Ms. Wolff's apartment for Violet, Doc, and me."

"What about me?" Old man Harvey asked, joining us.

I gawked at him. "Where did you come from?"

"The stork."

"I didn't hear the front door."

"The old biddies at the senior center don't call me 'mongoose' fer shits and giggles." He set a grocery bag on the table, pulling out a carton of eggs and setting them next to the stove. "Yer ex's Jaguar is parked next door again."

My shoulders tightened so fast my head nearly popped. "You're kidding!"

There could only be one reason Rex Conner was shacking up with Aunt Zoe's neighbor again, and it had nothing to do with Ms. Geary's famous cherry tarts. That son of a bitch was spying on me and the kids again.

"It's a natural-born fact." Harvey grabbed a frying pan from the cupboard, setting it on the stove. "Beatrice must have taken him back. I'd go ask her to be sure, but my britches are ridin' too high these days fer the likes of her."

"I thought I saw movement across the street when I checked for the paper earlier," Cooper said, taking his coffee cup to the sink. "What's for breakfast?" he asked his uncle.

Harvey held up a package of bacon and a bag of English muffins. My stomach growled in spite of my angst about my ex's fancy Jaguar.

"I need to put a restraining order on that asshole," I grumbled.

"I'll take care of Rex," Natalie said, patting my hand.

Scowling, Cooper came over to the table, standing over Natalie. "You're going to end up with a restraining order on you if he catches you near his car again."

She lifted her chin. "He won't catch me."

He placed one hand on the back of her chair and the other on the table in front of her, leaning in close. "But I might," he warned.

"You could try," she taunted back. "But I'm not sure you're *that* good."

The air practically crackled from the electricity rippling between them again. Holy hotcakes! If they didn't do something about this sexual tension soon, I was going to get zapped.

"We'll see, Beals." Cooper pulled back, looking as cool as an ice cube, and then turned to his uncle. "I'll hop in the shower and help you with breakfast when I finish." Without a backward glance, he strode from the room.

Natalie watched him go, her eyes burning holes into his backside. When her rubberneck snapped back to Harvey and me, we were both grinning at her.

"What?" she asked, dusting invisible crumbs from the table.

"How's that there sabbatical workin' out fer ya?" Harvey asked.

"It's great." She pointed her thumb at herself. "When it comes to men, I've got an iron backbone and steel ribs."

He pointed a spatula at her chest. "It's hard to see all of that iron and steel when yer headlights are shinin' in my eyes."

She glanced down, her cheeks paling one second and then flashing red the next. She crossed her arms over her chest. "Shit. I wasn't thinking this morning."

Harvey snort-cackled. "Nothin' like hooters and coffee to git an old boy's motor hummin'." He gave me a once-over. "You got yers hidden under that sweater. Doc must've slept in his own bedroll."

"Can it, old man, or I'll crack those eggs on your skull."

Snickering, he washed his hands and grabbed Aunt Zoe's apron from the wall.

Cooper returned ten minutes later. I'd downed a second cup of coffee in the meantime, and sent Doc a text to see what he was up to today. Natalie had put on a bra and Aunt Zoe's quilted red puffer vest, her chest doubly covered. Cooper glanced her way, but managed not to get his eyes stuck this time.

"Zoe said she'll be down shortly." Cooper moved over to the stove. "What do you want me to do?" he asked his uncle.

"Hold this." Harvey handed him the spatula and hobbled out of the kitchen, returning seconds later with a familiar-looking manila envelope.

"What's this?" Cooper frowned at the envelope that Harvey handed to him.

I barely held in my gasp as I realized what "this" was. Shit! What was Harvey doing, giving Cooper that right now? Shouldn't we have discussed a game plan first? Made sure I was out of the room, at least?

"Just open it," Harvey said.

Cooper pulled out the picture of that horned thing back in Slagton and the piece of paper that had been included with it. As he stared down at the picture, surprise flitted over his expression, followed by a tightening of his jaw. He cursed under his breath. Stuffing the picture and paper back in the envelope, he asked in a low voice, "Where did you get this?"

"It sort of showed up." Harvey's blue eyes met mine briefly.

Cooper caught our shared look. His lips thinned. "Bullshit."

"No tall tales this mornin', Coop. Someone called and left a message where to find it. Don't shoot the messenger."

"Who called?"

"They didn't say."

"Where did you find it?"

"Slagton." Harvey laid strips of bacon in the pan, his feathers seemingly unruffled by his nephew's snapping teeth. "Past the ol' company store."

"You didn't go back there alone, did you?"

"I'm a grown man."

"I went with him," I said. I couldn't let Harvey take the brunt of the heat, even though he'd technically dragged me along.

Cooper's gaze swung my way. "When?"

"Recently," I said, realizing that if I wasn't careful he'd realize somebody had messed with the tracking device on my phone—a certain somebody who had just kicked me under the table and was warning me to zip it under her breath.

"How recently?" he asked.

"What is it?" Natalie tried to run interference. She joined him at the counter, trying to grab the envelope from his hand. "A picture?"

"Nothing." Cooper tucked the envelope behind his back. "And if Uncle Willis and Parker know what's good for them, they'll forget they ever saw it."

"Forget what?" Harvey joked.

"I'm going to get the kids up," I said, escaping the room before Cooper changed his mind and decided to interrogate me further about the Slagton field trip.

"You can run for now, Parker," he followed me into the dining room. "But I know where to find you."

"Of course you do, Cooper." I climbed the stairs, looking down over the railing at him. "My phone is handcuffed to yours, remember?"

Or not.

Chapter Fifteen

My cell phone rang as I pulled into my parking spot behind Calamity Jane's. I cringed, afraid Cooper wasn't done bugging me about that damned picture from Slagton. There was no way he was going to let that whole fiasco go for long without some rubber-glove treatment.

I dug my phone out of my purse, letting the engine idle with the heater vent blowing on me. The drive to work was so short the warm air was just getting going.

It wasn't Cooper.

My heart pitter-pattered.

"*Bonjour, mon cheri*," I said in my best attempt at a sex-kitten voice at this ungodly hour of the day.

"No fair, Tish." Doc's voice was velvety in my ear. "I'm too far away to kiss your arm."

"My arm? I'd rather you start with my mouth. Where are you?" The Picklemobile wasn't in the lot. Neither were Mona's or Ray's SUVs, Ben's Subaru, or Jerry's Hummer, for that matter. I'd escaped from the house and Cooper early, but not *that* early.

"Down in Keystone at a client's place."

"Already?" I leaned back in my seat, frowning out the windshield at the pine trees blanketing the hillside in front of me. Doc must be as tired as Cooper after his late night at the Golden Sluice.

"I wanted to take care of things here so I could be back in Deadwood after lunch. They're calling for snow later."

Weren't they always this time of year and getting it right only half of the time? The Black Hills were notorious for giving the weather predictors the runaround. "Are you playing poker tonight with the boys?"

"Yes."

"Damn."

"You don't want me to play poker with them?"

I fiddled with my coat button—one that Elvis hadn't pecked off yet. "I'd rather you play with *me*."

I'd missed him next to me in bed more than I'd like to admit, even to myself. Having slept alone most of my life, it was surprising how quickly I'd grown accustomed to hearing his steady breath in the darkness, feeling his warmth next to me under the covers, knowing he was only an arm's length away.

"If it's any consolation," he said, "Coop just called and told me he cleared it with your aunt Zoe for us to have the game in her kitchen tonight so he can keep an eye on you."

Aunt Zoe was okay with Reid coming over again? She must plan on hiding out in her workshop. "Cooper needs to take a chill pill," I told Doc. "Where would I go on a snowy night?"

"I don't know, maybe Slagton again."

Oh. I grimaced. "He whined to you about that, huh?"

"That and about being woken up extra early because my girlfriend was screaming her lungs out in the room next door. He wanted to know what I usually do when you have nightmares—pinch you hard or slap you awake?"

"He better be careful. He tries either and I might wake up swinging."

His low chuckle tugged on my heart, making me miss him even more. "I reminded him of your deadly windmill move. He told me it was Lila haunting you this time in your nightmare."

"My brain made a mashup of Lila and her knives with Prudence's death scene, including the menacing guys with the potato sack masks."

"Damn. It's no wonder you were screaming."

Doc had experienced Prudence's death multiple times while hanging out in the Carhart house using his magic mind trick—what had he called it? Retrocognition, maybe? Both times had left him pale and shaken after he'd woken up from his trip to the past.

"Maybe you need to drink beer and play some poker with us tonight," he said. "Take your mind off your troubles."

"I'd rather take my mind off this crap by playing with you *alone*."

"I see." His tone lowered to an even deeper, sexier level. "And what would we play, Boots?"

"I always enjoy a rousing game of Twister."

"Twister with you is definitely entertaining, but you cheat."

"I do not."

"You do, too."

"How in the world can someone cheat at Twister?" I tried to sound innocent and slightly outraged.

"You purposely wear leggings or yoga pants when we play."

Shoot. He was on to me. "For comfort," I claimed. "They stretch better."

"They distract the hell out of me and you know it. You also like to bend over in front of me so I can see down your shirt."

"I wear a bra." Usually. "Besides, I have to put my hands on the dots. Whether or not you're peeking down my shirt is out of my control."

"Last time we played, you wore a thong and no bra."

"I had a camisole on."

"And only a camisole. I almost had a stroke trying to keep from touching you in front of the kids."

I laughed, remembering Doc's repeated curses under his breath that evening. My kids were used to my wearing camisoles and yoga pants around the house, especially during cleaning days, so they hadn't noticed the sweat dotting Doc's upper lip. But I had, which had spurred the temptress in me to tease even more.

"Fine, you big baby," I conceded. "What do you want to play?"

"How about another round of Frisk-the-Hot-Blonde-Against-My-Desk?"

A punch of lust made me blow out a breath. "Oh! That's a good game." I adjusted the vent, hot enough at the memory he was spurring to skip the heater.

"A very good one. How about you stop over at lunch today and let me remind you how good?"

"I thought you were in Keystone."

"I'll hurry. Are you wearing your purple boots?"

I looked down at my feet. "Nope, brown."

"I'll swing by your place on the way back and grab the others. Are they in your closet?"

"Yes, but they won't match my outfit."

"They always look absolutely stunning with your birthday suit."

I giggled. "You're hopeless when it comes to those boots."

"I'm a sucker for all things Violet. Harvey suggested I buy you spurs for Christmas."

"Oh, God, he would." I flipped my visor down, checking my teeth for food in the lighted mirror.

"I told him I have something else in mind."

That gave me pause. In the mirror, worry lines formed on my forehead. "What's that?" I was all over the place with ideas for him, trying to find the perfect gift that said, *I love you but don't feel stuck with me and my kids.*

"It won't be a surprise if I tell you."

"Don't make me seduce it out of you, Doc."

"You should try." I could hear his grin in his flirty tone. "Here's a tip: The more naked you are, the better your chances of success."

The lines on my forehead smoothed. "What time do you want me to come over?"

"Will one o'clock work?"

"Sure. You want me to bring you something for lunch?"

"Yeah, a paper bag surprise like last time."

I smiled. My underwear had been in that bag. "Tell me, big boy." I pulled my lip gloss out and touched up my lips in the mirror. "Did you dial my number to set up a booty call, or was there something else you needed to tell me?"

"Damn it. You distracted me again with your body."

"It's what I do best."

"No, that thing you do with your mouth is what you do best."

I closed the mirror and flipped the visor back up. "Which thing with my mouth are you talking about?" I'd done plenty with it when we were alone, and he was always very vocal with his appreciation.

"The thing where you tell me you love me with it."

A rush of that very love he was talking about filled me, flooding my heart until it overfilled and made my eyes water. I quickly swiped away the tears, not that he could see me.

"*Je t'aime*, baby." I purred those three little words in the language of love … well, one of them, trying to keep things light and flirty.

"Quit teasing me, Tish. I called to tell you about Ms. Wolff."

Zoiks! That certainly cooled my jets. "What about her?"

"I found something in your family history book last night that I need to show you."

Last night? After he dropped off Cooper? Eek. That book was so not my idea of bedtime reading material. "And it has to do with Ms. Wolff?"

"Sort of." I heard the sound of someone talking in the background. "I have to go," he said. "My client's calling me back inside. Keep your cute nose out of trouble this morning, Killer."

I blew him a kiss and hung up.

After hearing his voice, the day seemed brighter. I practically skipped across the parking lot and into the office, whistling like a Disney bluebird past Jerry's dark office, all of the way into the front room.

The sight of Tiffany sitting in Ben's chair made me skid to a stop, my whistle petering out.

I paused, looking around the room to make sure I'd entered the correct building. Had I stepped through a door to a parallel universe? One in which Tiffany and I worked together side-by-side instead of competing for men and sales?

"Good morning, Violet," she said, rising from the chair.

Her long, red hair looked even softer and wavier than usual this morning, not a single wild strand to be seen, dang her. How did she get her brow, eye, and lip liner so freaking perfect at this hour? It just proved my suspicion that she wasn't mortal. Her peach fuzzy cardigan sweater fit like a second skin, several of the buttons ready to pop loose and take out an eye. The pencil-thin skirt painted on her hips showed off the skinny bitch's lack of a baby tummy. As ex-girlfriends went, she was a real doozy to have to face when I wasn't packing mace, especially after sharing breakfast with a cantankerous cop. I'd sooner go nose-to-nose with a grizzly bear.

"What are you doing here, Tiffany?" And who let the razor-clawed she-cat inside the office? Nobody else was here yet.

"I stopped by to take our friend to breakfast."

"Which friend?" We didn't share any friends. Wait, did she mean Jeff Wymonds?

"Cornelius."

My lips tightened. Since when had we begun sharing custody of Cornelius? She'd tried to woo him away once or twice in the past, but his eccentricities had seemed to put her off. His quirks had put me off, too, at first, but now I think my kookiness outranked his, which is why he was *my* friend and not hers. Hell, I specialized in non-normal pals, some of them not even breathing anymore. I'd like to see the ultra-competitive, Jessica Rabbit wanna-be top that shit.

"Where is he?" I asked, looking around for my favorite Abe Lincoln doppelganger. Jerry's office had been dark, the door closed.

"He went upstairs to get dressed."

"Gotcha." Clothing was a good thing when it came to his hairy stick legs. I set my purse on my desk, trying to pretend Tiffany being in the office with me wasn't a big, sweaty-palm deal.

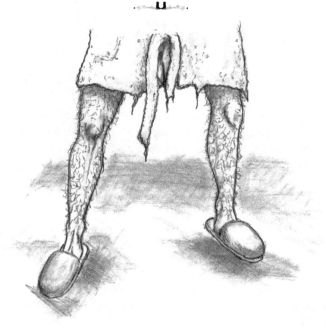

She rounded Ben's desk, leaning back against it with her arms crossed. "I hope you don't mind if I take him to breakfast."

"Cornelius is a free soul. Have at it." I wished her luck. His eclectic preferences in food made feeding him an adventure.

"I have a property I think he might be interested in seeing."

Of course! Now it made sense. I lowered into my seat, turning on my computer, straightening my pens. "Wonderful." I pretended her trying to steal Cornelius away from me didn't make me want to stick her head in a toilet and give her a swirlee. "Is it haunted?"

She leaned her head back and let out a loud, fake laugh. "You're such a riot, Violet."

She didn't know the half of it. She should have seen me yesterday with Detective Hawke and Prudence.

"It's not haunted," she said, her lips set in a smug smile.

"So, you're showing him a property that is ghost-free?" At her nod, I smiled back just as smug. She really needed to spend more time learning her prospective customers' tastes before she tried stealing them from other agents.

"It's a newer structure with a lot of potential."

"It sounds right up his alley," I lied. "I'll keep my fingers crossed it works out for both of you."

"I'd rather you kept your legs crossed," she said quietly.

So quietly, in fact, that for a moment I thought I'd imagined it. "What was that?"

"You heard me." Her teeth seemed to have grown longer, pointier, in the last few seconds, matching her claws. "Ray Underhill filled me in on your little strategy. Don't you think using sex is archaic?"

"Using sex for what?" I wanted her to spell out what she was accusing me of to make sure we were on the same page.

"Making sales."

Uh, hadn't she just done that with Jeff? Rather than point out the irony in her accusing me of using sex for gain, I shrugged. "Ray was pulling your leg." That no-good, lousy, stinking, rotten son of a bitch. "I haven't used sex to ensure any sales."

"What do you call Doc?"

Damned Ray and his stupid, fat bucket mouth. I lifted my chin. "I call Doc plenty of things, including my boyfriend." I also called him a god of sex, but that was only in my head when he finished taking me to the moon and back.

"I'm referring to the sordid arrangement you two had when he was shopping for a house."

We'd had a sordid arrangement? I must have missed out on that at the time in between worrying about Addy getting kidnapped and fighting for my life in a clown-filled haunted house.

"I don't know what you're talking about, Tiffany, or what sort of tales Ray spun for you, but Doc buying his house from me had nothing to do with sex." At least, I didn't think it did. Who would buy a house in exchange for sex? I mean, I was pretty good in the sack, but not thirty-year-loan worthy. "I was only his real estate agent at that time."

"Please, Violet. I saw the way you were looking at him the day I ran into you two at that house east of town."

The day she'd slapped Doc in front of me? How had I been looking at him? I remembered being shocked at the realization that Tiffany and he had shared more than a mere agent–client contract, but not much else.

"And the way you were dressed." From her wrinkled nose, I apparently had failed on the fashion front that day.

"Tiffany, I don't know what you're talking about." That was a teeny-tiny fib. I did remember trying to look good for Doc, hoping to land a compliment. My cheeks warmed at how pathetic and desperate I must have appeared to both Doc and her, but I held her stare.

"Two can play this game of yours," she said.

I was pretty sure she wasn't talking about Twister. "I'm not playing any game with you," I told her. "Jerry paid for that billboard ad without even telling me what he was up to. That's all. End of story."

"I'm no blonde, Violet."

Years of being on the receiving end of blond jokes had me extra sensitive to even the slightest derogatory remark about my hair color versus intelligence. "Obviously not, Tiffany," I said between clenched teeth.

"You think you're so cute with your curves and curls, but we all know the truth about you."

To which truth was she referring? That I used to stuff my bra with toilet paper back in junior high school? That I liked to gorge on peanut butter fudge ice cream and Humphrey Bogart movies? That I'd once had a sex dream guest-starring Captain Kirk *and* Dr. McCoy? That I channeled mentally unstable ghosts? That I'd killed not once or twice, but three times so far? That according to the rumor mill I'd murdered Ms. Wolff, too? That Detective Hawke thought I was a true-blue witch minus the flying monkeys?

My list of knuckle-chewing truths would soon be longer than Santa's "Nice" list at the rate I was going.

Rather than appear interested in her attempt to set me on edge, I gave her a bored stare. "My dad used to tell me that the truth will catch up to you every time, so there's no use running from it."

"I'm better than you," she said. "And I'll prove it."

Were we still talking about sex or did she mean better at real estate? I met her challenging stare head-on. "Good luck trying."

The back door opened. The tap of hard-soled shoes on the wooden floor broke up our silent standoff.

"Violet." Cornelius joined us. "I thought I could smell you."

Tiffany giggled, batting her lashes at Cornelius. "What does she smell like? Desperation?"

He stroked his pointy goatee. "Is that one of those fancy new perfumes?"

Tiffany wrinkled her upper lip at me. "No, it's a tired old one for Violet."

I picked up my stapler and threw it at her huge, inflated red head … in my fantasy. In reality, I pasted a smile on my face, holding her in my sights in case I decided to really take aim. "You two have a fun breakfast." *I hope you choke on your curds and whey, Little Miss Strumpet.*

"Would you like to join us?" Cornelius asked, something in his cornflower blue eyes urging me to agree. "We could share a can of sardines with toast."

I recoiled at the image of a small can full of oily little fish. "As appealing as that sounds, I'll have to pass. I have some paperwork to prepare for a couple of new clients." Speaking of fish, my smile widened to match the Cheshire cat's. "It's amazing how one little billboard can hook so many big fish, isn't it, Tiffany?"

Her sneer made her look quite ugly under all of that perfectly applied makeup. "I'll see you around, Violet. Probably with another one of your clients on my arm."

To demonstrate her point, she held her arm out for Cornelius to take.

He grimaced down at it as if it were crawling with bedbugs. Warily, he reached out and straightened her sweater sleeve so the seam was a long straight line. "There, that's better." He tipped his stovepipe hat at me and strolled out the back door, leaving a dumbfounded Tiffany to stumble after him.

I flipped off her back with both middle fingers. I would have flipped her off with my middle toes, too, but I had yet to be able to control those shorter digits. Practice, practice, practice.

Cornelius didn't return for the rest of the morning. I tried not to let Tiffany's client-napping attempt eat at me, but I did try to make Ray's fat gloating head blow up with my laser glare when he showed up to work right before I excused myself for my lunch date with Doc. With Jerry sitting in the same room, hating the horse's ass to death was all I could do before walking out the door with my chin lifted high.

The sight of the Picklemobile parked two stalls down from my Honda smoothed some of my bent tail feathers. As soon as I closed Doc's back door behind me, I bowed under the weight of my vexations, my silly anxieties about death, destruction, and dickhead Realtors making my chest tight. I panted and huffed as I stared down at my boots like I'd sprinted around the block twice before stepping inside.

Jeez-Louise! It was hard enough fighting off the monsters in my nightmares. Why couldn't I have my daytime hours free of back-stabbing bastards and sharp-toothed bitches?

"Did you come to huff and puff and blow my house down?" Doc's voice made me look up. He leaned one shoulder against the wall at the other end of the hall, his dark gaze raking over me.

I took a moment to soak him up. His black dress pants were topped by a dark red shirt rolled up at the sleeves, as if he'd had his hands buried in papers all morning. His tie hung loose, his top two buttons undone. His hair looked wavier than usual, like he'd run his fingers through it instead of a comb.

"Blow your house down?" I stood up straight, smoothing my suede skirt down over my hips. Fuck Tiffany and Ray and the rest of the world in general. I had Doc. Life was good. "Nah. I came to blow you ..." I pursed my lips and made a kiss sound, adding in a throaty voice, "... a kiss."

He waved me to come closer. "Bring me those lips."

I pushed away from the door. "Which do you prefer for lunch today, Mr. Nyce?" I licked my lips as I bridged the distance between us. "Do you want to melt in my mouth or in my hand?"

"You're such a tease, vixen." He unbuttoned my coat and slid it off my shoulders, tossing it behind him onto his desk chair. Then he grabbed me by the scarf hanging down each side of my neck, his knuckles brushing down the front of my satin shirt as he pulled me against him. "Let's start with your sweet mouth."

I went up on my toes and met him halfway, sliding my arms around his neck. He tasted like hot chocolate, giving me wicked ideas about whipped cream.

What started as a playful kiss grew heated within a couple of breaths. His hands grew bolder, along with his tongue, both teasing me with skilled touches.

"I miss your bed," he whispered between kisses. "Mine doesn't smell like you in the middle of the night when I wake up looking for something to warm me up."

"Spend the night after the poker game." I scraped my nails down his shirt, imagining his bare skin under my fingertips.

He groaned, his hands spanning my hips, fitting me tighter against him. "I can't."

"Why not?"

His lips trailed down the side of my neck, his tongue tickling me deep down inside. "There's no room at the inn."

I tipped my head to the side to give him more access to my skin. "There's the couch." After everyone went to bed, we could scratch this itch he was firing up inside of me while we were under Aunt Zoe's big quilt.

He chuckled under his breath. "That couch is a modern-day version of the rack, with springs instead of spikes."

"What if I promise to massage your sore spots all night?" I slid my hand over the front of his pants, giving him a demonstration of my rubdown abilities.

He reached down and stilled my hand. "Boots."

"What, Doc?"

Tugging on my hand, he pulled me into the front room. He pointed at my purple boots that were sitting on his desk next to a steaming to-go cup—that must be the hot chocolate.

"Boots, Tish. Put them on."

I grinned. "I thought you were joking about that."

"I don't joke about you and these boots." He crossed his arms. "I'm waiting."

I looked back and forth between him and my boots. "You want me to put them on right now?"

He nodded, glancing at his watch. "How long do you have for lunch?"

"An hour-ish."

"That should do. Get naked."

I took off my scarf and started unbuttoning my shirt. "Aren't you going to help me?"

"I want to rip that shirt off, not unbutton it. It's probably best I stick to watching."

"What else would you like to watch?" I asked, taking my time with the buttons to warm him up even more.

His Adam's apple bobbed. "You're playing dirty. I like it."

I paused with a couple of buttons to go, giving him a peek of my black satin bra through the shirt opening. "Maybe I should play hard to get to punish you for calling me a cheater this morning."

He knocked my hands aside and took care of the last two buttons in one swift sweep. "Don't even try it, woman." His gaze darkened as he pulled my shirt open, taking his time inspecting my chest. "Is this new?" He skimmed his fingers over the black satin cups, barely missing the mark.

"Yes." I sucked in a breath when his fingers skimmed over my bra again, this time right on target. "I thought you might like it."

His eyes lifted, searing mine. "Matching panties?"

Yes, but I hadn't bothered with the paper bag this time. I'd been too distracted by first Cooper and then Doc's bitchy ex. "I don't kiss and tell."

He hooked his finger in the center of my bra, pulling me toward him. "I bet I can make you."

I started unbuttoning his shirt. "Make me what?"

"Make you kiss …" he sank his hands into my hair, tipping my mouth up. I closed my eyes, waiting for him to dominate me, make me submit.

His lips brushed mine, touching me lightly, pulling back every time I tried to deepen the kiss. "And tell," he whispered in between seducing my mouth.

I clung to his shirtsleeves. "Doc."

His palms slid along my ribs, his thumbs grazing the underside of my breasts. "Tell me."

I slid my hands around his neck, pulling his mouth down to mine. I kissed him the way I wanted to be kissed, hard and almost bruising, showing no mercy as I slid my tongue along his. When I pulled back, he was breathing fast, too.

"There," I said. "I kissed you."

One dark brow lifted. "Matching panties or not? Tell me."

I took his hand and slid it down the inside of my waistline. "See if you can figure it out without peeking."

His eyes held mine as his hand slid further south, his intent smoldering in their dark depths.

I moaned in anticipation, my knees getting loosey-goosey. My grip on his shoulders tightened. His skin burned under the layer of cotton.

His fingers …

Someone knocked on his front door.

We both looked at the door, neither making a sound.

The knocking came again, faster and louder, longer in duration. "I know you're in there, Violet," Cornelius called. "I need to inform you of a change in status."

His voice was like ice in my matching underwear. Doc must have felt the arctic blast, because he pulled his hand free of my skirt and started buttoning his shirt.

I made a face at the door. "I'm busy," I yelled back, not willing to concede and button my own shirt yet. I walked over to the door, opening it a crack and peering out at my daytime roommate. "If this is about buying a piece of property from Tiffany, we can talk about it later."

His black brows drew together over his round sunglasses. "Tiffany?" He drawled out her name as if it were a new word in his vocabulary.

"Sugarbell," I said. When that didn't appear to hit home with him, I added, "The red-haired Realtor you went to breakfast with this morning." The one with whom he'd also possibly had a nooner if Tiffany had followed through on her threat to even the score.

"I know who she is, Violet."

"Then why are you looking at me like I'm speaking another language?"

"Because I cannot fathom why you'd think I would be buying anything from her, let alone property."

"She said she was showing you—"

"Violet." Doc's voice behind me cut me off. Before I could turn to see what he wanted, he pulled me aside, pointing at my open shirt.

I scowled, but buttoned up. Talking about Doc's ex was not how I'd planned to spend my lunch hour, dammit.

"Violet will be available in a minute," Doc said through a slightly wider crack.

"I'm glad you're here, Tall Medium," I heard Cornelius reply.

"Why's that?"

"I believe there's a hellhole next door."

"A hellhole?" Doc let out a small guffaw. "What are you—"

"It's in Calamity Jane's basement," I explained, fastening the last button on my shirt.

Doc's eyes were wide when he turned my way. "And when were you planning to share this dandy piece of news with me?"

"Probably after …" I glanced down at his pants. "You know."

"You were saving that for an encore?" He opened the door wider for our visitor to join us inside, frowning at me. "You and I really need to spend some time working on our communication skills in this relationship."

"You're one to talk." I jammed my hands on my hips. "Weren't you supposed to be showing me something just now?"

A grin crept onto his face. "I was about to, Boots, but then your visitor arrived."

"I wasn't talking about *that*, wise guy. I meant something from a certain history book. And FYI—Cornelius is *our* visitor, not just mine."

Cornelius closed the door behind him. "We need your help with the hellhole," he told Doc, interrupting any further discussion on Ms. Wolff, my family history scrapbook, and Doc and my relationship.

"Why do you need my help?" Doc asked him.

"Your ability to open doors into another realm might aid Violet in locating the source of the moans and periodic screams I detected last night with my EVP recorder."

Chapter Sixteen

I had an idea, but nobody liked it.

Not Aunt Zoe, not Natalie, and especially not Doc.

I hadn't told Cooper, so he had no clue what I was cooking up and I hoped to keep it that way for now. The damned detective had his nose in way too much of my business as it was.

Harvey, however, thought the idea had potential. He was more than happy to join me, although his enthusiasm wavered after I made him promise he wouldn't shoot anyone in the ass with Bessie, not even with rock salt.

"We need help," I told Aunt Zoe that evening, still trying to sell my idea to her.

"I agree, but not *his* help," she shot back. "And I don't care if Harvey agrees with you."

Natalie and I had joined Aunt Zoe out in her glass workshop after the supper dishes were cleared. Doc, Reid, Harvey, and Cooper were settling in for their weekly card game when we'd grabbed our coats and headed out back. Before I'd escaped through the back door, though, Doc had made me swear to join him for a private discussion in the Picklemobile later to finish what we'd started at lunch. Unfortunately, he wasn't talking about checking out my matching underwear, but rather discussing Ms. Wolff and my family history book or that damned hellhole, maybe both.

Earlier in Doc's office, Jerry had called me, interrupting our lunchtime chat about mysterious moaners and screamers. That darn billboard had worked its magic again, hooking another fish. Apparently, the night before, Jerry had arranged a post–lunch meeting with the potential client and forgotten to tell me about it. We needed to leave ASAP, which I did, giving Doc a quick kiss and making Cornelius a promise to listen to his recording when I returned.

Unfortunately (or maybe it was a good thing), Abe Jr. had been absent when we'd returned from the meeting. Listening to the racket going on inside of Calamity Jane's walls in the middle of the night would have to wait for another day. And since the Picklemobile had been missing from the parking lot upon my return to work, sex would have to wait, too. However, eating Aunt Zoe's sweet lemon meringue pie had not needed to wait, so I'd gobbled up an extra helping after supper to cheer up my dejected libido.

Now that I was sugar-sedated and my hormones had settled down for the night, I could focus on selling the idea I'd come up with on the way home from work.

"Come on, Aunt Zoe. What harm can come from just talking to him?"

"Plenty," she said.

"How about if I arrange it so the meeting takes place in public, somewhere like Bighorn Billy's?"

"Violet, don't you get it?" She pointed the pencil at me that she'd been using to sketch a potential design for another holiday piece. "Dominick Masterson is not your friend. He is a foe. His kind and yours are like chalk and cheese."

"But what if …" I started only to stop and frown. Chalk and cheese? "You mean we're both soft and porous?"

Natalie chuckled, leaning her hip against Aunt Zoe's worktable. "I think she means you're soft in the brain and growing more stinky by the day, while Dominick is mildly abrasive with a longer shelf life."

I grabbed Aunt Zoe's graphite glass reamer tool and aimed it at Natalie. "Call me stinky again, you bellybutton lint licker, and I'll shove this far enough up your ying-yang to tickle your tonsils."

"Please, Miss Cootie Queen. You really should have paid more attention in Anatomy 101." She snatched the reamer out of my hand. "Besides, you'd have to catch me first, and we both know that sloths run faster than you, especially after you've doubled up on dessert."

I stuck my tongue out at her.

"My point is," Aunt Zoe interjected. "You need to be careful around Masterson. He may not like he's on your side, but never forget that when the dust settles you are a threat to his existence."

She echoed what Doc had said earlier when I greeted him at the front door with my bright idea, only he'd also complained about Masterson using his slick charm to disarm me.

"I got it. Dominick is dangerous and I shouldn't turn my back on him, but what if he can give us answers that will save my ass?"

"Vi, honey," Natalie said. "I don't think there's a person alive that could give you that answer." She reached out and patted my butt. "This cute little derriere is one huge trouble-magnet."

"Keep it up, bucket mouth, and I'll sit on you with my huge magnet." I looked back at Aunt Zoe. "Aren't you even curious what Dominick can offer?"

"Not at the cost you're proposing," Aunt Zoe said, her face creased with frown lines. "It's too risky."

"I could ask Prudence for advice. She might have battled a *lidérc* before."

Natalie scoffed. "Prudence will kick you in the teeth just for asking, and then take a few choppers for her grotesque collection."

"Or ..." I crossed my arms, standing my ground. "She'll help me."

"No, Violet." Aunt Zoe's voice grew stern. "A *lidérc* is nothing to toy with and you know it. Even the more experienced executioners in our family line have avoided tangling with them."

"Doc was right." Natalie hopped up on Aunt Zoe's worktable. "You'd be making a potentially deadly deal with a devil. A very handsome devil, mind you, with a sexy-as-hell ass, long mouthwatering legs, broad shoulders ..." she trailed off with a starry-eyed look on her face.

I snorted. "You really need to get laid, horn-dog." Cooper's lousy flirting attempts seemed to have revved up her sex drive, leaving me to have to deal with a wacky nympho.

She shook off whatever fantasy had interfered with her train of thought. "But a trickster, nonetheless. Dominick is bad news. Hot and tempting bad news." She leaned back, resting on her palms. "Hey, maybe I should talk to him for you."

And have me risk being on the receiving end of Cooper's jealous wrath? I didn't think so. I was in enough trouble with the growly detective these days.

"No way. You'd stumble all over your tongue and then slip and fall in your own pool of drool." I turned to Aunt Zoe. "I'm running out of time here. The DNA results won't take forever. We need to think outside the box."

Her blue eyes narrowed. "Outside of the box doesn't have to include fraternizing with the enemy."

"You know as well as I do that nothing in this world is black and white."

"Violet, you don't know how to kill a *lidérc*, let alone capture one. Trading information on a timekeeper in exchange for capturing a *lidérc* is hardly even-steven."

"I'm not going to jail for something I didn't do."

She shook her head, refusing to give an inch.

"How about if I read up on how to catch a *lidérc*?"

"You? Read words?" Natalie guffawed. "Don't buy her snake oil, Zoe."

"Read what?" Aunt Zoe said. "If you'd taken the time to look at our family history book like I've asked you to many, many times, you'd know that the last executioner who tried to catch a *lidérc* went down in flames."

According to Layne, the executioner had actually jumped off a cliff, which would be better than burning to death.

"You're not going to bend on this, are you?" I asked.

She stood, facing off with me. "My job is to keep you alive to fight another day."

"Well, it's going to be pretty damned hard to fight while I'm rotting away in a jail cell, isn't it?"

Aunt Zoe sighed. "Come here, kiddo." I inched closer, wary. She grabbed me and pulled me into her arms, hugging me tight like when I was a little girl. She smelled like lemons and the chai tea she was drinking, homey and safe. "I don't want to fight with you about this," she said over my shoulder. "But I'm afraid you don't understand who and what you're dealing with here."

I rested my forehead on her shoulder. "You're right, I don't. But how will I ever learn if I don't stick my neck out now and then?"

"Fine." She pushed me back, scowling at me. "Call Dominick and arrange a meeting."

"Okay."

"But I'm coming with you."

"Deal," I said, relieved at the idea of her there to keep me from turning this into one of my grand fuckups. Plus, I knew Doc would be less ticked at me when he heard Aunt Zoe was going to be there to keep an eye on Dominick.

She sat back down in her chair, picking up her pencil again.

"Are you sure you don't want me to go along?" Natalie asked, swinging her legs. "I could try to seduce answers out of him, save you from having to stick your neck out."

"You need to seek counseling," I said.

"Or just have sex."

I shrugged. "I'm sure we could find some poor sucker to take the plunge." There was an easy target sitting about one hundred feet away at the moment, probably getting his ass handed to him by Doc at the poker table once again.

"Violet! You're supposed to help me stay strong and avoid men."

"Please, I'm only one person. That job would take a whole team of highly trained Special Forces men and women."

"I'm serious," she said, hopping off the table. "I want to stay strong for a year. While these last few months have been a little lonely at times, I've enjoyed not having to worry about how I look or compromise about my choices. And I've really loved not guarding my heart. It's been stomped on by one too many cheating bastards. Being single is so freeing. Now I know why you stayed away from men so long."

Uh, my staying away from men had nothing to do with any of the items she'd listed. Two children had been a surefire man-deterrent comparable to mace until Doc came along.

"I know what you mean," Aunt Zoe told Natalie, her focus on her paper. "Relationships take too much out of a person. That being said, I wouldn't mind a little friction now and then." She looked up and winked at Natalie. "If you know what I mean."

Natalie moved over to the back door, frowning out the window toward the house. "Yeah, I definitely do."

* * *

Long after the kids had gone to bed and Natalie had driven off, I sat in the front seat of the Picklemobile next to Doc. We were parked in Aunt Zoe's drive, which was as far as Cooper would allow me to range off the leash.

The pickup idled smooth and quiet, a testament to Doc's abilities under the hood and a new muffler. When I was driving the old girl around, she liked to belch and hiccup and sputter, backfiring every time I turned her off.

I adjusted the vent, warming my hands in front of the heat. "Who won the game?" I asked.

"Harvey."

"Seriously?"

"That old boy's a shark. He plays the going-senile angle, but I'm beginning to suspect he spent a lot of time in Vegas. He took all of Cooper's stash and half of Reid's and mine."

"Damn. I'm getting heated up with the wrong man tonight."

He chuckled, patting the middle of the bench seat. "Come here and warm me up, Killer."

I scooted over, settling into his side. The cab was heating up quickly, so I unzipped Aunt Zoe's quilted red vest. "This would be more romantic if we weren't sitting in my aunt's driveway."

"I'll take what I can get right now."

"I offered the couch, remember?"

"I'm not that desperate yet." He draped his arm over my shoulders, his fingers stroking me through my sweater sleeve.

I rested my palm on his thigh, feeling his muscles under his jeans. "We could steam up your windows for a while."

"That's not going to cut it. I've taken enough cold showers since you started your little game of seduction last July, Vixen."

"*My* game? All I did was stare at you like a love-struck groupie." Something Tiffany had confirmed earlier this afternoon. "You're the one who took advantage."

He laughed. "Oh, that is rich, considering all of the times you undressed me with your eyes."

My cheeks warmed, Tiffany's earlier words still stinging me hours later, damn it. "Doc, if I ask you something, will you give me an honest answer?"

His fingers stilled. "Sure."

I turned and looked up at him. "Do you remember that day I was showing you that house east of town and Tiffany showed up?"

"The day she slapped me?"

"Yeah." I lowered my gaze, playing with my zipper for a second or two, trying to form my words so I didn't sound pathetic. "Was it super obvious that I'd dressed to impress you?"

"You mean like a professional Realtor?"

I focused out the windshield, glad that the glow of the dashboard lights didn't show how red my cheeks must have been right then. "No."

He was quiet a moment. "I remember you said you were having trouble sleeping."

"I think I was dealing with nightmares because of the Hessler house." Between the stress of trying to sell it fast to save my job and the creepy clown décor, I was doing a lot of tossing and turning at night. Maybe that was after I'd heard the closing doors in the empty house, too, I wasn't certain.

"I picked on you about your red eyes and wild hair, which you'd left loose that day."

"That's right. Then after we left, we had a conversation about you not wanting to sleep with your Realtor."

His fingers began to stroke my arm again. "You said you weren't going to have sex with me."

"I had good intentions at the time.."

"I didn't."

"What do you mean?"

"I wanted to have sex with you."

"Even then?"

"I've told you before, Violet. From the day you tripped over my box of books, I wanted you. I knew hiring you as my agent was a mistake because I wanted you in my bed, but I couldn't resist."

"So you didn't think I was some sad, desperate single mom trying to entice you into my bed that day with the way I looked?"

"Sad and desperate? No. A single mom? Yes. Addy had made that clear to me by then, along with an eclectic list of your favorite things."

"I wanted to duct tape her big mouth shut."

His body shook with silent laughter. "I thought she was funny." He stilled, quiet for a few breaths. "I found the fact that you were able to successfully juggle kids and a career sexy as hell."

"I was dropping the ball a lot at that point on both fronts."

"From my viewpoint, you were a smart, competent woman with killer curves I itched to run my hands over, incredible hair that smelled like peaches, and lips that filled my head with wild fantasies day and night. Encouraging you to date Hessler made me take to the bottle many a night."

I captured his fingers and kissed them. "I wanted you to be jealous, but you seemed so unperturbed about me dating him."

"What could I do? I figured you deserved a normal guy, not some freak who faced off with ghosts on a daily basis. I thought that maybe I could settle for a flirty friendship between us, but then there was that kiss." He blew out a breath. "It knocked me for a loop. If Mona hadn't interrupted us, I would have taken you right then and there."

I laced my fingers through his. "Thank you."

"For what?"

"Wanting me when I was at a low point in my life."

"You've had me lassoed since day one, Boots." He kissed my temple. "What made you ask about that day in the house?"

"Something Tiffany said."

He sighed. "She's grasping at straws."

"Yeah."

"Don't let her see you bleed."

"I'll try not."

"I'm in love with you, Violet."

Tears filled my eyes. I blinked them away, swallowing the lump of emotion that filled my throat. Now was not the time to turn into a blubbering baby. Doc had just given me something more wonderful than any piece of jewelry or other expensive trinket. Something to treasure and hold close to my heart.

He cleared his throat meaningfully. "Now would be a nice time for you to reciprocate with your feelings for me, you know."

Grinning, I turned in the seat, wrapping my arms around his neck. I stared up at him in the semi-darkness. The scent of his cologne filled me with a deep hunger for so much more than kisses in a pickup cab.

"Doc?" I said, my expression dead serious.

"Yes?"

"I think you're really swell."

He let out a bark of laughter, and then leaned down so his forehead touched mine. "I'm going to make you pay for that one."

"If you say so, loverboy." I pulled his mouth down, taking my time kissing him. The windows needed a little steam to help block out the world, and by the time I'd finished showing him how crazy I was for him, we had his driver's side window mostly fogged over.

"Holy hell, Boots," he said when I pulled free and sat upright. He shifted in his seat, adjusting. "You have the most amazing mouth."

"That's just a little something to remind you of what you're missing by not sleeping with me on the rack tonight."

He shook his head as if to clear it. "You make it hard to say no."

"As long as I make it hard," I said, tongue in cheek.

He reached for me again, but I dodged his hand.

"Seriously, Doc. If you're not going to spend the night, we need to stop, or I'm going to crawl on your lap and make your horn honk."

His teeth glowed in the dash lights. "Is that what the kids are calling it these days?"

It was my turn to laugh. I wrapped his arm around me again, settling back against him. "Now, why did you ask me out to your pickup tonight, Mr. Nyce?"

He pulled me closer, toying with a strand of my hair. "Tell me about this hellhole."

"Didn't Cornelius fill you in after I left?"

"He played the recording from his EVP. He told me he suspects the sounds are coming from a hole in the basement, but before I could ask what made him think that, he got a call from his contractor and had to go to the hotel immediately."

I told him what I knew about the so-called hellhole, explaining that I figured it was more likely some sort of underground tunnel between buildings or a part of the sewer system.

"Did it smell?"

"No. Well, it had the usual musty sort of smell you'd expect."

"Hmmm. Did you hear anything coming from it?"

"No, but I'm a dud."

"Not really."

"Yeah, but sort of."

"You're more like a complicated, hot paranormal mess." When I frowned up at him, he added, "Which is the exact description of my dream girl."

Smiling, I kissed the underside of his jaw. "What are you doing tomorrow at lunch, Gomez?"

"I'm spending it with … a distracting blonde. Which reminds me, we need to talk about what I read in your family history book."

Oh, right. That was the original reason for our lunch date turned sex romp turned paranormal club meeting turned nothing.

"Do we really need to talk about that now?" I pulled his hand over so it rested on my breast. "Wouldn't you rather touch my soft parts?"

"Always, but first tell me what's going on with you and that book." His hand stayed put.

"What do you mean?"

"You avoid having anything to do with it."

I pondered that for several seconds. "I guess it scares me."

"Why's that?"

"It's too real. Every one of those women suffered the same fate as me—their lives were turned upside down due to a genetic anomaly. They had to learn to kill or be killed. There was no middle ground." I covered his hand with mine, holding him close as I explored my feelings about the stories of my ancestors who had come and gone. "The monsters they fought aren't just fictional beasts in any old book. They are real. Potential enemies I may have to face myself someday. They have the ability to do horrific deeds. Caly taught me that lesson. Their mission will be to either torture or kill me, or both." I leaned my head against his shoulder. "Do you have any idea how terrifying that is? How much I already worry for my kids? Any one of those creatures could come looking for me or Addy or Layne at any time. I won't know when or where, it'll just show up one day, ready to kill."

"But don't you want to know about those enemies before they arrive, weapon in hand?"

"To what end? According to Aunt Zoe, whatever methods the other executioners used to kill each foe won't work for me."

"You don't know that for certain and neither does Zoe."

"Maybe not, but one thing I do know is that what's on those pages will give me nightmares. Correction, give me *more* nightmares." I shuddered. "Last night, I scared my daughter so much with my screaming that she went to find you for help, but you weren't there so she grabbed Cooper instead. Addy was trembling when I lured her out from behind Cooper. A scared little rabbit. I did that to her."

"Violet, don't," he said, but I kept going.

"If I read that book, my mind will use what I read as fodder for new nightmares starring those creatures. I have absolutely no doubt about that, and since I can't stay awake 24/7, they will be there waiting for me when I slip into dreamland with their sharp teeth, glowing eyes, and who knows what else."

"Okay, Tiger." He kissed the top of my head.

"Besides." I smiled up at him. "You like to read about weird stuff like this. Why should I take that pleasure away from you?"

He traced the side of my face, ending at my neck. "Fine, I'll be your eyes on this front, but I'll need to share things from it that pertain to current events sometimes."

"All right. When that's necessary, I'll read or listen or look as directed. We'll be a team."

"You'll have to be forthcoming with me about everything you see and experience."

"Does that mean I have a new excuse to talk to you every day?"

"You've never needed an excuse." He leaned forward and brushed his mouth over mine. "Now, are you ready to hear about what I read?"

I leaned my head back against his shoulder, closing my eyes. "Let me hear it."

"A couple of centuries ago, one of the executioners worked with what your aunt Zoe or someone else translated as a keeper of the clocks."

"You mean a timekeeper?"

"The German word on the page was *der Zeitnehmer.*"

"Zite-namer?" I repeated, pronouncing it by sound. Maybe I should learn some German if I was going to keep at this gig. Or not. Hell, most days I had enough trouble with speaking plain old English.

"I'm guessing a 'timekeeper' is another name for the individual." Doc shifted slightly, his hand sliding down to my ribs, pulling me closer.

"So what happened?"

"The executioner wanted to go back in time to stop an event that had already happened."

"What event?" I asked, my eyes still closed.

"That's not important. What matters is that she found a timekeeper willing to help her return to the past."

"She traveled back in time?" I wondered how the timekeeper had done that. Did it have something to do with moving the clock hands?

"Sort of, but the way it was described was more like she stepped into another plane of existence, one where the timeline runs parallel to this realm."

I tried to picture parallel timelines, but struggled. How did that work? Was there someone named Violet living this life in another plane? Did she have her shit together more than I did? Did she have an equivalent to Doc, Addy, and Layne?

"Did the executioner fix what she'd gone back to change?"

"Yes." There was something in his tone that didn't settle well.

I opened my eyes, staring out the windshield at the front of Aunt Zoe's house, the only place I really felt safe. "There's a 'but' in there, though. What happened?"

"The executioner apparently died while in the other plane," he said quietly.

Did that mean her body was stuck over there, or was this just a mind thing? I didn't get all of this "realm" and "plane" crapola.

"How did she die?" I asked.

"Well, the problem with dying in another plane is that the person in the current timeline really doesn't have a way of knowing the cause of death. The author wrote that the executioner didn't return. It was assumed that she must have died."

I thought about that for a bit. Was she alone when she died? Did she realize she would leave her loved ones with questions and worries? With no closure? "What did she fix?"

"It turned out that fixing that problem changed the present for the worse."

I heard Prudence's voice in my head saying, *Time can be a tricky devil.* "Worse how?"

He hesitated. "Would it do any good to tell you the point I'm making is that messing around with timekeepers can result in death? We need to be careful if we go back to Ms. Wolff's apartment. There may be some doors in there that might be better left closed."

I sat up and frowned at him in the darkness. "Doc, what was the event the executioner was trying to stop from happening by going to the other plane?"

Even in the thick shadows, I could see the tension lining his face. "During a battle to save her family, her husband was kidnapped and murdered. His body was left outside of her door." He sighed. "In pieces."

Oh, God! My chest tightened with a bolt of fear, making breathing hard. I forced myself to take several slow, deep breaths until the restricted feeling eased.

"How did the executioner going to the other plane make the present situation worse?"

He took my hand, squeezing it. "Don't you think her dying was bad enough?"

"I don't know. That depends. Why do I have the feeling there's something you're not telling me? Some part of the tale you're leaving out?"

"The timekeeper warned her of the potential dangers," he continued, not answering me. "If we're going to try to go back and figure out what happened to Ms. Wolff, we need to consider—"

"How was it worse, Doc?" I interrupted. What in the hell was he leaving out? "I'm not going to drop this, so you might as well answer me."

He nodded slowly. "Okay. Her husband lived."

"So, he lived but she died?"

"Yes." He used his sleeve to clear a circle of fog from his window, peering out into the darkness.

That was sad, but the way Doc was acting made it clear there was more. "What else?" I pressed.

He looked at me, shadows adding hard edges to his frown. "Three of their four children were kidnapped."

"Oh no!" I covered my mouth, afraid of where this was heading.

"They were returned the next day." His voice lowered to a whisper. "In a basket. More pieces." He took my hand in both of his. "Violet, we have to be *very* careful dabbling with timelines."

Chapter Seventeen

Thursday, December 6th

A pounding noise woke me in the early morning darkness.
I sat up on the couch where I'd fallen asleep to *Rooster Cogburn*, letting John Wayne soothe my anxieties about the monsters roaming the outside world, lying in wait for me.

I rubbed my eyes. The television was hissing, the screen filled with ants running around in the snow. At least that was what Addy always called it. I frowned at the screen. That was weird. What happened to the Old West channel? The cable must have gone out.

Someone was pounding on the front door, making me jump. Who would be knocking on the door this early? Doc? Harvey? Reid? Had one of them forgotten something after the card game?

I stumbled toward the door in my bare feet, my slippers nowhere to be found. Huh. I tied my sweater tighter around me. I could swear I was wearing my slippers around the house last night before I settled in on the couch.

Moonlight blared through the half circle of glass at the top of the door, painting the foyer floor with half of a glowing wagon wheel. I hit the porch light and pulled the curtain aside, trying to see who had come calling so late.

The porch was empty.

I unlocked the door. It creaked open, the hinges complaining more than usual. A dusting of snow covered the porch. Through the screen door, I admired what looked like tiny, sparkling ice diamonds in the snow. The air smelled so fresh it burned the back of my throat.

A cloud covered the moon. The wind kicked up, rattling the bare branches of Aunt Zoe's big cottonwood tree out front. Cold air seeped in, curling around my bare feet.

"Hello?" I called into the shadowy night.

The wind whistled in answer.

Odd. I could have sworn I'd heard someone knock. I started to shut the door, but the sound of paper flapping stopped me.

What was that?

There was something sitting on the sidewalk at the base of the porch steps. I pressed my nose against the glass-top section of the storm door again, squinting out into the darkness. It looked like a wicker laundry basket. The kind with a lid on the top, like one of those big baskets that Marion hid inside of at the Cairo market in *Raiders of the Lost Ark*.

I needed a flashlight to be certain. I checked my sweater pocket for my cell phone, but it must have fallen out while I was asleep.

Bracing myself for the cold, I pushed open the screen door and tiptoed out onto the porch. I searched the yard, seeing nobody. There weren't even footprints in the snow. What the hell? Did the stork leave me another baby? I sure as hell hoped not. Raising two kids was turning me into an old lady well before my time.

I tiptoed down the porch steps, the snow freezing my feet. As I hit the last step, the wind kicked up, blowing my hair in front of my face. I pushed it aside, frowning down at the waist-high basket. The lid had a sprinkling of snow covering it like it had been sitting there for a while. A piece of paper fluttered against the wicker handle in the wind, making the flapping sound I'd heard earlier.

I caught the paper, tearing it free of the rope tying it to the basket. In the glow of the porch light, I read a word that still made me cringe: *Scharfrichter*. The thick dark ink had dripped, running down from the *S* and the *f* and the *t*.

Wadding up the paper, I stuffed it in my pocket. This game of sending me anonymous gifts needed to end. I crossed my arms, shivering as I stared down at the basket. What in the world had my mysterious Secret Santa sent me this time? The basket was big enough to hold a machine gun.

The snow and wind stopped all of a sudden, the silence growing cotton-thick in the dark world.

I grabbed the handle and lifted the lid as the moon peeked out from behind a cloud.

A whiff of rotting meat made me gasp. I gagged and slammed the lid back down before I could see what was inside.

What the hell?

The basket wobbled back and forth on the sidewalk and then toppled over, landing on its side in the snowy yard. The impact knocked the lid off, and a hand tumbled out onto the moonlit snow.

A small hand with child-sized fingers reaching up into the air.

I cried out, taking several steps back and tripped on the porch step. I came down hard on my ass, jarring my teeth.

As I sat staring at the hand, a strong wind came up suddenly, whistling past. It caught the basket and rocked it back and forth on the lawn in front of me.

A head tumbled out.

"Oh, my God!" I covered my mouth.

The moonlight grew stronger. I stared at the thing, my mind trying to make sense of the horror. Silvery blond hair whipped back and forth around the head. I caught a glimpse of wide sightless eyes and a face I knew too well.

Addy!

I screamed.

And screamed.

And screamed.

"Violet!" a man's voice shouted in the darkness.

I kept screaming, shaking so hard my neck felt like it would snap at any moment.

"Dammit, Parker! Wake up!"

Silence!

I opened my eyes. Cooper's furrowed face filled my vision.

"Cooper?" I whispered. My throat felt raw. So did my heart.

"You had another nightmare." He let go of my shoulders and stepped back.

I looked around, taking in Aunt Zoe's living room, the couch, the old quilt, the black and white western on the television, the blinking Christmas lights in the windows. Only a nightmare.

"Fuck," I breathed, covering my face. My cheeks were wet with tears. I fell back onto the couch, my whole body quaking.

"Are you okay?" he asked.

"No."

"You want some coffee? Or do you want to go back to sleep?"

I lowered my hands, drying my tears on Aunt Zoe's quilt. "There's no way I'm going back to sleep."

With a single nod, he walked away, his footfalls heading into the kitchen. I lay there, trying to chase the shocking image of my baby girl's head from my brain. This sort of shit was exactly why I didn't want to read that damned book. One story about an executioner dying and my asshole brain turned it into my kid being torn apart and left at my door.

By the time Cooper returned a few minutes later, I was sitting up, staring blankly at big Chuck Connors and his handy rifle as he played the part of Lucas McCain in *The Rifleman*. Maybe if I had a rifle like Lucas's, I would sleep better at night. Or I could just borrow Harvey's old shotgun, not that bullets would really keep my predators at bay.

"Here," Cooper said, holding out a mug for me to take. Steam rose from it.

"What is it? Hemlock?" I sniffed it, smelling vanilla and something else, maybe chai.

"Not quite. Zoe's bottle of poison was empty."

Hold the phone! Had Cooper made a joke? Was this another nightmare? I breathed in more steam, trying to soothe my throat, which still felt scratchy from screaming. "An empty poison bottle makes me worry about Reid."

His cheek twitched as if a smile were trying to push to the surface on one side. "It's some sort of tea. I didn't read the box. Move your feet." After I scooted aside, he dropped onto the other end of the couch.

"What are you doing?" I asked, frowning at him. The light from the television flickered over his face. From the side, his profile looked even more like granite than usual, rough hewn and cracked.

"What I agreed to do," he answered.

"What does that mean?"

He stared at the TV. "I lost at poker tonight."

"I heard." Unsure of what that had to do with his sitting on the couch with me, I sipped from my tea. The chai taste was subtle, the vanilla more of a smell than flavor.

"Your boyfriend and my uncle offered to give me back some of my money in return for a promise."

"Did you pinkie swear with them?"

His smile breached the surface this time, but only for a second or two. "Shut up, Parker."

"You really need to get better poker karma. What did you promise?"

"That I'd babysit you if you had another nightmare."

I sighed, feeling loved by two of my favorite boys. "That was sweet of them."

"Real sweet. They're both big suckers." He joked again.

Dang, he was in rare form tonight. I pinched my arm, making sure this wasn't a dream. "You're the one who lost at cards," I reminded him.

"That makes me a loser, not a sucker."

We sat there for a short while, watching *The Rifleman* together.

When a commercial came on, I looked over at him. "You can go back to bed, Cooper." I pointed at the television. "I have big, strong Chuck Connors and his fancy rifle to keep me safe."

He didn't budge, just rubbed his neck and watched the TV. "McCain's rifle isn't *fancy*, Parker. It's a modified Winchester model 1892. He has it rigged to fire when the lever is closed after a round has been chambered. This allows him to rapid fire without having to depress the trigger. It's a *badass* rifle. If McCain heard you call it fancy, he'd fill you full of lead."

I scoffed, setting my tea on the end table next to me. "Lucas McCain is a gentleman, Cooper. He'd never shoot a lady. If he heard me call his gun fancy, he'd just give me one of those handsome grins and ask me over to make supper for him and his boy."

"Maybe, but then he'd taste your crappy cooking and figure you for a villain out to poison him. He'd drag you back to town and have Marshal Torrance throw you in jail." He looked over at me with a shit-eating grin. "Right where you belong."

"You're a butthead." I took one of the couch pillows and threw it at him.

He caught it, laughing, and tossed it back. "And you're a pain in the ass."

The show started up again, snagging our attention.

I sipped at my tea, my muscles relaxing. The clarity of my nightmare lost most of its sharpness.

During the next commercial break, Cooper glanced my way. "What was it about this time?"

"What was what about?"

"The nightmare."

I finished the last swallow of tea and set the cup on the stand. "Aren't you cold?" I asked instead of answering.

He was wearing the same outfit as last night—sweatpants with bare feet and a bare chest. I, on the other hand, had my thick sweater wrapped around my flannel pajamas and a thick pair of socks. My slippers were on the floor below.

"A little," he admitted.

"Get under the quilt."

He frowned. "You're using it."

"It's a king-sized quilt, Cooper. I only need it for my legs and feet."

He hesitated.

"I promise I don't have cooties. Just use the other end."

He still resisted but I kicked the quilt his way. After he was mostly covered, I focused back on the TV. Some loud spokesman was trying to sell me a shower seat. As soon as I felt like I could talk without getting choked up, I told him about the nightmare.

When I finished, he blew out a breath. "Jesus, Parker. That's some fucked-up shit."

"Tell me about it."

"And this stemmed from what?"

I told him then about my family book and what Doc had told me, the story of the executioner and her family's tragedy.

He leaned his head back, staring up at the ceiling. "Damn. Here I thought cops had cornered the market on night terrors. You could write horror stories for a living."

"I'd rather stick to real estate."

"Have you thought about seeking counseling for these nightmares?"

I guffawed. "And tell a shrink what? That I'm an executioner and need help dealing with the mental side effects that come from facing off with monsters for a living?"

"You can't keep going like this. It's going to make you even more of a nut job than you are normally."

I wrinkled my nose at him. "Funny guy. You're on a roll tonight." Curling my legs tighter against me, I turned back to the television. "The nightmares had backed down again until this last week. Something is spurring them, and I need to figure out what before I have to start sleeping in the basement with Elvis to keep from waking everyone up."

"You'll make that chicken's heart pop with your shrieking."

"Maybe if we solve Ms. Wolff's murd—"

He snorted. "At the rate things are going, that's a big *if.*"

"Well, I can hope, can't I?"

"I suppose."

"Otherwise, I don't know what to do."

He shifted, angling more into the corner of the couch. "You could try sleeping pills."

"What if I get stuck in a nightmare because of them and can't wake up?"

He shook his head. "Jesus."

He'd already said that.

Another episode of *The Rifleman* started up, the rifle blasts comforting. I smiled. I must be hanging around Harvey too much if gun noises were working as a lullaby.

We watched the show, sinking into a comfortable silence again. I glanced over when the show came to an end. Cooper's head was tipped to the side, his eyes closed. I could see the blanket rising and falling over his chest in regular intervals.

I drew my phone from my sweater pocket and checked the time. Good, I had a few hours left until it was time to get up. Setting the alarm, I placed it on the end table. After turning the TV volume down, I settled into my corner of the couch. My eyes grew heavy after a while, and then darkness fell upon me again.

* * *

I didn't have any more bad dreams the rest of the morning at home, but I did run into a nightmare at work.

Rex Conner was sitting on the corner of my desk when I walked through Calamity Jane's back door. I skidded to a stop at the sight of my piece-of-shit ex in his swanky, tan wool overcoat and posh leather shoes. His blond hair looked freshly trimmed and styled, like he was ready for one of Jerry's billboard ads minus the stupid pencil in his mouth.

What kind of fresh version of Hell was this?

Since Jerry was leaning back in his chair, shooting the breeze with the son of a bitch, I had to pretend I didn't want to bash Rex's teeth in as I passed.

Hey! That gave me an idea for my debt to Prudence.

Then again, I might want to keep Rex's tooth for my own trophy case. I could take it out once in a while, polish it, and smile at the memory of how I'd acquired it.

I started to pull out my desk drawer when a thought made me pause. Trophies! Was that how Prudence's tooth fetish had started? Had she taken one from a longtime enemy? A hard-earned prize for the victor? A memento to remind her how fiercely she'd fought for her life and come out the winner? If that were the case, it was no wonder she'd been pissed that I'd taken her box of teeth. Those teeth were all she had to remind her of a profession about which she was still pompously proud, of a livelihood that had not only ended her life, but her family's, too.

That wasn't saying her need for trophy teeth hadn't gotten out of hand. But to give her some credit, if I had to rattle around an old house in Lead for over a century with nothing but time to think about what had been, I might wander just this side of the Deranged state line myself.

"Hello, Mr. Conner," I said, stowing my purse in my desk drawer. "Is there something you need from me?" Like a whack upside the head with my keyboard if he didn't remove his ass cheeks from my desk?

"Good morning, Violet," he said, his golden-brown gaze traveling down over my black textured sweater, leggings, and leather boots. "You're looking quite sophisticated this morning." His eyes lingered on my chest. "It's a shame I'm here for Mona instead of you."

Yeah, a real boo-fucking-hoo.

I looked pointedly at where he sat.

He raised his dark blond eyebrows, taunting me.

I turned to Jerry, who was watching us with a thoughtful pinch to his forehead. "Where is Mona?" I asked.

"She's on her way. Mr. Conner stopped by a little early."

"I had some errands to run before our appointment and finished sooner than I'd figured," Rex explained.

Bullshit. I'd bet Cooper's Colt .45 bedside lamp the jerk had stopped by ahead of time in hopes of catching me alone. Thank God Jerry had arrived before me.

The sound of the toilet flushing followed by running water made me groan inwardly. Oh, no. I shot a worried glance toward the back door. Please don't let that be …

Ray stepped out of the bathroom, fastening his belt. He joined our little Hadean breakfast club, his stupid sneer front and center. I balled my fist. Maybe I'd collect two teeth today for Prudence.

The horse's ass sized me up, his opinion of my outfit less than flattering judging by his wrinkled lip. "Did you stop by a funeral on the way into work, Blon …" he stopped, shooting a frown in Jerry's direction. "Violet," he finished.

I didn't bother with an answer and walked over to the coffee maker. Thankfully, I had an appointment with Rosy and the home inspector to walk through Cooper's house this morning. All I needed to do was show face here for a bit longer and then I could skip out, claiming I was meeting Rosy early for a pre-inspection brunch. Was nine o'clock too early to call it "brunch"? Better yet, I could say I was taking her out for coffee.

I returned to my desk, firing hate lasers from my eyes at my ex's blond head as soon as I was clear of Jerry's watchful gaze. I longed to grab Rex by the tie and string him up, demanding that he remove himself from my neighbor's bed or I'd cut off his balls.

Back in my chair, I turned away from where Rex lounged. Ray joined the chat session, sharing old war stories about college. Periodically, I could feel Rex's eyes on me. Being so close to the creep, along with having to smell his favorite cedar and cardamom cologne, made my skin crawl.

Ten minutes later, I gathered several papers I might need today and searched for my stapler. Where the heck was it? I liked to keep it close by in case I wanted to throw it at someone, mostly just Ray.

Rex glanced at me, his lids narrowing for a moment, and then he turned back to Jerry. When he shifted on my desk, making himself even more comfortable, I caught a glimpse of my stapler under the hem of his coat. Fishing it out, I stapled the papers. I started to set the stapler down and hesitated, my gaze darting from Rex's lavish coat to his name-brand leather gloves folded together neatly on my desk.

The temptation was too great to resist. While he wasn't looking, I reached over and stapled one of his gloves to his coat, managing to squeeze off three staples before he turned to look at me again.

I snarled at him, because smiling would have been a dead giveaway that I was up to something. His return smirk tempted me to staple his lips together next, but I resisted since I was already courting jail time for a murder I didn't commit.

Tucking the papers into my tote, I locked my computer and grabbed my purse. "Jerry," I said, giving Rex a wide berth. "I need to go meet my buyer early. I'm taking her out for coffee before we head over to the house for the inspection."

He gave me a thumbs-up. "Go get 'em, Champ!" I was surprised he didn't want to high-five me as I passed by.

I was halfway to my Honda when I heard the sound of Calamity Jane's back door closing.

"Violet," Rex called out from behind me.

I looked to the sky. "Father Odin, protector of the Nine Realms, help me to be strong against my freaking ex." I heard the sound of Rex's expensive shoes hitting the asphalt behind me. "And if you're feeling extra generous, grant me Thor's hammer to smash the jerk to smithereens."

Rex called my name again.

With Jerry not in attendance, I didn't have to be nice. "Go away, Rex," I said over my shoulder and kept walking, picking up the pace. If I could just make it to my car before …

He reached my door as I was pulling it closed, blocking it. "I need to talk to you."

I imagined planting my boot in his chest and sending him flying in a Jackie Chan–style kick. "We have nothing to discuss. Now move." I tried to shut the door on him, but he wasn't having it, no matter how hard I shoved at him.

"Damn it, Violet. Would you just stop pushing and hear me out?"

"Why should I?"

"Because you don't want me to talk to Addy and Layne the next time they're out building a snowman."

He had me there. I stilled, loathing him point-blank. "What?"

He straightened his coat, the glove I'd stapled to the hem hanging limp. "When did you start sleeping with that cop?"

My loathing turned to confusion. "What cop?"

"The shirtless one I saw out on your aunt's front porch yesterday morning."

Cooper was out on the porch without his shirt on? Crikey! Was he part polar bear? And why would Rex think … oh, duh. I thought about correcting him on who was sleeping with whom, but if Rex thought Cooper was sharing my bed, he might be more likely to back off rather than risk pissing off a cop.

"What business is it of yours?" I asked.

"He's covered with scars." He said it as if scars were only a small step away from full-on leprosy.

"Were you watching from Ms. Geary's bed with binoculars or a telescope?"

"Neither."

"Liar." Although to give him credit, Cooper was pretty scarred up.

"I thought you were screwing the guy who drives the Camaro."

I wasn't going to have this conversation with him of all people. "What do you want, Rex?"

His jaw dropped with a bit too much drama, if you asked me. "Are you having sex with both of them?"

Oh Lordy. Did he have any idea how juvenile he sounded? I didn't understand his obsession with who frequented my vagina. It wasn't like he'd unpacked his bags and stayed for long when I'd let him have a room at the inn. He'd spent a short time and then headed off to screw my sister's brains out, leaving me with two big "tips" I was still raising.

"Rex, my sex life is not a topic we are going to discuss. *Ever*. Now, what do you want? I have a job to do. Unlike you, I have two children to support."

His lips flatlined. "How long are you going to keep throwing that in my face?"

"Probably until I jam a stake through your heart."

"You're so passionate, Violet. It's a real turn-on. Now I get the black outfit." He leaned closer, his grin leering.

Those perfect white teeth so close to my face made my neck bristle. I resisted the urge to go "Prudence" on his choppers and knock one loose. Instead, I grabbed the glove I'd stapled to his coat. "Oh, look. You have something stuck to your coat." I tore it free.

"Hey!" He snatched the glove from me, frowning at the tear in the leather. "These are expensive gloves."

"More expensive than your coat?" I asked, pointing at the hole the staple had torn in the wool.

When he looked up from the rip, his nostrils were flared. "You ruined my coat!"

"I didn't realize there were staples involved. That's an odd way to keep from losing your gloves."

"You bitch," he snarled.

I lifted my chin. "Keep your nose out of my fucking business, Rex, or I'll ruin more than your damned coat."

"Fine, but you need to quit calling me at work."

"I don't know what you're talking about."

"Bullshit. You're trying to ruin my credibility and get me kicked off this research team to get me to leave town, right?"

Say what now? Why hadn't I thought of trying that? "Would that work?" I asked.

"No. I'm the lead, so I decide who stays and who goes."

"Damn."

"So this game of sending close-up pictures of female body parts to me at the lab needs to stop."

Naked body parts? That wasn't my style. I preferred blunt force trauma as a means of coercion.

I stuck my keys in the ignition. "It sounds like you have a stalker, Rex. I'm happy to report it's not me. Now step back a hair so I can try to not-so-accidentally run over your toes before I drive away."

"If it's not you, then who? Natalie?"

I highly doubted it. Natalie's preferences for revenge tended to focus more on prized possessions, like his Jaguar. For example, a baseball bat to the windshield or maybe a dead animal in the trunk. "Nat's too busy working to send you porn."

He crossed his arms. "I don't trust you, Violet."

"Excellent. The feeling is mutual." I reached out the door and shoved at his chest.

He allowed me to push him back this time. "I'm keeping my eye on you."

"Keep your eye on this." I held up my middle finger in his face. Cranking up the engine with the other hand, I warned, "Step one foot in Aunt Zoe's yard and I'll have the whole Deadwood police force up your ass so fast and hard that you'll be walking bowlegged for months."

I slammed the door and backed out of the lot, trading glares with the whoremongering bastard until I drove away.

On the way up to Cooper's place, I swung by the coffee shop in Lead and grabbed two drinks, remembering Rosy's favorite was a mocha with a shot of hazelnut syrup. After spending several weeks with her filming me for a reality series, we'd become fast friends. Then she'd hired me to help her buy Cooper's place and the rest was history in the making.

I let myself inside Cooper's house, dropping onto the black leather couch. I had about twenty minutes to spare, so I pulled out my phone and punched up Dominick Masterson's number, hitting Call before I could chicken out.

He answered promptly. "Violet. To what do I owe this honor?" His deep purring voice compelled me to pull my phone away from my ear and scowl down at it.

Doc was right. The guy was greasy with charm. I held the phone back to my ear. "I want to meet to discuss a possible deal."

"Fascinating. I've not made a deal with an executioner before."

That sort of surprised me. I'd figured him for an experienced, shifty devil. "Are you available tomorrow morning?"

"That depends."

I wanted to drop the kids off at school first. "How about nine at Bighorn Billy's?"

"Wouldn't you rather join me for dinner?"

No. I doubt I'd be able to eat with him sitting so close to me. He must not realize that my proximity to him set off my "other" being alarm, making my stomach buck. That detail would be prudent to remember for future safety's sake. If my enemy had no idea I was onto his true identity, it gave me a leg up.

"Dinner won't work for me," I said. "Breakfast will, though."

There was a long pause. Then he chuckled. "Breakfast it is. Don't be late. I have a schedule to keep."

"I won't."

"I look forward to hearing your offer, Executioner."

Why did he have to make it sound like sex would be on the table? Had he been chatting with Rex about my social life? "Splendid. I'll see you tomorrow."

I hung up before he could try to play any games with me. Dominick couldn't be trusted, but that didn't mean we couldn't help each other out now and then when the need arose. After this latest nightmare, my need was stronger than ever. I had to clear my name and remove this stress from my life. As it was, I was dreading going to sleep tonight, petrified of what dirty tricks Mr. Sandman would play on me once my eyes closed.

With time to kill, I walked around Cooper's place, tidying and dusting here and there. Rosy was due to arrive in ten minutes when my phone rang. I pulled it out, figuring it was her telling me she would be late.

Cooper's name was on the screen instead. I frowned. What were the chances he'd call when I was standing inside his house? Did he have hidden cameras? Was he watching me from his office right now?

I answered while searching the ceiling corners. "I swear I'm not anywhere near your locked basement room."

"What?" he snapped. That one word was so loaded with tension I was amazed my phone didn't short-circuit.

Dang. Here I'd hoped that sharing several episodes of *The Rifleman* in the middle of the night would warm him up for at least a day or two. "Never mind. What's going on?"

"I should be asking you that question."

"If this is about me being in your house, I have a legitimate excuse. Rosy and the home inspector are coming today."

"I know that, Parker. You told me last night before I went to sleep— the first time."

Oh, right. I'd forgotten. Between my nightmare and my confrontation with Rex, I was sort of sidetracked from the mundane. "So why are you snarling at me through the phone?"

"Where in the hell are you?"

"I told you, I'm at your house."

"Then why does the cell phone tracking software say you're in Nevada?"

"Nevada?"

"Do you need me to spell the word for you?"

"Don't bother. Spelling was never my strong suit."

"God, you are so not funny right now."

He needed to chill. "Cooper, I'm not in the Silver State."

"I fucking know that," he barked.

"You're not making any sense, Cooper."

"I'm not making sense?!" he shouted back.

Before he could howl at me anymore, I hit the disconnect button. "Stop yelling in my ear," I told my phone.

Seconds later, my phone rang again. I let it ring five times. "Are you going to be nice to me now?" I asked upon answering.

I heard a growl come through the line. Boy, oh boy, my favorite lawman was positively bristling. It's a good thing we had several big hills between us.

"You dicked with your phone," he said. "Didn't you?"

I heard the sound of a passing diesel engine. Was he standing outside? "I didn't do anything to your stupid tracking dealio, Cooper."

Natalie had, but he'd have to get me in a room down at the station under a bright, hot light to get me to admit that.

"Here's the thing, Parker. Whoever fucked with your phone screwed you royally."

"Why's that?"

"Because Detective Hawke is the one who checked on your location this morning and found that you'd relocated to Nevada."

"Shit."

"Bingo. I just got out of a meeting in which my ass was repeatedly reamed for not keeping a closer eye on you."

"Come on. We shared a couch, for crissake. It's just some glitch with the tracking software." I needed to get hold of Natalie and find out what she had done to my phone and change it back.

"I know that and you know that, but Hawke isn't so certain. And thanks in part to your recent witchy-witch game up at the Carhart house, he doesn't trust me to act as your guardian anymore."

"Oh, no."

"Oh, yes."

"What happens now?" I asked.

He sighed so hard I swear I felt the breeze from it clear up in Lead. "As soon as you finish with the home inspection, get your ass down here. And don't even think about dressing in costume this time."

I gulped. Down here? "You mean to the police station?"

"No, Parker, I mean 123 Sesame Street. Big Bird wants you to sing the fucking alphabet song with him."

"Oh, *now* you finally get a sense of humor, Cooper? It's a little late in the game."

He huffed several times, muttering several not very nice things about me. "Yes, I mean the damned Deadwood Police Station. Hawke and I will be here waiting for you."

The phone line went dead.

I keeled over after it.

Chapter Eighteen

Two hours later, I sat in an interrogation room down at the Deadwood Police Station under a bright, hot light.

"This is bullshit," I told my reflection in the two-way mirror.

"Yer hangin' the wrong cattle rustler," Harvey hollered, knocking on the glass. He came back over to the stainless steel table and eased down onto the chair next to me with a grunt. "I shoulda brought Bessie along."

"They wouldn't have let you in the front door."

He harrumphed and crossed his arms. "I'll tell ya what, if Coop doesn't get back in here soon, I'm gonna drain my lizard right in front of that fancy glass."

I recoiled. "Don't even think about it, old man." The room already stank like sweat and burnt hair. We didn't need to add the odor of urine to the overall bouquet.

"Tell that to my prostate. It's feelin' downright ornery so far this mornin'."

We waited in a shared annoyed silence. I glanced at my cell phone, checking the time every thirty seconds or so. Come on, some of us had jobs to return to before our bosses came looking for us. *Us* being only me, since Harvey was retired.

Before I'd left Lead, I'd texted Mona that I was going to be out for a while this afternoon taking care of some business, being as vague as I could so as not to rouse her suspicion.

Next, I'd called Harvey to let him know the home inspection was finished and he could return to Cooper's house whenever he wanted. He'd asked if I were interested in his making me some lunch quick before heading back to work. As tempting as his offer had sounded, I'd declined due to an anxiety-cramped stomach, telling him about my appointment with Cooper and Hawke. Then I'd asked if he knew what Natalie had done to my phone. I'd have asked her myself, but my calls were going straight to her voicemail today.

He didn't have a clue what dark magic she'd worked, and he decided right then and there without consulting me that I needed a bodyguard for my visit to the cop shop. When I told him that I doubted they'd let him get past the front desk officer, he bet me otherwise.

Now, ten bucks later, here we sat together in a torture cage inside the Deadwood Police Station.

"Thanks for coming along," I said, inspecting my cuticles.

"Ya didn't exactly give me much choice."

"What? I said you didn't need to come."

"You said one thing, but the quiverin' in yer voice said somethin' else." He elbowed me playfully. "We both know you could use a bodyguard for this kind of meetin'. Or at least a witness to vouch for your sweet buns when they charge you with assaultin' an officer."

"Leave my buns out of it." I frowned at him. "You think Hawke will try to get rough?"

"I'm more itchy about yer sharp teeth. Ya got a purty mean bite when you lock on. I should know."

"When have I ever bitten you?"

"I've asked you to remove your teeth from my hide plenty o' times."

"Your memory is playing tricks on you."

"My memory is fit as a fiddle. Just ask my poker-playin' pals. That reminds me, yer Romeo called while I was waitin' fer ya outside in the parkin' lot."

I'd phoned Doc before leaving Cooper's house, telling him what was going on in case I needed him to make bail for me … again. Although the last time, Cooper let me go free of charge. I doubted Hawke would be as generous once he got me locked up in the clinker.

Doc had told me he'd try to hurry up and finish early in Hill City, so he could be back here in case I needed him. When I told him Harvey was going to join me for my duet with Johnny Law, he said he'd stop by the bank and make sure he had enough cash to spring two jailbirds.

"What did Doc want?" I asked Harvey.

"He told me not to leave you alone with any cops."

"Was he worried I might bite one of them, too?"

"He reminded me there's a troublemaker on the police force who wants somethin' you have."

My mind flashed to the piece of paper someone had stuffed in my purse months ago when Cooper had thrown me in jail for an hour or so, the butthead. The words WE WANT WHAT BELONGS TO US had been scrawled on the paper, and the only place my purse had been all day before then, besides at my side, was in the evidence cage.

"Oh, God. I hadn't even thought about that." I'd been too worried about facing off with Detective Hawke.

"That's why you have Doc and me. We do yer thinkin' for ya."

That wasn't the only reason, especially when it came to *my* Romeo.

We sat for a few more minutes, making faces at each other in the mirror while we played what I figured was part of Detective Hawke's game of cat and mouse. He probably thought making us wait and wait and wait would make me more eager to talk, or at least more afraid of what he was going to do when he finally joined us. But he was wrong on both counts. I was just getting more pissed off.

"This is as ridiculous as pourin' water on a rusty wheel bearin'," Harvey said. "I'll give 'em two more shakes and then I'm gonna water the corner."

Thankfully, the door opened before Harvey got around to reaching for his zipper. Detective Hawke entered, followed by Cooper. Both men looked like ten miles of bad road, but Cooper at least still had his tie on straight.

"You shouldn't be here," Detective Hawke said to Harvey. He turned to Cooper. "Your uncle needs to leave."

"I already told him that." Cooper leaned against the two-way glass, his arms crossed.

"Then why is he still here?"

"He's part bull."

"What's the other part?" I asked.

"Mule."

I nodded. Cooper was spot-on there.

Hawke snorted. "You mean you can't control this old man?"

"Old man?" Harvey wrapped his thumbs around his rainbow suspenders, his chin jutting at Hawke. "Look at you, badge toter, puffed up like a pigeon in a bow tie and tux."

More like a turkey if he asked me. A turkey in a brown corduroy sports coat, striped shirt, baggy pants, and scuffed-up loafers. Sheesh, did he come straight from the set of *Barney Miller?*

"Yeah," I said. "We don't need no stinkin' badges to be tough."

Harvey grinned at me. "Been watching *Blazing Saddles* again?"

"I can't get Lili Von Shtupp singing 'I'm Tired' out of my head this morning."

"Did ya have another nightmare?"

I nodded, glancing at Cooper. A stab of guilt poked me at the exhaustion lining his face.

"See, Coop?" Hawke turned to his partner. "This is why your uncle has to go. He's distracting the suspect, especially with those god-awful suspenders."

"Oh, you're one to talk, Ralph Lauren," I said. "Did you choose that outfit in the dark?"

Harvey glared up at Hawke. I had a feeling he was imagining where he'd like to aim Bessie. "Coop, this fool ain't gonna last eight seconds on my back. Ya better round up the other rodeo clowns and get 'em ready to drag him out of the ring."

Hawke gave Harvey a beady-eyed glare. "That's it. Either you leave now of your own free will, or I'll have some of the boys drag you out of here."

I latched onto Harvey's arm. "Since this is an unofficial meeting that I agreed to attend, Harvey stays or I go."

"You won't be going anywhere if I handcuff you to the table," Hawke threatened, pulling a pair of cuffs from inside his blazer.

"Back it down a notch, Detective," Cooper said, his gaze bouncing between his partner and me. "It's not going to hurt anyone to have Uncle Willis in here with Parker. He'll be good." Cooper stared at his uncle. "Won't you?"

"As sure as a chicken has feathers." Harvey's gaze was still locked onto Hawke. "Now, we all know Violet didn't put a spider in Ms. Wolff's biscuit, so what's this roundup about?"

"I'll tell you what it's about." Hawke pointed his handcuffs at me. "Parker slipped her leash."

There were several things about that statement that fried my hiney. "I'm not your damned pet, Detective."

"You're a prime suspect in a murder case."

"I'm innocent until proven guilty."

"That's a formality we'll overcome as soon as the DNA evidence comes back from the lab, mark my words."

"Oh, no!" I overacted with a loud gasp. "Look how I shudder in fear at your words." I held my hands in the air, shaking them.

Honestly, my heart did race a little at his threat. So much hinged on a single strand of hair.

"You should, you witch."

I scoffed. "Are we going to resort to name-calling now? That's real mature. What is this, auditions for *Kindergarten Cop Two*? Is there a casting director hiding behind that two-way mirror?"

"Actually," Harvey said, scratching his beard. "I'm purdy sure there's already a second movie in that franchise."

I raised one eyebrow. Really? I didn't remember seeing it. "Is Schwarzenegger in it?"

"No. Dolph Lundgren took his place."

"Young Dolph or old Dolph?" I asked, remembering something about how intelligent Dolph was in real life. I could use a big strong genius like him to take on Mr. Black.

"The old one," Cooper said, rubbing his eyes. I couldn't tell if he was tired or frustrated. Probably both.

Harvey grunted. "But the big Swede still looks like a stack of bricks that'll make yer knees wobble."

" 'My name is Drago,' " I said in a fake Russian accent, stealing one of Lundgren's lines from *Rocky IV*. "Soon, the whole world will know me."

"Will know *my name*," Cooper corrected my quote, skipping the Russian accent.

"Ya know," Harvey said. "If we add a few inches to Coop, and about sixty pounds of bulk, we'd have us a Dolph Jr."

"That's enough!" Detective Hawke roared. A vein pulsed on his forehead. "This is a serious meeting. You two need to remember that or I'll lock you both—"

"Parker," Cooper interrupted Hawke. His voice had that hard, take-charge tone that usually made my neck bristle. "Where's your phone?"

I pulled it out of my purse.

"May I see it?"

He was actually asking for once? What a concept. I almost asked what the magic word was, but decided not to push my luck. I unlocked it and held it out to him.

He punched some buttons. His forehead wrinkled. "Whose number is this?" He held the phone out to me, showing me a telephone number starting with a 702 area code. "That's a Las Vegas area code," he added.

Vegas? I took the phone back and checked my contacts. "It's Cornelius's."

"According to our tracking software, he's in Goldwash, Nevada, right now."

"You're kidding. He was just at Doc's office with me yesterday." I hit the Call button.

Detective Hawke paced back and forth between us, periodically huffing in my direction.

Cornelius answered before it even rang on my end. "Who is this?" he asked.

"You know who it is, Cornelius." I'd recently made sure my name appeared on his phone's screen when I called so we'd stop having this stupid who's-who conversation. "Are you in Nevada?"

"Violet, your paranormal skills are growing at an incredible rate. Did you dream about me being here?"

Before I could answer, he added, "Or did you use remote viewing to see me?"

I opened my mouth, but he interrupted with, "Or was it mental projection?"

I gave him a second to add another option. When he didn't, I spoke up. "None of the above. Did you fly down to visit your friend who owns the haunted hotel again without telling anyone?"

Cornelius had called me before from Goldwash. Apparently, he had a friend who also ran a ghost-happy hotel down there.

"You're amazing!" he shouted loud enough for all four of us in the room to hear him.

Cooper rolled his eyes. Harvey snickered. I chose to ignore Hawke's derogatory remark about my character.

"Did you use telepathy to tap into my thoughts?" Cornelius asked. "Wait! Don't answer that. Tell me what I'm thinking right now."

"You're thinking that the next time you leave the state, you're going to let me know."

"Because your littermate believes I'm your boyfriend?" he asked in a whisper.

"Sure."

"Ah-ha! I knew it. Ever since the séance on Thanksgiving, our minds have been tethered."

Tethered to Cornelius? He'd sprain my brain within a day or two. "If you say so."

"Yes, it all makes sense now. This explains why I keep thinking about women's underwear."

Uh, no, it didn't.

"I have to go, Cornelius. I'll talk to you later." I hung up and set my phone on the table, wrinkling my nose at it. Sometimes I wondered about that man. "Cornelius has taken a trip south," I told both detectives, adding, "For some reason," probably having to do with Natalie's skilled fingers, I thought, "your fancy app is tracking him, not me."

"Way to go, Coop." Hawke jammed his hands on his hips. "You programmed in the wrong damned number."

Cooper's steely eyes nailed me to my chair. "Yeah. I guess I did. We'll have to fix that, won't we, Parker?"

"Or we could just rely on me checking in," I offered.

"She's not reliable." Hawke squished that notion flat. "She's a witch. She'll trick you."

I groaned. "Detective Hawke, how can you not see how absurd the whole idea of me being a witch is? This is not Salem, Massachusetts, in the 1690s."

"Then explain what happened up at that house."

"You mean the Carhart place?"

"Of course I mean the Carhart house! You did something to me up there."

"I didn't touch you."

"You messed with my head."

No, that was Prudence's doing. "Be reasonable, Detective. Do you really believe people have the power to get inside others' heads and dabble with their thoughts?"

I hadn't before Deadwood. Then I met Prudence and Wilda and Harvey's grandpappy, to name a few.

"Then explain why I'm having a recurring dream about getting my throat sliced open by men wearing burlap masks."

Harvey and I exchanged wide-eyed looks.

"I saw that!" Hawke said, rushing us. He leaned across the table, shoving his nose in my space. "What did you plant in my head, Parker? Did you use some kind of hypnosis?"

"I swear, Detective. I did nothing to you in that house." In fact, he was the one who'd slapped me ... with Prudence's help, of course.

"I don't believe you."

I doubt there was any way I'd ever convince him otherwise.

I focused on Cooper. "One has to wonder if the stress of this job is getting to your partner. Maybe the chief needs to put Detective Hawke on a mental health leave for a while."

"Oh, you wish I'd go away, don't you?" Hawke bit out. "But I'm not going anywhere. I'm your worst nightmare."

No. Last night's Fear-Fest starring Addy was currently my worst nightmare. Rather than correct Hawke on where he stood in my nightmare lineup, I tried to diffuse the tension swirling in the room with more trivia. "Who said that 'worst nightmare' line?" I asked Harvey. "Was it in a Batman movie?"

Harvey cocked his head to the side. "I think it was Rambo."

"This is all fun and games for you, Parker, but it's going to get very real very soon. When that DNA evidence comes back, I'll be knocking on your door with handcuffs ready to slap on you. You've managed to slip the law for the last time."

"I haven't been trying to slip the law, you dipshit." I knew provoking him was foolish, but a scrappy, hot-blooded woman could only take so much.

"You're a disease," he said, "and I'm the cure."

Harvey raised his hand. "I know that one! It was Sylvester Stallone in *Cobra*."

"Dang it!" I smiled through the anger making my cheeks warm. "You beat me to it. How about this one?" I focused on Hawke, squinting. "Go ahead, Detective Hawke, make my day." I might have been imitating Dirty Harry, scratchy voice and all, but I meant what I said.

A loud snort came from Harvey. "Ya have to at least make it a challenge, girlie."

Hawke slammed his fist on the steel table. The boom made Harvey and me both jump. "Stop fooling around!" His eye twitched as he scowled at me. "According to the lab, we'll have the DNA results within a week. If I were you, Parker, I'd get my papers in order, because you're going to go away for a long time after I'm through with you." A smug grin crept onto his face. "Your conviction is going to earn me one hell of a promotion."

What?! Was all of this shit about pinning the murder on me and locking me up so that he could climb a step on the career ladder? What a fucking egotistical prick. Prudence was right when she called him a … what was the word she'd used? Oh, yeah.

I stood to leave and delivered my exit line: "Whatever you say, snollyguster!"

Detective Hawke barked at me.

He actually barked—twice—with bared teeth, wrinkled lips, and all. German shepherds could have taken a lesson from him.

I blinked in surprise, leaning away from him. The back of my knees hit my chair, and I fell into it.

"What the planets?" Harvey's jaw hung low. "Is that line from *Rin Tin Tin*?"

Cooper came off the wall, exchanging raised brows with me.

"What?" Hawke looked from me to Harvey and back. "Why are you two staring at me like that?"

Son of a dog biscuit! He didn't realize he'd barked at me. I leaned forward and repeated, "Snollyguster."

He barked again, loud, spit flying in my direction.

I flinched, feeling like my hair had been blown back that time.

"Boy, howdy!" Harvey smacked his thigh. "You're a real law dog now."

"Detective Hawke." Cooper grabbed him by the shoulder. "Can I have a moment alone with Parker and my uncle?"

"Why?" Hawke's face turned beet red. "What's going on here? Why are you all looking at me like I'm some sort of mutant? She's the freak!" He pointed at me.

"Snollyguster," I shot back.

Hawke barked at Cooper, flinging spit in his face.

Cooper wiped away the spit with the back of his wrist and then glared at me. "Cool it, Parker."

"Tell him to quit calling me names."

"Hawke," Cooper said in a calming voice. "Remember what the chief said. Let's keep it professional here."

"Why do you need a minute alone with *her*?"

"Because you're being too aggressive with the suspect. I would like to soften her up about another idea for keeping tabs on her."

"I'm being aggressive? She's the one who—"

"Snollyguster!" Harvey cut him off this time.

Hawke barked again, spit sprinkling Cooper's tie.

"Goddammit, Uncle Willis!" He whirled on both of us. "You two sit there and keep your lips closed."

"What is going on?" Hawke's eyes darted all around. His right cheek twitched several times. "I feel weird." He rubbed his throat. "Why is my throat sore all of a sudden?" His beady gaze settled on me. "It's you! You're making me think I'm sick." He clung to Cooper's arm. "I told you she's a witch. She's put a hex on me."

I opened my mouth to use the magic word but Cooper nailed me with a laser glare. "Don't!" He turned back to Hawke. "Go get a drink of water. I'll finish this and see them both out."

Hawke nodded, holding his twitching cheek. "My face hurts. I'm gonna go sit down."

"Good idea."

He opened the door, turning to me once more with an angry glare. "You'd better find an ace attorney, Parker."

"Okay, snollyguster."

His barks echoed down the hallway.

Cooper slammed the door shut behind him. "What the fuck, Parker?"

I pointed at the cameras in two corners of the room.

He walked over to each, clicking them off. "Okay, now talk."

"Ya sure you don't want her to bark for treats like yer partner?" Harvey wheezed in laughter.

I tried to keep a straight face for Cooper's sake, but the memory of Hawke's rabid expression each time he barked made me burst out laughing.

It took a minute for the two of us to sober up. Cooper stood, arms crossed, waiting for us without even a hint of a smile. Apparently, this was the T-800 Terminator robot version of Detective Cooper, not the human one I'd watched *The Rifleman* with on the couch last night.

When I could speak again without giggling, I wiped the tears from my eyes and told Cooper and Harvey about Prudence using that word to describe Hawke. How she'd told me to use it when I needed a distraction.

"She must have planted that nugget in his melon while she was rattlin' around in there," Harvey said, his tone awed. He shot me a frown. "Did she plant anything in mine?"

"Not that I know of."

"I doubt there's much fertile land left inside your dried-up old brain," Cooper muttered.

"Yeah, well this ol' dried-up brain kicked yer ass at poker last night, boy, and don't ya forget it."

"Hell." Cooper plowed his fingers through his hair, leaving shark fins. "This nightmare just keeps getting worse."

Sort of like my nightly adventures.

"So," Cooper said, rubbing his jaw. "It appears that Prudence was able to plant a trigger word in Hawke's head as well as share her dying moment with him."

"Yep." I rested my forearms on the table, wondering if I'd ever be as talented as she was in this demon-killing business, even after her death. "She doesn't like lawmen."

"I'm picking up on that."

"And she was particularly disgusted with Detective Hawke and his infatuation with himself."

Cooper looked at me with a no-shit smirk. "I'm sure you weren't much help talking him up."

I shrugged. "It wouldn't matter what I said. Prudence has a low opinion of pretty much everyone, including me." Especially when it came to my inability to do my job well in her eyes. "So, now what do we do?"

"About what?" Cooper asked.

"Do you have to stay handcuffed to my side day and night? If so, sleeping on the couch is going to get old."

"You joke, but Hawke wanted to put an ankle bracelet on you and keep you under house arrest this morning."

"That boy's rudder is broken clean off," Harvey said. "Did you see how much he's twitchin'? Yer really rattlin' the heat now, girlie."

"It feels more like I'm 'battling' than 'rattling' the cops most of the time," I grumbled.

Cooper guffawed. "That's rich, Parker, coming from you. By the way, I have a message for Nyce that I need you to deliver."

"What?"

"His idea of paying another visit to Ms. Wolff's apartment is not going to happen."

"Why not?"

"Detective Hawke has taken up residence in the Galena House."

"Since when?"

"Last night. He's camping on Ms. Wolff's living room floor."

"Why?"

"Because he has a gut feeling you're going to break in and plant evidence that might keep your ass out of jail."

* * *

I warned Natalie not to come over that evening, but she didn't listen to me. Lucky for her, Cooper opted out of supper at Aunt Zoe's in lieu of packing up more of his stuff. After making me pinkie swear to stay home all evening and not give him any more headaches at work, he enlisted Doc's and Harvey's help, offering beer and pizza in exchange for muscles and pickups. He'd recently rented a storage unit to use until I found him a house.

I'd told Doc that I hoped I could find Cooper's dream home soon, because I wasn't sure the warden would let me sell real estate from prison. I laughed at my own joke. Doc didn't. The news that I'd delivered for Cooper about Ms. Wolff's apartment being occupied nightly hadn't gone over well, although Harvey's reenactment of Hawke's barking had smoothed the wrinkles from Doc's brow for a few minutes.

After a supper of Aunt Zoe's homemade butternut squash soup, grilled chicken breasts, and store-bought dinner rolls that Natalie picked up from the Piggly Wiggly on her way over, Natalie and I parked on the couch with the kids. They found a holiday special and we all snuggled together under the big quilt while visions of flying reindeer and unhappy toys filled the television.

Aunt Zoe had returned to her workshop after supper, finishing up an order for special ornaments for what she described as a winter wonderland–style wedding. The romantic in me imagined something akin to the red sparkly dresses and white faux-fur muffs from *White Christmas*.

Natalie grinned when I described it to her during a long set of commercials. "Let me guess, the bride and groom are singing 'Walking in a Winter Wonderland' as they ride off in a horse-drawn sleigh into the starry night."

"Wouldn't that be pretty?" I said, playing happy-ever-after in my mind with a certain dark-haired man, minus the singing part since I couldn't stay on key to save my life.

"You'd freeze your butt off and end up with pneumonia," Ms. Practical said.

"We could snuggle under a blanket."

"Yeah," Addy chimed in. "Like we are now." She burrowed into my side. "I'd ride in the sleigh with you, Mom."

I smiled and kissed the top of her head. That was sweet, but she wasn't part of this daydream, except for throwing rice at us as we rode away.

"The horses might poop on you," Layne added, sharing Natalie's outlook.

I frowned at him and then over his head at Natalie's smiling face. "You two are both pooping on my parade."

Addy reached over and tugged on Layne's ear. "Yeah, quit being such a mean boogerhead."

He slapped her arm away. "You're the boogerhead, brat."

"That's enough," I said, giving them *the look*. When they both settled down again, I leaned back into the couch cushions. I started up the winter wonderland fantasy again, moving on to a warm, white-sandy beach under the moonlight with a certain hot body leaning over me.

"I wonder," Addy started, and then hesitated, her little forehead pinched.

"You wonder what?" Natalie asked.

Addy glanced at me from under her lashes. "I wonder if Mom will ever get married."

"Why would she do *that*?" Layne asked.

"Because she's in love with Doc and that's what you do when you're in love, right, Natalie?"

A shadow passed over Natalie's features. "Not always, kiddo."

"Mom doesn't love Doc," Layne said, frowning at me. "You don't, do you?"

Before I could answer one way or another, Addy said, "She does, too. Why else would she let him come over for supper every night?"

"Cooper and Harvey come to supper all of the time," Layne said, a sneer pinching his face. "Does she love them, too?"

"Well," I started, but Natalie's laugh stopped me.

"Trust your aunt Nat, you two. Your mom is not in love with Detective Cooper." She lowered her voice and added, "She thinks he has mean cooties."

"His cooties are nice!" Addy told me, defending Cooper to me.

"But not as nice as Doc's," Natalie wiggled her eyebrows at me. "Right?"

"Everything about Doc is nice," I agreed.

"See," Addy told Layne. "She loves him. Now they'll get married and have babies."

I did a double take. "Say what now?" The thought of pregnancy made me feel like paying a visit to the porcelain goddess.

"They are not going to get married," Layne insisted. "Besides, Doc said he wouldn't marry her, remember?"

Whether Addy remembered or not, I sure as hell did.

"That's not what Doc said, you dork," Addy spat.

"I'm not a dork." Layne pulled his punch, giving me time to block it and keep them from an all-out brawl.

"Layne, what have I told you about hitting your sister?"

"But she keeps calling me names."

"Addy, enough with the name-calling. Treat your brother with love and kindness. 'Tis the freaking season for it, for Santa's sake."

"Fine, but Layne's wrong."

Natalie and I exchanged curious glances. "How is he wrong, Addy-bug?" Natalie asked.

"That's not exactly what Doc said."

I was all ears at that moment. Even my heart was eavesdropping from behind my uvula.

"What did he say?" Natalie pressed.

"He said that he wouldn't marry a woman unless her kids wanted him to marry their mom."

Oh!

Well.

Really?

Wait.

Did that mean he'd be willing to get married someday? That he wasn't allergic to wedding bells? That if I ever was brave enough to broach the subject of tying the knot he wouldn't run for the hills and never look back?

I looked down at my hands, wishing both were wrapped around shots of tequila right about now.

"Which means," Layne said in a pissy tone, "that he isn't going to marry Mom because we don't want her to marry him, remember?"

"We don't?" I asked.

"No." Layne looked up at me, his face set. "We're okay with you having a boyfriend, though."

It didn't take a sledgehammer to pound his feelings on the subject into my head. Doc was okay to have around for now, but not permanently. Got it.

"I don't know," Addy said.

"You don't know about what?" Natalie asked.

"About Doc."

"What don't you know about Doc?" I asked.

"Well, I really like him, but ..."

"But what?" If she said she liked Jeff Wymonds better, that was too freaking bad. There was no way in hell her mother was going to marry Jeff just so she could have her best friend as her sister.

"But what if he doesn't really like kids?"

"Why wouldn't he like kids?" I asked.

She shrugged. "I don't know. Because we fight a lot." She looked up at me. "What if he gets tired of us and wants to send us away?"

My heart panged at the worry filling her eyes. I pulled her close, kissing her head. "You're not going anywhere, baby. Remember, you promised to stay with me until I'm old, and I'm going to hold you to that." I looked up to find Layne watching us. "You, too, young man. I need you both forever. Nobody will ever EVER convince me to send you two away from me, understand?"

He nodded.

"Yes, Momma," Addy said, smiling up at me. "I really do like Doc a lot, though."

I messed her hair. "Me, too."

"I told him—"

"Shhhh," Layne cut her off. "The show's back on."

I wanted to hear what she'd told Doc, but apparently the conversation about my future as a married woman was over. Both kids' focus locked onto the television screen again.

Natalie looked at me over their heads, reaching along the back of the couch to squeeze my hand and offer a smile and wink.

I smiled and squeezed back, glad to have her tonight for company.

Later, after we put the kids to bed, I told her how the phone tracking conversation with Cooper had gone, including him knowing "someone" had messed with my phone. I suggested she head out before he came home and drilled us both with those steely eyes in between chewing on us with his serrated teeth.

She agreed, sliding on her coat. After a glance up the stairs she waved me to follow her outside on the front porch. "I have something to tell you and we don't need little ears listening in."

I grabbed Aunt Zoe's padded red vest again. My pea coat was in the laundry room, needing three new buttons sewed on—damned Elvis! I zipped the vest up to my neck and closed the front door behind me. Jack Frost had already gone to work sparkling up the place. The Christmas lights in the window added a happy glow to the dark night. The air smelled like wood smoke, making me want to hurry back into the warm house.

"What is it?" I jammed my hands in the vest pockets, wishing I'd thought to grab some gloves, too. "You want to weigh in on me getting married?"

She shook her head. "But if you don't choose me as your maid of honor, I'll shave your head the night before the ceremony."

I chuckled. "Deal. What's up?"

"Last night around two in the morning, I heard something again."

Galena House ghosts? Then I remembered Cooper's news. "I told you that Detective Hawke is staying down below you, remember?"

"It wasn't Hawke."

Her tone left no doubt about it. "What did you hear?"

"Music."

"What sort of music?"

"Old country stuff. Golden oldies like Hank Williams Sr. and Patsy Cline."

"Maybe it was Freesia or the other resident who lives there." I couldn't remember the old lady's name, but she made one helluva tasty sugar cookie.

"I figured you'd say that," Natalie said, "so I snuck out into the hall and went to each of their apartments, listening at the door." She looked toward the street for a moment before turning back to me. "It wasn't coming from the other apartments."

"You sure you weren't hearing it through the vents?"

"Positive." She leaned closer. "It was coming from the attic."

"How did you figure that out?"

"I went up there."

"Really? You're braver than me."

"That's not news, chickenshit." She dodged my jab, chuckling. "Come to find out Freesia has some antique furniture up there under sheets. Back in the corner there is one of those big old-fashioned radios with the dials and a light-up little window. It reminded me of the one my grandma had. Do you remember it? She kept it in her dining room."

"Yeah, she told me how her whole family would sit in front of it with popcorn and listen to weekly radio programs before they could afford one of those newfangled televisions."

"Exactly. It looked sort of like hers, only the glass over the dial wasn't fogged."

"So, you think someone went up in the attic and turned it on in the middle of the night?"

She frowned. "It was unplugged."

"No way."

"Yes way."

"Are you sure there weren't batteries inside?"

"Violet, I'm not an idiot. I checked the thing out. It's totally old school, batteries NOT included."

"So, it was playing golden oldies on its own?"

She nodded. "And here's the freaky part. I tried turning the dials, but the station stayed the same and the volume didn't change."

"What the hell?"

"But when I turned to leave, it clicked off."

Goosebumps peppered my skin. "Was it still lit up?"

"Nope. The whole thing went dark and silent, like it hadn't been cranking out tunes seconds before. I tried to turn it back on, even plugged it in, but it was dark and dead."

"Are you sure you hadn't imagined it?"

"I'm positive. There's only one explanation for it." She stuffed her hands in her coat pockets. "It's a haunted radio."

That sounded so corny, but I believed her. "Did you see anything unnatural before or after the radio went quiet?"

"No."

"Did you smell anything funny? Like rose water perfume or old shaving cream?" I remembered reading about paranormal investigators picking up on scents like those before their ghost meters went crazy.

"Nope, no weird smells, no moving sheets, no sounds."

"That's weird."

"Spooky, too."

"What did you do?"

"I got the hell out of there, raced back down to my apartment, and locked the door behind me."

"If it was a ghost, would a locked door matter?"

"Shush." She shuffled her feet. "The whole thing sort of reminded me of *Poltergeist*, you know?"

"But that was a television that turned on and off."

"I know that, but it was close enough." She shuddered. "It took me a while to fall asleep."

"I don't know that I could have."

"I kept the lights on in my place all night." She snorted. "I haven't done that since I was a kid."

"Do you want to sleep here tonight?"

"Where? On the couch again? No thanks. Those springs get more pokey by the day, I swear."

"Addy and I could squeeze you into my bed."

"No, you're having enough trouble sleeping as it is. Besides, I don't feel like facing off with Cooper tonight. I need more sleep to handle him."

"You could stay at Doc's," I suggested. "Or with Harvey in Cooper's house."

She shook her head, pulling her keys from her pocket. "I need to get back on the horse. If I don't fight my fears, I'll start wigging out at my own shadow."

"Okay, but if you change your mind, there's always Aunt Zoe's couch in her workshop."

"Thanks."

"For all you know, Nat, this might have been going on for years. Maybe old Jake Tender likes to listen to music in the middle of the night when he gets lonely. Next time, you should ask him for a dance."

"Maybe I will, smartass."

"Did you say anything to Freesia about it today?"

"Yeah, first thing this morning when I woke up. It seemed to be news to her."

"Did she know whose old radio that is?"

Natalie nodded. "She told me the furniture in that part of the attic all belonged to Ms. Wolff."

Chapter Nineteen

Friday, December 7th

Bighorn Billy's Diner was busier than I'd figured it would be for a weekday morning in December, especially considering the Black Hills hadn't been hit with enough snow yet for the serious snowmobilers and skiers to pour in.

Dolly Parton was singing "Jingle Bells" through the overhead speakers as the waitresses served up steaming plates of eggs, biscuits and gravy, pancakes, and several other drool-inspiring dishes. I was tempted to order something more than plain toast and scrambled eggs, spurred by the aroma of fried meat and carbohydrates filling the air, but I knew better. Dominick would undoubtedly set off my "troublemaker" radar as soon as he arrived, making me queasy. The last thing I wanted to do was hint at my innate alert system by throwing up in his lap. Not to mention how un-cool that would be as a representative of the Executioner clan. Prudence would surely take back my matching club jacket.

Aunt Zoe sat next to me in the booth seat, sipping on coffee as we waited for our breakfast guest before ordering. The soft scent of her lavender soap should have been calming along with her mellow personality this morning, but I had a fidgeting problem. I had come to realize this after she'd taken away the fork I'd been tapping on the table and then put a hand on my knee to still my bouncing leg.

"Thanks for letting me borrow your red vest again," I said, straightening my spoon next to my coffee cup.

"It looks good on you. Maybe you should keep it. I have plenty of other coats." She smirked. "The vest has no buttons for Elvis to rip off, so it should stay in good shape."

I growled under my breath, calling that chicken several unsavory names. Why couldn't my kid be happy with a gerbil?

"It could be worse," Zoe said, laughter in her tone. "Addy could be into snakes."

Speaking of snakes, I told her about Rex's shenanigans yesterday, something I'd completely forgotten thanks to my visit to the Deadwood Police Station.

Now it was her turn to growl and swear. "That boy doesn't know when to pull up stakes and ride off into the sunset, does he?"

"He has an odd obsession with my sex life. I don't get it. When I was in his bed, I wasn't enough."

"He wants what he can't have. Now you're a challenge."

While we were on the subject of obsessions and challenges, I asked, "What's going on with you and Reid?"

She stopped with her coffee midway to her mouth. "What kind of a question is that?"

"A perfectly normal one from a family member who loves you dearly."

With a sigh, she lowered her cup. "I'd rather not talk about it."

"And I'd rather hear an honest answer."

Her gaze narrowed. "What makes you think anything is going on with us?"

"You invited him over for supper and didn't once threaten to fill him full of holes." I drew invisible circles on the table. "One of those alone is enough to make me scratch my head, and when you put them together, it makes me curious if maybe you've recently received dire news about your health … or his."

She rolled her eyes. "You're being silly. I invited him over because I wanted to hear what he had to say about that incident on the Mickelson Trail. That's all there is to it."

"That's one hundred percent phony-baloney you're trying to sell me. You could've called him on the phone and asked."

"I wanted you to hear his answer, too."

"Oh, really?" Come on! Did she think I was born yesterday?

"Yes, really. Violet Lynn, quit looking at me like that."

There was no reason she couldn't have relayed the information to me and we both knew it. "I don't believe you."

She lifted her chin, tucking a strand of silver-streaked hair behind her ear. "Believe what you want. I told you my reasoning, so let's move on."

I wasn't ready to move on. "Man, you're so stubborn."

"I'm only stubborn on Friday mornings in December." She sipped her coffee and then asked, "Are you ready for your parents' visit tomorrow night?"

No. Not even a little. I'd been too busy being distracted with an accusation of murder by the local boys in blue. Well, Detective Hawke actually leaned more toward brown.

I sat back, scowling at my hands. "I'll go grocery shopping tonight and pick up what we need for dinner."

"That's not what I asked."

"I just wish they'd wait another month to meet Doc."

"Why? What will another month change? Isn't it better to get it out of the way?"

"Not really. It'd be better if I could choose the time and setting of this stupid meet and greet."

Her forehead furrowed as she looked at me. "What is it that has you so worried? Is it that they'll realize Doc has a sixth sense? If so, there are no ghosts at my house that will trigger any reaction from him in front of them, so you can stop fretting about that."

"It's not that." I fiddled with my coffee spoon. "It has nothing at all to do with his ability or his personality. I think he's perfectly capable of charming the pants off of them." I snorted. "Especially Susan."

Aunt Zoe grimaced. "Yeah. We'll have to keep an eye on her."

"I'm more concerned about what they're going to do and say to him."

"Your parents are kind people, Violet."

"I know that, but you know how they are. My mom will undoubtedly say something inappropriate about my history with men in front of Doc, and dad will probably grill him about his long-term intentions for his daughter and grandchildren."

She patted my arm. "Have you considered that maybe it'll be as simple as enjoying pleasant conversation over good food?"

I raised one eyebrow. "Have you met my mother?"

She laughed. "It could be worse."

"How?"

"You could be pregnant with twins again. You remember how *that* went over with the two of them?"

Dear Lord, yes. My mother had mock-fainted, requiring a cold washcloth to return upright to her chair. She'd gone on to give an Emmy-winning performance in drama for days on end. Dad, on the other hand, had said absolutely nothing after I dropped the bomb. He'd walked away from the table and disappeared into his workshop, shutting out the world and me. A week later, he'd emerged with two cribs to show for his tool-filled therapy.

I groaned. "You're right, this isn't so bad. If only Susan wasn't going to be with them."

"She's not going to miss this. You know she feeds on turmoil."

Did I ever. Screwing up my world was her favorite treat. "It's not fair that Doc has to meet all three at once." Although technically, he'd already sort of met Susan.

"Honey, it's perfectly normal to be thrown to a family of wolves when you're getting serious in a relationship."

"Are we getting serious?"

She scoffed "Don't you think that's a pretty silly question at this point?"

"No, I don't. For all I know, this level we are at right now could be as deep as Doc wants to dive into my shark-filled waters."

"Maybe it's time *you* ask him about his long-term intentions."

"Oh, okay, sure. I'll do just that." I squirmed in the booth seat at the idea of talking to him about such a thing. "What do I say? 'Doc, when you say you love me, does that mean you plan on sticking with me through sickness and health, 'til death do us part? Or is that just another way to charm me out of my underwear again?' How does that sound?"

She covered her eyes with her hand and shook her head. "Oh, Violet. What is it with you and relationships?"

"They're too hard. It's easier to smother them before they grow into adulthood." I blew out a breath. "Besides that, all of the 'what-ifs' give me heartburn."

"How about for now you let sleeping dogs lie?"

"What's that mean?" The only dogs I knew were law dogs and they kept biting at my heels.

"Instead of worrying about how things may or may not end up in the future with Doc, enjoy the here and now."

"I was trying my best to do just that, and then the kids had to go and bring up Doc's comment on marriage again." On the way to the diner, I'd told her about the scene in front of the television last night. "Now I'm all flustered and afraid I'm misreading his signs."

"Misreading how? The guy is obviously crazy about you."

"Yeah, crazy with a capital C to want to stay with a woman who is consistently on Deadwood's top ten Usual Suspects list."

"Violet," she started.

I held up my hand. "I don't want to talk about this anymore. I'd rather talk about the horrible monsters I need to kill." I aimed a glare at her. "Besides, we were supposed to be talking about your relationship with Reid."

She sniffed, looking into her coffee cup. "I took a roast out of the freezer for tomorrow's dinner before we left the house this morning," she said, blatantly changing the subject. "But we may need more meat if Willis and Cooper join us."

I gave up on digging any deeper into her love life. "Cooper said he was going to skip it."

"Well, Willis told me that he wouldn't miss this show for nothing, not even for a box of shotgun shells and a lap dance."

I chuckled. "That ol' boy needs to find another source of entertainment."

"Why? You keep him plenty preoccupied with your escapades and adventures." She grinned. "He was still snickering this morning on the phone about your trip to the police station. He said Hawke's bark was in fact meaner than his bite."

"I don't know about that. Last night, I dreamed that Detective Hawke was biting me."

"Like a zombie movie bite?"

"More like werewolf. I said Prudence's magic word and he turned into a German shepherd. Only instead of only barking at me, he attacked and tore out my throat."

She flinched. "Sleeping on the couch probably isn't helping with the nightmares. How about we move Addy into my bed and you can at least toss and turn in comfort?"

"Cooper would probably appreciate that."

Last night, he'd shown up as Hawke's snout moved south and ripped out my guts, shaking me awake again. This time, he'd brought me some lemon tea and settled into the recliner under Addy's rainbow-colored comforter.

"Did he stay and watch TV with you?"

I nodded. "He let me choose between *Bonanza* and *Gunsmoke*."

"That's a no-brainer." She ran her finger around the rim of her coffee mug, a far away smile on her face. "I've always had a soft spot for Festus, especially in the episodes when he'd sing."

"I'm well aware of your admiration of Ken Curtis's pipes."

"You know he was a lead singer—"

"With the Sons of the Pioneers from 1949 to 1952," I finished, shoulder bumping her. "You used to play some of their records for me on that old record player in your office when I was a kid, remember?"

"Oh, yeah. Your great-grandmother loved listening to them."

My memories of my great-grandmother were not as warm and fuzzy as Aunt Zoe's. The old woman had always given me a strong case of the heebie-jeebies, but now was not the time to dwell on her and her creepy rune stones that repeatedly foretold of me carrying death in my pockets. Those were her words, not mine. Aunt Zoe might swear on my great-grandmother's *magistra* skills and praise her knowledge about how to keep our family's executioners alive, but to me she would always represent the boogeyman.

Aunt Zoe glanced toward the door, doing a double take. "Now there's a handsome devil if I ever saw one."

I followed her gaze. Dominick Masterson stood inside the front door, peeling off his leather gloves and stuffing them in the pockets of his long black wool coat. His dark hair was fashioned in the latest slicked-back style without looking greasy like Ray's always did. His narrow pinstripe shirt and dark dress pants were tailor-made and fitted. Several of the females in the room stared, admiring the view. I wondered if they knew he was back on the market. Actually, marriage was probably a mere technicality in their eyes, certainly not a showstopper.

" 'Handsome devil' is a fitting description for Dominick," I said under my breath. "And he's come down to Deadwood, willing to make a deal."

"Hold on tight to your soul, baby girl."

Dominick scanned the room, his dark gaze landing on me. I waved at him to join us.

"Here we go," I said, forcing a smile to my lips.

He stopped a waitress on the way to our booth, whispering something in her ear and following it with a wink. She tittered and headed off toward the kitchen.

"Hello, Violet," he purred in his deep, silky voice. "You brought company. Who is this lovely creature?"

Queasiness spread in the pit of my belly. I swallowed some water, doing my best to keep the ball of nausea right where it was. "Dominick, this is my aunt, Zoe Parker."

His white teeth made an appearance, dazzling as always. He held his hand out for hers, which she gave without hesitation. "It's wonderful to meet a relative of Violet's." His gaze sized her up and down, his brows rising in appreciation. "Especially one so lovely as you."

"My, oh my." Aunt Zoe licked her lips. "Aren't you a smooth one?"

He leaned closer, whispering, "I have my rough edges, too."

Aunt Zoe's cheeks darkened. She leaned toward him, her voice sultry when she replied, "You'll have to show them to me some time."

Come again? I gaped at my aunt, who was staring up at Dominick like she wanted to skinny dip in his eyes.

He raised her hand to his mouth, kissing the back of it. "Sounds like a deal, beautiful."

"You know where to find me." She licked her lips again. "At the corner of—"

I elbowed her in the ribs. Good and hard.

She grunted, pulling her hand free of his. "That hurt, Violet!"

"Sorry about that." I made a show of taking off her red vest. "I'm getting warm and needed to slip out of this."

While Dominick took off his coat and hung it on the hook at the end of the booth, I gave Aunt Zoe a what-the-hell gesture. She grimaced back, shrugging, and mouthed *I don't know.*

In other words, whatever shiny magic Dominick was using to "wow" the womenfolk, Aunt Zoe was as susceptible as everyone else.

Great, I was on my own. Not only that, I was going to have to make sure Aunt Zoe didn't end up selling her soul to the attractive devil while I was at it. Doc was right. I should have brought Harvey along, too.

Somehow, Dominick made sliding into the seat opposite us look cool and sexy. I envied his charisma. If I practiced more in the mirror, maybe I could "wow" the pants off Doc with just a smile. Wouldn't that be a fun private-party trick? I tucked that away for later daydreaming and focused back on the man across the table ... or whatever he was.

"I've seen you before," he said to Aunt Zoe. "Don't you own the glass gallery on Main Street in Deadwood?"

She nodded, keeping her eyes averted while still rubbing her side. "I've been there for a long time."

"My ex-wife enjoyed shopping for unique glass pieces there. She'd often use one of your stunning vases as a centerpiece when we'd throw dinner parties."

"Your wife had good taste," I said, pulling his focus back to me.

"Of course she did." His dark eyes locked onto mine. "She married me, didn't she?"

I held my ground. "Yes, but then she up and left. What was she thinking?"

I was serious. I'd like to know if his wife had even been capable of thinking anymore when she "left" him, or if he'd made her go away for good by way of a dirt nap?

"Clearly, she wasn't thinking." His tone was even, his demeanor unruffled by my question. "Or she would have stayed to see what happens next."

I took the bait. "What's going to happen next?"

He took his time answering, staring at me so long I had to blink. My stomach lurched like a drunken sailor, but I didn't let it show.

"For starters," he finally said, "our waitress is going to deliver my hot chocolate."

Sure enough, as if on cue, the waitress he'd spoken with on his way to our table walked over and set a mug down topped with a swirled dome of whipped cream. She blushed and tittered as he flirted with her, and then pranced away.

"That's not our waitress," Aunt Zoe told him, blinking like she'd just woken up.

He shrugged, pulling a golden spoon from his shirt pocket, steaming it with his breath. "She'll do in the meantime." He polished the spoon with his napkin.

"You forgot sprinkles," I said. The absurdity of the moment almost rattled a laugh out of me, but I managed to keep my lips pinched tight.

He raised one dark brow. "Whipped cream is my dessert of choice, Violet. I prefer it on all of my sweets." His pupils seemed to grow larger as he stared at me. Then his focus lowered to my mouth.

A fresh wave of nausea made me swallow several times quickly. Something was going on here. Was it just his over-the-top flirting making me want to vomit, or was he attempting to use some kind of influence on me? Experimenting to see my reactions? Whatever it was, I needed to nip this in the bud or move to the next booth over.

I crossed my arms. "Knock it off, Dominick."

"What?" he feigned innocence far better than my kids, but I was an ace at sniffing out hogwash.

"This flirting game you're playing with me."

"Maybe I find you attractive." He dipped the spoon in the whipped cream, looking in Aunt Zoe's direction as he licked it off his spoon provocatively. "Along with your aunt."

I heard Aunt Zoe sigh like a lovesick puppy.

Maybe I should have her wait in the car. "I'm not your type."

"My last five wives have been blond and curvy."

Last five? Had there been more before those five? More important, what had he done with them? I leaned forward, lowering my voice. "But none of them were your enemy."

He leaned forward, too. "Which makes you even more interesting."

My stomach cramped, making me tense up. I breathed through the pain, sitting back to keep the distance. Next time, I needed to meet him in a large auditorium, or maybe at a football field.

"You're just trying to get me off my game," I said. But it wasn't going to work.

He dipped into his whipped cream again, slowly licking the spoon clean. Aunt Zoe rested her chin on her hand, openly ogling him, her brain once again a steaming pile of lusty mush.

I suddenly realized what Dominick was doing. This wasn't a matter of merely seducing the others in the room to stroke his ego. It was his show of power. With what appeared to take very little effort, he had gained control of an impartial crowd in a setting that I'd figured would be safe for this meeting. On top of that, he'd neutralized my backup, aka Aunt Zoe, turning her into one of his heart-eyed minions.

"And what game is that?" he asked, his smile cocky.

Before I could answer, our regular waitress returned and took our orders. She offered Dominick a refill on his whipped cream, making it clear she was available to personally serve it to him via various body parts. Her bawdy invitation along with another flare of queasiness made me recoil.

He winked at her. "Maybe later, darling."

She giggled and left with an extra sway in her hips, which Dominick didn't even seem to notice.

Aunt Zoe did, though, judging from the squinty-eyed glare she aimed at the departing waitress. I pinched her thigh under the table. She turned that glare in my direction and then seemed to realize that she was once again under his spell. She shook it off.

"Don't you want to go wash your hands and freshen up before we eat?" I said to her, hoping that some cold water and distance from Dominick might snap her fully out of this lust-filled stupor.

"Yes, I do." She grabbed her purse, shooting me a worried frown. I flashed a thumbs-up back at her.

"So," Dominick said, after she left. He reached for my hand. "We're finally alone."

I pulled my hand back before he could touch it. "Cut the shit, Don Juan. I don't have time for any more of your showing-off today, so let's get down to the reason we're really here."

He smirked. "You noticed my demonstration?"

"I'd have to be blind and drunk to have missed it." I pointed at him. "And I don't appreciate you messing with my aunt's head, so when she returns, leave her alone."

"I can't help it if I'm drawn to her. She's a very striking woman. I imagine she would provide great pleasure for her sexual partner in and out of bed."

Jeez! Really? Did he have to go there? "She's off limits to you."

"But she's lonely. We could enjoy each other's company for a while. I could ease her frustrations, make her feel wanted again."

That was Reid's job, not Dominick's. "She's taken."

"Does she know it?"

I didn't know that answer. "We're done talking about her."

"Fine," he pouted, taking a sip of hot chocolate. "What do you need from me in exchange for finding and capturing my pet?"

By pet, I assumed he was referring to the *lidérc*. I doubted Dr. Otto Sugarloaf would have referred to it so affectionately. Otto was the one on whom the parasitic entity had caught a ride to the US in the late 1800s. It had ruined his career and life in his home country, and it had gone on to destroy him here as well. I'd need to be careful not to end up suffering the same fate as poor Otto.

"I want to know about the timekeeper."

"Which one?"

Which one? How many were there? I'd heard of one other, but that was it. "Ms. Wolff."

"Ah, the one who no longer is."

"Yeah, her." I crossed my arms. "Out of curiosity, how many timekeepers do you know?"

His lips pursed. "Come now, *Scharfrichter*."

I winced at the sound of my title spoken aloud, glancing around to make sure nobody appeared to be eavesdropping. There were still plenty of glances and outright stares in Dominick's general direction, including a handful of men now who appeared to be admiring him as well, but I doubted any spoke German.

"You know there are tales I cannot tell," he continued. "At least not for the price you're offering today."

"I would think the capture of your *pet* would be worth some serious trade currency."

He shrugged. "In some circles, sure. But you are hardly in a position to bargain for more at the moment."

What did he know about my bargaining position? And how?

"Now, what would you like to know about Ms. Wolff?"

"Who killed her?"

One dark eyebrow lifted. "Is this a trick question?"

"No."

"I don't understand what you're getting at."

"I'm not getting at anything. I just want to find out if you know who took her out of commission."

He stirred his hot chocolate with his golden spoon. "Of course I know."

"Who?"

"You."

I blinked. "Come again?"

He took a sip of hot chocolate. I had a feeling he was taking his time answering just to toy with me. "You are the one who killed the timekeeper."

"No, I didn't."

"But she wore one of your marks."

"My marks? Which particular mark?"

He mimicked slicing his neck.

I cringed. "Anyone could have done that to her," I said, not liking my so-called mark one bit. I'd prefer to leave a V cut into someone's clothes, like Zorro's Z.

"Not true," Dominick said.

"You're saying that my kind are the only ones who do the ..." I did the neck slicing trick.

He gave a wishy-washy nod. "Mostly."

"Ah-ha! So somebody else could have killed her."

He appeared to contemplate that through a mouthful of hot chocolate and then swallowed. "Probably not. Why would anyone else take out a timekeeper?"

"Why would I?"

"Only you know that answer, *Scharfrichter*."

I winced again at the name on his lips. "Okay, enough about who killed who, let's move on to what a timekeeper does."

He grinned. "A timekeeper keeps track of time."

"Keep it up, wiseass, and I'll shove that golden spoon of yours up your nose."

His head tipped back as loud, deep laughter rippled throughout the room. Several females' heads turned. I could have sworn I heard a collective sigh.

"Ah, Violet. You are such a refreshing breeze after dealing with the previous one of your kind."

"You knew my predecessor?" How well had he known Prudence? Did he know she was still around? How old was Dominick?

"I knew her. There are only so many places to hide in these hills, and she was a sight to see, especially that night ..." He stopped, checked himself, and then smiled. "Well, gentlemen do not speak of such things."

Yeah, but Dominick wasn't really a man, was he? Let alone a gentleman. I needed to take another trip up to visit Prudence, apparently, and find out her history with Dominick.

"From what I've been told," I said, returning to the reason for our meeting, "a timekeeper keeps track of where and when."

"Exactly."

"What does that mean?"

He held up his finger.

I frowned. Where and when meant one finger?

The waitress appeared, food in hand, and I realized he had been telling me to wait.

She handed me my plate, more or less shoving it in my direction while worshipping Dominick with her smile. The eggs almost landed on my lap. His pancakes were covered with a mountain of whipped cream and strawberries.

She dabbed her finger in the cream and stuck it in her mouth. "Delicious."

"Yes, you are," he flirted back.

"Someone please shoot me," I muttered.

Aunt Zoe returned to the table, shooing away the waitress. She slid into the booth next to me and frowned at the amount of whipped cream and strawberries stacked high on Dominick's pancakes compared to her own spritzing of cream and one lousy strawberry.

"Don't worry," I told her. "Dominick is going to give the waitress a big tip when we're done." It'd probably be covered with whipped cream when he gave it, too.

I pushed my eggs around on the plate, my stomach not really interested in me putting them in my mouth and sending them south.

"Would either of you like a bite?" he asked, holding out a piece of pancake dripping with cream.

I held out a hand, my stomach clenching.

"Yes!" Aunt Zoe said, eating from his fork as he smiled at her with his charm on high beams.

I pulled her back to my side of the booth. "Damn it, Dominick. You said you'd stop doing that."

"Okay, okay, but I can't help it. Your aunt is very tempting, and I'm hungry for someone who can hold my interest during the day as well as the night."

"Too bad. You can't have her. She's out of your league."

He winked. "That makes her more of a challenge."

"No."

"As you wish." He closed his eyes for a couple of seconds and then returned to his mound of whipped cream.

Aunt Zoe looked at her plate of untouched food and then me, her forehead creased. "That's weird."

"What?"

"I swear I took a bite of pancake."

After hitting Dominick with a quick glare, I patted her arm. "I'll explain later. Eat up."

While Dominick and Aunt Zoe ate, I pushed my eggs around some more on my plate and nibbled on my toast. Aunt Zoe nearly choked on her pancake when I claimed to have a small appetite in the mornings. I waited for Dominick to finish his whipped cream before pressing him for more information. By then, the restaurant was mostly empty.

"So, what does it mean?" I asked. "How do you keep track of when and where with a clock?"

"You need to stop thinking of clocks as a means for keeping track of the hours in a day." He dabbed the corners of his mouth with his napkin. "Instead, think of them as keeping track of time spent in a location. For example, we are here eating, so our clocks would be ticking away here. However, if we were to expire or go somewhere else, our clocks would no longer be tracking time in this location."

I took a drink of coffee, suspecting I was going to need the caffeine to make sense of this before he was done.

Aunt Zoe pushed her empty plate aside. "So, when the clocks are no longer working, what does that mean?"

It was good to have her back by my side. In the future, we'd have to be more careful around Dominick.

"That depends on the clock," he said. "But usually it means the clock's subject is no longer with us."

"You mean dead?" I asked.

"Not necessarily. Subjects come and go, depending on their role. When they move back and forth, between here and there, the clocks tell the timekeeper."

Okay, I sort of understood the *here* and *there*, but—"How will the clocks tell them?"

"By cuckooing or chiming, depending on the clock."

"You're saying," Aunt Zoe said, her brow lined, "that if a clock is chiming, that means someone is coming or going."

"Correct. The chime represents a state of change."

"And if it is silent," Aunt Zoe continued, "someone is no longer here, meaning they're dead or somewhere else."

"That is also correct."

But Prudence had said the cuckooing was the toll of the death bell. Why would she say that?

"And if a clock is ticking away," Aunt Zoe said, "the clock's subject is here doing his or her thing."

"Or its thing," I added.

He nodded. "See, it's quite simple."

Yes and no. For example, I didn't really understand where "there" was, and part of me wasn't sure I wanted to know because of who or what might be waiting *there* for me.

I rubbed my temple. "How do you know who the clock's subject is?"

"By the carvings."

Ah-ha! So that was why the carvings on each were unique—like snowflakes.

"Do you have a clock?" Aunt Zoe asked him.

"Of course not."

She frowned. "Why not?"

"Because I am not a traveler."

"Only travelers have clocks?" I asked.

"Only travelers need to be monitored."

"Why?"

"Because they cause ripples." He smirked. "As well as other problems."

I thought of the bone eater and the problems it had caused when I brought it back with me to Harvey's ranch. "Are executioners considered travelers?"

"Yes."

"So, I have a clock."

"Most likely."

My palms grew sweaty. Where was it? Who was watching it? Was that how Ms. Wolff had known about me? Was one of the clocks on her walls mine?

"Where do the clocks come from?" Aunt Zoe asked.

"From the clockmaker." He said it as if it were common knowledge.

"Is this clockmaker local?" She dug deeper.

"That I do not know, as I am not a timekeeper."

"You certainly know a lot about them," she said, her gaze wary as she watched him.

"I've been around for some time."

My turn. "So Ms. Wolff was keeping track of all of those different travelers?"

"If she was doing her job, then yes."

"And those clocks represent all of the travelers in this area?"

"I doubt it, as there is more than one timekeeper."

That's right. I knew that. "Where is the other timekeeper?"

He steepled his fingers. "That information I cannot give away, especially to a killer."

"I didn't kill Ms. Wolff."

He shrugged. "Whether you did or not, I cannot risk telling you any more information on other timekeepers. It would be bad form."

Okay, then maybe he could answer this: "Was Ms. Wolff dabbling in something she wasn't supposed to?"

"Aren't we all?"

No. Yes. Maybe. Was I? I should ask Doc if there were rules listed in my family history book that I needed to know about so I could decide whether to break them or not.

"Could Ms. Wolff have been killed because of her involvement in something risky and I am now suspect by association?"

"I suppose, but it's not normal."

I laughed. "Nothing about this conversation is normal."

"Maybe it's not normal to you yet," he said. "But that too will change if you live long enough."

If I lived long enough? I tried not to focus on that comment too much. "Recently, when I was in Ms. Wolff's apartment, there was a clock cuckooing. Then the phone rang. When I answered it, someone told me to open a door. What did that—"

"You heard the phone ringing?" he interrupted, his tone suddenly higher.

"Yeah." I shared a raised brow with Aunt Zoe before turning back to him. "Ringing along with the cuckooing."

"And you heard the voice through the phone?"

"Yes."

He leaned forward, his elbows resting on the table as he stared at me. The bout of nausea swelled into my throat, but I swallowed it. "What are you, Violet Parker?"

"We've already gone over this part."

"Yes, but a *Scharfrichter* is not a timekeeper. They are two very different beings."

"Different beings?" I parroted.

"Did you open the door?" he asked.

"Hell no."

"Why not?"

"I didn't like the sound of his voice." It had been too creepy for me to even think about letting him through, reminiscent of the big bad wolf. "Plus, he was rude and he didn't say, 'Please.'"

Dominick's jaw fell open. "You jest?"

"No, why?"

"You needed to open that door."

"It's not my job, remember? I'm a different *being* than a timekeeper. Besides, I couldn't open it."

"Why not?"

For one thing, I didn't know how. More important, "Because I kind of broke that door and now it doesn't work anymore."

"That might cause a problem."

"Not for me." I had a feeling that letting the caller through would have been a bigger problem.

A smile slowly spread up his face. "Fascinating. You were chosen."

"What's that mean?" For some reason, I had a feeling he wasn't talking about my name being drawn for a Secret Santa game.

"Ms. Wolff chose you. That must be why you can hear timekeeper-related sounds and are able to answer the calls—tools of the trade, so to speak."

So Prudence was right? "Why would she choose *me*? I had no idea who she was until I showed up and found her dead."

"I'm more interested in why she would choose anyone. It's highly unorthodox for a timekeeper to do this."

"I'm telling you, she didn't choose me for anything like that. She simply wanted to give me information, but I took too long to get there."

"Are you sure about that?"

"About what? Her wanting to give me information?"

"No, are you sure that you took too long to get there?" He pursed his lips. "Maybe you took exactly long enough. Had you thought of that?"

Huh? No. Why would I …"What?"

"Violet, timekeepers are experts at manipulating time. I find it more likely this was Ms. Wolff's plan all along."

Her plan? How would she …?

I leaned my head on Aunt Zoe's shoulder. Sweet juju beans! This was going to crack my brain. She patted my cheek and nudged me back upright.

"Time can be a tricky devil," he added with a wink.

I froze. Where had I heard that before? Oh, yeah! Prudence had said that, too.

He looked at me with total earnestness, no charming smile or flirty eyes. "There is one thing you should remember, *Scharfrichter*."

"What's that?"

"If you use the clocks to control your enemies, you may find out time is no longer on your side."

Chapter Twenty

I was still scratching my head about timekeepers and clocks later that evening in Aunt Zoe's warm and cozy kitchen. Outside, the weatherman's predicted snowstorm blew in and blanketed the world in white, cold fluff.

All afternoon at work, while dark clouds had piled up on the western horizon, I'd struggled to stay focused on real estate crap. But Dominick's words had replayed over and over in my brain.

Snow was already starting to fly when I'd parked in Aunt Zoe's drive next to Harvey's pickup. Inside, the warm house had smelled like a carnivore's fantasyland. The old buzzard had thrown together a beef stew that knocked my socks off. For a side, he'd whipped up and baked some homemade cornbread. It was a shame Harvey kept turning down my marriage proposals. If I hadn't had the foresight to change into some lounge pants and a pink fleece shirt before supper had been served, my seams would've burst by the time I'd licked my bowl clean.

"Dang, that was so good," I said after cramming the last buttered cornbread crumb in my mouth. I leaned back in my chair, holding my stomach. "I don't think I can move for the next hour."

"You want a beer?" Doc asked, rising from the chair next to me.

"I'm still nursing my lemonade, thanks."

"I do," Natalie said and downed the last drops from her current bottle. "Will you grab me another, Doc?"

Cooper looked over from where he stood at the sink washing supper dishes. "That'll be your third, Beals."

"What's your point, policeman?" she asked. "In case you haven't noticed, I'm not behind the wheel."

"Drink that third and you won't be getting behind the wheel later either, especially in this weather. I'll have to take you home."

I smirked. As if getting Natalie alone in his Durango would be a hardship.

"I'm not going home tonight," she told him. "Didn't you hear? We're having a snowbound slumber party. I hope you brought your flannel pajama pants with the little handcuffs on them." She grinned. "Your butt looks so darn cute in those."

Cooper returned his focus to the sink full of suds. I could swear his cheeks were pinker as he scrubbed the stew pot, but maybe it was my imagination.

"We're having a slumber party?" Reid asked. He was sitting next to me instead of where he would've probably preferred—next to Aunt Zoe. She'd made a point of keeping two chairs' worth of space between them when we were all settling in to eat, using Harvey and Cooper as a buffer.

"We are, but you're not," Aunt Zoe said, setting a plate of still-warm lemon squares in the center of the table. "You're going home."

"I need to see a man about a mule," Harvey said, standing. He squeezed my shoulder as he passed on his way to the dining room. "Save me a couple of yer aunt's lemon bars, Sparky."

"I'll try, but you'd better not stop to smell the roses while you're looking for your mule-man." After Harvey left, I asked Aunt Zoe, "Why can't Reid stay? It's dangerous to drive in the snow, especially on these hills."

I had no doubt Reid would be able to make his way through the snow without a problem, but after Dominick's flirting game this afternoon, I wanted Reid to have a chance to earn some bonus points with her.

"His truck has four-wheel drive and snow tires." She gave me a warning glare. "Besides, there's nowhere to sleep." Before I could mention the available space in her queen-sized bed, she added, "Unless you have room in *your* bed, because mine is full."

"Who's sleeping with you, Zo?" Reid asked.

"Not Dominick," I joked, earning a zip-it scowl from her.

"Natalie is," she said, carrying a stack of dessert plates.

Reid turned to me. "You mean Dominick Masterson?"

I nodded, earning an even deeper scowl from my aunt for tattling.

"I thought Natalie was going to sleep on the couch," Doc said. He opened the fridge door and grabbed two beers. With a raised brow, he held out a third toward Reid, who gave him a thumbs-up.

"Cooper is on the couch tonight," I told Doc. "Addy and Kelly are going to bunk in Addy's room."

Jeff had called this afternoon and asked if Kelly could spend the whole weekend with Addy. He had a romantic trip planned. I agreed to Kelly staying over, cutting him off before he could fill me in on any details on this romantic romp, including who or where and especially what. I didn't have the brain space for nipple rings and locker room talk after my morning lesson on timekeepers. I thought about asking if he'd decided to leave me for Tiffany, but then opted to wait for him to bring it up so I didn't sound desperate.

"Actually, Layne offered his bed to Cooper," Aunt Zoe told me, doling out plates and forks.

"Where's Layne going to sleep?" Doc asked.

"On the floor in a sleeping bag," she said. "He wants to have a boys' slumber party,"

Cooper glanced my way, drying his hands. "The kid insisted, but if you'd rather he be in his bed …"

"It's fine," I said. It was kind of Cooper to appease Layne's male bonding need, because I didn't want to share the male I planned to bond with later in the dark.

Natalie grinned at Cooper. "Would you look at that? The wild, rough-n-tough cop is finally getting domesticated. I like it."

"Pipe down, Beals," he shot back.

"Seriously, I think it's really sweet, Coop." The look in her eyes as she stared at him bordered on smoldering. I could practically see her sabbatical notion curling at the edges from the heat.

If she was going to keep bumping along on this no-sex wagon, she needed to tug on the reins a few times before her horses broke free and ran over someone—namely Cooper. While I was game for poking at Cooper now and then after months of his being a pain in my ass, our late-night western marathons had softened me up toward him some. The guy had enough problems with unsolved murders, ghosts, and now a barking partner. She didn't need to add acute sexual frustration to his teetering plate.

I cleared my throat, gaining her attention, and mouthed the word *sabbatical.*

A shadow passed over her features, and then she nodded. "I'm gonna take some of these to the kids." She grabbed a few lemon squares and plates, escaping to the living room where all three kids and Elvis the chicken were watching an animated film about a troop of Santa's elves.

"I'm feeling a little left out," Doc said, returning to the chair next to me. He draped his arm over the back of my chair, smiling broadly at Cooper. "You never come to my slumber parties anymore."

Cooper scoffed. "That's because you just want me to come over and lose at poker so you can take all my money."

"That's not true," Doc said, sipping his beer. "The last time you were at my place, we switched to blackjack and Martin took your money, not me."

Reid snickered. "Who'd have figured we'd find a game you suck at even more than poker?"

Cooper wadded up the dishtowel and threw it at Reid, who laughed even harder. "We should do that again some night, Coop. I made enough off of you to take Zo out to a nice restaurant for dinner and drinks." He pointed at Aunt Zoe. "Which you still owe me after that last knock-out blow, darling."

Reid had a glass jaw that Aunt Zoe knew well. Last month, she'd clocked him a good one to keep him out of harm's way when we were hunting the *lidérc* up in Lead. In exchange for his forgiveness, she owed him a dinner date, which she kept finding ways to dodge.

"You haven't forgotten about that yet?" she replied.

"Oh, no. One of these days you're going to run out of excuses."

Doc's fingers slipped under my hair, caressing the back of my neck. A tingling zing rippled down my back, leaving goosebumps in its wake. I ran my hand along his thigh under the table, shooting him a flirting glance. He strummed my neck again, his gaze lowering to my lips.

Unbeknownst to the kids, Doc was spending the night in my room tonight. If it weren't for a houseful of people, I'd suggest he and I sneak off to my boudoir now. I had a few bedtime stories I wanted to act out for him while wearing a flimsy lacy number I hadn't shown him yet. But there was a houseful of people, so I had to play it cool for a while longer and settle for a few bites of sugar instead of sex.

I lifted a lemon bar, mock-toasting Aunt Zoe. "*Bon appétit.*"

Doc stopped my hand before the lemon bar reached my mouth. "Tish, that's French." He leaned over and took a big bite of my lemon bar, stealing almost half of it. His dark eyes creased with laughter as he chewed and swallowed.

"You have sugar on your lips, Gomez." I licked mine, trying to tease him into sharing.

He took the bait, leaning closer, zeroing in on my mouth.

"Jesus. You two are making my eyes bleed." Cooper interrupted Doc's descent. "Somebody go get my gun."

"A hose would work better," Harvey said, returning to his chair. His gold teeth showed through his beard as he grinned across at Doc. "Careful, boy. Sparky's actin' hot to trot tonight. She's rarin' to get heiferized, so ya might wanna keep yer powder dry."

I gaped at Harvey, my cheeks flash heating. "I am not wanting to get *heiferized*." That wasn't entirely true. I was interested in taking part in the process of getting "heiferized," but not the actual stork delivery results.

Doc's laughter filled the kitchen. "Willis, you have a true gift with words."

"More like a true gift with manure," I muttered, shoving the rest of the lemon bar in my mouth.

"If Cooper is in Layne's bed," Reid said to Aunt Zoe. "I can crash on your couch."

"That's where Willis is sleeping," Aunt Zoe shot back.

"You sure you wouldn't rather switch with me?" Cooper asked his uncle. "That couch is hard on a body."

"No, siree. Them there lumps fit my back just right. I sleep better on it than yer bed."

"I suppose you could sleep on the couch in my workshop." Aunt Zoe gave in to Reid. "If you insist on staying."

"You can't keep me at arm's length forever, Zo."

"Wanna bet?"

"Yeah, I do." Reid's gaze hardened. "Now, what's the deal with you and Masterson?"

"There is no deal."

Harvey butted in. "From what Sparky is hintin' at, it sounds to me like good ol' Dominick is sufferin' from Cupid's cramps."

Aunt Zoe scowled at me. "Way to go, mouth."

"Don't blame me." I pointed at Harvey, who was cramming a second lemon square in his mouth. "Blame him."

"I'm blaming both of you."

"What did Masterson have to say?" Cooper asked me, grabbing a lemon square and dropping into the chair next to Reid.

I told Doc most of the scoop earlier over the phone. Other than him, only Aunt Zoe and I knew what had gone down, and she had some blank spots in her memory thanks to Dominick's thick fog of charm.

Before I could start, Addy and Kelly ran into the kitchen with their empty lemon square plates, setting them in the sink. Elvis followed on their heels, dressed in a green plaid, chicken-sized sweater vest, which my mother had found online and purchased. Add a Sherlock Holmes hat, pipe, and magnifying glass, and Cooper could have a new partner that squawked instead of barked.

"Mom," Addy said, stopping at my side. "Can Kelly and I play with Elvis in my room?"

"Hmm. I don't love that idea."

"How about if it's just for an hour, and then I put her back in her cage in the basement?"

"What do you think, Aunt Zoe?"

"You promise to clean up any messes?" Aunt Zoe asked Addy.

"Yeah, but Elvis hasn't had an accident in over a month. I think she's finally potty trained."

I huffed. "Now you need to teach her not to leave eggs in my shoes." I'd had to trash a pair of ankle boots earlier this fall when I crushed an egg down deep in the toe while in a rush to get out the door for work.

"Sheesh, Mom. I'm not a magician, you know." Addy moved to Doc. "Do you have to work in the morning?" she asked him.

"I'm taking the day off so I can meet your grandparents."

I cringed. Maybe I should have a beer ... or six.

"Good." Addy gave Doc a coy smile, both of her dimples showing. "Will you come over in the morning and make French toast for us? I was telling Kelly how you put the cinnamon swirls in it and it tastes soooo good."

"Sure, Squirt." He reached over and tweaked her chin.

"I can make you breakfast, Adelynn," I said, not wanting Doc to feel put on the spot to feed my kids. Plus, after my conversation with the kids last night about Doc and marriage, I was a tad nervous about how the morning might go if Addy or Layne found Doc in my bed. Doc might want to escape to his nice, quiet house for a while if things blew up in my face.

"No offense, Mom, but your French toast sort of sucks. Let's go, Kelly." Addy grabbed her friend's hand. "Come on, Elvis," she called as she and Kelly ran out of the room. Elvis clucked and strutted after them.

"No offense, Killer," Doc said, chuckling.

I grinned. "Show off."

Natalie returned from the living room, sliding into her chair. "What did I miss?" she asked, avoiding looking in Cooper's general direction.

"Sparky was about to tell us what happened between Dominick Masterson and Zo," Reid told her.

"Great." Natalie grabbed two lemon bars, settling into her chair. "Start with what he was wearing. Masterson always dresses to impress."

"Do you want to give her a rundown of his outfit?" I asked Aunt Zoe, fighting back a grin. "Or did you even notice that he was clothed when he was wooing you with all of that whipped cream?"

"You'll do just fine, smarty pants."

"What whipped cream?" Reid's eyes were in gunslinger mode.

I started with Dominick's arrival in Bighorn Billy's, included his love of whipped cream, and ended with Aunt Zoe and I making our exit shortly after his warning about Father Time turning on me. Since Reid was sitting with us, I tempered the part about Aunt Zoe, sharing only enough to get the point across that Dominick had her under his spell with what appeared to be minimal effort. By the time I finished, the plate of lemon squares was empty and a quarter inch of snow had accumulated on the back porch railing.

"What were ya thinking?" Harvey asked Aunt Zoe. When she glared at him, he held up his hands. "I'm serious. What was goin' through yer mind when he was doin' that to ya? I'm curious if it felt like when Prudence was in my noggin'."

"All I can remember is thinking how attractive Dominick is … was," she said, glancing at Reid.

That was the same answer she'd given me on the way back from the diner.

She tucked a loose silver strand from her braid behind her ear. "Did you ever have a crush on someone so strong that just the sight of them made you stop in your tracks and stare?"

No, never, not me … said the woman who had nearly lost her best friend over a fiery crush on the tall, dark, and lemon bar–stealing medium sitting next to her.

My gaze slid to Cooper, another sucker with a crush. He appeared to be studying the label on his beer bottle.

"Yes," Natalie answered, snaring Cooper's attention.

I laughed out loud.

"What is that laugh for?" she asked me.

"Aunt Zoe just described almost every crush you had from sixth grade through high school."

"You're one to talk, ya big tart."

"Hey, I'm not the one who ran into that steel post because I was so busy smiling at Joel Soderdale when we walked past him."

"That's no fair. Joel had sparkles in his eyes." She explained to Aunt Zoe, "He had these intense blue eyes with little silver specs in them. They were mesmerizing."

"They were pretty cool," I had to agree. "He snagged a lot of girls because of his eyes."

"And long, dark eyelashes," Natalie added.

"And killer cheekbones," I remembered.

"Anyway," Aunt Zoe continued. "That's how it felt. I was

overwhelmed with ... well, lust." She glanced down at the crumbs on her plate, her face darkening. "I wanted him, plain and simple, even though Violet was doing her best to bury her elbow in my ribs." She looked at Harvey and then Reid with a pinched forehead. "I had no control."

Natalie nodded as if she knew that reaction by its first name. "That must explain why every time I see Dominick, I stop and stare at him."

"Right." I snorted. "I'm sure that's it."

She smiled and flipped me off.

I shot a glance at Cooper to check his temperature after Natalie's comment. His face was a rigid, unreadable mask, aka "detective mode." I could practically hear the co-pilot in his head announcing over the loudspeaker that all emotion shields were in place and secure.

"The point is," Aunt Zoe cut in again, fiddling with her fork. "I couldn't resist Dominick, no matter how hard I tried. Hell, nobody in that room could." She pointed her fork at me. "Except Violet."

When all eyes locked onto me, I shrugged. "Dominick makes me sick to my stomach. I was fighting back bouts of nausea from the moment he walked up to our booth, even more so when he tried to touch me."

Doc shifted in his chair. "Tried to touch you where?"

"Only on the hand. That was after Aunt Zoe had escaped to the bathroom."

"Why you?" Reid asked Aunt Zoe.

"Nice, Martin," Cooper said, shaking his head. "It's no wonder you're still single."

"Don't get me wrong, Zo. You're a beautiful woman, but why did Masterson focus on you when there were other women in the restaurant throwing themselves at him?"

She chewed on her lower lip. "I have a theory about that. I'm Violet's Achilles' heel. Dominick tried to ensnare her, but couldn't. Through me, though, he can manipulate her."

She'd mentioned that idea to me on the way home. I grew even more bristly about it the second time she said it.

Right then, I remembered something else I hadn't told her before. "There was more to it than that. Dominick told me he saw sadness in you that he wanted to fix. He was certain he could make you happy for a while in exchange for your making an entertaining companion for him." I left out the bit he said about "entertaining" both in and out of the bedroom.

"Yup," Harvey said. "A fine heifer will perk me up fer months."

Cooper stood. "You have cows on the brain, Uncle Willis." He took his plate to the sink.

Natalie chuckled. "Harvey's right, though. A new love does tend to put a bounce in your step." She cast a swift glance in Cooper's direction, looking away before anyone who wasn't watching her like a hawk would notice.

However, the magnification on my "hawk" binoculars was set at 10x, so I saw enough to wonder if she was having second, third, and fourth thoughts about her sabbatical.

"Could he?" Reid asked Aunt Zoe.

"Could he what?"

"Make you happy?"

She stared at him for a long silent moment, and then shrugged. "Dominick is very attractive, but underneath it's all the same Hell, merely a different devil."

"A very dangerous devil," I added, sending Doc a worried frown. Dominick knew where Aunt Zoe worked. If he set his sights on her when I wasn't around, she might be toast.

Doc returned my frown.

"Sparky?" Harvey said. "That day Ms. Wolff called ya, how long did it take from when ya hung up on 'er until we showed up on her doorstep?"

"A half an hour, maybe a little longer. Why?"

"Somethin' is stickin' in my craw about what Zoe's loverboy said."

Aunt Zoe harrumphed. "He's not my loverboy."

"Which part?" I asked Harvey.

"The bit about Ms. Wolff dabblin' with time." He stroked his beard, his head cocked to the side.

Cooper leaned against the counter, crossing his arms. "So, let me get this straight. The clocks in Ms. Wolff's apartment that are ticking represent subjects who are existing here amongst us." At my nod, he continued, "And if a clock is stopped, the subject is no longer with us, but not necessarily deceased." I nodded again. "And if it's cuckooing or chiming, then …"

"Change is occurring," Doc answered for me. "Something is either coming or going."

"Or trying to," I added.

"And those clocks that you heard chiming for a couple of days meant that something kept trying to come through or leave." He didn't ask, merely stated it. "But then you didn't open the door, which is apparently something a timekeeper is supposed to do, so what then? It left?"

"I guess."

"Where did it go?"

I raised my hands, palms up.

"This is insane, Parker." Cooper pinched the bridge of his nose, near the crooked part. "I'm going to need a bottle of whiskey for it to start making sense."

Natalie tapped on the table. "So, Dominick thinks Ms. Wolff gave you some of her timekeeping abilities?"

"That's what he insinuated."

"How is that even possible?" Reid asked, giving Aunt Zoe a troubled glance. She was frowning at the table, her mind seemingly elsewhere at the moment.

"I have no idea," I answered for her.

"Did ya leave yer brains in yer other coat tonight, Sparky?" Harvey asked.

"Maybe I did, ol' man." I looked around at each of them, ending with Cooper. "Listen, who knows if any of this is even true? Dominick can't be trusted. He might have been intentionally misleading. Maybe all executioners can hear the sounds I heard in Ms. Wolff's apartment."

"That's not normal behavior for executioners," Doc spoke up. When I turned his way, he added, "At least according to your family history book it's not."

"Define normal." I remembered a Morticia Addams quote that had always stuck with me, adding, "What is normal for the spider is chaos to the fly."

His lips curved. "You, *cara mia*, are far from normal."

"How's it all tie together?" Cooper asked, still pinching the bridge of his nose.

"All of what, Coop?" Harvey asked.

"This timekeeper shit with the remains found on the Mickelson Trail and the picture that you and Nosy Parker here picked up from Slagton."

"For the record," I said, "I only rode along on that trip."

Harvey made chicken sounds at me.

"What's the story behind that picture, anyway?" Doc asked.

Cooper sighed, lowering his hand. "I'll make all of you a deal. If I tell you about the picture, you promise not to go back to Slagton to sniff around more without me."

"You want to pinkie swear again?" I held up my pinkie.

He glared in return.

"Okay, fine." I lowered my hand. "But I'm sort of shocked you're not going to give us the 'police business' runaround."

"That picture isn't police business. It's *my* business."

"This just keeps getting better," Natalie said, rubbing her hands together.

"When I was back there asking around about the victim you three musketeers found in Uncle Willis's safe, one of the locals mentioned he'd been out hunting somewhat recently and seen a strange creature. He explained that it walked upright, but had thick horns, like a bighorn sheep."

Natalie shuddered. "That reminds me of that pink-eyed thing from *Amityville Horror.*"

"At the time," Cooper continued, "I could smell liquor on the guy and figured it was the moonshine talking, but I decided to give him the benefit of the doubt. I gave him my home phone number and told him to call if he ever saw it again, suggesting he take a picture if he could. I didn't expect anything to come of it, which is why I gave him my home number. The last thing I need at work these days is another one of Parker's Bigfoot sightings coming in, you know?"

"I wish it was good ol' Bigfoot I was seeing," I muttered.

"What makes you think this creature back in Slagton is tied to Violet?" Aunt Zoe asked.

Reid joined Cooper at the counter, getting a coffee cup from the cupboard, adding, "We still don't know for sure that the Mickelson Trail remains weren't left by some cougar or mountain lion."

"Think about it. Parker shows up in town and weird shit starts happening, including one fucked-up murder after another."

"So this is my fault?"

"No, more like the result of your presence. Apparently, these things were living here with us all along. Then you came and got things stirred up."

"She's been stirring up trouble since we were kids," Natalie said, giving me a wink.

I shot her with my finger gun.

"It comes in waves," Doc said, his tone sobering. "Nature always seeks to restore balance."

I looked at him. "What do you mean?"

"Think about it. Before you, there was Prudence. That collection of teeth didn't come from her scouring the seashore somewhere. She was taking care of business here in Deadwood, cleaning up, dealing with whatever trouble was coming out of the woodwork, including taking out humans." When I frowned at him, he added, "Not all of those teeth were from other beings. The question is, had she gone too far in her vengeance?"

"Then she got murdered," Natalie said. "Playing along with your theory, that means her death was necessary for balance to be restored."

"Maybe," Doc said. "Or Prudence's death just put things on hold for more than a century, which is a hiccup in the long skein of time."

"So, if I went away ..." I started, trailing off.

"I don't think it's as simple as you leaving and Coop's problems going away." Doc took my hand in his. "A balance has to be found first. Clearly, if these other beings are roaming and killing at will, you're needed here. If you were to leave, things could grow considerably worse."

Aunt Zoe nodded. "My grandmother talked of the balance often, warning me to watch for shifts in the scale." She leaned forward, pushing her empty plate away. "Doc, based on what you've deciphered in the book, do you think the appearance of these other creatures is directly due to Violet's presence? That she is some sort of magnifier that summons them from their usual hunting grounds?"

"I haven't come across anything yet in the book about executioners having any kind of summoning power."

"Didn't Dominick say that the hunters would be coming for me?" I said, trying to remember exactly how that conversation went.

Doc nodded at me. "But I think it's usually the other way around with an executioner. You're called because the threat is here." He looked across at Aunt Zoe. "Your niece has been living a regular life for decades. Why the sudden change? Why was the executioner awakened in her now? Does it have something to do with that first brush with death in Wolfgang's house? Or did something else trigger it? Something far beyond her control?"

Cooper focused on me. "Why did you move to Deadwood?"

"Ha, ha," I said dryly.

"I'm serious, Parker. What prompted you to move to Deadwood?"

I shrugged. "I felt the need for a change."

"But why Deadwood?" Doc pressed.

"I felt like I needed to be here with Aunt Zoe."

"You were being called to action," Natalie whispered. "How freaking cool is that?"

"Trust me, spudnut," I said. "It wouldn't feel very cool if you were walking in my boots."

Doc rubbed his lower lip. "Zoe, you've said before that sometimes the executioner genes skip a generation or more, right?"

She nodded.

"While I've been studying your family history book, I've been creating a timeline. At first, I was only noting the estimated life span of the executioners, but then I realized that some of them started fighting at a very young age and others were older—in their twenties, thirties, and beyond when they made their first kill. That made me wonder if it's not a matter of which generation pulls the short straw, but rather that every generation has the genetic makeup to become an executioner. The trigger is an external force, rather than internal, that lights them up."

I sat back, letting his words simmer. That would mean I really had no control over any of this, that I was being directed sort of like a puppet. Did that mean if I lived long enough to see the balance returned, I'd have to be killed off like Prudence? Or could I slink back into regular life and live happily ever after as plain old Violet Parker, struggling single mom and crappy real estate agent?

Doc squeezed my hand. "That's only a theory. I could be way off, of course."

I doubted that. His theories were more often than not close to the mark.

"What if somethin' were to happen to Sparky while the balance was still catawampus?" Harvey asked. "Would another killer from her line be called into action?"

"You mean Zo?" Reid asked.

"Either Zoe," Harvey said. "Or a smaller version of Sparky."

We all looked up at the ceiling.

Addy.

I grimaced, locking onto Aunt Zoe's blue eyes. "If anything happens to me, take her away from here. She's too young. She'll have no chance." Hell, I didn't think *I* had much of a chance. So far, Lady Luck had been in my boat. If she jumped ship, I'd be walking the plank in no time.

Aunt Zoe nodded once.

"Back in seventh grade," Natalie said to me, all mirth gone from her face. "We made a blood contract."

I remembered.

"I meant what I said then, Vi, and I still mean it now. For you and your kids."

My eyes grew watery.

"What did she say?" Cooper asked.

I frowned, blinking away the tears. "That she'd die for me to keep me safe."

At the time, I was dealing with a she-bully who was twice my size and sat next to me in science. She was threatening to beat the crap out of me if I didn't take the fall for her pouring dish soap in the teacher's goldfish tank. The gravity of Natalie's promise held a lot more weight now. If only it were school bullies I were facing.

"It's not going to come to that," Aunt Zoe said, her voice confident.

"How do you know?"

"Because you're a smart girl."

"Lucky to boot," Harvey said, apparently reading my mind. "You've dodged more bullets than Coop."

"That would explain all of his scars," Natalie said.

Wanting to move on from the idea of Addy being next in line for the slaughter, I changed the subject. "Okay, if Dominick is right about Ms. Wolff somehow giving me the ability to detect travelers who come and go, then what exactly did she find out before she died? What was it that motivated her to give me these abilities?"

"Hey, Mom?" Layne walked into the kitchen with envelopes in one hand, pausing our pow-wow.

I pasted a smile on my lips. "What honey?"

"I forgot to give you the mail. I got it when we got home and stuffed it in the front pocket of my backpack."

I held out my hand for the envelopes he was holding.

"Most of them are Christmas cards," he said, handing them over. The envelopes were all opened, which was no big deal since I had always allowed the kids to open holiday cards for me.

"But this one is different." He held out another opened, card-sized envelope for me to take.

Something in his voice made me frown. "What do you mean, it's different?"

"Look." He pulled out a plain white card and opened it. Inside, a picture of him holding up a glass egg had been taped to the back of the front cover.

My stomach dropped.

I knew that picture! It was *THE* picture. The one that had been stuck in Ms. Wolff's dresser mirror.

I took the card, holding it out for Cooper to see.

He came closer, his mouth flat-lining. "Was there anything else with it?" he asked Layne.

"Just this." Layne pulled a piece of folded paper from the envelope.

Cooper opened the paper, his gaze narrowing to slits.

"What's it say?" Doc asked.

I was afraid to find out.

Cooper handed it over.

Doc held it out for me to read at the same time.

It is time. You will need this, Scharfrichter.

"What's that mean?" Layne asked, pointing at my "other" name.

"It's just a weird German word." I took the paper from Doc and crumbled it in my fist. "It's nothing."

"Layne," Aunt Zoe said, her voice light and smiley. "Do me a favor, kiddo, and go see if you can find that special I recorded about the Maya civilization. Reid told me earlier he'd like to watch that with us."

Layne frowned at me for a few seconds, long enough that I didn't think he'd take Aunt Zoe's bait. Then he gave in and disappeared into the living room.

"I'm spending the night, then?" Reid asked Aunt Zoe.

She nodded, not looking thrilled about it, but Reid smiled anyway.

I tossed the crumpled note on the table. "I wish whoever was sending me this shit would stop playing hide and seek and just knock on the fucking door."

"Careful what you wish for, baby doll," Aunt Zoe said. "Remember the story about that mummified monkey's paw by W.W. Jacobs? Granted wishes sometimes come with hellish consequences."

Chapter Twenty-One

Saturday, December 8th

Life never seemed to go as planned for me, especially when I really needed it to. I grabbed a syrup-coated plate and stuck it into the sudsy dishwater, washing it as I stared out the kitchen window at the sparkling snow.

Take last night, for example.

After dealing with the Dominick shit and the timekeeper crap, I had the business with Layne's picture.

Who had returned it to me? Was it Mr. Black? Had I been wrong all along and Mr. Black hadn't taken Layne's picture from Ms. Wolff's apartment that day? Could he have been distracting Freesia at Ms. Wolff's door while someone else was inside swiping it?

The questions surrounding the picture had made me dizzy. My solution was to sleep on it … next to Doc. But then life stepped in and shook my snow globe yet again.

About two hours before I'd planned to sneak Doc up to my room, there was a loud crash overhead, followed by little girl squeals and a particular chicken's squawks. I raced up the stairs, barging into Addy's room only to pinch my nose and rush back out, followed by the two girls and Elvis.

Call it a mother's instinct or an executioner's sixth sense, but I'd known there was a reason I didn't want Addy taking Elvis up to her room. When I demanded an explanation from my kid for why her room smelled like someone dumped perfume all over the place, my daughter told me that Elvis knocked an old bottle of my perfume off her desk. On its way to the floor, it hit one of the metal drawer knobs and the glass top shattered. While Addy ran to grab a towel from the bathroom, the perfume leaked out and soaked into the carpet, leaving her bedroom smelling like a good ol' whorehouse. At least that's what Harvey told me when he joined us upstairs to find out what the commotion was.

At bedtime the room still reeked in spite of the carpet cleaner that was supposed to neutralize odors and the window open a couple of inches. There was no way I could let the two girls sleep in there, so I ended up giving up my bed to them. Doc mentioned walking home through the snow, but Harvey offered to sleep in the makeshift whorehouse since his smeller didn't work so well anymore. The old goat had high hopes that the aroma would spur happy dreams full of good-time memories, including someone named Nevada Nelly with a penchant for spurs. I handed him an extra quilt and left before he could share any further details.

That left the couch for Doc. Unfortunately for him, rather than crawl into bed with the girls after everyone had settled down for the night, I opted to squish in next to him. Although he didn't seem to mind too much, especially when I slipped off my robe and crawled under his blanket in just my camisole and underwear. We fooled around a bit under the covers, rubbing and teasing enough to get him breathing hard and me achy with need, but then Addy came down crying because she had a bad dream. Playtime was over.

By the time I returned to the living room after Addy was back to sleep, Doc was passed out as well. Giving up, I grabbed another blanket and made myself comfortable in the recliner for the night.

This morning, I'd woken to daylight coming through the living room windows and the smell of French toast in the air. After peeking out at the six inches of winter wonderland glistening in the sunlight, I headed for the shower. I heard Addy and Doc talking in the kitchen and smiled as I climbed the stairs, enjoying the warm comforts of Doc in our home.

Then I remembered who was coming for dinner today and groaned. Too bad my father had a heavy-duty four-wheel drive Blazer with studded snow tires that six inches of snow would barely even slow down.

Fast forward several hours to me elbow deep in sudsy dishwater as Aunt Zoe worked her magic at the stove. The house was quiet thanks to Doc taking all three kids to the Rec Center to burn off some energy, which I suspected had more to do with getting them out of our hair as we prepared for company. Harvey had headed back to Cooper's place to shower, shave, and put the finishing touches on the homemade pies he'd made yesterday to bring to the meal. Cooper and Reid had gone to work, leaving Natalie, Zoe, and me to clean and make dinner.

With an hour until hurricane landfall, aka my parents' arrival, Doc dropped off the kids. I let the water out of the sink and dried my hands, meeting him in the dining room.

"How was the Rec Center?" I asked.

For over a month, Doc had been taking my kids to the Rec Center to do something other than swim and play air hockey. My suspicions were based on my kids' continual differing stories every time I asked them what they'd done while there. However, Aunt Zoe insisted I keep my big nose out of it and allow Doc the opportunity to make his own memories with my children. I knew she was right, but that didn't stop me from inquiring whenever they came home.

Doc gave me a quick peck on the mouth. "We had fun."

"Doing what?"

He grinned. "Rec Centering."

I crossed my arms. "You care to elaborate?"

"Not today, Tiger." He shook his keys. "I need to go shower and shave at home before your parents arrive."

"Hey, Doc, will you do me a favor?" Natalie caught up with us at the door.

"Sure."

"Will you go to my apartment before you come back and bring the two paper bags full of wine and beer that I forgot on the floor by the door? I have some of Violet's dad's favorite beer in there." At his nod, she handed him the key to her place. "Thanks!"

I went as far as the front porch, taking in the crisp, pine-scented air, deep blue sky, and glittery snow. It was going to be a beautiful day, I told myself. Everything would work out just fine and dandy. Doc would charm my parents. The food would be delicious. Harvey would be on his best behavior. My kids would end up with great memories of another family get-together. I would survive to see another day.

I looked up at Doc. "I'll see you soon?"

"Is that a question?"

"I wouldn't blame you if you wanted to make a run for it."

He took my face in his hands and gave me a soft kiss. "I wouldn't miss this for the world, Killer. I'll be back in two shakes."

I waved him off, and then marched back inside and started giving orders to the kids to bathe and get spruced up for their grandparents. Natalie trailed up after the kids to oversee the troops.

Not twenty minutes later, the doorbell rang.

In my mind, it sounded like the toll of the death knell.

"They're early," I said to Aunt Zoe.

She tossed me her oven mitt. "Check the roast for me. I'll get the door."

After looking at the roast, I grabbed a bag of fresh lemons and the squeezer from the drawer. I'd sliced and pressed a few lemons when I realized I wasn't hearing any voices in the dining room or living room. Maybe Aunt Zoe was helping my parents carry food in from the Blazer. It wasn't like my mother to show up empty-handed for a family meal.

Two lemon squeezes later, Addy came running into the kitchen. "Hey, Mom?"

I smiled down at her, noticing her freshly washed hair and clean face. Natalie had done well. "What, honey?"

"Who's that man Aunt Zoe is kissing on the front porch?"

I did a double take. "Kissing?"

"Yeah, she's out there without her coat kissing some guy. Grammy always says going out without your coat is a good way to catch a cold."

I set the lemon squeezer down on the counter. "Are you sure it's not Reid?"

She jammed her hands on her hips. "Don't you think I'd know it was Reid if I saw him?"

Maybe not if his face was lip-locked onto Aunt Zoe's. I wiped my hands on the dishtowel and headed for the door to see for myself. Trying to be discreet, I peeked out the front window next to the door.

I gasped. "Oh, no!"

"What's wrong, Mom?"

"Never mind." I pointed at the stairs as I grabbed the door handle. "Go upstairs right now."

"But I already—"

"Right now, Adelynn Renee!"

As she stomped up the stairs, I yanked open the door and stepped outside on the porch, closing the door behind me.

"Get your lips off of her, dammit!" I punched Dominick Masterson in the arm.

A car door slammed somewhere close by, echoing through the cold, crisp air.

He released Aunt Zoe, holding her steady as she swooned against him. "Hello, Violet."

When he looked in my eyes, a wave of nausea rocked me back a couple of steps.

"What are you doing here?" I grabbed Aunt Zoe's arm, hauling her from his clutches. "You promised me you wouldn't come near her."

"I've changed my mind."

"You can't change your mind! Not about this."

"I want Zoe." He spoke as if it were a fact, pure and simple, and I should not only understand but bow to his will.

"She's not a toy, Dominick. You don't get to just have her because you want her."

I heard the front door creak open behind me. "Hey, Vi," Natalie started.

Criminy! I didn't need another female falling under his stupid-cupid spell. I shoved Aunt Zoe toward Natalie. "Take her inside, Nat."

"What's going on? Is that—"

"*Now*, Natalie! I'll explain later." After the door clicked shut behind me, I faced off with good ol' slick Dominick. "If you don't leave my aunt alone, I'm not going to capture your damned *lidérc*."

He adjusted his dashing blue scarf that I'd seen Aunt Zoe tugging free during his kiss. "We made a deal, *Scharfrichter*."

"And you staying clear of my aunt was part of that deal."

"Since when?"

"Since I included it at the restaurant." I was reaching there, because we hadn't officially agreed on that stipulation.

His dark gaze narrowed. "Fine, we can play this your way. However, if you fail to bring me the *lidérc*, the deal is off and I will return for her."

"Hi, honey," a familiar voice said from the base of the porch steps.

Mom!

Oh, hell. *Now* my parents show up? Their timing couldn't have been worse.

I peeked around Dominick's shoulder. "You're early." I gave him a wide berth as I stepped down the stairs Doc had shoveled and salted earlier. It wasn't wide enough to keep my stomach from cramping for a moment.

I gave my mother a hug, careful of the bowl of what looked like coleslaw in her hands. She smelled like summer wildflowers, same as always. "You look really pretty with your hair like that," I said. Her blond hair had strands of various-colored ribbons twirled down through her wavy locks, reminding me of a 1970s record album cover. I envied her lack of crazy curls everywhere.

She looked toward the porch and frowned. "Where did your friend go?"

I turned. Dominick was gone. I glanced around the yard. Totally gone.

"Maybe he went inside." I shot a worried glance at the front door, hoping Aunt Zoe or Natalie hadn't let him inside. "You look nice in that color of green," I told her, leading her up the steps. "It matches your eyes."

"Thank you. Susan picked it out for me. You know how smart she is when it comes to fashion."

Was my mom referring to Susan's street-hussy summer line of clothing or her pole-dancer fall collection? I pinched my lips together, having promised my father the last time we talked that I would work harder on not fighting with my backstabbing sister in front of my mother.

"Where is Susan?" I asked, fingers crossed she'd decided to skip coming up here to steal my boyfriend.

"She drove separately."

Damn! Maybe she'd slide off the road and careen over a cliff on the way up to Deadwood. One could hope.

The door opened as we crested the top step and Natalie stepped out to welcome my mother inside. "Hello, Hippity-Hope. You look smokin' hot, wild child."

"Nat!" My mom loved Natalie as much as me, I swore. Probably more since Natalie didn't fight with Susan all of the time. She looked Natalie up and down. "And you look as gorgeous as always," she said and hugged her. "Punched any boys lately?"

"Only one, but he's made of steel, so he didn't even blink."

Over Mom's shoulder, I mouthed to Natalie: *Where's Aunt Zoe?*

Natalie thumbed toward the house.

I prayed that meant Dominick wasn't in there with her.

"Let's get out of this cold," Natalie said, leading my mom inside.

I was following behind them when my dad called my name from around the front of the house. I slipped and slid back down the steps and along the sidewalk in my slippers. He stood at the back door of his Blazer holding out a casserole dish for me to take.

"Hey, Pops." I kissed him on the cheek, and then took the dish from him. "When you have your hair longer and wavy like that you remind me of Quint." Only my father had a solid sprinkling of gray around the temples. He was a tad thinner than my brother, too, especially now that Quint had bulked up some in the muscle department, but Dad still looked as big and strong as when I'd been a little girl riding high in his arms.

"Where do you think he got his good looks?" he jested, winking at me. His hazel eyes looked yellowish-green in the bright light. He shut the back door of his Blazer. "Your mom likes it better a little longer. She says I look more like the rowdy boys from her younger, hipper days."

Ah, my mom, Hope Parker, the flower child. She used to love to put me in headbands and bell-bottoms when I was a kid, even though it wasn't the style. Every now and then she'd paint a daisy on my cheek, too, and claim I looked "far out." The things I'd do to make my mom happy back then were bananas.

"Hey," Dad said as we neared the porch steps. "Who was that guy your aunt was kissing out here when we pulled up?"

Shit, he'd seen Dominick's public display of bewitchment. "That's just an old friend of hers."

An old troublemaker was more like it. I should've known Dominick would be back for more. Aunt Zoe was one hell of a catch with her classic, graceful beauty, not to mention her brains and wit. Reid had really messed up when he'd let her go way back when, but I might be a tad biased.

"That's some friend." Dad opened the door for me even though he was balancing three times as many dishes and bowls as me. "He practically had her bent over backward."

"How was the drive up?" I asked, changing the subject.

Inside the house, Dad paused to wipe off his boots and share his load with Layne, who acted as if his britches were full of Mexican jumping beans at the sight of my dad.

I left the two of them to their usual bonding routine, joining Aunt Zoe in the kitchen. She was doing my job squeezing lemons. I set the casserole dish down on the counter next to her. "Are you okay?"

She nodded, her face set in a frown. "That son of a bitch didn't even give me a fighting chance."

"I warned him off." I handed her half a lemon. "I told him if he tried messing with you again, I wouldn't deliver his precious *lidérc*."

"Thank you."

"Don't thank me yet. He countered that if I didn't deliver the *lidérc*, he was going to come back for you."

She sighed, shaking her head. "I shouldn't have gone with you yesterday. I got cocky, figuring I could handle it, but I underestimated him."

"Both of us did. Trying to keep Dominick under control is like holding a tiger by the tail."

"A very sexy tiger," she added, squeezing the lemon half.

"With very sharp teeth."

"And an amazing mouth."

"Aunt Zoe," I chastised.

A small grin flitted over her face. "Sorry, but he is as good as his word in that department."

Well, he'd apparently had a lot of time to practice. "Better than Reid?" I pressed.

Her grin faded. "No. Reid still wins, hands down. He has the whole package deal going for him, damn it."

Good! I needed to make sure she kept thinking that way.

"I'm going to figure out a fix," she told me, grabbing another lemon half. "A way to block Dominick from getting into my head."

"That's the spirit," I whispered as my dad joined us.

Layne followed on Dad's heels, a bounce in his step. For years, my father had been the leading man in Layne's life. Quint stepped up whenever he was home, but his photojournalist job kept him away a lot. Layne thought my dad was the bee's knees and wanted to be just like him when he grew up. He'd even used shoe polish to "dye" his sandy blond hair black once, so he'd look more like Dad.

"Hey, Sis," Dad said, setting down the dishes and bowls. He came over and joined us at the counter, planting a kiss on Zoe's temple and then pulling me into a warm hug. "How are my two favorite girls doing? Keeping out of trouble?"

I soaked up his hug. "You know me, Dad. I'm always extra good."

He let me go and walked over to the tray of vegetables sitting on the table. "Sure you are, especially at getting into trouble." His grin reminded me again of my brother. "Who's your new boyfriend?" he asked Aunt Zoe.

"He's not my boyfriend, Blake. Just someone I met recently who's extra amorous."

"Really?" Dad picked up a carrot, giving me one of his you're-busted looks. "Violet seemed to think he was an *old* friend."

I shrugged. "What do I know? I try to keep my nose out of Aunt Zoe's love life."

She let out a loud, good-natured guffaw. "You're hilarious, Violet."

"What? I sort of do."

"I doubt that." Dad took a bite of the carrot, crunching on it. "So, when do I meet this doctor of yours?"

"He's not a doctor," I said, licking my suddenly dry lips. "And you need to promise me that you won't harass him about his long-term plans for me and the kids."

"Come on. No harassing?" Smile lines fanned from the corners of his eyes. He moved over to the roast Aunt Zoe was pulling out of the oven, inspecting it over her shoulder. "The whole reason I drove your mother through the snow and ice was to pick on the new guy."

"I mean it, Dad. Promise me you'll—"

The doorbell rang.

"I'll get that," I told Zoe, giving Dad a poke in the shoulder. "But we're not finished here."

"Whatever you say, Goldilocks." He reached for a piece of the roast, but Aunt Zoe smacked his hand, laughing as he pinched her in the ribs.

I headed for the front door, looking up the stairwell. What had Natalie done with my mother? And where were Addy and Kelly? Layne was sitting in the living room, his face glued to the television.

The doorbell rang two more times as I pulled open the door. "I'm coming. Hold your ..." The sight before me made me snarl without thinking. "And here I'd hoped Satan had called you back to Hell for the holidays."

My sister's smile was so fake it looked plastic. "That hurts, *big* sis." Susan fake pouted for a second or two, and then linked her arm in

Cornelius's, who stood next to her in his Abe Lincoln garb while holding out a bouquet of blue and pink dyed Gerber daisies. "Look who I found." She leaned into him, squishing her perky boob against his shoulder.

Cornelius gave me his usual crooked smile. "Hello, Violet. Your littermate was waiting for me at the end of the drive."

"Of course she was. She's accustomed to picking up men curbside." The man-stealing bitch. "When did you get back?"

"I caught a flight late last night." He shoved the daisies at me. "This is the day I'm to meet your family, correct?"

I'd forgotten that Susan had made a point of inviting Cornelius, my pseudo-boyfriend, to dinner. "Uh, yeah, sure." I stepped back. "Come in."

Susan pushed me aside, pulling Cornelius into the foyer after her. She took off her long coat, wearing her usual mini-skirt and thigh-high black boots. Today she'd added a gold sweater that fit like a bathing suit. I rolled my eyes, taking Cornelius's coat and hat.

"We've got a problem," he whispered to me when Addy and Kelly came down the stairs and distracted Susan.

"You're telling me. Doc is coming today, too." When he stared at me, I added, "The tall medium."

"Oh, that is another issue then. Would you like me to leave?"

"Of course not. Stay and have dinner with my family. But mum's the word on me and my abilities."

"Which abilities would those be?"

I smirked. "The breathing fire and tightrope walking ones."

"Ah. You're referring to your occupation in real estate."

I opened my mouth to correct him and then closed it. That did sort of describe me at work, especially with Jerry putting up those damned billboards left and right.

He straightened his sleeves. "That was a joke, Violet."

"Helloooo," my mother said from the top of the steps. "You must be Violet's new man."

I cringed. "Here we go." I turned to correct my mom.

But before I could get a word out, Susan butted in. "Mother, meet Doc." She latched onto Cornelius's arm again, melding into his Siamese twin.

He bowed. "Hello, Violet's mother. You can call me Cornelius."

Mom stopped two steps from the bottom, her gaze roving from me to Cornelius. "But I thought you go by D …" she gasped. "My, what beautiful cornflower blue eyes you have."

"Thank you. I borrowed them from my grandfather."

She smiled. "He must be as interesting to look at as you."

"Even more so now that he's been dead for over a month," Cornelius answered in earnest. "We opted out of embalming him, though. He always had a fondness for coffin flies."

"Coffin flies?" my mom squeaked.

And we were off.

Rather than correct my mother's mistaken assumption about Cornelius being my boyfriend, I threw up my hands and escaped to the kitchen with his daisies. I'd let him keep her and Susan preoccupied while I figured out how to clear up the Doc confusion without embarrassing anyone other than Susan, the stinking floozy.

Ten minutes later, while Aunt Zoe arranged Cornelius's flowers in one of her own purple glass vases, I was telling my dad about some of my new clients as he sliced the roast when the doorbell rang again. I glanced at the clock. That had to be Doc. It was almost time to eat.

"I'll be right back," I told Dad and headed for the front door.

Harvey waited for me on the other side of the door with a stack of pies, a neatly trimmed beard, and slicked-back hair. He looked different than usual, so much so that I just stared at him for several seconds.

"Are ya gonna move yer hiney aside or make me eat my dessert on the porch?"

I took one of the pies from him and stepped aside. "What kind of pies did you make?"

"That one there is cherry. These two are sweet potato and peanut butter."

"Did you bring—"

"The jar of hot fudge is in my pocket."

"You're the best!" I took the other pies from him and set them on the sideboard so he could shuck his coat. "You really need to bite the bullet and marry me one of these days. I'd make a great wife."

"Violet?" my mother said from behind me, her tone uncertain.

I turned.

"I thought you said Mr. Cornelius was your boyfriend."

"Well, I—"

"But you were just talking to this ... uh ... slightly older man about getting married."

"Yeah, it's complicated. Cornelius isn't the real Doc. Susan is confused." There, that was simple enough. I handed her Harvey's cherry pie and grabbed the peanut butter. "Help me take these pies to the kitchen."

Harvey let out a low whistle, making Mom and me both turn his way. He ogled my mother up and down. "My, aren't you as purty as a fence-corner peach." He grinned at her with both gold teeth showing. "Sparky, did ya order her from one of those mail-order magazines, because she looks like she walked right off the pages of a catalog."

Shit-criminy, talk about laying it on thick. "Mom," I said, nudging my head toward ol' Sugar Tongue. "Meet Willis Harvey. Harvey, this is my mom, Hope Parker."

She tittered. "Well, it's sure nice to meet you finally."

Finally? Had the kids talked about Harvey to her?

She set the pie down and hugged Harvey, surprising both Harvey and me. "You're a smidgeon older than I'd expected, but if Violet wants to marry you, you must be young at heart. Why does everyone call you 'Doc'? Did you used to be a doctor before you retired?"

Oh, dear.

Something crashed in the kitchen, followed by Aunt Zoe yelling, "Violet!"

I left my mom and the pies with Harvey, racing to see if Aunt Zoe was okay. Sliding into the kitchen, I asked, "What happened?"

Dad pointed the knife he was using to slice the roast at the back door. "Your aunt saw her new-old friend standing at the back door, dropped a pan in the sink, and then ran into the living room."

Dominick waved at me through the back-door window.

"You want to grab the door, Goldilocks. My hands are greasy and ..." Dad stared at Dominick, the knife lowering as my father's smile widened. "You know, he seems like a really good guy. We should let him come to dinner."

"No!" I rushed out the back door, slamming it behind me. Grabbing Dominick by the arm, I dragged him down the steps and through the snowy backyard. As soon as we were around the side of the house and out of view of everyone inside, I let go of him and bent over the evergreen shrubs at the edge of the property line, dry heaving several times.

After I wiped my mouth, I whirled on him. "I told you to leave."

"I forgot to give you the message I came to deliver." He looked over at the bushes with a frown. "Are you feeling ill?"

Extremely, especially since Susan had arrived. "You're bullshitting me about a message. You just came back to see Zoe."

"It's not a lie. When I saw your aunt earlier, I forgot I'd come to see you, not her." He rubbed his hands together. "She's such an amazing specimen."

I huffed, still not buying that his crush on Aunt Zoe had made him forget his reason for showing up on her doorstep. "Fine. You've got the hots for my aunt. Now what's your message?"

"One of the hunters has arrived."

It took several seconds of shivering in the cold in my wet slippers for his message to sink in. "You mean one of my enemies has arrived to hunt me?"

He nodded.

"Why are you telling me this?"

"I thought you should know."

And I appreciated that, but—"Why would you go out of your way to help me?"

"I want my *lidérc* back, and you are the only one who can capture it, *Scharfrichter*."

Right. He needed to make sure I stayed alive long enough to fulfill my side of our deal. "When you say *arrived*, do you mean here in the Black Hills?"

"I don't know its exact location, but I've received information that it is here amongst us."

"Like on this plane?"

"Yes, that is another way of saying it."

I crossed my arms, my whole body trembling from the cold. The winter sun did nothing to warm me, especially now that I knew another enemy had arrived to take me out.

"So, what do I—"

"Violet?" my mother called from the back porch.

I took a couple of steps back and peered around the side of the house at her. "I'll be right there, Mom."

I turned back to wrap up my meeting with Dominick only to find him gone once again. Scanning the yard, I scratched my head. Dang. I needed to learn that disappearing trick of his.

Before my mom came to investigate further, I ran back to the porch where she waited. "Violet, we need to talk about your boyfriend."

"Inside, Mom. I'm freezing."

She followed me through the back door. "Why in the world were you outside without a coat? You're going to catch a cold."

I kicked off my wet slippers. "How many times have I told you that you can't get sick from being in the cold without a coat?"

"Maybe not, but you can certainly—"

The doorbell rang.

Frick-n-frack! That had better be Doc.

I looked around for Aunt Zoe. She was still missing. Dad was almost finished with the meat, stacking it on the tray inside a circle of roasted potato wedges.

"Where's Harvey?"

My mother shot a worried glance toward the dining room. "He said something about needing to water the flowers."

The doorbell rang again.

"Stay here with Dad," I told my mom. I grumbled on the way to the door. "What am I? The flippin' doorman?"

It wasn't Doc.

"Hey, Sparky." Reid held out a dozen red roses for me to take. "These are for Zo, but if I give them to her, she'll probably throw them back in my face. Maybe you can give them to her for me."

I frowned, stepping outside in my bare feet. Holy shit-ski, the porch boards were freaking freezing! "What are you doing here?" I asked him after I'd closed the door.

"I was sort of hoping to have dinner with your family."

I rubbed my chin, remembering something Aunt Zoe had told me about Reid and her relationship in the past. "Now you want to come to dinner? Years after Aunt Zoe asked you repeatedly to meet her family?"

"That's the idea." He smiled, his mesmeric, dark blue eyes appealing his case.

"Did she invite you to come today?" I asked.

He scoffed. "No, but I figured I'd break the ice and show up anyway."

Wow, that took some balls, but I had a feeling if Reid walked in the house, Aunt Zoe might break something else … over his head. "Maybe we need to think about this and come up with another plan." Especially after the mess with Dominick this morning.

The door opened behind me. Before I could turn to see who had joined us, the door slammed.

"What in the hell are you doing here, Martin?" Aunt Zoe asked.

Shit, too late.

"Hey, Zo. You look amazing in that color of purple." Reid was talking faster than normal. "I brought you some flowers." He turned to me, nudging his head in Aunt Zoe's direction.

"Oh, right." I shoved the bouquet at her. "These are for you." Feeling like a third wheel, I bowed at Reid and then Aunt Zoe. "I'll leave you two to talk alone and go melt my toes over the stove."

On my way through the door, I ran into my father's chest.

"What's going on out here?" he said, setting me aside and joining Aunt Zoe on the porch. "Are you playing musical men today, Zoe?"

"Musical men?" Reid said, frowning. "What's he mean?"

Uh-oh. I stepped back outside onto the cold porch boards. "I'll explain later, Reid. My dad is confused about …" I ran out of words then and just smiled extra wide for a finale.

Aunt Zoe sighed. "Damn it, Martin. You picked a hell of a time to come courtin'."

"Reid Martin?" my dad asked, his eyes narrowing.

Reid nodded, holding out his hand. "You must be Zo's brother, Blake. It's nice to finally meet you."

Dad glared down at Reid's hand. "Are you the same Reid Martin who broke my sister's heart a few years back?"

"Blake, don't," Aunt Zoe said, grabbing my dad's sleeve.

"Probably," Reid said, lowering his hand, his face lined with uncertainty. "I'm sorry about that. I was an idiot."

"It took her a long time to get over your lousy hide," Dad said, bristling in spite of Aunt Zoe's attempts to keep him calm.

Reid looked from my father to Aunt Zoe and back. "And for that, I'm truly sorry. I had recently divorced and was struggling with a lot of self-doubts."

"But now you think you can just come back here with some flowers and Zoe's going to take you back with open arms?"

Reid scoffed. "I know better than that."

"You're damned right she's not. You have a lot of nerve, buddy."

"Blake," Aunt Zoe said, her voice stronger. "I've got this. Please go back inside."

My dad hesitated, but then nodded, stepping back. "Zoe, don't let him mess with your head again."

I grimaced. It might be too late for that. I grabbed my dad by the arm, pulling him back inside. "Dad, let Aunt Zoe deal with Reid."

"Fine," he said, but he turned back before I could get the door shut and hollered out, "but I like the other guy you were kissing today better!"

Oh, double fudge. I shut the door, leaning against it for several seconds as my dad stalked away, growling about Reid being a no-good, shiftless heartbreaker.

Hmmm. That hadn't gone so well.

Harvey stepped out of the bathroom and looked my way, his bushy brows rising. "What did I miss?"

"My dad almost decking Reid."

He rubbed his hands together. "Woo-wee! Things are startin' to get excitin' now."

I led Harvey into the kitchen to give Aunt Zoe and Reid some privacy. Dropping into one of the chairs, I made the introductions to my dad.

My mom leaned on the counter next to my bottle of tequila. It looked less full than the last time I'd snuggled with it. She raised her coffee mug at Harvey. "You're a little older than I'd like for my daughter, Mr. Harvey, but if you'll marry her, I'm happy. I've been waiting for years for Violet to finally settle down." She took a swig of what was undoubtedly my tequila in her cup. "Hell, I'd pretty much given up on ever getting a son-in-law when it came to her."

"Hope," my dad said, picking up the bottle. "How much tequila have you had already?"

Her shrug looked loosey-goosey on her shoulders. "Only a few fingers or more. It goes down really easy with a drop of lemon." She pointed at the pitcher of lemon juice Aunt Zoe hadn't finished making into lemonade. "Since I skipped breakfast, it started burning nice and warm right away."

"Oh, man," I said, lowering my foot to the floor. "Don't tell me Mom's drunk already."

Harvey wheezed. "This just keeps gettin' better." He joined her at the counter. "So, do ya prefer I call ya 'Ma,' or would you rather I use your first name after I marry yer daughter?"

"Hold up," Dad said, giving Harvey a thorough once-over. "Is this your new boyfriend, Violet?"

Aunt Zoe came stomping and snarling into the kitchen before I could answer my dad. "The nerve of that man to show up now with roses." She tossed said flowers on the counter, grabbing a vase from the cupboard. "What gives him the right to get huffy about me kissing another man?"

"He gave up that right years ago," my dad said, cheering her on.

"Damned right he did." Aunt Zoe picked up the tequila bottle. She grabbed a glass from the cupboard and filled it with enough of the liquor to knock a full-grown man on his ass. "If I want to get my heart kicked around again, I'll give him a call. Until then, Reid Martin needs to back the hell off. I'm real tired of men getting in my head and messing everything up."

"I'll drink to that," my mother said, grimacing as her gaze darted back and forth between Harvey and me.

I sighed. Dang it, things were going downhill like a runaway Olympic bobsled. I looked up at the clock. Where in the hell was Doc? He needed to show up on his white horse and whisk me away from this temporary bout of insanity.

"Maybe you three should go set the dining room table," I said. "Let Harvey and me—"

The doorbell rang.

Aunt Zoe swore.

Mom giggled.

Dad frowned at me. "You'd better get that."

I nodded, my toes stinging as I crossed the dining room floor. They were finally starting to thaw and now being poked with hundreds of tiny needles.

I opened the door, ready to throw myself in Doc's arms and tell him we had to make a run for it.

Two police officers stood on the porch with their thumbs hooked in their utility belts.

"Hey, Rocky," the tall thin officer said, using an old nickname I'd earned after breaking Cooper's nose. "You have a minute?"

I stepped outside on the porch and closed the door behind me, staying on the scratchy welcome mat, which was a shade warmer than the frozen floorboards. "What's going on?"

"Is Natalie Beals here?"

There was no use denying it since her truck was parked in front of the house. "Sure. Why? Are her parents okay?"

The other cop nodded. "Everyone is fine. We sort of need to take her to the station for a little bit."

Sort of? "Why? What did she do?"

"That's police business, Ms. Parker. Could you go get her for us?" When I sputtered and started to object, he lifted his hand, silencing me. "I can see you're having a party in there. Now, we can make this a big noisy deal that will upset everyone, or you can go get Natalie and we can slip away without anyone even noticing."

"Are you throwing her in jail?"

The thin one snickered. "No, Rocky. That cell is reserved for you."

I balled my fists, my temper crackling and sparking. "That's really funny, you overdressed meter maid."

"Calm down, Ms. Parker," the other officer said. "Nobody is going to jail. We need to talk to Natalie down at the station for a few minutes, then we'll bring her back to your get-together without causing a scene."

I looked back at the door, thinking about my mother and Aunt Zoe already hitting the bottle. The sooner I could make these two policemen go away, the better. "Fine. Wait right here. I'll be out with her in a minute."

Inside, I raced up the stairs, slipping on one with my frozen foot and falling on my chin. "Son of a beeswax!"

"Are you okay, Mom?" Addy asked from the top of the stairs.

"I'm fine." I got back to my frozen feet. "Where's Natalie?"

"She's talking to Abe Lincoln's ghost in the bathroom mirror."

In the mirror? What the hell?

"Mom, why are there two policemen standing on the front porch."

I grabbed Addy as I passed, pulling her along with me. "They're looking for a lost dog and need Natalie's help."

"How sad. Kelly and I can help, too," Addy offered.

"No, they only want Natalie."

Sure enough, I found Natalie and Cornelius standing in the bathroom looking at each other in the mirror. I started to ask what in the ever-lovin' Hades they were doing, but then shook my head. We had a bigger problem. I closed the door in Addy's face.

"Natalie," I whispered, turning on the bathtub faucet to drown out my voice in case Addy was listening under the door. "You have company."

Cornelius looked from the bath to me. "Is bathing together one of your pre-dinner family traditions? Because I'm not sure all three of us can fit in that small tub."

"What did you say?" Natalie asked, coming closer.

Cornelius walked over to the tub and picked up the bottle of pink bubble bath. "This won't do. I get a rash from bath bubbles. I prefer lavender oil in my water. It allows the spirits to join me in the tub if they are so inclined."

I gaped at him. Bathing with ghosts? That was bonkers.

Shaking off my stupor, I shut off the water and grabbed Natalie by the wrist. I pointed at Cornelius. "Wait for me here."

"Okay," he said as I reached for the door. "But I'll be honest, Violet. Unless this is a new method you plan to use to channel ghosts, I don't think your tall medium will approve of us bathing together."

I didn't bother replying and left him standing by the tub. Natalie let me drag her downstairs. I shoved her coat into her hands, glad to see she was already wearing her tennis shoes.

"Am I going somewhere?" she asked as I hauled her toward the door.

"Yes." I opened the door and pulled her out into the cold. "These two officers need to take you to the station."

"Why?" she asked, and then greeted both of the cops with a hug, asking the non-snickering one how his wife was doing.

The policemen gave her the same explanation they had me. Natalie went willingly, assuring me she'd return shortly after she found out what was going on at the station. I had a feeling that Cooper might be behind this, so I kept my knuckle chewing to a minimum and went back inside.

"Who was that?" Susan asked from the living room, joining me in the foyer.

"The grim reaper," I answered, glaring at her. "He came to take you to the dance. Why don't you grab your coat and head on down the road with him."

"As insults go, that was plain stupid," she said.

"Yeah, well I'm a little preoccupied with other pains in the ass right now, so you'll have to wait your turn."

She followed me through the dining room. "Where did you hide your boyfriend?"

"In the upstairs bathroom," I answered, joining the kitchen crowd.

My mom's eyes were looking extra bright, a sure sign of her being well along the road to Tipsy Town. Aunt Zoe was still swearing about men and their head games, while my dad and Harvey worked on putting the rest of dinner together.

"Who was at the door," Harvey asked while drizzling leftover pan drippings from the roast over the puffed-up Yorkshire pudding pastries. I hadn't seen that done before and licked my lips in anticipation.

"Nobody important." I handed Susan a stack of dinner plates. "Make yourself useful outside of my boyfriend's bed for once."

My mother gasped. "Violet Lynn!"

I winced. "Sorry. That slipped out."

"Try harder," my dad said, giving me a stern look.

I pinched my lips together and focused on putting the final touches on the lemonade I'd started what seemed eons ago, squeezing the lemons a little too hard and getting more pulp than usual with the juice. The poor lemons had to take the brunt of my day's mounting frustration whether they liked it or not.

And where in the mother-humping hell was Doc, dammit?

Twenty minutes later, the table was set with plates and food when the doorbell rang yet again.

"That had better be Doc," I muttered to Harvey as he sliced the pies. "Do me a favor and tell the kids to wash their hands for dinner, please."

"10-4, Sparky." He looked me over. "You doin' okay?"

"I don't think so."

"We'd better fill yer gullet before yer head pops."

I strode through the dining room, breathing in the delicious aroma of roasted meat and bread. Harvey was right. If this wasn't Doc, I was giving up on life and stuffing my mouth with as much food as I could fit inside of it.

I opened the door and sighed, closing the door with me on the freezing side again. "Cooper, please tell me you're here to break bread with my family and not give me bad news."

Cooper's face pinched up tight. "Yeah, you see, about that." He blew out a breath. "I'm here to tell you Nyce will be a little late to dinner."

"No shit. He's already a lot late. Where is he?"

"At the police station."

I blinked. "What? Why?"

Cooper sighed. "It's all a misunderstanding that's being worked out as we speak."

"Explain."

"Detective Hawke caught Nyce coming out of Natalie's apartment about an hour ago."

I nodded. "I know. She gave him her key so he could grab some drinks she forgot."

"Well, Detective Hawke is a little high-strung right now, as we've both witnessed, and he knows Nyce is your boyfriend."

"And?"

"He cuffed Nyce and took him to the police station."

"You've got to be kidding me."

"Unfortunately, I wasn't at the station at the time Hawke brought him in, or I would have been able to get Nyce out of there. But since I was gone, things escalated due to some insults Detective Hawke said about you, and Nyce ended up in a jail cell."

"That pompous, pig-headed prick!" I stomped my cold feet.

"Nice alliteration, Parker."

"Hawke needs to be put back on his leash."

"Calm down."

"You need to talk to your boss about him. This is harassment."

"I will talk to the chief on Monday when he's back at work. But right now, Hawke is the ranking officer so it's been a bit tricky."

"So, that's why those two cops came and took Natalie to the station."

"Yes. Doc requested that someone bring her in so she could give a statement verifying that he merely was doing as she'd asked." He shifted his feet. "She was almost done writing her report when I left to come fill you in on the whole mess."

"Damn it. Of all the—"

"Violet!" Rex Conner called out from across the street.

I cringed. No. This couldn't be happening. Not today.

"Go away, asshole!" I yelled, making Cooper wince.

Rex stormed up Aunt Zoe's sidewalk, his face an ugly mask of anger. "You've crossed the line, sweetheart." He stopped at the bottom of the steps, glaring up at me and then Cooper.

"Now is not a good time, Rex." I moved to the top stair.

I heard the creak of the front door behind me. Glancing back, I groaned at the sight of my dad stepping out to join us.

"Now is as good a time as any," Rex snapped. "And I'm glad your boyfriend is here to witness this."

My boyfriend? Doc wasn't here. He was ... ohhhh, he meant Cooper. I'd forgotten that Rex had seen the detective out on the porch shirtless getting the paper the other morning.

"I want to file charges against Violet," Rex told Cooper.

Cooper joined me on the first stair step. "For what?"

"These!" Rex held up a pair of pink satin panties. "Why don't you explain to your lover why you enjoy sending me the panties that you've obviously been wearing while getting off?"

I recoiled. "You've made a mistake."

"There is no mistaking this, Violet. They are stiff and they smell like sex."

He'd smelled a stranger's panties? I gagged a little.

Rex shook the underwear at me. "You purposely sent them to my boss's address with a note to me inside. That's grounds for harassment, bitch."

Harassment was turning out to be the word of the day.

With my cheeks burning, I looked back at my father's fury-lined face. "I swear, Dad, those are not my underwear."

Cooper moved another step down. "What proof do you have that those are Violet's?"

Rex sputtered, then his mouth melted into an ugly sneer. "Who else besides her would be trying to get me fired so I'd leave the Black Hills?"

"Maybe you need to stop and think about this some more," Cooper suggested. "At least, remove yourself from Zoe's yard."

"I'm not going anywhere until Violet admits she's fucking with me."

"I am not fucking with you, Rex. Nor do I ever plan to again. Now get off my aunt's lawn or I'll shoot you for trespassing."

"You can't shoot him for trespassing, Parker." Cooper held out a calming hand toward Rex. "How about you head down to the station with me? You can write up a statement about what happened and we'll keep it on file."

"Oh, you'd like that, wouldn't you, loverboy? I follow you there and these disappear." He shook the panties at Cooper. "I'm a lot smarter than the other idiots Violet has screwed. I'm the one who walked away, remember, not the other way around. You keep that in mind the next time she tells you how juiced up she is for you and wants to ride you to town."

"You son of a—" Something bumped into my shoulder, knocking me sideways into Cooper. I realized what had hit me the second my father tackled Rex, knocking him flat on his back in the snow.

Cooper shoved me aside and leapt down the steps after my dad, diving into the mix.

My dad landed two solid blows to Rex's breadbasket in spite of Cooper's attempt to pull him free. "Those are for both of my daughters, you piece of shit."

"Oh, crap." I stumbled down the steps, not sure what to do as the three of them rolled in the snow.

Finally, Cooper got a solid grip on my dad's arms and was able to drag him off Rex, tugging him back several feet.

I walked barefoot over to the pink panties, picking them up with a cottonwood twig that had been sticking out of the snow. While my dad growled and cursed, I held the panties out in front of Rex.

"These," I said, shaking the stick in front of Rex, "are not *my* panties. And he," I pointed the underwear toward Cooper, who was still gripping my dad's arms, "is not *my* lover. Get that straight in your scientist brain, you dipshit."

A scuffling sound on the porch made me turn. Cornelius, Susan, and Harvey were all standing on the porch, along with my mother, who was leaning on Harvey's shoulder. Please, please, please let Aunt Zoe have seen Rex out the window and removed my children far from the scene of this unbelievable clusterfuck.

"Rex," I heard Susan coo with a sigh of happiness.

"Blake," my mother said, her voice high and giggly. "Why are you playing in the snow with those boys?"

Oh, Mom was definitely flat-out drunk. This would go down as another tragic family dinner that would undoubtedly be blamed on me. Hell, now I might as well blow the ship to smithereens since it was already sinking with me at the helm.

"While we're on the subject of my sex life," I said, pointing the panties at the porch. "Cornelius is not my boyfriend, nor is Harvey my fiancé. They are both good friends of mine and that's it." I flicked the panties at Rex. They landed on one of his expensive Italian loafers. "And to set the record straight for one and all, my boyfriend is Doc Nyce and he's not here at the moment."

"Where is Doc?" Harvey asked, looking at his nephew.

I answered for Cooper, "At this very moment, Doc is at the police station defending my honor." He was also in the thick of fighting a breaking and entering charge, but they didn't need to know that minor detail.

I dropped the microphone … or rather in my case, the stick. There. All of my secrets were out. Well, not quite all, but the ones about my real boyfriend were flapping in the frigid breeze blowing across the snow. Damn, my toes were cold.

Marching over to the porch steps, I gave a final bow. Actually, it was more of a clumsy curtsy. "Here's a thought," I said. "After Cooper gets this cocksucking bastard off Aunt Zoe's lawn, how about we go inside and enjoy dinner like a normal family while we wait for my boyfriend to get out of jail?"

Chapter Twenty-Two

Several hours later, Cooper dropped Natalie off at Aunt Zoe's place. He didn't stick around to enjoy any more of my family fun, relaying through Natalie that Rex was not going to press charges against my father for assault. That was smart of Rex, considering I could press a few charges of my own if he wanted to play that game.

"Where's Doc?" I asked before Natalie could even take off her coat.

"He went home to take a shower and wash off the stink of jail."

"I know that stink all too well."

She chuckled, then sobered. "He told me he feels like shit for letting you down. He knows how big of a deal today was supposed to be."

"But he didn't let me down. This wasn't his fault. He was just in the wrong place at the wrong time."

"I told him that, but he thinks if he'd controlled his temper around Hawke, he wouldn't have ended up in jail."

"He was defending me." I sighed. "Hasn't he figured out yet that being with me means control is a figment of his imagination?"

"Man, don't I know that from experience." She giggled when I tugged on her hair. Looking over my shoulder, she frowned. "Dinner is over, I take it."

I nodded. "Aunt Zoe and my parents are in the kitchen and the kids are upstairs playing. Harvey had to leave. He said he has a hot date tonight."

"Damn, that old man sees way more action than I ever did before this sabbatical. What about Cornelius?"

"He was suffering from jetlag, so I sent him to Calamity Jane's to get some sleep."

"And Susan?"

"Satan's concubine got bored when it was just her family here. She left, claiming she had some important things to do."

"She probably had to go home and feed her hellhounds."

"Or find another innocent soul to annihilate. But there are plenty of leftovers in the fridge. Mom even made up plates for you and Doc."

"Man, I love your mom."

"Yeah, well, she's still pretty drunk, so maybe you should see what she set aside for you before writing a love sonnet about her." I peeked out the window. "Shit. It's really starting to come down."

Outside, the flurries that had been wishy-washy all afternoon were getting serious. I glanced at the clock. Nightfall was coming and my parents really needed to hit the road and drive back down to Rapid. It appeared that my wish from earlier this week might be granted—the meeting between my parents and Doc would be delayed.

I should be dancing a jig about that, but for some reason it made my chest tight. I thought of Doc sitting in that filthy jail cell all afternoon, knowing we were here waiting for him.

I wouldn't miss this for the world, Killer.

"Damn it," I grumbled, grabbing Aunt Zoe's red puffy vest, looking for my snow boots. Where had Addy left them? She had a bad habit of walking off in my shoes and leaving them God knew where. "Screw it." I grabbed my purple boots, sliding them on over the yoga pants I'd put on after eating too much for dinner.

"What are you doing?" Natalie asked when I held her shoulder to steady myself while sliding on one boot and then the other.

"Something that I may live to regret." I zipped up the vest. "Go get my dad and tell him it's time to hit the road."

Ten minutes later, I followed my parents out the door. I meant to ask Natalie if she was the one sending Rex the dirty underwear, but we hadn't had a moment alone after she went to round up my parents. I doubted she did. That wasn't her style, but maybe her sabbatical had shifted things in her brain.

"If Cooper comes home," I told Aunt Zoe as she followed us as far as the porch, "let him know where I am and that I'll be back in a while."

She gave me a thumbs-up. "Good luck!"

I hopped in the back seat, directing my dad along the snowy neighborhood streets of Deadwood's Presidential District. My mom was still floating high on tequila currents, but after the drunken nap she'd taken after dinner, she was beginning to sink down to earth. A little.

"Pull in behind that old green pickup," I said, pointing at the Picklemobile sitting in Doc's drive.

Dad turned into the drive and parked. "Now what?"

I'd told him we were taking a short detour on his way home, but I hadn't mentioned where or why. "Shut off the Blazer and follow me."

"What about your mother?"

"We'll bring her along."

Dad helped my mother out the door. When she stumbled, he caught her.

"Maybe she should stay back," I said, not wanting either of them to fall and get hurt on the slick sidewalk.

"I am not staying in the Blazer," my mom said, only a slight slur left in her voice. "I can walk. Just give me a moment to get my feet under me."

True to her word, she lurched up the sidewalk alongside Dad, stumbling only once on her way up the porch steps.

I rang the doorbell, chewing on my lower lip. My stomach fluttered as we waited at the door.

"Who lives here?" My mother's whisper was loud enough to be heard across the street.

"You'll see," I told her, pushing the doorbell again. *Come on, open the door.* These thin yoga pants did little to block out the cold. I leaned over and tried to peek in the dining room window. The curtains were closed, but I could see light around the edges.

"How's your shoulder, Blake?" Mom asked.

He rolled it forward and backward. "It's a little stiff."

"How about I give you a hot-oil rubdown tonight?"

He wiggled his eyebrows at her. "Hubba-hubba."

"For Pete's sake, you two, knock it off." I tried to give them a stern look, but ended up grinning. "Your child is present."

"How do you think we got you, Goldilocks?"

"There are two things I try not to do each and every day," I told him. "One is look directly into the sun; the other is think about how I was conceived."

Mom giggled, shivering. "You tackling Rex was so sexy."

I guffawed. "I'm surprised you even remember it, Mom. You were already several shots of tequila to the wind by then."

I hit the doorbell again. I thought about pulling out my key and letting myself in, but maybe Doc didn't want company after the hoopla down at the station.

A thudding sound came from inside.

"I think I hear someone," Dad said. He put his arm around Mom and tucked her against his side, kissing her temple.

The lock clicked and the door opened.

Doc's hair was wet and finger-combed, his T-shirt damp in spots, his jeans crisp. He smelled fresh out of the shower, soapy clean with a hint of cologne. "Violet? What are you doing here?" He looked over my shoulder at my parents, his smile polite. "I was about to head over to your aunt's."

I nudged him aside and stepped inside, waving at my parents to follow. Doc shut the door behind us and leaned against it, his gaze guarded.

"Doc." I licked my cold lips, diving in headfirst. "These are my parents, Blake and Hope Parker." I latched onto Doc's arm, pulling him closer, and slid my arm around his waist. "Dad and Mom, this is Dane Nyce. You can call him 'Doc.' " I smiled up at him, resting my hand on his chest. The feel of his steady heartbeat under my palm spurred me to take an even bigger step. "He's the guy you've been hearing about from the kids, the one I'm in love with."

Doc's eyes widened in surprise as he stared at me. Then he recovered and held out his hand to my dad. "It's nice to finally meet you, Mr. Parker."

"It's Blake." My dad shook his hand. "Addy and Layne have been talking you up."

"Your grandkids are a lot of fun." Doc sent me a sly smile. "I think your daughter is really swell, too."

I laughed at his echo of my own words of love from the other night and pinched his side, making him grin wider.

My dad sent me a raised brow before focusing on Doc again. "How was jail?"

Doc groaned. "It smelled like humiliation with a spritz of urine." He focused on my mother, holding out his hand. "Mrs. Parker, you are as lovely as your daughter."

Mom's smile filled her whole face. "You're so young and normal." She took his hand, leaning over to me. "He's very tall and handsome," she whispered to me but all could hear.

"Mom, you said that out loud."

"Did I?" she giggled.

I pulled Doc's hand from hers, placing hers back down to her side. "Yes."

"Am I still talking out loud?"

I grimaced at Doc. "She self-medicated with tequila today."

"Like mother, like daughter," he said, catching my hand. The heat in his gaze when he raised my knuckles to his lips practically singed my split ends. Then he lowered my hand and focused on my parents again. "Would either of you like anything to drink?"

"Yes, but we'll have to take a rain check," my father said. "The snow is really coming down and we need to hit the road."

Doc nodded. "I'm sorry I missed dinner."

Mom was still gawking at Doc. "He has a nice, strong jaw and very broad shoulders."

I rolled my eyes. "You're still talking out loud, Mother."

"Violet explained the circumstances at the police station to us," my dad said to Doc. "Had we known it would take so long to spring you, we would've come down and kept you company." His gaze narrowed. "Out of curiosity, Doc, how many times have you been in jail now?"

"Today was a first for me."

Dad smirked at me. "You've got him beat by far, Goldilocks."

"Funny, Dad. Ha ha."

Mom reached up and took Doc by the chin, turning his face to one side and then the other. "I bet he would make adorable babies," she whispered nice and loud.

"Mom!" My cheeks warmed. I knocked her hand away from Doc's chin. "Your volume knob is broken."

"I don't know, Hope." Dad rubbed his jaw, sizing up Doc. "Do you think he's the marrying type?" A grin teased the corners of his mouth.

I nailed my dad with a knock-it-off squint.

Dad snickered. "Layne says you have a nice car."

"It's a '69 Camaro SS," I told Dad. "He rebuilt it himself."

"I had some help," Doc said.

"That's not a nice car," Dad said, "It's sexy as hell."

"I had sex in a Camaro once," my mother said and then hiccupped.

"Mom! Please stop talking."

"Yes, you did, baby." Dad chuckled, looking at her with that hubba-hubba glint in his eyes again. "Where do you think your brother was conceived, Goldilocks?"

I recoiled. "Come on! Please stop talking about having S-E-X before I go blind."

"I like this one best, Violet." Mom patted Doc's chest as if we were picking out a new couch. "Wait." She made a fist and knocked on Doc, listening for a couple of beats. "Yeah," she turned to my dad. "He's the real deal."

"This *one*?" Doc looked at me with raised eyebrows.

"Mom got confused during my musical boyfriend game today, but I cleared it up after Dad punched Rex."

"I heard Zoe's porch was ringside seating."

Dad squeezed his right hand slowly, grimacing. "I've been waiting to lay out that son of a bitch for over a decade."

Mom hiccupped again, bumping me to get my attention. "He has a sensual aura around him," she said, circling her palm in front of Doc's chest. "It reminds me of your father's aura when the moon is full and he gets frisky."

"Oh, sweet Lord!"

Doc chuckled, squeezing my hand. "Your parents are great."

Great at embarrassing me! My parents needed to say good-bye now and drive home before they said something even more mortifying. I walked over and opened the front door. "Oh, darn. The snow is coming down harder. You two had better go."

"I think that's our cue to leave, baby," Dad said, reaching for my mother's arm.

Before he caught her, Mom stumbled forward and wrapped her arms around Doc's waist. She looked up at him, her smile bordering on goofy. "You promise to join us for Christmas, Doc?"

Doc loosely hugged her, patting her back twice while staring at me. "I wouldn't miss it for the world."

I unwrapped my mother from Doc, leading her over to the door where my father waited. "Good-bye, Mom." I kissed her cheek. "I'm sorry I drove you to drink today."

She blew a tequila-scented raspberry in my face, waving me off. "I'm so glad you're not marrying Mr. Harvey. He's a nice man, but just a teeny tiny bit too old for you." She gave me a hug and kissed my nose like I was a dog. "Your doctor is a keeper. Don't screw this up like you usually do, Violet."

"Thanks, Mom. Your words of wisdom are legendary as always." I leaned her against the doorframe, turning to my dad.

Before I could get a word out, he pulled me into a surprise hug. "You're a good egg, Goldilocks." He pushed me back, holding onto my shoulders as he stared down at me. "We need to talk about the occupational hazards that come with your latest career change." His hazel gaze held a warning. "You've always been one hell of a scrapper, but this is tougher than anything you've tackled before."

I wasn't sure what to say. He had to be referring to my executioner gig, but since my mom was leaning nearby, I couldn't clarify. "Okay," I said, frowning up at him.

"Walk us out," he added.

I nodded.

Doc shook my father's hand again and closed the door behind us, leaving me to walk my parents out to the Blazer alone.

"Be careful," Dad said after settling Mom in the passenger side and shutting the door.

I followed him around to his side. "You mean with Doc?"

He shook his head. "With the *others*. Your aunt told me you've been enlightened about our family history."

"More like enlisted," I muttered. "Better yet, drafted."

He hugged me tight, kissing the top of my head. "I don't want to lose you."

"I don't want to be lost."

"I'm here if you need me, Goldilocks. For anything. Anytime."

The husky emotion in his words made my eyes water, taking me back to childhood for a second or two. "Thanks, Daddy."

After planting a kiss on my forehead, he let me go and handed me the plate of leftovers my mom had made up for Doc. "I like him," he said, thumbing toward Doc's house.

"Me, too."

"He sort of reminds me of your brother."

"Yeah." I glanced over at the empty porch, deciding tonight was as good of a time as any to show my dad all of the cards I'd been holding close to my vest. "Except I don't think Quint can interact with ghosts."

My dad stilled. "Really?" At my nod, his brows raised. "A medium?"

"Good guess."

"Your aunt isn't the only one who's boned up on our family history." Dad shoved his hands in his coat pockets. "Mental or physical?"

I blinked, surprised at that question coming from my father. "Uh, a mental medium."

"Interesting. Does he know what you are?"

"Yep."

"And he didn't run?"

"He's sticking around. He's determined to protect me and the kids."

"You don't say?" Dad looked at Doc's house. "Your mom is right. He's a keeper. Don't blow it this time," he teased, tousling my hair. "Now get inside before you catch a cold."

Smiling, I returned to Doc's porch, waving good-bye as my parents rolled off down the road. Doc held the door for me.

"My mom made up a plate for you." I handed it to him. "There's plenty more at Aunt Zoe's, but I brought it for you in case you were hungry."

"I am." He set it on the side table where he kept his keys and wallet.

I unzipped the red vest. "So what did Haw—"

"For you." He grabbed me by the vest lapels and hauled me against him, surprising a gasp out of me. His mouth took mine, seeking, needing, demanding. He backed me against the door, pressing his full length against me. His lips were soft, his body hard. When he rubbed against me, a rush of heat blasted clear to my boots.

"Holy hell," I whispered to the ceiling as he moved to my ear, licking, sucking, making me feel lightheaded. My body tightened south of my stomach, pleasure tempting just out of reach.

"I want you, Violet," he said, kissing the shell of my ear.

I clung to his shoulders as the blood raced through my veins. "I noticed."

"I need you naked."

"Okay." He'd get no fight from me.

He pulled back, frowning down at me. "We're not doing this against the front door. I don't want any interruptions this time."

"Wherever. However." I touched the front of his jeans. "I don't care so long as you're inside of me."

He palmed my hips, lifting me. "Wrap your legs around me."

I did, my arms, too. I clung to him as he carried me up the stairs, kissing his mouth, his jaw, his neck the whole way. He set me down in his bedroom, closing and locking the door behind us.

I started to take off my vest.

"Wait." He held out his hand.

"Why?"

"Before you distract me, I need to tell you that I'm sorry."

I kept the vest on. "For what?"

"Not being at your family dinner."

"It wasn't your fault."

"It was." He jammed his hands in his pockets. "I knew better, but I lost my temper. Coop had warned me that Hawke wouldn't hesitate to use me to get back at you, and I fell into Hawke's trap anyway."

"What happened?"

"He insinuated you were screwing Coop, only he used much more derogatory terms for you, the screwing part, and Coop."

"You know Cooper and I are not …" I wrinkled my nose, not even able to voice it.

"Yes." He crossed his arms. "But Hawke came at me on two fronts simultaneously—you and my friend. It had double the impact and for some reason I snapped."

A protector through and through. Did Cooper realize what he had in

Doc? Did I? I took a step toward him, wanting to touch him and show him that I did. "You're only human, Doc."

He smirked as I drew near. "Coming from an executioner, I'm not sure if that's a compliment or an insult."

I peeled off my vest, tossing it aside. "A compliment, trust me." I paused to look at him, taking in his broad shoulders under his T-shirt, his strong arms crossed over his chest, his low-slung jeans riding on his hips, his long legs. "And one hell of a human, at that."

"You're distracting me, Violet."

"I'm not touching you … yet."

"You don't need to. Your eyes alone can flummox me."

"Is there something else you need to say, Doc, because I'm running out of patience."

"Yes. Thank you."

"For what?" I rubbed my hands together, planning my attack. "I haven't even started."

"Bringing your parents to meet me. I know how much you wanted to keep me hidden."

Hidden? I looked up into his dark gaze. "Not hidden, Doc. That makes it sound like I'm ashamed of you, and that couldn't be farther from the truth."

"Then besides your sister and her tendency to steal your boyfriends, why the hesitation? Your parents seem perfectly normal."

"Well, 'normal' is a word I like to use loosely when it comes to them, especially my mother."

He chuckled. "She's funny."

"She was tipsy."

"Even better to make the first meeting less awkward."

I hesitated, not wanting to bare everything about my insecurities over Doc meeting my parents. But it was probably better to cough up the real reason I worried about his meeting them, since Christmas was around the corner. I'd have to go through it all over again when he showed up with me for what would probably be another family dinner catastrophe.

"Here's the thing, Doc." I met his inquisitive gaze head on. "I didn't want you to meet my parents because my mom has a broken filter and will let my past screwups when it comes to men slip out. She doesn't have a lot of faith in my ability to find someone for the long term." I licked my dry lips. "Or at least someone for longer than a month or two. But to give her some credit, she has good reason for her lack of faith. I have a history of loving and leaving guys before things get too serious."

"What is too serious?"

"Me, standing here in your bedroom, being honest."

He nodded. "So your mom shares your past mistakes. That's the past, not the present. I can handle that."

"Maybe you can, but I struggle with my dirty laundry being aired in front of anyone, especially the guy I'm trying like hell not to scare away."

"I have dirty laundry from the past, too, Violet. We all do."

"Yes, but you don't have someone shouting through a megaphone about it from rooftops."

He chuckled. "True. Is that the only reason you didn't want me to meet them?"

I shook my head, swallowing a lump of cowardice and pushing on to the next wall I needed to break through on this truth journey.

"I was worried about my dad."

"That he wouldn't like me?"

"No, that he *would* like you."

"And that's bad because?"

Shit, this was hard. I clung to Aunt Zoe's words about my being different from Tiffany in Doc's eyes. "My parents are old-fashioned. Don't get me wrong. They have no problem with premarital sex or anything like that, but I haven't introduced them to a man in my life besides Rex. I usually only tell them I am dating Mr. X or that I am no longer dating Mr. X, sometimes sharing the follies that come with my dating experiments."

"I'm the first guy they've met since Rex?"

"Officially, yes." I wrung my hands together, building up the courage to push through this last part.

Don't screw this up, a voice in my head said.

You're not helping, another said, shutting the other voice in a closet.

"Doc, my dad is going to expect something of this." I pointed back and forth between him and me.

One of Doc's eyebrows rose, but he said nothing, waiting.

"He was good tonight." I thought about Dad asking Mom if she thought Doc was marriage material. "Well, mostly good, because I told him to watch what he said to you. But when you go to Christmas, I can't guarantee he'll hold back. He's sort of ornery that way."

He smiled. "That explains where you get it."

I gave him a pretend squint, and then went back to wringing my hands. "He's going to expect a long-term commitment, even though you and I have only been dating for a little over four months."

"We aren't dating, Violet."

I stilled. "We aren't?"

He shook his head. "The word *dating* implies that we are periodically going to movies, dinner, or other events. I've dated in the past. That is nothing like what we are doing here."

"What are we doing then?" To lighten the mood, I added, "Mating?"

He chuckled. "I do enjoy the mating part, but that's not what's going on here." He sobered, capturing my hands and tugging me closer. "You just introduced me to your parents as the guy you are in love with."

I winced, hiding my face in his chest. "I felt bad that you were stuck in jail all day because of me. I wanted them to understand that you were more to me than some guy I'm sleeping with every chance I get."

"Violet." He cupped my cheeks, tipping my face up. "Why were you worried about me meeting your dad?"

I bit my lip, lowering my lids for the plunge. "He's going to …" I started in a whisper, and then paused to swallow. My heart hammered in my chest so hard it made my head pound. I forced myself to look into his eyes. "He's going to talk about marriage."

Doc stared down at me, his face a blank slate. "And that's a problem for you because … ?"

"He'll scare you off."

One dark eyebrow lifted. "So his talking about marriage isn't a problem for *you?*"

"Me?"

"Yes, you're the one who just told me you are a love 'em and leave 'em type of girl."

Oh, right. "No. That's different."

"Why?"

"Those other guys were … well, because you are … you."

His hands slid down to my shoulders. "So the problem is supposedly mine?"

Supposedly? Yes.

"Why do you think it's my problem?"

"Because of Tiffany." My voice croaked a little while letting that deep-down truth free.

He nodded slowly. "There it is. I knew it." A smile curved the corner of his lips. "How many times have I said that you are different from Tiffany?"

I shrugged. "Maybe once or twice."

He let out a bark of laughter. "Bullshit. I've said it several times and you know it."

"Okay, maybe three or four times."

Shaking his head, he said, "You are so damned complicated, woman."

"I'm sorry."

"Don't be. It's one of the things I love about you. You're a puzzle I'm constantly trying to solve. As soon as I get the sides all pieced together, you blow into the room and send the pieces flying."

That didn't sound like something to love, especially for a guy who liked to be in control of his world.

I needed to finish saying what I'd started with this whole truth dump since Doc now planned on attending Christmas festivities with my family. "Doc, in the future, when my father talks to you about marrying his daughter, if you can just play along and know that I don't expect you to follow through, I'd appreciate it. That would reduce my anxiety about you being around them tenfold."

"No."

I frowned. "What do you mean, no?"

"I'm not going to lie to your father. That goes against my morals."

"Okay, then maybe you could—"

"Violet, I'm not allergic to marriage."

The M word made me gulp. Here it was, that moment I'd been dreading for months. "Oh."

"I left Tiffany because of her obsessive, competitive nature. I got tired of her games. It just so happened that she brought up marriage when I was on my way out. One had nothing to do with the other."

"Oh," I said again, my mouth too dry.

"You and I are not dating here."

I stared at him barely breathing. "What are we doing then?"

"We are building a relationship based on love and trust." His gaze lowered to my boots. "And desire."

"Okay." My heart thudded in my throat, still not certain if it should start pounding for joy.

"If your father asks what my intentions are toward you," he continued. "I'll tell him that I'm going to do everything in my power to make his daughter happy and feel safe."

I nodded. Those were both good things.

"If that leads to marriage," he said, "then so be it."

If? IF? What did he mean, *IF?!*

Doc grabbed the hem of my sweater and lifted it over my head, tossing it aside. "I'll also tell him that I'm head over heels for his daughter."

He scooped me up and took me over to his bed, lowering me onto it. "That I can't stop thinking about her day and night."

He pulled off one of my boots. "That I adore her two kids."

The other boot came next. "That I feel incredibly lucky she has set her sights on me."

He grabbed the waist of my yoga pants and dragged them down and off in one tug. "That I will take a bullet for her without thinking twice."

His gaze ogled me from head to toe, centering on my panties. "But I *won't* tell him that I often fantasize about stripping her naked and burying myself between her soft thighs."

My libido sat up and roared.

He snagged my underwear, yanking them down. They went the way of the rest of my clothes.

"That my favorite place to be is inside of her, making her cry out in pleasure."

The front hook on my bra didn't slow him for a moment. He let it fall open, leaving me lying there in my birthday suit, my brain sputtering from his verbal onslaught.

"And I won't tell him that the thought of losing her love feels like a knife piercing my chest." He unbuttoned his jeans, stepping out of them.

He crawled on the bed, hovering over me, his knee parting my legs. "Or that every time she looks at me with those stunning green eyes my heart races."

His head dipped, his tongue trailing up my cleavage. I buried my fingers in his hair, moaning as his tongue circled one breast and then the other, teasing without hitting the mark.

"Or that her sexy voice is one of my favorite sounds."

His hand slid down my stomach, dipping lower.

"Doc," I whispered and moaned, lifting my hips to meet him.

"Especially when she says my name while I'm making love to her." His fingers explored, teasing, rubbing, making my body hum.

He nuzzled my ear, his alluring scent and expert touch twisting together to make one hell of a tornado of need churning inside of me. I grasped his shoulders, writhing under his touch as my body tightened, pleasure spinning faster and faster.

"And," he whispered in my ear as his fingers strummed and delved, filling me. "I would never tell that I lie awake at night, thinking about all of the places on her body that I like to lick." He pulled his hand away, making me cry out in complaint. "And taste."

His lips moved lower, his tongue taking over where his fingers had lit me up seconds before. My fingers laced through his hair, holding on for dear life as he licked and sucked and turned me inside out.

There were no more words then, only moans and my loud cry when I arched off the bed. Then I sank back down while waves of pleasure rippled through me.

He stood long enough to peel off his shirt. Then he was back, pulling me to the edge of the bed.

"My boots?" I asked, knowing how much he liked me to wear them during sex.

"There's no time for them tonight, vixen."

I sat up. "You sure."

He shed his briefs. "Positive."

"I could bend over for the soap," I flirted.

"Not this time." He fell onto the bed next to me and pulled me on top of him. "I want to watch your face as I make you mine tonight."

I straddled him. "Possessive. I like it."

But first, I wanted to show him how much his words made me burn for him. I leaned over him, kissing him slowly. I sucked his tongue into my mouth, tangling mine with his while I linked my fingers in his and held his hands flat against the mattress. He groaned, moving his hips, searching for me.

"Not yet," I said.

I rubbed my bare chest over his, teasing him with brushes of my body from top to bottom. My kisses were wet and wild in the pre-feeding frenzy.

"Violet," he gasped after I slid along his length. His voice was husky, guttural with want.

I reached down and cupped, stroked, gripped. "Is this what you fantasize about?" I whispered, my teeth tugging on his earlobe.

"Yes," he groaned. "Now, please!"

"Not yet." I wasn't done showing him how much I loved him. I circled his lips with my tongue and then stared down at him until his gaze met mine. His lids were heavy with lust, his eyes dilated with desire. Seeing Doc locked in the throes of passion nearly made me lose hold of my own control.

"Doc," I said.

"What?"

"I only kept you from my family out of fear of losing you." I lowered my mouth, kissing him slowly, making love to his lips.

He took me by the face, pushing me away enough to say, "I'd walk through Hell for you, Violet. You won't lose me that easily." Then he kissed me back.

While his tongue was busy stroking mine, I slid down onto him.

His breath caught, his eyes widened.

I smiled against his lips, lifting and lowering again.

His head tipped back, his eyes closing. "Oh, God, Boots," he rasped. His hands spanned my hips and helped me along, pulling and pushing, faster and faster.

He beat me to the punch this time, bowing under me, all of his muscles locked as he cursed at the ceiling. I kept rocking my hips, drawing it out for him. When he finished shuddering and returned to earth, he flipped me onto my back and shoved me inch by inch up the bed until my body locked around him. I moaned and quaked, my hands clenching onto his shoulders, my body pulsing.

Then there was silence, broken only by our heavy breathing.

Outside his window, the snow fell.

Doc's body spanned mine, keeping me warm as the heat of desire waned. "Violet."

"Yeah?" I ran my fingernails up and down his back.

"I love you."

I smiled at the ceiling, my heart kicking up its heels in joy. "I love you, too."

"Does the idea of marrying a medium scare you?"

My heart stopped mid-kick. "Uh, no."

"Good."

I waited for him to say something else, like maybe ask if I wanted to marry a medium anytime soon, but nothing else came. I kept stroking his back, realizing that I was okay with no proposal. It was too soon. We had a lot to work through before that next step, including two kids who weren't ready for me to turn a lover into a husband. Just knowing marriage was an option for the future was enough for now.

But that didn't stop me from asking, "Does the idea of marrying an executioner scare you?"

"A bit."

My fingers paused. "It does?"

"I've seen you in action, Killer. I'd be lying if I said that your skill with a weapon doesn't make my balls tuck up a little, especially when you're swinging your war hammer."

I chuckled.

He lifted his head. "But it's sexy as hell at the same time."

His cell phone rang from somewhere in the room. He pushed off the bed, grabbing his phone from his dresser, looking down at the screen. "Damn. Playtime is over, I guess," he said, answering with, "Hey, Coop."

He glanced over at me. "Yeah, she's here."

"Got it. Give us about fifteen minutes." He hung up and tossed the phone on the bed next to me, pulling on his briefs. "We have to get you home, Cinderella."

I sat up, noticing his phone case. I lifted it, holding it up in the light. On the case was my picture from last Halloween in my Morticia Addams costume. Someone must have taken the shot while I wasn't paying attention, probably Natalie. I vaguely remember her taking some pictures of her cousins, who were visiting at that time. At the bottom of my picture were the words: *Cara Mia.*

"What's this?" I asked, holding up his phone.

He shrugged on his shirt, his smile sheepish. "Natalie sent me that picture. I liked it."

"You made a phone case with my picture?"

"Yep."

"Why, Doc," I said, grinning. "You are such an old romantic."

"What can I say, Tish? I'm smitten."

I went up on my knees, naked still, holding out my arms. "Come here, Gomez."

His eyes narrowed as he neared. "Why?"

"I want to show you how much I love you."

"We don't have time for sex. Coop's waiting."

Cooper could chill. I caught Doc's arm and pulled him closer, sliding one hand around the back of his neck. I kissed him with all of the emotion I could muster. While I worked my magic, my other hand slid south, my nails scraping over his briefs, bringing him back to life. I leaned back, smiling. "Who said anything about sex?"

He stared down at my mouth. "Uhhh."

I slid off the bed and kneeled in front of him. Hooking my fingers in his briefs, I tugged them down. "If I do this right, it should only take a few minutes."

I winked up at him, licking my lips.

His Adam's apple bobbed.

I took him in hand ... and followed with my mouth.

I did it right.

It didn't take long at all.

Chapter Twenty-Three

Sunday, December 9th

Not even the sight of Cooper standing at the coffee maker first thing the next morning could drag me down after the trip to the moon in Doc's bedroom.

"What is that piercing sound coming from you?" he said, glaring at me. He'd added a faded red flannel shirt to his usual early morning attire of sweatpants. "It's like wind is leaking from your ears."

"It's called whistling." I bumped him aside, reaching for a mug. "Some detective you are."

"Why are you whistling after yesterday's debacle?"

I shrugged. "When life gives you lemons, grab some tequila and salt and have a fiesta." Actually, I preferred limes with my shots.

"Shut up, Parker." He moved to the table, dropping into a chair.

"Ah, what's wrong, Mr. Grumpy Pants?"

"Considering your situation, I can't see any reason for you to be whistling. We're all fucked."

How was *he* fucked? I was the one who would be charged with murder and forced to wear bright orange for decades.

I shrugged off his doom and gloom. "If you must know, I'm whistling because I got laid."

He cringed. "Jesus, Parker. Stop, please, before you make my ears bleed."

"You should try it sometime," I continued. "Maybe then you'd stop acting like you have a golf club jammed up your ass."

He set his cup down on the table with a clunk. "You're as bad as living with my uncle."

"Not quite. If I was even close to Harvey's level of candor, I'd be giving you the nitty-gritty details of my sexual escapades." I grabbed the milk from the fridge. "Including smells and tastes."

He pointed at me, giving me a gunslinger squint. "Don't even think of it."

"Listen, Coop. If you're going to share coffee with me every morning, we might as well drop the niceties." I poured the milk and took it back to the fridge.

"That's 'Cooper' to you. Better yet, 'Detective Cooper' first thing in the morning."

"Hey, you asked why I was smiling when shit is about to hit the fan. I could give you some mumbo-jumbo like they write on those motivational calendars." I dropped into the chair opposite him. "Or I could tell the truth and only the truth, so help me God."

He squeezed the bridge of his nose. "Are you done?"

"For now." I sipped my coffee, grinning like a monkey with two bananas.

"Good. What time am I picking you up today?" he asked.

We had houses to see in spite of the snow, which had quit falling shortly after Doc and I had returned to Aunt Zoe's last night. While eating leftovers, Cooper had offered to drive today. I'd hesitated, since we'd be riding in one of the Deadwood Police Durangos, which might encourage more nicknames from the other cops. However, Doc reminded me of the steep hills and snow-packed roads, and the meaty snow tires on Cooper's vehicle.

"Natalie said she'd be ready around noon. Does that work for you?"

He scowled at me. "Does she really need to go with us?"

That earned a frown from me. "Don't you enjoy her company?" And by "enjoy," I meant pined for her every waking moment.

"You know I do. But ..." Lines filled his face.

"But what?"

"We might run into someone, and I'd rather she not be there if that happens."

"You mean Detective Hawke?"

"No."

Who else would he ... I met his steely gaze. "Oh."

He nodded once.

"So, you don't want Nat to see you pull a Scooby-Doo and leap into my arms when a wispy villain appears?"

His eyes narrowed.

"Come on, Scoob," I said in my best Shaggy imitation. "Like, you can do this, man."

"Hilarious, Shaggy."

I leaned forward, grinning in spite of his scowl. "We could have

Natalie wear big round glasses and an orange sweater and yell, 'Jinkies!' when the ghost appears."

"Parker," he warned.

"How about if I promise to pack some extra Scooby snacks for the day?"

"That's it. I don't care if you are Nyce's woman, I'm going to teach your son to start leaving the toilet seat up."

I laughed, looking up as Aunt Zoe walked into the kitchen in her robe and slippers.

She paused, looking back and forth between Cooper and me, her brow wrinkling. "Violet, dear, are you delirious with fever?"

That made me laugh harder.

"She got laid," Cooper told her, draining his coffee in one gulp.

"Ah. That is one of the side effects of leaving her alone with Doc for too long."

He stood, taking his coffee cup to the sink. "I'm going to hop in the shower if neither of you need it."

I was still chuckling as he left the room. "Good morning," I said, puckering up for Aunt Zoe.

"Dang," she said, coming closer and lowering her cheek to my lips. "Doc must have really gotten the job done."

I fanned myself, sighing dramatically.

She headed for the coffee maker. "Must be nice."

"Yes, it was. Doc Nyce." I giggled.

"Is there tequila in that cup?"

"Not yet, but the day is young." I sobered, a smile still warming my cheeks. "We talked about the M-word."

"You and Cooper? How's Doc going to feel about that," she joked, joining me at the table.

"He didn't ask me to marry him or anything like that," I said quietly, glancing over toward the dining room to make sure we didn't have little eavesdroppers. "But he made it clear that he's not averse to it."

"Great. Did he have someone in mind?" She grinned.

"You're on fire this morning," I said, squeezing her hand.

"When you're hot, you're hot."

"We should call the fire department and have them send the captain over with his hose."

"If he brings that hose anywhere near me, I'll tie it in a knot."

"You might've already done that when you gave him hell on the porch yesterday and sent him packing."

She groaned and massaged her temples. "Don't remind me of that disaster. That son of a bitch thinks that because I've let him come over for supper a couple of times he has a leg up on any other man interested in me."

I rested my chin on my palm. "Does he?"

She huffed at me. "Yes, dammit."

"Are you going to tell him that?"

She shook her head. "Reid is trouble."

"Not as bad as Dominick."

"That's debatable on several levels."

I took her hand, holding her knuckles to my cheek. She smelled like the candy apple lotion my mother brought her yesterday as a thank-you gift for hosting dinner. "I'm here if you need me."

"I do need you, at least until I figure out how to block Dominick." She patted my cheek, grinning at me. "Then you can keep your cute nose out of my love life, Violet Lynn."

I scrunched up my face at her. "Fat chance, hot stuff."

"So you and Doc are okay?"

I faked a swoon.

"That good, huh?"

"Yeah."

"And the kids?"

I shrugged. "As far as they are concerned, it's status quo for now."

"Great. You need something to be going right for you with everything else in your life being so screwed up."

"Hear, hear." I finished my coffee, heading for the sink.

"What's on your plate today?" she asked.

"House hunting with Cooper and Nat."

"Natalie is going along, too?"

I nodded, leaning against the counter.

"Are you playing cupid?" she asked. "If so, you might make an even bigger mess than what happened when Nat thought she liked Doc."

I held up my hand. "I promise *not* to play cupid today."

"Then why take her along? Or was that Cooper's idea?"

"Actually, he's sort of not in favor of it."

"Really?"

"He's worried about seeing ghosts with her as a witness."

"Ahhhh. But you're going to include her anyway?"

I smiled. "It's good for Cooper."

"Maybe." One of her eyebrows lifted. "But is it good for Natalie's sabbatical?"

* * *

Old Man Winter had coated Deadwood's Presidential District in a white, sparkling cloak. The deep blue sky made the cold air seem fresher, cleaner. I'd forgotten how happy snowy mornings in the Black Hills made me. Then again, there was the Doc factor still making me whistle under my breath while memories of yesterday in his bed kept those cockles in my heart superheated.

Cooper skidded and spun up Lincoln Avenue. Doc had been right. Being in the passenger seat with Cooper at the wheel had my palms much drier, especially since slipping backward down the hill would result in the police department's vehicle being banged up and not my Honda.

"This is only like four blocks from Doc's place," Natalie said from the back seat as Cooper pulled into the driveway of a 1930s California–style bungalow that Mona had recently put on the market. Natalie sat behind Cooper, sipping on the coffee she'd made him stop for after what she said was a "busy night." What she meant, I wasn't sure yet, but I had plans to find out before the day was over.

"I thought the two boys could have play dates together," I joked.

"Shut up, Parker." Cooper was still scratchy when he picked me up at work, but more like a month-old, worn dish scouring pad that was starting to stink. Not that he stank, because he'd used my soap again this morning—mint chocolate, if my nose was working right.

"You're a broken record today," I told him as he parked and shut off the engine.

The three of us stared out at the one and a half story house with its sloping roof and dormer window facing the road. A partial front porch had been glassed in for the winter.

"It's pink," Cooper scowled.

"You can repaint the siding whatever color your spiky heart desires."

"The chimney is missing a few bricks."

"A few bricks short of a chimney," Natalie said, laughing at her own joke. "That reminds me of you, Vi."

"Stick to your day job, peanut gallery," I said. "Which is why we brought you along." I turned to Cooper. "You should have brought the police rig with a cage for the laughing hyena in the back seat."

"She would have chewed through the wire in no time."

"True. Her teeth aren't super sharp, but her bite can pulverize." I pointed toward the house. "Nat, can you fix that chimney pretty easily?"

"That depends on the shape of the chinking between the brick."

"That means Layne's superglue won't do the trick," I jested to Cooper.

"This is a busy road," Cooper complained.

I looked up and down the empty street. Had we been in the Old West, a tumbleweed would have rolled across it. "You're right. Interstate 90 is a wagon trail compared to this bustling freeway."

"In the summer, Parker, this road is loaded with tour buses and cars heading up to Mount Moriah."

"Like you're ever home in the summer." Natalie took my side.

"Yeah, what she said."

He stared in the rearview mirror. "Keep it up, Beals, and I'll handcuff you to the oh-shit handle behind Parker's head."

She chuckled. "Now you're just flirting with me, Coop."

I reached for the door handle. "Should we—"

Cooper hit the automatic door lock. "Hold on a second, Parker. While I have both of you captive, I have a question." He looked from me to Natalie in the mirror. "Which one of you two messed with the tracking program I put on Parker's phone?"

"Ummm" was my brilliant answer.

"I don't know what you're—" Natalie started.

"Don't, Beals." He turned in his seat and hit her with a hard direct stare. "Do not treat me like Detective Hawke. I want an answer."

I opened my mouth to take the blame, but Natalie cut me off. "It was me."

"Why?" he asked.

She held his stare, not shying away. "Because it's Violet."

"Where's the line?"

"Which line is that?"

"The one at the border of how far you'll go for Parker?"

She shrugged. "I haven't reached it yet, but if I do I'll send you a postcard."

He turned back to the front. "That's some loyalty."

"It's called love, Coop. You should try it some day. You might smile more often." She leaned forward, sniffing between us. "By the way, what's that smell? Do you have an air freshener hidden somewhere in here? It smells like mint chocolate ice cream."

"He used my soap again," I told her, still watching Cooper to see if he was going to keep his rubber gloves on or return to being my client.

He cast a smirk in my direction. "Parker doesn't have any regular soap."

"You can blame Doc for that," Natalie said.

"Hey, no picking on Doc when he's not here to defend himself." I pulled on the door handle, looking at the mint chocolate–scented detective. "What do you say, Cooper? You want to take a look inside?"

He hit the unlock button. "It's pink."

"It's more of a salmon color," Natalie said, handing her coffee to me to stick in the cup holder.

"There's a nice garage for your Harley. Focus on that, Grumpy Pants." I pushed open the door.

Cooper got the door for Natalie since it could only be opened from the outside. The two of them trailed behind me onto the porch, waiting while I fished out the key. I led the way inside, pausing to take off my boots on the rug provided. Natalie followed suit. I grabbed a pair of booties from the sideboard next to the door, holding them out to Cooper.

Pushing them away, he took off his black snow boots and set them outside on the porch.

The front door opened to a cozy living room with polished wood floors and several thick white shag rugs. I could see Mona's usual professional touches, like the vase of silk flowers on the ornate tile mantel, the subtle smell of cinnamon from the bowl of potpourri on the bookcase next to the door, and the beaded throw pillows she often used to dress up a couch.

Natalie crossed to the fireplace, pulling out the flashlight she'd brought along. She checked out the fireplace and then up the chimney. "The chimney looks like it's in good shape on the inside."

An open dining room adjoined the living room, the table set with holiday napkins and plates, another one of Mona's touches.

"This is adorable," Natalie said, following me into the dining room. She paused to take a closer look at the dinner plates, holding one out toward me. "Look, Vi, they have tiny Santas in sleighs circling the edges. We should get some of these for your kids."

"You mean for them to break?"

She rolled her eyes and set the plate down. "You're such a mom."

Cooper brought up the rear, his focus darting around the room, his face rigid, unreadable.

The small kitchen was cute as a button, lined with well-crafted built-in cupboards with windowpane glass fronts. The sink was farm-style with a curtain hanging below that matched the other window dressings.

"Maybe I should sell my place and grab this one up," Natalie said, sliding open a barn-style door to reveal a compact pantry.

Cooper grunted and moved on without us. I left Natalie to her nook and cranny inspection and found him a few minutes later upstairs in a long open room, ducking his head due to the sloped ceiling.

"It's a little low," I said and promptly bumped my head. "My kids would love this, though."

"Maybe *you* should move in here."

"I'm partial to Aunt Zoe's." At least until Doc offered his place.

I pondered that idea for a moment, trying to picture my kids in his place. For starters, they'd touch everything, stain his carpet with juice, and bounce on his furniture. Maybe we'd just live at Aunt Zoe's until Layne and Addy were old enough to leave the nest.

If you live that long, a voice whispered in my head, sending chills down my back.

"Zip it," I muttered.

"I didn't say anything," Cooper said.

"I was talking to the voices in my head," I kidded, but not.

He studied me. "When it comes to you, Parker, I'd buy that you really are schizophrenic."

"Says the man who sees ghosts." I placed my hands on my hips. "What do you think?"

He walked toward the stairwell. "I think it's pink."

I shadowed him down the steps. "Cooper, you can paint it come spring."

"It's too small."

"Uh, last I counted, there was one of you. How much space does one man need?"

"More than this pink dollhouse has to offer."

"At least there are no ghosts," I said when we returned to the living room.

He turned to me. "What makes you so sure about that?"

"You're not acting skittish."

"Nyce taught me a few tricks."

Oh, yeah. Doc had been working with him. I leaned closer, whispering, "Is there a ghost here?"

He stared over my shoulder for several beats. "There's an old lady in a gray wool dress sitting in the chair next to the fireplace."

"What?" I whirled around, my heart thumping. "Which chair?" There were two bracketing the fireplace.

He snickered. "Got you."

Natalie joined us. "What's going on?"

"Parker needs a Scooby snack."

"Paybacks are hell, Detective." I bumped him out of my way as I headed for the door. "Cooper doesn't like this place," I told Natalie, sliding on my boots.

"Why not?" She joined me, pulling on her boots.

"It's too pink for his masculinity."

"But it's so cute."

He held the door for us, eyeing Natalie. "Trust me, Beals. A man doesn't want to bring women to his house and have them ooh-ing and ahh-ing about the ribbon curl designs on the mantel."

"How many women do you plan to bring here, Coop?" she asked, fiddling with a string hanging off her coat.

"Who's counting?" he asked.

I wasn't sure if that was supposed to be a rhetorical question or if he really wanted to know who was going to be counting the women—as in Natalie.

"Your uncle," she shot back.

Actually, she was probably right about that.

Natalie waited on the porch while Cooper pulled on his boots and I locked up.

When I turned around, I caught her staring at his butt as he bent over to slide his foot inside his boot. I cleared my throat, thumbing toward the porch steps when she looked my way.

Go! I mouthed.

After pretending to punch herself in the eyes with both hands, Natalie stomped down the steps.

After we all piled inside and I'd handed Natalie her coffee, Cooper started up the Durango and let it idle in the drive. "Where to next?"

"Just a minute." I dug through my papers for the address of the next house.

"Do they monitor your mileage on these vehicles?" Natalie asked him.

"No. They figure we're sticking close to town."

"That's pretty trusting."

"We're cops." Cooper messed with the buttons on the radio as he waited for me.

I snorted. "That badge pins onto crooked cops the same as honest ones."

"Speaking of crooked cops," Natalie said. "Have you ever screwed around in one of these?"

"What do you mean by 'screwed around'?" he asked, glancing at her in the rearview mirror.

"Like do doughnuts in an empty parking lot?"

"That would be reckless driving."

I scoffed. "Do you even know how to relax, Cooper?"

"I relax every time I empty cartridges at the shooting range."

Blah blah guns blah. "You should seek counseling about your need to pull triggers."

"So should you."

"What's that—"

Natalie interrupted me. "How about having sex in the back seat?"

I whipped around. "Natalie!" Was that an invitation?

"What? I saw it once in a movie. The two cops were making out and accidentally locked themselves in the back seat since the doors only open from the outside. It was funny."

"Does Cooper seem like the kind of guy who'd accidentally lock himself in a police car with a woman?"

"I don't know. But I do know from experience that he can be pretty charming when he tries."

Natalie must be talking about that night at the Purple Door Saloon and whatever went down between them. I glanced over at Cooper. His face could have been a carving up on Mount Rushmore.

"Well, Cooper?" she prodded.

"Of course not." His voice was terse enough to snap a stick.

"Maybe you should," Natalie said under her breath, taking a sip of her coffee while staring out her window.

I shuffled my papers, making noise to break the awkward silence in the vehicle. I tried to remember why I had thought bringing Natalie along would be a good idea. Harvey's ear flicking was less squirmy to endure.

"Here it is," I said and rattled off an address. The house was on south Main Street in Deadwood, near the junction to Central City.

We crunched and slid down Lincoln Avenue, weaving our way over to Main Street. Traffic was light thanks to the snow and it being Sunday, making the drive less harrowing. The sun had everything dripping. The periodic static outbursts from the police radio broke up the awkward hush that filled the cab.

The next house was larger, as in four bedrooms and two baths, which should make Cooper the Curmudgeon less snippy. And it wasn't pink. We parked streetside in front of the white, early 1900s Colonial Revival with a full porch blocked in with multiple columns. The house was boxy without a lot of fancy architectural touches. Its curb appeal was its stateliness. Large rectangular windows bordered by dark green shutters broke up the house's upper floor. A separate two-car garage sat to the left up a steep, snow-coated drive.

Before Cooper had a chance to get out, a call came in for him on the police radio.

I stepped out and opened the back door on my side for Natalie. She slid across and climbed out, coffee in hand.

"What the hell are you doing?" I whispered as soon as I shut the door.

"What? Haven't you ever wondered that?" She took a sip from her cup, frowning at me over the plastic lid.

"No, and you're on sabbatical."

Cooper's door opened.

"My body is abstaining, Vi. Not my mind."

He came around the front of the Durango, waiting for me to lead the way up the salt-sprinkled stone steps cut into the retaining wall. A recently shoveled sidewalk led the way to the porch. The salt crystals crunched underfoot as we made our way across the wide lawn.

Natalie didn't follow us onto the porch. "The foundation looks a little rough. It could be deteriorating out from under this old place," she said while frowning down at the base of the porch. "Fixing that alone will cost you an arm and a leg." She headed out of sight around the side of the house.

I opened the front door, leading Cooper inside.

He stopped on the threshold long enough to take off his boots and leave them outside the door and then joined me, sniffing.

I grimaced. "Don't do that."

"Do what?"

"Sniff."

"Why not?"

"Doc used to do that when I took him through houses."

"Do you have an issue with sniffing?"

"Only in that it was often followed with creepy ghosts that would sneak up on me and try to knock Doc on his ass."

"Did you come across a lot of ghosts while house hunting?"

"More than I would have liked." I smirked. "And Doc would always want me to bring him back again another time. At first, I thought he was Grade-A nuts."

"And now?"

"Now I know he's nuts because he still likes me in spite of this executioner shit."

"Isn't that the truth?" Cooper chuckled when I pretended to box him in the eye. He sobered quickly. "But what about the ghosts part?"

I shrugged. "I've gotten used to there being wispy folks here and there, although they do still make me want to hide under the covers since I usually can't see them." Especially after a certain little girl ghost and her clown doll trapped me in an elevator.

"You're better off not, trust me."

He moved past me into the living room, leaving me frowning after him. What did these ghosts look like? Was it just the fact that he was seeing dead people that threw him off balance, or was it something more?

We'd made it to the kitchen where Cooper was admiring the cold, stainless steel lack of hominess when the front door opened and closed.

"We're in the kitchen," I called out to Natalie.

The clomping of heels made me pause. She knew she was supposed to take off her boots in these places.

Wait, Natalie was wearing snow boots. They didn't clomp like hard heels do.

"Hey, Coop," a soft, purring voice said from the dining room entryway.

We both turned to stare at Tiffany Sugarbell, who was wearing a black sweater dress under her white, wool-blend wrapcoat. White knee-high leather boots completed her ensemble. Who dressed like that on a snowy day while house hunting? Sheesh! Then again, she didn't appear to have a client with her. Wait a second. What were the chances of her just happening upon a house I was showing to Cooper?

"Hello, Miss Sugarbell." Cooper leaned against the counter, looking from Tiffany to me. He crossed his arms. A hint of a smile lifted his mouth. "What brings you up to Deadwood today?"

"I have a lunch meeting with Violet's co-worker."

Ray! That horse's ass.

I pasted a fake smile on my face. "Ray's not here. You can probably find him at Calamity Jane's. You know, our office."

She laughed, long and fake, like her hair extensions. "Oh, I know that. I just happened to be on my way to drop paperwork off for Jeff Wymonds and saw Cooper's police car outside and put two-and-two together."

The bitch could add. Good for her. That meant she could keep score for Jeff while he drove in touchdowns between her stupid long legs.

Whoa! *Back 'er down, Tiger.* I should probably seek therapy for this buried hostility. Two shots of tequila should do it.

Swallowing the acid bubbling in the back of my throat, I fought to keep my smile hanging front and center. "Let Jeff know I'll drop off Kelly later this afternoon when I'm finished showing Detective Cooper a few more homes." I turned away, facing Cooper, adding, "Thanks for stopping by, Tiffany."

He raised one brow.

I bared my teeth.

"Oh, before I leave," Tiffany said. "Did you hear the news?"

Why her? Why today? Why any day?

Sighing, I leaned against the counter next to Cooper and braced myself. "What news?"

"Calamity Jane Realty is now ranked second as the top-selling real estate business in the northern Black Hills."

We were moving up in the Realty world. That should make Jerry's day. "Good for us."

"Apparently, filling billboards with a frizzy-haired blonde in silly poses has worked to your boss's advantage."

"Shit," I heard Cooper say under his breath. "Not the hair."

I took a moment to breathe and make a conscious effort not to charge her like a pissed-off rhino and show her some more silly poses—like my foot jammed up her conceited ass.

"Yep," I managed to get out between tight lips. "Jerry knows how to market."

Cooper gave me a that's-all-you-got look.

What? She'd caught me off guard. I needed some time to stretch my insult muscles and sharpen my tongue before a match.

Tiffany tossed her long, shiny red hair over her shoulder. "Imagine what he could do if he started with someone a little less bulgy who has a modicum of class."

Fury flooded my brain, making my tongue sputter.

"Hey, Tiffany's here," Natalie said, standing in the entry between the dining room and kitchen. She raised her coffee cup toward Doc's ex. "Damn, girl. You look like you stepped off the cover of a magazine."

Tiffany smoothed her hand over her hair. Her upper lip curled as she took in Natalie's jeans and long-john thermal shirt under her heavy work coat. "Hello, Natalie." Her tone was snooty, just like her stuck-up nose. "Was that you I saw skulking around outside?"

Natalie nodded. "I was checking out the foundation for Violet."

"Where are your tools?"

"I left them at home today. What are you doing here?"

"I came to say hello to our friend."

"You mean Coop?"

Tiffany laughed. "Oh no, he's way more than a friend, right Coop?"

Cooper shrugged, staying out of this.

"I was talking about our little Violet here." Tiffany's smile was positively smug when she turned on me. "She and I have a bond now that we are both sharing billboard space over on Interstate 90."

"A bond, you say?" Natalie's smile looked amazingly real. I needed to take some lessons from her. "Isn't that the sweetest thing since chocolate-covered fried Twinkies?"

"I wouldn't know. I don't eat fried food."

"Yeah, raw and bloody is more your style. Well, any new friend of Vi's is a friend of …" She stepped into the kitchen, only to trip over her own feet, flailing and stumbling into Tiffany.

Tiffany screeched, shoving Natalie away. She gaped down in horror at her no-longer-pristine coat. Coffee ran down both sides of her white wool coat, dripping onto the toes of her white leather boots.

I covered my mouth, holding in the giggles bubbling up my throat.

"I'm sorry, Tiffany," Natalie said, righting herself. She looked down at her squished coffee cup with a wrinkled brow. "I've been so clumsy lately. Violet, hand me those paper towels. I'm sure these coffee stains will come right out."

Tiffany's mouth opened and closed several times before uttering, "You bitch!"

"Come on now," Natalie said, brushing coffee drips off the white wool with her hand, not bothering with a towel. "Accidents will happen."

Tiffany batted Natalie's hand away. "You're making it worse! What's on your hands?"

"Oh, shucks. I meant to wash that old grease off when I came inside, but I got distracted when I heard your voice."

"This is a four-hundred-dollar coat!" Tiffany wailed, making Cooper and me wince.

Natalie stared at the stain, nodding. "Good point. Make sure you let the dry cleaner know how much it cost so they don't ruin it with some cheap stain remover."

Tiffany stomped her boot. "You did this on purpose!"

"Oh, Tiffany. How can you think that?" Natalie stuck out her lower lip in a fake pout. "It was an accident, but I really appreciate your catching me so I didn't dump coffee all over this beautiful hardwood floor." She smiled at me. "That would have been a real disaster, huh, Vi?"

Nodding, I pinched my lips together harder, looking toward Cooper. He watched the scene with a straight face and slightly narrowed eyes, like he was mapping out a crime scene.

"You know," Natalie continued, setting her crushed paper coffee cup on the counter. "I swear I saw a coat just like that at a thrift store down in Rapid a couple of months ago."

"I don't shop at thrift stores." There was that snooty tone again.

Natalie's smile had a hard edge with frosty overtones. "Now that Violet is taking over your market share, you might want to start."

Tiffany's jaw dropped. "Oh! You are such a ... a ... ahhh!" She shoved Natalie back a step and strode out of the room.

"Let me know if you need my tools for anything, Tiffany," Natalie called at her departing back. She added under her breath, "I have a pair of needle nose pliers I'd like to use to pluck out her uppity nose hairs one by one."

Tiffany's heels clomped all of the way to the front door, which she slammed so hard the mirror over the dining room fireplace rattled.

I burst out laughing.

"Well," Natalie said, turning back to me. "That got rid of that rat. I'll send you a bill for my exterminator services later." She walked over to the sink, washing her hands under the faucet. "So, the foundation looks pretty solid except on the north side," she told Cooper as if that whole scene hadn't just happened. "But there appears to be some dry rot under the eaves in the back."

I blew her a kiss. "I love you, Nat."

She winked back. "Seventh grade. You and me. Blood promise." She dried her hands on a paper towel. "Besides, bullies suck."

Cooper rubbed his jaw, staring at Natalie with an intensity that practically shot sparks. "I hope you never come swinging for me, Beals."

"Watch your Ps and Qs and you'll be good." She stuck her hands in her back pockets, her smile cocky.

His gaze traveled down over her shirt and jeans. "Maybe I don't want to be good." His voice had a rasp that made me look twice. "Maybe I'd rather be bad."

Had he really just said that?

Natalie's face darkened a shade. One of her eyebrows crept upward. "I thought you liked to be good, Coop. You know that cop mumbo-jumbo you gave back at the other house about not driving recklessly, breaking rules, and dating local girls."

Uh, hold the phone. I distinctly remember there being no mention about dating local girls in that conversation. I thought about slinking away into the dining room to leave them to hash this out without me, but I was too damned curious to see what happened next to move.

"You inspire waywardness, Beals."

She tipped her head to the side, her lips pursed. "Are you screwing with me, Coop?"

"Is that an invitation?"

"You know what I mean."

"What do you think?" He pushed off the counter, strolling toward her.

Her gaze narrowed as he neared, but she held her ground. "I think you're a hard man to read."

He straightened the collar of her coat. "And I think you've been on sabbatical too long."

She flinched the tiniest bit as his words hit home.

Cooper glanced over at me. "Let's take a look upstairs." Without another word, he left the room.

Natalie watched him leave, her face stormy with emotions.

I moved over by her, cleaning up the coffee spots on the floor. "That was interesting."

"Was he actually flirting for real just then?" she whispered, fanning her thermal shirt. "Have I been on sabbatical so long that I'm starting to see things that aren't really there?"

"It's hard to tell for sure with Cooper," I said, stepping carefully in this minefield. "His jagged teeth and sharkskin usually keep me standing several feet back from his tank."

"He's been acting weird lately, I swear," she said. "I keep getting mixed vibes from him. I always feel like I have something on my face and he just doesn't want to tell me."

She was getting warm. "Speaking of weird shit," I said. "Are you the one sending Rex dirty underwear to get him fired?"

Her nose scrunched up. "No. I applaud the effort and would love to see it succeed in ousting him, but that's too gross for me. I prefer to get my messages across via blunt force trauma, like with a crowbar to his Jaguar."

Hmmmm, who was it then? Did I have a porno-loving guardian angel?

We found Cooper upstairs in the master bedroom. He was staring into the dresser mirror, his focus on the window.

"It looks like they've put a lot of work into restoring the molding," I said, walking over to check out the window and see if there was something he could see outside. It faced the street. I made sure Tiffany's Jeep was nowhere to be seen before turning around and realizing that I was now the center point of Cooper's reflected focus.

I smiled.

He didn't, his face growing taut as he looked at me.

"Cooper?" I said, turning away from the mirror to stare at him.

"Don't move," he said, using his cop voice on me.

I obeyed, barely breathing.

"What is it?" Natalie asked, stepping further into the room.

"There's someone standing next to Violet."

"A ghost?" She moved next to Cooper.

"If you're not seeing him, then yes, a ghost."

I didn't know what was scarier—that Cooper was using my first name or that a ghost was standing next to me.

"Are you kidding, Cooper?" I asked. "Like at the other house? Because if so, this isn't funny."

"Not this time."

"What's it doing?" Natalie whispered, like the ghost wouldn't be able to hear her if she kept her voice down.

"I think he's sniffing her neck."

"He's what?!" I cringed, waiting for it to appear in front of me and make me scream.

"Is he old or young?" Natalie asked.

"Older. I think. He's wearing a button-up vest and stiff shirt collar that shows his tie. He sort of looks like the guys in those old Charlie Chaplin movies from the 1920s."

"What's he want?" I asked, my voice higher than usual. Why me? Why couldn't it pick on Natalie?

"How should I know, Parker?"

"Ask him," Natalie said.

"What do you want?" Cooper snapped at the ghost.

Natalie sighed. "That's not how you talk to ghosts, Coop."

"How in the hell am I supposed to know how to speak to ghosts?"

"Is he still smelling me?"

"Uh, yes."

"Why did you 'uh' first?"

He grimaced in response, making the panic flying in my stomach flutter faster. "Because he's holding a shotgun."

There was something Cooper wasn't telling me, damn it. "Do something about him."

"What am I supposed to do?" he growled back. "I left my proton gun at home."

"Really, Cooper? You pick the worst times to try to be funny."

"Violet, calm down," Natalie said. "The ghost can't hurt you."

Easy for her to say since she wasn't getting sniffed ... or worse. "We don't know that for sure."

Cooper's grimace deepened. "I think he's trying to strangle Parker with one hand. Or line her up for a kiss."

"Oh, God!" I blocked my face.

"You can't interrogate him like you have him down at the station," Natalie said to Cooper. "You need to be nice when you talk to him. Make him want to talk."

He frowned down at her. "I don't know that we want this one to try to talk."

"Cooper!" I snapped.

He turned back to me, focusing on the space to my left. "Is there something you need from us?" He turned to Natalie. "How's that?"

"Better."

"He's walking toward me now," Cooper said, his face tightening as his eyes followed something in the empty air.

"Good," I said, brushing off my neck and face like I'd been covered with ectoplasmic slime. "It's your turn."

"Now what?" Cooper asked Natalie.

"Try asking him another question."

"Give me your name," he ordered.

"Coop, could you stop being a cop for one moment?"

"Will you please tell me your name?" he asked through gritted teeth.

"Well?" Natalie pressed.

"He's saying something."

"What?"

"I don't know."

"Is he speaking a foreign language?" I asked.

"I can't hear him."

"What do you mean?"

"I mean there is no sound coming from him, Parker."

"Is he a mime?" I asked.

"No, he's not a damned mime."

"Don't yell at me in front of the ghost."

He blew out a breath. "I'm sorry. This is new for me. I'm not Nyce."

"It's still new for me, too," I said, "and we're in this together. Take your frustrations out on your other partner. The one trying to frame me for murder."

"If you two girls are done bickering," Natalie said, "ask the ghost if this is his house."

"Of course it's his house," I said.

"We don't know that," Cooper defended Natalie. "He could have been visiting and died here. Didn't you say this place used to be a boarding house at one time?"

"No, that was that old place over in Central City."

Cooper took a step back, his steely eyes widening.

"What are you doing?"

"He's reaching toward my face."

"You need to let him pass through you," I said.

"Why?"

"I don't know. That's what Doc does."

"Yeah, well that's Nyce's gig, not mine." He stepped to the side, his head slowly turning toward the door. "He's leaving."

Natalie moved to block the doorway, licking her finger and holding it up in the air.

What the planets? "What are you doing, Nat?"

"Trying to see if there is a temperature change. They always talk about ghosts being cold on TV."

"Natalie, that's a bunch of …"

"I can feel him!"

"You should be able to," Cooper said. "He just passed right through you."

"How cool was that?" she said, grinning.

I looked at Cooper. "She's lost her marbles."

He nodded. "Let's get out of here."

"But he might come back," Natalie said.

"Trust me, we don't want him to."

"Why not?" I asked.

"Because half of his head was blown off."

Yikes! And he was sniffing me? Oh, gross. "I need a shower."

We didn't waste time escaping to his Durango. After voting two-to-one to call it a wrap for the day, we took the "one" back to the Galena House.

We sat in front of the big boarding house for a moment, catching our breath.

Something flickered in my mind, something Natalie had said earlier.

"Nat, you said you had a busy night." I turned in my seat to look at her. "Did you hear footsteps again on the stairs?"

Cooper frowned in the rearview mirror. "Our officers aren't giving you trouble, are they?"

"No," she said, looking from the mirror to me. "It was the old radio in the attic again."

"What are you talking about?" Cooper asked, so she filled him in on the old radio and how it played on its own. When she finished, he asked, "And this is the second night it's happened?"

"Well, I wasn't there Friday night, but Freesia said she heard it that night and went up to check it out. It stopped as soon as she entered the attic."

"And last night?" I asked. "Did it stop when you entered?"

"Yes. But when I turned to leave, it started up again. Then I approached it, and the stupid thing kicked off again. I did that two more times and then just gave up and went back to my apartment."

"Did it keep playing?"

She nodded. "It finally stopped around dawn. I zoned in and out a few times, but each time I woke I could hear it overhead."

I turned to Cooper. "You think Big Jake Tender liked old country music?"

He leaned his head back against the headrest, closing his eyes. "We should ask Nyce what this means. I'm out of my league here."

A sharp knock on my window made me jump and turn.

Detective Hawke's face filled my view.

Cooper whispered, "Keep your mouth shut, Parker. Let me handle this." He rolled down my window.

I crossed my arms, glaring at the bonehead. I so wanted to do a Three Stooges move on his big honking nose for throwing Doc in jail yesterday, but I obeyed Cooper's orders.

Hawke gripped the windowsill, his smile smug and calling for a kiss from my boot heel. "Hey, Coop. How's our number-one suspect doing?"

"What's going on, Hawke?" he asked, ignoring the question.

"Nothing, just coming home a little early today. The boys down at the station have everything under control." Hawke waved in at Natalie. "Hey, Nat. Feel like inviting me up for some dinner and a movie?"

"Beals is coming home with us," Cooper said.

"Another time, gorgeous," he said to Natalie with a wink. He patted the roof above my window. "You better take Parker home and put her back in her cage."

I glared at Cooper to keep from grabbing Hawke's fingers and bending them backward until something snapped.

"I'm taking her back to her office," Cooper said calmly. "She'll get herself home from there."

"Make sure she doesn't fly off on her broom."

"We're done here," Cooper said. He started to roll up the window. "I'll see you in the morning, Hawke."

"I'll see you on Tuesday, Parker," Hawke said, stepping back with that smug grin still filling his melon.

"What's on Tuesday?" Natalie called from the back.

Cooper left the window open a couple of inches so Hawke could reply.

"I called my old pal from the lab and made a deal. Lab results by Tuesday in exchange for tickets to the next three Broncos home games." He rubbed his hands together, his gaze locked onto me. "It looks like we'll have a murderer in jail by mid-week."

Chapter Twenty-Four

Detective Hawke popped my balloon, the pea-brained snollyguster. The passenger side window closed the rest of the way, blocking out the cold air and Hawke's obnoxious laughter as Cooper shifted into gear and rolled away.

"Fuck," I said, leaning back against the headrest. "What are the chances I'm going to get out of this mess?"

Even Cooper's worry lines had wrinkles. "I know a lawyer who might be able to help delay things a little, give Nyce and me more time to figure out who really killed her."

"I'm not going to let this happen, Vi." Natalie reached up and squeezed my shoulder.

"What does that mean?" Cooper asked, scowling at her in the rearview mirror.

"Exactly what I said, Coop. I didn't stutter."

"Natalie," he started.

She sat back. "Don't 'Natalie' me in that cop voice of yours, dammit. You do what you can do in your capacity as a detective to help Violet, and let me do what I can as her best friend."

"Nat." I turned around to look at her. "I can't allow you to get in the middle of this."

Her laugh was short. "I've never been anywhere but in the middle, right next to you."

"You won't be any help if you're in jail, Beals. And don't think for a minute that Detective Hawke will take it easy on you. His bloodlust for Parker has him acting irrationally."

"Oh, ye of little faith," she muttered, making a snarly face at the back of his head. "Who said I'm going to do anything illegal?"

She was beginning to sound like a woman on a mission. I jumped on her bandwagon. "You have something in mind?"

"As a matter of fact, I do. Cornelius said something to me the other day in the bathroom that gave me an idea."

"You mean when you two were looking in the mirror?" I remembered wondering what in the heck they were doing.

"Yeah. He told me that mirrors are often considered portals for spirits. When I asked why, he went on about the properties of silver on the back of old mirrors, electromagnetic fields, conductivity, ultraviolet light, and more scientific crapola. The point he was making was that ghosts can easily pass through mirrors into our world."

"And you believed him?" Cooper clearly didn't.

It was my turn to scowl. "Cooper, tell me something. Why were you looking in that dresser mirror today when we joined you in the upstairs bedroom?"

He glanced my way while navigating the narrow street. "I could see the ghost in the reflection."

"And then the same ghost appeared next to me outside of the reflection, didn't he?"

A frown was his response.

"You're in this with us now whether you like it or not," I told him. "That means you have to stop being pissy about being able to see ghosts. You need to open your black and white mind and accept that there is a lot of ectoplasmic gray surrounding you." I focused back on Natalie. "So, what's your idea?"

"Last night while I was messing around in the attic with that radio, I found an old mirror covered by a sheet. You need to do a séance with that mirror."

Cooper shook his head. "It's not going to work."

"Jeez, Coop." She crossed her arms, glaring at him. "You are one huge downer some days."

"I'm not trying to play devil's advocate here, Natalie." He glanced at me. "I'm just saying between Hawke and the officers he has assigned to monitor Ms. Wolff's apartment, there is no way anyone can get in there without him knowing about it."

"We can go in the middle of the night," she suggested.

"The stairs are creaky as hell in that place. He'll hear and come to investigate."

"So we keep him distracted," she shot back.

"I'd rather slip him a roofie," I muttered. And then leave him for the coyotes to gnaw on out in the Badlands.

Cooper slowed for the stop sign at Deadwood's Main Street, hitting his blinker. "How are you going to distract him?"

"Vi, I need to borrow that little black dress of yours."

A heavy sigh came from Cooper. "Let me do it. I can get him out of there without you having to sleep with him."

Natalie scoffed, her cheeks darkening. "Who said I was going to have sex with the big bozo? Man, Coop. You have one of the worst opinions of my character." She kicked the back of his seat hard enough to make him bounce, telling me, "This guy really pisses me off sometimes."

Cooper turned in his seat to look at her face to face. "I'm sorry, Natalie. I just ... When it comes to you I ..."

She pointed out the windshield. "Green light."

Cooper faced forward and hit the gas.

After a couple of more huffs, she said, "My idea is to take Hawke down to Rapid for dinner and dancing, keeping him out very, very late."

"Well," I chimed in, "if anyone can shoehorn Hawke's ass out of that apartment, it's you, Nat. Especially if you slip into a sexy dress and coat those baby inner tubes you call lips with something red and glossy."

She blew me a loud kiss with her baby inner tubes.

"I still don't like it," Cooper snapped.

"Why not?" she pressed.

He hesitated.

Come on, I willed him with my eyes. *Say it. Tell her the truth.*

"Because the roads will be icy when you drive home. It's too dangerous to be out."

Chicken!

"Uh, in case you've forgotten, Coop, I've lived here in the hills all of my life, too. I know how to drive in winter."

"Why don't you let me do the distracting? I can take Hawke to a bar, talk shop with him, and get him wasted."

"Because you need to help Vi and Doc look for ghosts. You're the only one who can see them."

"To what end?" I interrupted their bickering. "If we do this, Natalie, what do you think will come of it?"

"I think Ms. Wolff is up in that attic, listening to her old radio. Using the mirror, Doc and Cornelius and you could somehow draw her out like you guys did with Cooper's great-grandfather. With Cooper's ability to see ghosts, he can try to communicate with her. If that doesn't work, maybe Doc can work his magic and draw her to him, experiencing her death first hand. Either way, we'll have our murderer by the time sunrise comes around, and Cooper can help us figure out how to lock Detective Hawke's jaws onto the real killer."

As ideas went, that was better than what I was pondering, which centered on barreling toward the Mexican border in a 1969 Camaro SS with my kids and Doc in tow while boning up on my Spanish. How many pesos equaled a US dollar these days?

"When do you want to do this?" I asked.

"Tonight."

"No," Cooper said, slowing for a red light.

Natalie rattled off a string of curses. "For once, Coop, could you stop being such a fucking naysayer and take a leap of faith."

"That's not a leap of faith," he shot back at her, meeting her glare in the rearview mirror. "That's a desperate scramble at best."

I rubbed the back of my neck, weighing her idea with more optimism than Cooper. "I'm not sure I can get Cornelius to join in with so little prep time. He always has a checklist of items he needs for the séance. A process that he insists upon following."

"There's always kidnapping," she said. "Make him wing it."

"Yeah, but—"

"Vi, when you took on the bone cruncher that night behind Harvey's place, did you have a battle plan, or did you just take a run at the son of a bitch?"

That was definitely adrenaline-fueled running and swinging, and we all three knew it.

"Okay," I said. "But we need to get Doc on board. Without the master of ceremonies, we might open the wrong door." *Again.* Doc was still trying to fix my last screwup with Mrs. Hessler and Wilda. Lo and behold, I could make things worse.

"Are you seriously contemplating Beals' plan?" Cooper asked me, pulling in behind Calamity Jane Realty.

"Cooper, I don't exactly have tons of options."

"Don't overthink this for once, Vi," Natalie advised. "Trust in your abilities. Believe in yourself."

He shifted into park, letting the Durango idle. "That's it, end of discussion," he said to me. "Go back to work, and take your Obi Wan wannabe with you."

I got out, opening Natalie's door.

She scooted toward me, but then paused midway across. She gave me the hold-on finger and leaned forward between the front seats. "I'm sorry I yelled at you, Coop," she said and then smirked. "Even though you have such a shitty opinion of my reputation."

"Natalie, I don't—"

She cut him off. "That's not important right now. What is important is that I know you're trying to help Violet in your own law-abiding way. But the time for proper procedure has come and gone. If we don't find out who really killed Ms. Wolff, Violet is fucked. Not only that, but her kids are fucked, too. Hell, we're all fucked, because whether or not you believe in monsters, they're out there. We need Violet to kill them. If she ends up in prison, you can bet your ass that I will follow the Wile E. Coyote Acme handbook and stop at nothing short of TNT to break her out so she can finish what she was born to do."

He turned, his face inches from hers. He held her stare, his expression rigid. "I'll think about it, Beals."

"Good. You do that, and I'll give you a couple of hours to get used to the idea before I come looking for you." She pulled her hood up. "Meet us at Zoe's for supper and we'll hash out the details with Doc." Before he could reply one way or another, Natalie leaned forward and kissed his cheek. She sat back with a tight smile. "Oh, and don't buy the ghost house. It needs too much work."

Sliding out beside me, she shut the door and rushed through the cold for Calamity Jane's back door.

Cooper grimaced at me through the passenger window. I shrugged. What could I say? Natalie was a force of nature. He needed to understand that if he was going to try to lasso her. Besides, she was right. We needed to find Ms. Wolff's killer pronto, and using his methods would take too long.

I watched his taillights as he drove away. With or without the stubborn detective, I was going up to that attic tonight to try to find answers using my own way.

* * *

Doc listened quietly while Natalie and I laid out our plan during supper, his expression contemplative as he watched me. Cooper kept his objections to himself this time, his silence stony.

"Coop," Aunt Zoe said, pushing away her plate of mashed-up turkey potpie. She'd been picking more than eating for the last twenty minutes. "What are the chances of you talking to the chief tomorrow morning about Detective Hawke's erratic behavior and getting him suspended for a few days?"

I didn't give Cooper a chance to answer. "What good will buying us more time do if that lab report comes on Tuesday? The chief can read it as easily as Hawke."

She set her fork down. "I'm trying to come up with another option."

"Why? We have a perfectly good plan."

"Violet, what if the entity turning on that old radio isn't Ms. Wolff? Have you thought about that?"

Of course I'd thought about that. I'd just not voiced it to Natalie or anyone else, figuring I'd try to be prepared for whatever came through, good or bad. "Then we're no worse off than we are currently."

"We could be," Doc said, rising and walking over to the sink. He stared out the window into the darkness beyond.

I stared at his back, noticing the tension in his posture. "Have you ever experimented with ghosts and mirrors, Doc?"

He turned around, leaning against the counter with his arms crossed. "I've never needed mirrors to interact with them."

"I bet Cornelius has," Natalie said.

"Maybe you should call him and see," Aunt Zoe said to me.

"No. We need to surprise him into joining us tonight. If we give him time to think things through, he may balk."

"As he should," she said, taking her plate to the trash and scraping the remains of her dissected turkey potpie into it. "I don't like it. It's too rash. Something will go wrong."

Natalie's phone rang. She took it out of her pocket. "It's Freesia. I'll be right back." She left the table and headed into the living room, answering as she walked.

"What's the worst that could happen?" I looked to Aunt Zoe first for that answer.

She set her plate in the sink. "You release an entity that kills all four of you." When I grimaced at her, she shrugged. "And that's just for starters."

Next, I looked to Cooper. "Let's hear yours."

"My what?"

"Worst-case scenario."

He took a drink of lemonade before answering. "Hawke is onto us and arrests all of you on some trumped-up charges. You get fired and still wind up in prison; Beals is arrested for trying to spring you from the big house; Nyce destroys his reputation and his customers' trust; and Curion is hired by the police department to act as their paranormal liaison."

Well, his imagination was thorough if nothing else. "And what about you?"

He rubbed the back of his neck. "I'm forced to walk away from law enforcement for good."

"But if you behave, they might let you keep your guns."

He glared at me without comment.

"What about you, Doc? What's the worst thing you can think of that could happen?"

His dark gaze had a haunted look. "You go into that mirror, Killer, and you never come back out."

A replay, in other words, of what had happened to my ancestor. A chill ran down my spine, my nightmare with the basket ricocheting through my thoughts.

He smirked, adding, "And the real bitch of it is that I'm really starting to like you, too."

I lifted my chin. "You think you can get rid of me that easily?"

Before he could answer, Natalie came blowing back into the kitchen with a victory smile in place. "Freesia's in."

"What's that mean?" Cooper asked.

"She's going to help me keep Hawke distracted down in Rapid tonight."

Perfect. Natalie wouldn't be stuck having to fend off Hawke's big mitts on her own if he got grabby. Although, knowing Natalie, she'd slug him so hard he'd have to go looking for his jaw in the next town over.

"I need to go through your closet," she told me.

"Have at it," I told her.

As she left the kitchen, Doc called after her, "Not the purple boots!"

She laughed, her footsteps pounding up the stairs.

I looked at Cooper. "Feel better?"

He leaned his elbows on the table. "I'll feel better when tonight is over and I'm not stuck trying to figure out how to get your ass out of another one of your grand fuckups."

"Ah, isn't that sweet?" I grinned at Doc. "Cooper is worried about little ol' me."

"Shut up, Parker."

"Violet," Aunt Zoe said, leaning next to Doc. "What's the worst you fear could happen tonight?"

I sobered, looking from her to Doc to Cooper and then back. "The worst? That I find out there's nothing I can do to stop Hawke and wake up tomorrow morning knowing I'm going to lose all of this." I spread my hands wide. "You, my kids, Doc, Nat, and Harvey." I glanced at the detective across the table from me. "Hell, even Detective Grumpy Pants here."

Cooper flipped me off.

"Hawke will stop at nothing to destroy my life," I said, joking aside.

I swallowed a lump of emotion rising in my throat. Executioners didn't cry, I reminded myself. They dusted themselves off, picked up their weapons, and ran screaming back into battle. I just needed to figure out what weapon I was going to need tonight.

"Put yourself in my boots," I said to all three of them. "If everything you cherish was about to be stolen from you, wouldn't you do whatever it takes, reckless or not, to stop the thief?"

* * *

Much later that evening, Cornelius answered the door to the upstairs apartment at Calamity Jane Realty wearing a short, loosely tied pink robe with not much underneath from what I could tell. I shielded my eyes from the sight of his hairy, spindly legs two seconds too late.

"Violet!" Surprise made his voice higher than usual. "Did I request a late-night protein shake?"

His black hair was wet. A minty, rosemary scent hovered in the air between us. Shaving cream, maybe? His goatee did look like the edges were more defined. I must have interrupted his shower. Thank God he'd opted for a robe when he answered the door or my third-eye chakra might have gone blind.

"Nope." I pushed past him, stepping inside. The studio apartment was bigger than I'd imagined, with warm beige walls, original molding, hardwood floors, and pendant lighting throughout. "Wow, this is nice," I said, admiring what I imagined was the handiwork of my old boss, Jane. Although, to give Jerry's money-making brain credit, he might have put work into the place to spruce it up for a renter, but I'd have thought I would have heard about it over the last few months.

I walked over to a piece of luggage sitting open on the floor next to a Murphy wall-bed. Picking out a pair of black jeans stacked on top and a matching sweater, I tossed them to Cornelius. They landed at his bare feet. The tops of his toes were hairy, too.

He looked down at the clothes. "Am I going somewhere?"

"Yep."

His gaze was narrow when he lifted it to me again. "You're not going to bury me in a shallow grave, are you?"

I jammed my hands on my hips. "Why on earth would I do that?"

"Because you have been possessed by a malevolent spirit and are on a mad killing spree."

Now I knew Cornelius's worst-case scenario for tonight.

"No, I'm not going to bury you in a grave, shallow or deep." At least not tonight. With Cornelius, one never knew what might come to be.

"Then why do I require clothing?"

"The Tall Medium is waiting for us below." So was Harvey, who'd insisted on acting as our getaway driver on this madcap adventure as soon as he'd caught wind of it from Aunt Zoe. By "caught wind," I meant that he'd stopped by the house on his way home from a holiday shindig at the senior center and promptly heard a lungful of hot air from Aunt Zoe about what we were planning to do at the Galena House.

"Is the Tall Medium wearing white or black tonight?"

Why did that matter? Did he want to be twins?

"Brown flannel, actually. And blue jeans." I'd run my hands over both when he arrived at Aunt Zoe's, greeting Doc like he was covered in Braille.

"An earth color. Wise choice. Concentration and common sense will rule his actions."

That seemed fitting for Doc.

"Are we going to a movie?" Cornelius asked, pulling on his jeans in front of me.

I turned away before I could see any other hairy spots on his body, closing my eyes to be safe. "Do you ever go to movies?"

"No."

"Then why would we?"

"There's always a first."

I heard the sound of a zipper. "I have a surprise for you tonight," I told him.

"Will I live to see tomorrow?"

I opened my eyes a crack. Good, he was dressed. "Do you want to?"

He walked past me and grabbed a pair of socks and shoes, sitting on the bed to put on both. "It's probably for the best."

I certainly hoped to see the sun rise again. I checked my watch, which reminded me of an accessory we might need. "Did you fix your one-horned Viking helmet?"

He pointed to the small kitchen.

I grabbed it, and then returned to the door where he joined me while slipping his coat over his shoulders.

When I reached for the doorknob, he caught my arm. "What's going on, Violet?" His cornflower blue eyes searched mine, serious, curious, with all traces of Cornelius the Cryptic absent. "Are you in trouble?"

"Yeah, I am. Big trouble, and I need your help luring a ghost through a mirror portal in the attic of the Galena House tonight."

Natalie and Doc had decided to aim for midnight, and then keep trying until three, which was an hour after the bars closed. Natalie and Freesia would take their time getting Hawke home, keeping him out as long as they could manage.

Cornelius walked to the small kitchen area and grabbed what looked like an old-time doctor's bag off the counter. "We're going to need to stop by my hotel and grab my PK amplifier."

"What's that?"

"It will increase the base power of your psychokinetic abilities."

"Okay, but what will it really do?"

"Make it so one of us can see the ghost."

"Oh, we don't need that then."

"Why not?"

"Because we already have a PK dealio."

"Really? What model?"

I led the way out of his apartment. "It's a PK-Cooper."

"A PK-Cooper?" He locked the door behind us, following me down the stairs to the first floor.

"Yep. But I need to warn you, it's a little fussy about tonight's mission."

"Are you getting a spark at all from it?"

"Oh, yeah, plenty of those." I held the downstairs door open for him. "But don't worry, that won't affect his ability to see dead people."

Cornelius stopped, frowning down at me. "Did you say 'his'?"

* * *

Harvey parked his pickup a block down the street from the Galena House, letting it idle while we waited to hear from Natalie or Freesia that they were well out of the area. This gave Doc and me plenty of time to fill Cornelius in on the plan for tonight along with Natalie's experiences with the old radio in the attic.

As soon as I'd received an all-clear text from Freesia, saying they were past Sturgis on their way to Rapid City with Hawke securely trapped, I pulled up Cooper's cell phone number. He was also waiting down the street, sitting in Aunt Zoe's pickup, keeping an eye out for cops who might have been ordered to monitor the boarding house in Hawke's absence.

I texted Cooper, asking if we had an "all clear" to enter the Galena

House.

He wrote back: *Elk ear?*

What about it? I typed. Was that code word for something? We hadn't come up with a code word, had we?

What about what?

An elk ear?

What in the hell are you talking about, Parker?

You said elk ear.

LOOK AT WHAT YOU TEXTED ME!

I scrolled up my phone. Sure enough, my *all clear* actually read *elk ear.* What the hell was wrong with my phone? Was it possessed now, too?

Doh! I texted.

Give Nyce your phone!

I did as ordered, handing it to Doc who was sitting in the front of the pickup with Harvey.

No sooner had Doc taken it from me it rang.

"Hey, Coop," Doc said into the receiver, listening while looking back at me. "For you, maybe," he said, grinning, "but when she speaks French, I'm a goner."

Cooper said something that elicited a chuckle from Doc, and then an "Okay." He handed the phone back to me. "We're all clear."

"Ya sure ya don't want me to tie 'er up to the hitchin' post in front of the place and keep an eye out for trouble? I brought Bessie along to keep us company tonight."

"I think down the street is a better post," Doc said. "Then if you see a cop drive by, there's time to let us know and maybe even intercept if we need more time to get out."

Cornelius leaned closer to me. "Could we go to jail for what we are about to do?"

"It's a definite possibility."

"Excellent. I'm keen to speak with the ghost residing in that jail cell while you're present. If there are handcuffs involved, secure yourself to me. I'll swallow the key."

Or I could just run like hell into the trees.

Harvey dropped Doc, Cornelius, and me off in front of the Galena House, rolling away before anyone drove by and caught sight of us.

Natalie had left her key ring with me, showing me the keys to the front door, her apartment, Ms. Wolff's place, and the attic. We stepped inside the old boarding house, closing out the cold dark. I showed Doc the attic door key and sent him and Cornelius up ahead while I waited for Cooper to join us.

He showed up a minute later, slightly winded. He must have run from where he'd left Aunt Zoe's truck on the next street up.

"Where did you learn how to spell?" he asked, closing the door behind him, wearing only his gray thermal shirt and jeans. He'd apparently left his coat in the truck. "A correspondence course through the damned mail?"

"Shut up, Cooper. It's your fault. I think you broke my phone when you put that tracking dealio on it." I led the way up the stairs, around the landing to the attic door. The door stood ajar. As I climbed the stairs in the narrow, chilly stairwell, I could hear Doc and Cornelius moving around above me. Cooper locked the door behind us.

The attic was a large square, the same footprint as the Galena House foundation. I'd been in it before with Freesia and Cornelius and found it to look and smell like any other attic I'd ever been in—cobwebs, dust, and stale air. Nothing had changed, except for the number of "ghosts" in the room. That's what Freesia had called the sheet-covered furniture when she'd shown us around months ago. Someone had taken the sheets off a wrought-iron chair, the large radio Natalie had told us about, and a dresser that looked familiar for some reason.

Doc joined me in front of the dresser. "What's wrong?" He caught my hand, linking his fingers with mine.

"This dresser is spurring a memory."

"You've been up here before, right?"

"Yeah, but it was covered by a sheet then."

"Was it in Ms. Wolff's apartment the time we did a séance there? The day you took on the juggernaut?"

That was it! The dresser had been there in her bedroom along with a twin bed. The frame for that must be under one of the sheets. I shivered. "Yeah, it was on the other side of the mirror."

"Do you want me to cover it back up?"

"No, it's only furniture, and that big white bastard can't reach me anymore." I'd vaporized the juggernaut's ass in the present day and I'd sealed him up somewhere in the past as well.

"Listen, Killer." Doc turned me to face him. I could see the same uncertainties that had been lining his face in Aunt Zoe's kitchen. "I need you to do something for me tonight."

"Is this going to be R-rated again or should we aim for triple X this time?" I teased.

His grin made a brief appearance. "I need you to avoid touching Cooper at all times."

I frowned over at where Cooper was inspecting the back of the old radio, checking out the plug, testing it with the coiled extension cord Natalie had apparently left for us to use.

"But he's so scratchy and jagged. How can I resist reaching out to him and getting my skin shredded?"

Doc's hands framed my face. "There is a chance that if you touch him, he will be pulled along with you."

"And that would be bad because?"

"I don't know how to get him back."

"But you can get me back, right?"

"Maybe."

"Doc."

"I hope so. I can usually feel your presence, sort of keep tabs on you." He paused, frowning. "Usually."

"That's not real comforting. Shouldn't this be more of a pep-rally sort of speech? You know, a 'go get 'em, tiger,' sort of thing?"

"Cooper is a wild card. I don't know if I'll be able to locate him if he goes in and gets separated from you."

"Okay, no touching. Got it."

He leaned down and kissed me. It was a tender, loving kiss, and it pretty much melted my already gooey heart. When he pulled away, he touched his forehead to mine, his eyes closed. "Come back to me tonight, Killer."

"Like I told you before," I whispered, taking his hand and kissing his knuckles. "You're not getting rid of me that easily."

"Oh, hell," Cooper complained. "Knock off that shit, you two."

I grinned up at Doc. "Coop's jealous that I got some action last night."

"I'm not jealous," came from the other side of the room.

"According to an article I read," Cornelius said, opening his doctor's bag. "The scent of pumpkins increases the flow of blood to the penis in lab rats and humans."

Cooper dropped the cord, cursing.

"Hey, that gives me an idea," Doc said, winking at me.

"I swear, Nyce. I will shoot you." Cooper moved his flashlight beam around the walls. "Maybe even twice."

"You're carrying?" I asked Cooper. I didn't like hanging around ghosts while Cooper's gun was loaded. Prudence had almost shot me with his gun the last time.

Chuckling, Doc dropped a kiss on my forehead. "According to Willis, Coop carries everywhere, including the shower."

"We need to find soap that smells like gunpowder for Cooper's Christmas stocking."

"I think I'll shoot both of you," Cooper said, frowning at the wall. "Do any of you see an outlet?"

Doc left me to help him.

"Violet," Cornelius called from where he stood next to the radio.

I joined him, shining my flashlight on the old radio. It was dark, no lights behind the glass, no music. When I twisted the knobs it stayed dark.

"What do you think?" I whispered.

"I don't think you need to whisper," Cooper answered, plugging the cord into an outlet behind a sheet-covered block of furniture.

Cornelius pulled a stethoscope from his bag and put it on, holding the chest piece on the fabric covering the front of the radio.

"Do you hear anything?" I asked after a few seconds. Since I doubted the radio had a heart, I wasn't sure what he might be listening for, but I was open for discussion.

"Nothing," he said, wrapping up the stethoscope and dropping it back in his bag. "Your friend is certain this radio was playing and she wasn't merely dreaming?"

"Both she and Freesia witnessed it on multiple occasions."

"Here's the mirror," Doc said, carrying a large ornate, gold-framed mirror over to us. He leaned it against the side of the radio. "You want the sheet off?" he asked Cornelius.

"Not yet. We need to keep the portal closed until we're ready." Cornelius stood, looking around the large room. "Did you check for any dolls?" he asked me.

"Dolls?" I asked. "Why would I look for dolls?"

"They can be used as containers to trap ghosts that come through the portal."

"You mean like the doll starts talking?" I cringed at the thought.

"That is the idea, yes."

"Yeah, that's not going to work for me." I shivered, zipping Aunt Zoe's red vest up to my neck. "I'll be too creeped out to focus on the candle flame."

Doc squeezed my shoulder. "We'll skip the doll."

"We need to create a spirit-friendly environment to try to lure the ghost to us, which is far safer than going in after it," Cornelius said, looking around the room. "If this furniture belonged to the dead woman we are trying to contact tonight, we should uncover a few of the items and set them up within sight of the mirror." He frowned at me. "It's unfortunate you didn't give me time to grab my EVP recorder. Radios have been known to be excellent conduits for channeling ghosts."

While Doc and Cooper moved a couple of chairs closer as well as an antique end table, Cornelius extracted candles from his doctor's bag, along with a bundle of sage. Next came a jar of something dark and gelatinous. He handed the jar to me.

"What's this?" I asked, shining my flashlight on it. It was reddish purple in the light. I had a morbid thought. "Please tell me it's not congealed blood."

"Hmm. I don't remember keeping any congealed blood in this bag." He frowned at it. "Not after the last one broke."

He took the jar from me, opened the lid, dipped his finger inside, and then stuck it in his mouth.

I took a step back, ready to gag if it was blood.

"Grape jelly," he announced, capping it again.

What? "You use grape jelly to lure ghosts?"

"No, I use it as a dip for celery sticks. I stuffed it in my bag when I was moving to your building so I wouldn't forget it."

I smacked my forehead. I should have known.

"Where do you want the mirror positioned?" Doc asked.

Cornelius pointed at a beam coming up through the floor behind us. "Set it up so the radio is the focal point." He handed me a lighter, pointing at a small pile of candles. "Set them up in a circle."

"How big?"

"You need to fit inside of it."

"Will you be with me?"

"Not this time."

When I finished setting out the last candle, he drew a triangle on the floor with chalk inside of the circle of candles I'd set up.

"Why a triangle?" I asked.

"The triangle is a spiritual doorway or gateway." He pocketed the chalk. "It represents the joining of earthly and spiritual realms. Light the candles."

As soon as I finished lighting the last one, he said, "Violet, you mentioned on the way here that you brought an item that ties you to this spirit."

I fingered the picture of Layne in my pocket. "Yes."

"Good. Sit inside of the triangle and wait for us to finish preparations. No, face the mirror. You need to be looking into the portal."

I did as told, frowning at my reflection. Purple boots, green jeans, red puffy vest. I wondered what my choice of colors meant for tonight. I tried to flatten my wild hair so that the sight of me wouldn't scare Ms. Wolff away.

Behind me the old radio sat dark, quiet. I crossed my fingers inside of my pockets, fighting the doubt demons taunting me.

Cornelius positioned Cooper outside of the circle of candles in front of me but slightly to the right of the triangle's vertex so that he didn't block the mirror. Doc took the vertex to my left and Cornelius took the one on my right. All three of them faced inward, toward me, making me the center of attention.

"Now what?" I asked, wishing I could be sitting on the outside for once.

"Where is the object that will link you?"

I pulled out Layne's picture, holding it up for him to see.

"Hold the photo in your lap and focus on it."

I frowned at my son's sweet smiling face, my heart thudding hard in my chest. Focus how? On what in particular?

"Coop," Doc said. "Keep an eye on her, but don't touch her."

"Got it," Cooper shot back.

"Tall Medium," Cornelius said, settling his one-horned Viking helmet on his head. "You know what you need to do."

"Yes," Doc said.

"You may begin."

I wiped my sweaty palms on my jeans, worrying my lower lip.

In the still of the attic, I could hear the wind whistling outside. The walls creaked and popped. Something flapped outside the window, reminding me of the paper on the basket in my nightmare.

No, I wasn't going to think of that. I was going to focus on my son, alive and well, on his way to becoming a man. With Doc in the picture, Layne would finally have someone to turn to with questions that made me scratch my head ... or cringe.

Cornelius began to hum, a deep rhythmic reverberation that lulled the anxiety bubbling low in my stomach.

I peeked at Doc out of the corner of my eye. One of his knees was raised, his forearm resting across it with his head lowered. A glance the other way found Cornelius sitting cross-legged, his usual position. His one-horned Viking helmet sat slightly crooked on his head, his face a picture of concentration.

I chanced a look-see in Cooper's direction and ran into a pair of steely eyes staring back at me. He squinted a warning, for what I had no idea. Probably to quit fucking around and get to the business of catching ghosts.

Taking a deep breath, I shook the tension from my shoulders and settled in for the ride. I conjured a single candle in my mind, the flame flickering in the blackness. As I focused on the flame, making it grow and curl at the tips, Cornelius's humming began to fade, replaced by a whispering sound.

I strained to hear it, letting the candle flame shrink to a single blue teardrop. The whisper grew louder, the sound becoming rhythmic. There was a beat there, one I recognized. I focused on the sound. The flame became a skinny blue line. I heard the sound of cymbals, then a soulful-sounding horn. The whispering grew louder, turning into a chorus I knew well from my memories of hanging out in Aunt Zoe's workshop. The old record player. The crackling sound of a timeworn vinyl record. The Sons of the Pioneers singing in harmony.

I-ayyyyy. Yippee-i-oooooo!

I crooned along with them in a deep voice, "Ghost riders in the sky."

I opened my eyes.

Cooper was gone, his spot near the vertex of the triangle empty.

So was Doc.

Only Cornelius remained. He'd removed his Viking helmet, though.

In the mirror's reflection, I saw the radio. Its glass was lit with a soft yellow glow. The music poured from its speakers. I turned around to look at it, expecting it to be dark in my world.

But it wasn't. It was lit up, just like in the mirror. The song ended, leaving the scratchy sound coming from the speakers. I knew that sound—a needle at the center of a spinning vinyl record. Dead air.

I pushed to my feet, stepping over the candles to move closer to the radio. Was it a record player, too? I didn't see a way to open the top. I turned the knobs. Nothing changed. The lights glowed. The static continued.

A door slammed downstairs.

I looked toward the stairwell. Light reached up through it. Hadn't Cooper locked that lower door? Where had Doc and Cooper gone? Had Harvey contacted them? Did we have trouble coming?

The light in the stairwell flickered a few times, then held steady.

Mournful violins began to play on the radio, giving me chills. If this was what Natalie had been talking about playing throughout the night, it was no wonder she was having trouble sleeping. There was something eerie about the golden oldies echoing from the radio. I sort of wished I had my war hammer right about then.

I turned back to the triangle in the circle. Cornelius still sat humming away. I hesitated. Should I stay and wait for Doc and Cooper to return?

Something crashed downstairs.

What was that?

"Doc?" I called down the stairwell.

No answer.

Shit. I searched the attic, looking for answers on what to do next. There was no way I was going to do something stupid and go down there alone. Nope. No way in hell.

"Parker!" I heard Cooper shout from below. "Come here!"

What was going on, damn it? Was Doc okay? Was the crash something to do with him?

I tiptoed down the stairs, peeking out into the lit hallway. It was empty. I stepped out onto the upper landing. "Cooper?" I called. "Where are you? Where's Doc? The radio is working. You guys need to get up here."

A creak came from the wide stairwell leading to the first floor. I walked around to the top of the stairs, seeing nobody below. "Cooper?"

A door clicked shut downstairs.

I hesitated on the top step, confused, uncertain, on the verge of goosebumps.

The sconce on the wall next to me dimmed and then brightened enough to make me squint when I looked at it. It flickered before returning to normal.

Up in the attic, the song changed. The theme song to *Rawhide* resonated down around me.

Rollin', rollin', rollin' …

I stood a moment, trying to make sense of my surroundings. Everything looked the same, but the building felt like an echo of its usual self. The railing under my hand felt cool, solid and real. I clung to it, a touch of reality, as I made my way down the stairs.

Halfway down, I peered over the railing. Ms. Wolff's door stood open a crack, a wedge of light leaking out into the hall. Was Hawke back? Did Natalie drop the ball for some reason?

"Cooper?" I whispered, tiptoeing down the stairs and over to her door. The small brass knocker was swinging slightly, like the door had only just opened—or someone had just used the knocker.

Upstairs, the *Rawhide* whip kept cracking. Frankie Laine's voice flowed through the old boarding house with that scratching hiss of a worn 78 record.

Through the crack in Ms. Wolff's door, I heard something creaking steadily. It reminded me of my great-grandmother, sitting in her rocking chair while her gnarled fingers fidgeted with her bag of rune stones.

Inching the door open, I eased inside the apartment, the bright hall light overhead keeping my unease at bay. The music from the attic faded, replaced by steady ticking sounds. Lots of ticking sounds.

I walked into the dining room, frowning at the wall of clocks. They were back, all of them. Had Hawke found …

It all made sense suddenly.

Shit. I'd really screwed this up. I hadn't lured Ms. Wolff through the mirror, she'd lured *me*. The music, the crash, the creaks, the door slams. I'd followed her trail of breadcrumbs thinking I was chasing Cooper and Doc.

Damn, she was good. Leaving Cornelius behind was brilliant. Had I woken to find everyone gone, I'd have realized more quickly what was going on here.

The urge to return to the attic flooded me. Doc was going to be worried. I needed to backtrack and start over again. Maybe I should sit with my back to the mirror this time.

I turned to head back upstairs, but the door was shut.

I'd left it open, I was certain.

I walked over to it and pulled on it, twisting the knob one way and then the other, but it wouldn't budge. Fuck.

The overhead hall light blinked on and off several times. Was that a sign? Was the power fluctuation something one of Cornelius's paranormal gadgets would have picked up if we'd brought them? Or was someone trying to communicate using the electricity in the building?

"Please open the door, Ms. Wolff," I said aloud, hoping that if it was a matter of communicating, she'd be reasonable.

The rhythmic creaking sound reached my ears again. It came from the other end of the hall, beyond the dining room full of clocks. Fear kept me glued in place. If my great-grandmother were sitting in that rocking chair in the living room, I'd know I'd stumbled onto the *lidérc*'s newest lair. Damn it. I should have brought my war hammer.

You can do this, I cheered to myself. When that didn't make my feet move, I pulled Layne's picture from my pocket. I needed to do this for him and Addy. I had to see who was waiting for me in Ms. Wolff's living room. And why.

Taking a deep breath, my feet began to move again. I walked deeper into the apartment, rounding the wall and stepping into the living room. A sense of déjà vu struck me as I stood there looking at the rocking chair, which rocked on its own. I even remembered the creaking as it moved back and forth, or at least I thought I did. This all seemed so familiar—frighteningly so.

The rocking chair slowed to a stop.

"Where are you?" I asked, sounding brave, as if I wasn't worried about my bladder letting loose at any minute. I cleared my throat. "Show yourself."

The old country music started again, only it sounded even more scratchy, like it was being piped into the room.

I crossed my arms, tucking my trembling hands into my chest. "I don't have time for games tonight. Show yourself and let's get this over with."

The music grew louder, enough so that I could pinpoint the source: the antique phone.

It sat on the end table beside the rocking chair. The lamp next to it seemed to spotlight it. The receiver was off the hook.

I moved to it, picking up the receiver and holding it to my ear.

"Drifting along with the tumbling tumbleweeds …" crackled through the earpiece.

Chills spread up my arms and down my back.

"Hello?" I whispered, even though the tumbleweeds continued to roll along in verse.

In my peripheral vision, something moved.

With the phone still to my ear, I slowly turned my head, my heart slamming against my ribs.

In the shadowy corner of the living room, not ten feet away, stood the white-haired juggernaut. He was watching me.

My breath seeped out of my frozen throat, whistling like a dying breath. My body started to shudder, my muscles quivering so hard that my knees grew rubbery.

As we stared at each other, his snake-like eyes seemed to glow brighter. His body took on a more solid form, separating from the shadows, becoming more real. He took a step toward me. The lamp lit half of his craggy face, deepening the shadows around his eyes, adding more angles and ridges. In his hand was the medieval battle-ax I'd faced and dodged before, the blade shiny. Recently sharpened?

From my viewpoint, he looked to be straight out of Hell.

"Scharfrichter." The name rolled off his tongue syllable by syllable.

My paralysis broke.

I screamed, stumbling backward, and tripped over my own boots.

Chapter Twenty-Five

Our plan had a flaw.

A big one with white hair, snake-like eyes, and a deadly weapon. I tried to catch my balance as I stumbled, my arms flailing, but still fell on my ass. Prudence would have been so proud.

Twisting and pushing up at the same time, I sprung toward the door like a sprinter off the blocks. Head down, hell bent, I was getting back up to that attic immediately.

I'd made it two steps and rammed the top of my head into something solid in the empty air that sent me spinning sideways into the dining room table. My feet tangled with a chair and down I went again, rolling into the wall, jarring several clocks above me.

What the hell had I hit? The juggernaut? He must have moved at lightning speed. I sat up, blinking, searching for it. Where was he? My gaze darted to the living room, the bedroom doorway, the ...

Through the legs of the dining room table and chairs, I saw something move. Breath held, I lowered my head, peering between the legs, and saw blue jeans and a gray thermal shirt.

Gray thermal ... *Cooper?* I scrambled to my feet and raced around the table.

He sat up, holding his hand over his left eye. With his other eye, he glared up at me, his face contorted in pain and anger.

"Cooper! You scared the shit out of me. What are you doing here?" I glanced toward the front door, which was still closed. More important, "How did you get in here?"

He got to his feet, his mouth moving, but no sound came out.

Cocking my head to the side, I stepped closer. "What?"

His mouth moved again, his right hand waving in the air to emphasize his point. He was tense, no doubt about it. As I continued to watch him, trying to figure out what he was saying and why I couldn't hear him, he stopped and shook his head. His chest rose and fell in agitated huffs. He pointed at the eye he was covering and then at my head.

Oh. He was what I'd plowed into during my haste to escape. I must have rammed my head into his face. No wonder he was so pissed.

I pointed at my ear. "I can't hear you. It's like you're on mute. Can you hear me okay?"

He nodded, his mouth set in a hard line.

I reached out toward him. He reared back.

"Hold still, damn it. I'm testing something." I reached again, touching his shoulder and then poking his chest. "Hmmm, I can feel you and see you, I just can't hear you. Can you feel me?"

He lowered his hand covering his left eye, his teeth gritted as he undoubtedly cursed me.

I crossed my arms, trying not to cringe when I looked at the damage I'd done to the left side of his face. The area around his eye was already turning a dark reddish blue, showing the signs of turning into one hell of a shiner "That's not my fault, Cooper. It was an accident."

His face darkened, his mouth moving a mile a minute. He jabbed me in the shoulder, hard, bruising.

"Hey! It's not like I did it on purpose. I couldn't even see you standing there. Next time, stay the hell out of my way when I'm freaking out. I'd have thought you'd learned that lesson in Mudder Brothers when I broke your stupid nose."

His eyes narrowed, the fury tightening his face scaring me a little. His right hand chopped the air as he let loose on me, but I only heard the tick-tock of the clocks on the dining room walls.

I watched him, feeling like he was on the other side of a wall of glass, or a television screen—a silent movie in the making. I was impressed with the amount of emotion the pissed-off detective could portray without making a single sound. Thanks to that lack of sound, I didn't feel like jumping in and going head to head with him nearly as much, not even when he flipped me off with both birdies inches from my face.

Holding up my hands, I said, "Sorry, Cooper, but I don't read lips well."

I left him then, making for the front door. It was still locked. Shit. I strode back over to him, ignoring his glare.

"I saw the big white juggernaut," I explained. "He was standing over in that corner. Did you see him?"

He looked in the direction I pointed, shaking his head.

"Shit. I was hoping you'd seen which way he'd gone. He was carrying that damned battle-ax of his." What had his twin brother called it? A scythe? Whatever. I was calling it an ax.

Cooper pushed me aside, not very nicely either, and headed toward the bedroom.

I followed. "Cooper, stop! Where are you going? We need to get out of here and back to the attic. I screwed this up somehow."

He pushed open the door to Ms. Wolff's bedroom. The light was on in there. We stood in the doorway, looking in at the full wall of clocks, the bed, the dresser, the unbroken mirror—everything was just as it had been the first time I'd stepped into this room that day Cooper showed me Layne's picture in her dresser mirror.

The mirror … I looked at the dresser. Layne's picture wasn't there. I felt in my pocket. Because I had the picture.

I pulled it out, frowning down at it. If I had the picture …

Cooper grabbed my arm, tugging me away from the doorway into the living room.

"Damn it, Cooper." I tugged back. "You almost made me drop the picture." I shoved it in my pocket.

He stopped so fast that I ran into him.

Shoving him to the side, I growled, "Don't stop right in the—"

The words froze on my lips.

The juggernaut stood on the other side of the living room, seeming even larger than before. He was a hulking presence compared to the woman at his side, who was close to my height but willowy. Her hair was long and white, her cheekbones high and strong, reminding me of the drawings in my kids' history books of Sacagawea, the Shoshone woman who helped Lewis and Clark, only with every part of her faded white. Her eyes matched her companion's, though, with snake-like slits for pupils.

"Cooper," I whispered, stepping closer, bumping into him. "Do you see them?"

If he answered, I couldn't hear. He tucked me behind him, shielding me. I would have suggested we make a run for it, but they were standing between the door and us. There was no way we'd both make it past the juggernaut and his blade, at least not in one piece.

"What are you doing?" I asked when I saw Cooper reaching for his concealed gun. "That's not going to work." I grabbed his arm.

He shook me off and enunciated two words: *Stay. Back.*

"No, listen. Unless you're Doc, what happens to you in this place happens in the other normal world. Trust me, you can't beat that thing with his ax. This is my fight."

"To whom do you speak, *Scharfrichter?*" the woman spoke, her voice strong, no quiver of age or timidity.

I stepped out from behind Cooper, batting away his attempt to grab me and pull me back behind him again. Instead of answering her, I asked, "Who are you?"

"You know who I am."

Her voice sounded familiar. "Not definitely, but I could hazard a guess or two."

The juggernaut leaned down and spoke in the woman's ear. She nodded, moving over to the rocking chair. "Does this help?" she asked, rocking.

The wave of déjà vu flooded over me again.

"Ms. Wolff." I didn't ask. I knew it, clear as my own name.

While the juggernaut was looking at Ms. Wolff, Cooper made a run at him. He tried to slam into the big guy, but flew right past him and disappeared through the wall behind him.

I frowned. What the hell?

As I stared at the wall, Cooper stepped back through, his eyes meeting mine. The confusion written all over his face undoubtedly matched mine.

Then it made sense.

Oh, shit.

Cooper stepped toward the juggernaut, reaching out to touch its back, but his hand passed through it. He confirmed what I'd already guessed— he was a ghost on this plane of existence, able to see and hear, but not speak or touch ... well, not touch anyone besides me. How in the heck did that happen? Why couldn't I hear him?

"The time has come, *Scharfrichter*." The finality in Ms. Wolff's tone snared my attention. Her English was very good, what sounded like a Slavic accent coming through only here and there. I tried to remember what she'd sounded like when she'd called me that day so long ago, but a lot had happened since then to blur my memory.

"The time for what?"

"You brought the picture, I presume."

I fingered Layne's picture, wondering how she knew I had brought it. "What picture?"

"Do not waste *my* time with games."

Cooper returned to my side, frowning down at me. Only now, it was more of a worried frown than pissed off.

I pulled the picture from my pocket and held it up. "Yeah, I have the picture."

"Excellent." She turned to the juggernaut, speaking in what must be their language. It rolled off her tongue, sounding almost musical.

He nodded and took a step toward me.

I grabbed Cooper's sleeve, holding my ground otherwise.

"You have been chosen, Executioner," the juggernaut said in clear English, not even a hint of an accent.

Chosen for what? I covered my throat with my hand. Chosen to die by a sharp blade?

Wait a second! The juggernaut I'd battled in this very apartment in the past had a distinct accent. This one sounded different. I gulped. "You're Mr. Black, aren't you?"

He nodded once and held out the battle-ax toward me, handle first.

When I just stared at the weapon, Cooper nudged me.

I looked over.

Take it, he mouthed.

I tentatively stuck my hand out, afraid it was a trick.

Mr. Black held my guarded stare as I gripped the handle and took it from him. "Why are you giving me this?" I asked him. Were we going to battle fair and square, unlike when I'd taken on his brother?

"Death is required," Ms. Wolff said from the rocking chair. "The loop will not be complete without the sacrifice."

"Death?" I grimaced. Something felt wrong here. Very wrong. "Whose death?"

"Mine, of course," she said.

I looked down at the ax in my hand, putting one and one together. "You want *ME* to kill you?"

"It's not a matter of want, *Scharfrichter*, it's a matter of need."

A matter of need …

A scene replayed in my head. The big bad wolf breathing through the antique phone in this very room, answering my question of who killed the timekeeper. *Scharfrichter*, it had said.

I fast-forwarded to a couple of days ago with Dominick at breakfast: *You are the one who killed the timekeeper … she wore one of your marks.*

I looked down at the medieval ax, turning it in my hands. The lamplight glinted off the blade part of the ancient weapon. I killed the timekeeper?

Cooper grabbed my wrist. When I turned to him, he shook his head, his steely gaze troubled. He didn't have to mouth the words for me to get his gist. If I did as they said, then I was fucked. I might as well just leave the Galena House and head straight to the police station and check myself into a jail cell.

"I can't do this," I told Ms. Wolff. "I'm not a killer."

Ms. Wolff laughed. It had a musical lilt to it. "That is quite amusing coming from this *Scharfrichter*, yes?" she said to Mr. Black.

"She does not understand the gravity of the situation," he told his counterpart.

"You're right," I said, lowering the blade to the floor. "I don't. I don't understand how I'm standing here talking to you right now," I said to Ms. Wolff. I turned to Mr. Black. "And I don't understand why you are standing here not trying to kill me like your twin did. None of this makes any sense."

Mr. Black spoke to Ms. Wolff in their language.

"There is no time for that," she replied.

"You must make time for it if she is to follow through as needed."

"Make time for what?" I asked.

Ms. Wolff sighed. "Fine, but this will make us rush through the end."

I exchanged raised brows with Cooper.

"Carnage is coming," she explained. "A bloodbath such as we have not experienced in many generations. The cages have been opened and your skills as a *Scharfrichter* will not be enough to contain the waves of upheaval and ruin. We must act now to build your strength by means that those behind the butchery will not expect, or you will be slain by the next solstice. Now, do your job and cut off my head."

I laughed.

And then I laughed some more.

I couldn't help it. It was laugh or run screaming toward the door and pound on it until somebody woke me up from this nightmare.

Cooper grabbed me by the shoulders and turned me to face him. He pointed his index and middle fingers at my eyes and then pointed back at his own.

I nodded and stared into his steely eyes. Hiccups of laughter continued to bubble up and out, out of my control initially, but the longer I looked into Cooper's familiar gaze, the more I quieted.

Finally, I was back at the reins. I took a breath and turned to Mr. Black. "Why don't you kill her?"

"I cannot."

"Why not? Your twin brother slayed three others like her in this very apartment. I saw it with my own eyes." Well, I actually only saw him swing at the last one and then the head fall to the floor and shrivel up, but now was not the time to split hairs. Why did he slay them? I was about to add that question to the list when Mr. Black spoke.

"Because a timekeeper cannot slay another of their kind."

Another of their … "You're a timekeeper?"

He nodded once.

I frowned. "As in the 'other' timekeeper? The one I've been looking for since I found Ms. Wolff's body?"

The same Ms. Wolff who was sitting in the rocking chair, impatiently rocking away right this moment.

"It is one of my many roles," he answered.

"Why didn't you approach me before now to tell me who you were?"

"Because you are a *Scharfrichter*."

"What does that mean?"

"You would have tried to kill me, as you did the other like me."

He was right about that. His twin had me swinging at shadows.

"I did not want to experience that fate at your hands, so I had to choose the right time."

"So you're not some kind of morbid killer with a fetish for body parts?" That was what Ray had told me about Mr. Black.

"I am a killer," he said as if announcing he was a plumber. "But I do not collect body parts, nor was the other like me my 'twin brother,' as you say."

What was he then? That wasn't important now. "So you're a killer *and* a timekeeper?"

"Those are two among many roles *der Zeitnehmer* plays," Ms. Wolff said. "Now, can we continue with the process before we miss the window in time?"

Window in time? What did that mean?

"I'm not going to kill you," I told her again.

"It is what you do."

"I don't just go around randomly killing, I do it when it's necessary."

"This is necessary," Ms. Wolff said.

"You must execute her in order to expand your abilities," Mr. Black explained. "Without them, we will no longer exist."

"When you say 'we,' do you mean you and me?" I asked. "Or you and her?"

"I mean all of us. You do not understand the enemy you will soon face."

I turned to Cooper. "So if I have this straight, I must kill Ms. Wolff in order to obtain the skills of a timekeeper, which will be necessary in order to have a chance at surviving the wave of evil and death coming our way. Is that what you're getting here? We could use your little police notebook to keep track of this shit."

He scowled at me.

"I don't like it either, but I'm not really seeing an out yet."

Turning back to Ms. Wolff, I said, "Why did I need to bring a picture of my son?"

"As a reminder."

"A reminder of what?"

"To return to finish the second loop."

"I don't understand."

She sighed, clearly exasperated with my tiny part-human brain. "Tethering is a two-loop procedure."

Tethering? What had Prudence said about tethering? That it was bad juju, right?

"Without the second loop, the process will not be sealed and all will be lost. My death will be a waste."

"So we did this once before during a first loop?"

"Yes."

"How come I don't remember it?" That would explain my déjà vu sensation.

"Because you have been an apprentice, if you will. You had my abilities, but not the knowledge of how to use the skills correctly. After we complete the second loop, you will remember all. This is the process that must be followed."

"So what am I supposed to do with this?" I held up Layne's picture.

"Place it in the mirror in my bedroom where you found it."

I paused to think that through. If I put it in the mirror, Cooper will find it and then tell me about it, which will start me freaking out about how Layne is connected, and then Mr. Black will show up and take the picture again. I grimaced. Thinking about that too much was going to hurt my brain.

My focus shifted to Mr. Black. "You took the picture from the mirror?" At his nod, I added, "And you are the one who mailed it to me with that cryptic note."

"It was required for the final loop."

"But what if I hadn't brought it?"

"There was no chance of that."

"Why not?"

"Because you already brought it the first time."

"But this isn't the first time."

"Correct. It is the second."

I scratched my head, glancing at Cooper. "Are you getting this?"

He pinched the bridge of his nose, his lips moving in what I guessed were swear words probably aimed unfairly at me.

"To whom are you speaking?" Ms. Wolff asked.

"Myself," I said. "Were those really strands of my hair the police found in your hand?"

"Yes."

"Shit." I frowned at Cooper. "I'm fucked."

"Not if you complete the second loop," she said.

"Come again?"

"The first loop requires your hair for the tethering process to begin. If you follow through with the second loop, the hair will no longer be in my possession at death."

"Your problem with the lawman will no longer be," Mr. Black said.

I paced between them, ax still in hand. "So, you're saying that if I kill Ms. Wolff a second time right here and now, then the hair Detective Hawke is using to build his murder case no longer exists?"

"Correct."

"You both know about this situation of mine with the law then." It wasn't a question and they didn't bother answering. Of course they had known. "This is blackmail."

"*Nein*. It is a necessity, *Scharfrichter*. Accept your responsibility."

"Why are you doing this?" I asked her. "Why are you willing to sacrifice yourself to help me?"

"I told you, our strength is no good separated."

"Why not kill me and take mine?"

"That is not how it works. Executioners are bred, timekeepers are made."

"But ..."

"I am tired, *Scharfrichter*," she said. "I have been here a long time. I have loved and lost more times than I can remember. You have no idea how fortunate you are to have a short lifetime." She gripped the arms of the rocker. "I no longer desire to continue in this world, but you do. You want to live, to watch your children grow old. Of greater importance is the fact that your existence is necessary to bring balance yet again, but mine is not. If I can offer help via a sacrifice, then so be it."

"I don't think I can kill you."

"You already have once," she said. "Take the photo of your son to my bedroom now. We are out of time."

I did as told, my thoughts twisting in turmoil. When I returned to the living room, Cooper blocked my path. He shook his head.

I closed my eyes, torn between what was morally wrong and what Ms. Wolff insisted had to be done.

"Violet Parker?" I heard Ms. Wolff whisper with a hitch in her breath.

What? I looked at Ms. Wolff. She was holding the antique phone to her ear. The one that had no dialtone when Cooper and the cops listened. The one that I'd heard ringing a month later and had picked up to hear the big bad wolf ordering me to open the door.

"I need to talk to you," she continued. Her voice echoed in my head, replaying across time.

Cooper turned to stare at the timekeeper, too. Mr. Black stood off to the side, peering out the window.

"It's about what you are," she repeated what she said to me that cold October day on the phone.

"*Nein, Scharfrichter.*"

I remembered my question that followed: "Nine what?"

"I must see you immediately. Come to the Galena House on Williams Street, apartment four. Knock seven times."

Why seven times, I wondered just as I had then.

"You will come now," Ms. Wolff said, loud and clear. "I will be dead soon."

Shit. Shit. Shit. This wasn't really happening, was it? I squeezed the all-too-real handle of the battle-ax.

"Do not delay!" She paused before adding, "I will be waiting." Then she hung up.

"Oh God," I said, my stomach fluttering.

"Now," she frowned at me. "Kill me."

"What if I don't?"

"You will die," Mr. Black said.

"What? Why?" By his hand?

"We are tethered, *Scharfrichter*," Ms. Wolff answered for him. "If you do not kill me and return to your time, the loop will break and we will both die."

"So my body up in the attic will just keel over."

"Your body is here. You will never return to the attic."

Fuck me. It was like the story in my family history, the one Doc told me about. Tears filled my eyes, frustration and fear overflowing. I was trapped.

I looked at Cooper. "And the executioner was never seen again," I whispered.

He stared down at me, his face tense. The area around his left eye was swollen now, turning blue around the edges. He scrubbed his hand down the right side of his face, his lips moving. But his words never reached me.

"I don't know what to do," I fretted, chewing on my knuckles, my gaze darting from one player to the other in this macabre game.

Cooper took me by the shoulders. When I frowned up at him, he mouthed: *Do. It.*

Then he released me and walked through the bedroom doorway, turning his back on me as he stared into the dresser mirror.

"Now, *Scharfrichter*," Mr. Black said. "You need to return in order to complete the loop."

"How do I know you're not lying to me?" I said, whirling on him. "That you're not using me as some sort of tool to accomplish a deed that will set me up for something even worse than a life in prison?"

"Violet," Ms. Wolff said. Her use of my name snared my attention. "We are not your enemy."

"Then who are you?"

"We are sentinels, acting as your allies. Who do you think sent you the war hammer?"

"You?"

She shook her head, pointing across the room.

I frowned at Mr. Black. "But you've been asking about my son," I said, remembering Eddie Mudder's warnings about the "other" juggernaut asking questions. "You were watching him play in the schoolyard. Why?"

"He must not be harmed."

Harmed by whom, if not Mr. Black?

"*Scharfrichter*," Ms. Wolff snapped. "Come here."

I moved closer, glancing toward the bedroom to see if Cooper was watching. Only Cooper wasn't there. He was gone!

I peered into the room. Where was he? The closet door was closed, the room empty. What had Doc said? If Cooper followed me into another plane, Doc didn't know if he'd be able to find him to pull him back? I needed Cooper to stick close to me so I could make sure he got back, dammit.

"*Scharfrichter!*"

"I'm coming!" I felt pulled along, rather than walking of my own volition. As I neared her, Ms. Wolff scooted forward in the chair.

"Lift the weapon."

It shook in my hands as I raised it.

"Higher."

I didn't want to, but I couldn't seem to stop myself from doing as ordered, getting it ready to swing. I shook my head, looking into her pale face. "I can't do this."

"You will."

"No."

"It won't hurt me, *Scharfrichter*." Her smile was sad. "It will free me."

"This is not what I—" My vision tunneled, black shadows eating at the edges. "Want," I said, my voice sounding far off and crackly, like the old radio in the attic.

The ax fell.

"No!" I screamed as the blade sliced.

I tumbled with it into the darkness.

Chapter Twenty-Six

Monday, December 10th

The next thing I remember," I told Doc, staring out his office window at the gray early morning sky, "was Cooper shaking me, ordering me to snap out of it and stop screaming."

I heard his chair creak behind me. "You have no memory of leaving Ms. Wolff's apartment?"

Shaking my head, I turned away from the outside world and walked over to the empty chair next to Cornelius. "One minute I was in the living room with Ms. Wolff and Mr. Black." I lowered myself onto the seat. "The next I was standing outside the door of her apartment, screaming my head off, as Cooper so kindly put it."

I was careful not to mention the bit about killing the timekeeper in front of Cornelius in case Hawke decided to put him on the stand someday. As far as Cornelius was concerned, our objective had been to communicate with Ms. Wolff's ghost, and that objective had been met.

Things had moved quickly after Cooper found me, with Doc and Cornelius packing up and hauling me out into the cold. Harvey was waiting out front in the warm pickup, frowning several times in the rearview mirror at me as he drove us back to Calamity Jane's to drop off Cornelius, and then home. When we pulled up, Cooper was still sitting in Aunt Zoe's pickup, frowning out the windshield.

We all filed inside where Aunt Zoe waited with cold beer and hot tea. I fell into a kitchen chair, sipped on the chai tea placed in front of me, and told the whole ghastly tale to Doc, Harvey, Aunt Zoe, and Cooper. My story came out in broken pieces, a lot of details skipped because exhaustion and the shock of what I'd done made my head fuzzy. When I ended in tears, Doc had decided to call it a night for me, telling everyone that we needed to see how things looked come daylight. Thankfully, Aunt Zoe had put Addy in her bed for the night, leaving mine open for company.

Doc led me up to my room, stripped me down, and slid a nightshirt over my head. Then he crawled into bed with me and pulled me into his arms. I fell asleep within minutes while he stroked my hair, whispering sweet nothings in my ear. I slept hard, nightmare-free. My imagination must have been running low on energy and decided to take the night off.

I'd woken to an empty bed and the smell of fresh coffee. Aunt Zoe was sitting at the table when I stumbled bleary-eyed into the kitchen, her mug of coffee steaming. She didn't ask too many questions, only if I were heading into work and what I needed her to do for me besides getting the kids up, dressed, fed, and to school. That was enough as far as I was concerned.

Doc joined us, fresh from the shower. He told us Cooper was already up and gone, and that the detective had left me a message—*Do NOT call or text me today!*

Huh. Here I'd thought we were best buddies after last night. Apparently, Cooper was still pissed about that black eye.

Doc drove me to work extra early, but instead of going into Calamity Jane's, I followed him into his office where we were supposed to meet with Cornelius and fill him in on what had happened in the apartment.

The guest of honor must have been watching for us. We were in Doc's office only minutes when the back door opened and Cornelius joined us, wearing his pink robe, striped pajama pants, and his round sunglasses. He had a protein shake in hand and was quite chipper considering how little sleep he must have had, which I figured explained the need for sunglasses at our early morning meeting.

"What do you think?" Doc asked Cornelius, bringing me back to the present. "How would you explain what Violet experienced?"

Abe Jr. stroked his goatee, his brow drawn over his sunglasses. "It reminds me of a haunting."

"What does that mean?" I asked him.

"A haunting is an event that occurs on a time loop, but doesn't actually include any interaction with the living." At my frown, he added, "Think of it like a video recording that keeps playing over and over. Only in this case, you interacted with the recording, which is unusual. The question is, did your interaction change the outcome of the loop?" He held up one long skinny finger. "Or, was this all part of the haunting loop, just a part that was not witnessed before last night?"

Trying to make sense of that made my head throb over my right eye.

"Another possibility," Cornelius continued. "Is retrocognition."

"Remind me what retrocognition is," I said to Doc.

"He means you were able to see and experience events from the past with no prior knowledge of them."

"But ..." I started, thinking about how Ms. Wolff said I'd been there before.

Doc held up a hand, stopping me from going any further. He nodded knowingly and turned to Cornelius. "How do you explain Detective Cooper? Violet could see and touch him, but not hear him. The other two in the room seemed to not know he was there."

"If we continue with the haunting theory involving a loop in time, it would make sense the others involved couldn't see or hear him. He was not part of the haunting loop, merely a visitor observing."

Doc steepled his fingers, leaning back with a thoughtful frown.

"Another possibility," Cornelius said, "could be the detective was having an OBE."

"OBE?" I asked.

"Out-of-body experience," Doc explained.

"But his physical form was in that apartment just like mine." At least I thought it was. He sure felt real when I head-butted him.

"He could still go in and out of his physical form," Cornelius said. "Which might explain his going through the wall and this Mr. Black character." He took a drink from the straw in his protein shake. "Another possibility is the concept of reciprocal apparition, wherein you and the detective were able to see and respond to each other in a different astral plane than this one."

"But why Cooper and not Doc, or you?"

Cornelius shrugged. "The detective was able to go into a trance, possibly, and detach from his physical surroundings. Or there's the chance that you were able to connect to his mind via telepathy and imprint your visions of the apartment and all that occurred, making him an observer only, able to view but not actually participate."

"Why did I keep hearing the radio playing old music?"

"There is a school of thought that believes in RVP." When I gave him a "huh" look, he added, "Radio voice phenomenon."

"You can hear the voice of the dead through a radio," Doc clarified.

"Only in your case," Cornelius said, "it wasn't so much the voice of the dead, but a channel for you to access a haunting and project yourself into it."

I buried my face in my hands. "I can't believe there are words for all of these things."

"Whether or not traditional science is willing to accept the paranormal world," Cornelius said, "it's all around us. Some of us are better at seeing and hearing it than others. You, Violet, are the strongest physical medium that I have come across. Not only that, your sixth-sense abilities far exceed in multitude and variety those of anyone else I've known personally."

Great. I was a freak extraordinaire.

"Did you find all of your answers last night?" he asked me.

"What do you mean?"

"You said you had to make contact with a particular ghost. Was one of the two in the apartment who you were looking for?" At my nod, he added, "And did the ghost give you the answer you needed?"

"Yeah, she did." I knew who killed Ms. Wolff now. So did Cooper. How that was going to pan out with Detective Hawke and the others we'd know tonight when Cooper got off work. Mr. Black had said that my hair would not be in Ms. Wolff's possession if I completed the second loop. Without my hair, Hawke had nothing to tie me to her murder.

But, was Mr. Black lying? Using me to kill Ms. Wolff for his own means? Or was I really now not only an executioner, but a timekeeper as well?

Cornelius stood. "Excellent. Then our mission was a success." He threw his empty protein shake in Doc's garbage can. "Now we can focus on the hellhole under your office building."

Oh, yeah, I'd forgotten about that uncanny problem. "Why? Did you hear more weird noises coming from it?"

"No. It's been sealed off."

"What do you mean?"

"Your old boss doesn't want us going down there."

"How do you know that?"

"She has sealed the closet door."

"Sealed how?" Doc asked.

"The knob turns, but the door appears to be stuck."

"Why would Jane do that?" I thought aloud.

"I could hazard several guesses," Cornelius answered. "But I think the most likely answer is one of two possibilities. There is activity in the hole and she wants to keep something from coming out."

"Or us from going in," I finished for him. I wasn't a fan of either answer.

"You're reading my mind again, Violet. What am I thinking now?"

I sighed. This mind-reading game of his made me want to yank on his goatee. "You're thinking about the color green."

"Unbelievable," he said. "You must have sensed that I'm trying to choose a color for the third-floor hallway in my hotel, and know that green is the color of nature and therefore represents harmony."

"Yep." I shot Doc a what-are-the-chances glance. "That's what happened."

"Oh, that reminds me." Cornelius turned to Doc. "I read a paper concerning research that showed the child of two mediums has a 48.75 percent chance of being born with the combined extrasensory abilities of both parents. Now might be the optimal time to mate if Violet is in estrous."

I gasped, my cheeks warming.

Doc grinned at me. "Well, I don't have any pumpkins handy, but we could give 'er a whirl."

Cornelius nodded. "I'll leave you to it then." And he did, exiting via the back door, leaving Doc and me alone.

"Damn, Killer," he said, his grin fading. "Cornelius is right. You really knocked this one out of the park."

"Did you talk to Cooper this morning about what he witnessed?"

"A little. He's still shaken up, I think, even though he's trying to hide it." He smirked. "And his eye hurts."

I groaned. "In spite of Cornelius's ideas, I don't understand how I could hurt Cooper yet nobody else could even see him."

"Cornelius has a lot of solid theories and the terms he tossed around fit the puzzle, but when it comes down to it, I think there's one answer that stands out above all others."

I knew the answer. "I'm an executioner."

"An executioner," he said, rising and coming around to the front of his desk. "And now a timekeeper, too." He caught my arm and tugged me to my feet. "I have a feeling there will be things that occur from here on out that might not even have names in the paranormal community. Events that will leave us scratching our heads."

"I'll be happy if everyone just keeps breathing."

He pulled me closer, his arms wrapping around me. "Me, too, Killer."

I buried my face in his neck. He smelled like a sunny day in the woods, making me want to lie down on a blanket next to him and stare up at the trees. We could pretend everything was normal. He was just a boy and I was just a girl in a world with no monsters, ghosts, or paranormal hunters coming to remove me from the picture.

Hunters—that reminded me of something. "What do you think Ms. Wolff meant about the cages being open?" I asked him.

"Your guess is as good as mine, but I doubt she's talking about hamsters running amok."

"Or chickens."

I felt his quiet laughter under my cheek. "Speaking of poultry," he said. "Elvis left an egg in my shoe last night."

"Ahh, she's adopted you." I lifted my head, resting my chin on his chest. "I need a let's-make-up gift for Cooper, so he doesn't hate me forever and a day for that black eye."

He kissed my forehead. "My little bruiser. I warned him about you."

I turned in his arms, resting back against him. For a few seconds, I stood there soaking up his warmth as I watched traffic roll by outside the window.

"Doc, did Cooper remember the strands of hair in Ms. Wolff's hand before I brought it up to the group last night?"

Doc hadn't until I'd told him about it after the séance when we had a moment alone. Aunt Zoe and Harvey didn't either. Cooper didn't indicate one way or another when I'd explained to everyone around Aunt Zoe's table that the hair had been the main reason why I'd returned to that apartment. It *appeared* that finishing the second time loop had indeed erased that piece of evidence from existence along with everyone's memory about it—everyone's but mine.

However, I'd know for sure if that key piece of evidence against me in the Ms. Wolff case still existed by the end of today.

"He remembered the hair," Doc said. "But Coop was struggling to figure out the details of how he returned to his physical form. He said he looked in Ms. Wolff's bedroom mirror and saw something flicker behind him, like a glitch on a computer screen or TV. Then he was standing inside the bedroom with several clocks missing and Hawke's sleeping bag on the floor next to the bed. He heard you start screaming and found you in the hall outside of Ms. Wolff's door."

I covered Doc's hands with mine, lacing my fingers through his. "That was you, wasn't it? Cooper returning to the normal world, I mean."

"I'd been able to keep tabs on his energy initially as he followed you downstairs and into the apartment. But then you nose-tackled Coop and I lost him."

Chuckling, I smiled up at Doc. "I didn't nose-tackle Cooper."

"Those were his words, not mine."

"Cooper's a drama queen."

"I'll tell him you said that next time he complains."

"Oh, God. No! He'll bite me."

"Well, you are very soft and tasty." He nuzzled my neck for a moment before continuing. "I couldn't sense Coop after you two made contact until he stepped in front of that mirror. Then he was back in view and I pulled him through immediately before I lost him again."

I knew what that felt like. Freesia had once pulled me through a mirror, the same one, in fact, that Doc had used to snag Cooper. The very mirror that I'd shattered last month and no longer existed. How could Doc use that mirror to … Never mind. Time certainly was a tricky devil.

"What about me?" I asked. "Did you lose me?"

"I never had you."

I turned in his arms, facing him again. "What do you mean?"

"When we're playing with realms and timelines, all I can hope to do is keep up with you. I can try to second-guess your next step like I did at the Hessler House with Wilda and her mother, moving things out of your way and protecting you within the limits of my abilities."

Oh, jeez. With all of this Ms. Wolff stuff, I'd forgotten about Wilda and her mother. Could I dare to hope they'd moved on from Deadwood, not to be heard from again? Probably not.

"But," Doc continued with his explanation. "There are no guarantees."

No guarantees. That was sort of my motto now, according to Ms. Wolff. I blew out a sigh. "I'm a killer, Doc."

He tipped my chin up, his smile tender. "Yeah, but I still think you're really swell."

I chuckled. "You're pretty special yourself." I wrapped my arms around his neck. I pressed against him, letting him warm me to the core. "So, where do we go from here?"

"I'd say my backroom with the door locked tight, but I have a client coming in about ten minutes."

I wiggled my eyebrows at him. "All we need is five."

He kissed me, his tongue tasting my lower lip before he pulled away. "Don't tempt me, woman."

"Me? Tempt you? Never." I batted my eyelashes at him. "But I am wearing my boots today, and I don't believe you've seen these panties I have on yet. They have these cute little bows on each hip."

With a groan, he turned me around and marched me to the door, grabbing my purse and coat along the way. "I'm spending the night again in your bed," he told me.

"Do I have a choice in the matter?"

"Nope." He helped me with my coat. "Harvey is moving into my house and bringing ol' Red along. I'm going to give them a couple of nights to settle in without me there."

I took my purse from him. "What about Cooper?"

"If you're in the clear, he told me he'll head back to my place tonight."

Cooper had crashed on the couch last night, according to Aunt Zoe.

"Hmmm." I looked Doc up and down, admiring his form in his gray pants and dark red button-up shirt. "I suppose I could make room for you under my covers again."

"That'd be mighty generous of you, ma'am." He leaned closer, running his finger along my jawline. "I'll make it worth your while."

I deliberately licked my lips. "I'm your huckleberry."

He laughed and planted a soft one on my mouth. "Call me later, Boots."

"Happy number crunching." I closed the door behind me.

I walked next door, about to step inside Calamity Jane's when a gust of wind stole the hat of an older man across the street, tumbling it toward me. I caught it, crossing the street to hand it to him. "Thank you," he said, continuing on his way with the hat jammed on tight.

I turned to head back to Calamity Jane's.

"Hey, Parker!" I heard a voice that made me cringe.

The sight of Detective Hawke striding my way made me growl.

"You need to come to the police station."

"Now?"

"The sooner the better."

Shit. My heart clutched itself and stumbled around in my chest. "I thought this wasn't going to happen until tomorrow."

"What's going to happen tomorrow?" he asked.

"Isn't that the big day?" I remained purposely vague.

"What the hell are you talking about?"

Wait, what was he talking about?

I searched his face to see if he was messing with me. Could it have really worked? Was I actually free and clear of Ms. Wolff's murder, at least for now?

"Your birthday?" It came out a question by accident.

"Tomorrow isn't my birthday."

"Oh, I thought … I thought that was why you went out with Natalie and Freesia last night." As far as I knew they had all gone to Rapid to get him out of his apartment, but maybe tripping through time had caused a bigger ripple than I'd thought.

"We went out to celebrate Nat's upcoming birthday," he explained. I bristled at his shortening of Natalie's name.

"That's right. I was confused."

"I'm not surprised. You seem to get 'confused' on details, especially when it comes to the murders around here, which I find awfully convenient."

"I'm sure you do."

He gave me his best gunslinger glare. "It's probably all of that eye of newt you've been sniffing, Witch."

Well, damn. Playing around in the past hadn't changed that part of our relationship. That made me wonder what else hadn't changed.

"Don't you think for a minute, Parker, that I've forgotten about the hex you put on me."

Which in particular, dickwad? I bit my tongue.

"I have some crime scene photos you need to see."

"Why?"

"Cooper thinks you might have some insight."

"Detective Cooper said that?" Aloud? To someone else? I looked up at the sky. Where were the flying pigs?

"Yeah," Hawke continued. "But I suspect your insight is tied to the fact that you are responsible, at least in part."

Of course he would. I gave him a polite smile. "I'll make an appointment through Detective Cooper to see those pictures of yours."

"You just make sure that's all you do with my detective. If I catch wind you two are up to any hanky-panky, I'll have him put on leave so fast it will make both of your heads spin."

I could only imagine how Cooper would have reacted to that monologue. Rather than leaning closer and biting his head off, I started to walk away. But then one last question for the big buffoon sprang to mind. "Detective Hawke?" I called to his back.

He turned around. "What?"

"I was just wondering about something."

"Hurry up with it, Parker. Some of us have murders to pin on our number-one suspect."

"I'd expect that from you, *snollyguster*."

He barked three times. Spit flew through the steam of his breath, the barks echoing in the cold morning air.

"That sounds good to me," I said, giving him a thumbs-up.

"What sounds good?" His upper lip was still wrinkled in a snarl.

"Taking a look at those pictures of yours sometime. See you later." I turned away, adding under my breath, "Law dog."

Mona was in the office when I stepped inside.

"Hi, Vi." She did a double take when she looked up at me. "You look tired."

"I had a rough night."

"Nightmares again?"

I nodded. Only this time the nightmares had happened while I was awake.

"Maybe you should take the day off."

I liked the sound of that, but … "I need to take care of some paperwork for those three new clients Jerry's billboard hooked."

She scowled. "I hate to say it, but that billboard of his seems to be working for both Ben and you."

"And all of us, judging from our recent second-place ranking."

Ray came in, and I got lost in my paperwork, doing my best to ignore the glares he kept shooting my way. I didn't know what I'd done to earn his sneers this morning. I couldn't remember yanking on his chain recently, only Detective Hawke's.

Natalie called a short time later. I stepped out the back door, shivering in the cold while she filled me in on her evening with Detective Hawke. Lucky for her, Freesia had helped to divert the big buttinski's attention. I gave Natalie the lowdown about what had happened at the Galena House, catching her up to date. After she agreed to come to supper tonight, I hung up and returned to work.

Jerry and Ben were out most of the morning. If Mona or Ray mentioned why, I wasn't paying attention. My mind was back in Ms. Wolff's apartment, replaying the scene time and again, trying to figure out if Cornelius was right about something. Doc had mentioned Cooper seeing glitches, which had spurred a memory of my own. Something I would describe as a glitch had occurred each time the song changed on that old radio. Was last night's adventure a "haunting"? As in one long recording playing over and over that I was part of somehow? Or had I gone back in time and repeated the second loop?

By the time lunch rolled around, my head was throbbing in spite of the acetaminophen I'd taken. The three cups of coffee since I'd started working probably hadn't helped.

Ray stood and stretched, making a point of interrupting me. "Blondie, I'm heading to lunch."

I frowned across at him. "And I care because?"

Mona had run down the street to grab something to eat and would be back any minute now. I didn't need to cover for Ray, so what was with the announcement?

"Jerry and I are meeting with your good buddy today."

I sat back, crossing my arms. "And which buddy is that, Ray?"

"Tiffany Sugarbell. She has a proposal for Jerry that I don't think he's going to be able to resist."

I'd done enough mind-reading with Cornelius this morning. "Let's have it, Ray. If you gloat on it much more, you'll choke and I'll be damned if I do the Heimlich maneuver on you."

"I'll keep it simple for you: There's a new girl in town. Say *Adios*, Blondie."

My gut torpedoed south. Great. Just freaking wonderful. Now I'd have two back-stabbing little bitches to face off with every day.

I huffed. Fine, bring it. If I could take on a bone cruncher and a *lidérc*, I could handle Ray and Tiffany tag-teaming up on my ass.

"Okay." I smiled at Ray and raised my cup of coffee to him. "*Adios*, motherfucker."

He stalked over to me, his over-tanned face puckered up tight. "You're going down, Blondie. And I'm going to enjoy watching you fall flat on your face."

I rolled my eyes. "Ray, your ass must be so jealous of all the shit that keeps coming out of your mouth."

The front door jingled. Mona was back.

She took one look at Ray and me and scowled. "Ray, isn't it time for you to go to lunch?"

"Yeah, Red. I was just on my way out." Under his breath he added, "Just like you, Blondie."

I laughed. "That's a good story, Ray, but in what chapter do you shut the hell up?"

Mona looked over, her eyebrows lifted.

"Nice mouth, Violet," Ray said, pretending to be offended.

I flipped him off to his face right in front of Mona. "I'd tell you to go fuck yourself, douchebag, but that would be cruel and unusual punishment."

Mona's brows rose even higher, her lips pressed tight.

"Wait until Jerry hears about this," Ray said and headed for the back door. "He's going to jump all over Tiffany Sugarbell." He slammed the door behind him.

Mona lowered her glasses. "If he jumps all over her, I'm going to rip him to shreds."

With a heavy sigh, I lay my head on my desk. "Maybe I should go back to school. They say the healthcare industry is growing like crazy."

"Come on, Vi. You're not going to give up that easily, are you?"

"Tiffany's claws are really sharp."

"True, but I have one hell of a bite."

I raised my head.

She smiled, showing her teeth. "It's just getting interesting now."

I nodded slowly. "I'll have your back if you have mine."

"Deal." She looked me over. "Go home. Get some rest. The real estate world will make it a day without you."

I took her advice and packed up, squeezing her shoulder on the way out.

I called Natalie as soon as I got home and asked her to pick up the kids, then crawled into my bed, hugged the pillow that still smelled like Doc, and went to sleep.

* * *

Something smelled very cheesy and delicious. I sat up in bed, my room dark and cool. Someone had shut my bedroom door, but the aroma of baked cheese had seeped through the cracks.

I scrubbed my hands over my face and made my way downstairs, drawn by not only my stomach's need for food, but also the sound of laughter. Pausing in the kitchen's entryway, I smiled.

Doc was helping Layne set the table while Addy was playing tic-tac-toe with Natalie, giggling while Natalie tried to tickle her to distraction. Aunt Zoe was looking over Harvey's shoulder as he stirred something on the stove.

Norman Rockwell, eat your heart out.

Doc looked up at me. His gaze warmed, his smile smoldering at the corners. "Look, Layne. Your mom has bed head."

Layne turned around at the same time the doorbell rang and laughed. "Your hair looks like a crazy lady's, Mom."

"She is one wild woman," Doc said and winked at me.

"Don't forget nutty like squirrel poop," Natalie added, which made both kids break out in giggles.

I wrinkled my nose at her and went to answer the door, smoothing down my hair on the way.

Cooper stood on the porch.

"Why did you ring the doorbell?" I asked.

"Isn't that what visitors do?"

"Yeah, but you practically live here." I held the door wide.

He stepped inside and handed me an envelope. "Good news," he said as he took off his coat.

Doc must have heard us, because he joined us in the dining room. "What is it?"

"I think we're in the clear," he said. "There was no mention of hair or a lab report all day. When I searched the evidence log, there was nothing there either."

I fell back against Doc, relieved. While I'd tested Hawke earlier, I was still worried he might be toying with me.

"But my eye hurts like a son of a bitch, Parker."

I cupped my hand around my ear and leaned toward him. "What was that, Cooper? Your lips are moving, but I can't hear you."

He glowered at me. "Would it kill you to say you're sorry?"

"Fine. Cooper, I'm sorry I gave you a black eye."

He nodded. "You're forgiven."

"Really?" That seemed too easy. I'd expected the mention of handcuffs at least.

"No. I'm still pissed." He pointed at his black eye. "You have no idea how much shit I had to take today because of this."

"You didn't tell them I did it, did you?"

"I didn't need to. They all know I've been hanging around you and came to the same conclusion about Rocky Parker."

I grimaced.

"What's that?" Doc asked, pointing at the envelope in my hand.

"It was stuck under Parker's windshield wiper."

I opened it slowly, expecting a cryptic note. Finding a Christmas card from Mr. Stinkleskine instead made me sigh in relief. I handed it to Doc and headed for the kitchen. "Wash your hands, Cooper. It's time to eat."

Natalie looked up at the sound of his name, a small smile hovering on her lips. When she caught me staring at her, she lowered her gaze back to Addy's game of tic-tac-toe.

The phone rang as we were all sitting down to eat the three-cheese macaroni casserole covered with bacon bits. Aunt Zoe got up to get it. "You're late, Martin," she said into the phone, not even bothering with a "Hello."

I shot Doc a raised brow. She'd invited Reid for dinner?

"Oh, I'm sorry. One minute." She held the phone toward me. "It's for you."

I took it while sitting. "Hello?"

"Good evening, *Scharfrichter*."

I knew the voice immediately. "Mr. Black."

Everyone but the kids froze, their eyes on me.

"We need to talk," he said.

"About what in particular?"

"Keeping track of time and those within it."

"Will this be my first lesson?"

"Call it what you will."

"When and where?"

"I'll be in touch as soon as I find somewhere safe."

Safe from what, I wondered.

He hung up before I could ask.

Nice. He must have been taking phone etiquette lessons from Cooper.

I walked over and put the phone back on the charger. "That was my new friend from work," I told everyone, keeping things light and easy due to little ears in the room. "He's going to catch me up to speed on fun and games with clocks sometime soon."

Aunt Zoe sighed. "This is highly untraditional."

"So am I, according to Prudence."

"Who's Prudence?" Addy asked.

"Another work friend of your mom's," Natalie said.

I sat back down to supper. Doc squeezed my leg under the table, leaning over to kiss my temple. His show of support made me almost as happy as the mound of cheesy macaroni covered with bacon bits on my plate.

Aunt Zoe excused herself to turn on some holiday music for ambiance as we chowed down. I paused midway through my pile of cheesy goodness to look at the people around me. Damn, I was a lucky little executioner. Now if I could just make it through New Year's in one piece.

I started to dig back into my macaroni and paused, listening.

Funny, I didn't remember a cuckoo sound in *Jingle Bells*. The cuckoo kept going after the song ended. I lowered my fork, my heart starting to pound in rhythm with it.

"Do you hear that?" I asked Doc, quietly.

"Hear what?"

Uh-oh.

"I'll be right back," I told him and left the table.

I was standing at the hall closet when Doc joined me. "What's wrong?"

I pointed down at the clock in the box.

"What about it?"

I lifted it and set it on the dining room table. "Do you see that?"

"No. What?"

I frowned. "It's cuckooing."

"Shit."

Cooper joined us. "What's going on?"

"The clock is cuckooing," Doc told him.

"I don't hear it."

"Violet does."

"Oh, hell." Cooper muttered. "Someone is trying to come through."

I nodded, chewing on my lower lip.

"Oh, no," I whispered a couple of heartbeats later.

"What?"

"It stopped."

"That's good, isn't it?" Cooper asked.

"Maybe," I said.

I stood watching the clock hands, waiting, praying.

Please don't let the hands start moving.

Please give me a little more time.

Please …

The second-hand twitched. It began to move one small jump at a time.

"It's here." I frowned up at Doc. "Now what?"

He squeezed my hand. "It's time to kick some ass, Killer."

Cooper swore. "Out of the frying pan and into the fire."

The End … for now

Next up in the Deadwood Mystery Series: The Purple Door Saloon with
Violet and Natalie in ... *Deadwood Shorts: Tequila & Time*
(AVAILABLE NOW!)

Tequila is a slippery devil ...
Tequila is a slivvery depil ...
Tequila issa slipperppery debil ... depil ...

Recipe for drunken laughter:
Take two best friends since childhood;
Add four shots of tequila each;
Sprinkle in a handful of secrets;
Shake.

Given the right amount of *Tequila & Time*, even the deepest secrets
between two friends will rise to the surface.

About the Author

Ann Charles is USA Today bestselling author who writes award-winning mysteries that are splashed with humor, romance, paranormal, and whatever else she feels like throwing into the mix. When she is not dabbling in fiction, arm-wrestling with her children, attempting to seduce her husband, or arguing with her sassy cat, she is daydreaming of lounging poolside at a fancy resort with a blended margarita in one hand and a great book in the other.

Facebook (Personal Page):
http://www.facebook.com/ann.charles.author

Facebook (Author Page):
http://www.facebook.com/pages/Ann-Charles/37302789804?ref=share

Twitter (as Ann W. Charles):
http://twitter.com/AnnWCharles

Ann Charles Website:
http://www.anncharles.com

More Books by Ann

Books in the Deadwood Mystery Series

**WINNER of the 2010 Daphne du Maurier Award
for Excellence in Mystery/Suspense**

**WINNER of the 2011 Romance Writers of
America® Golden Heart Award for Best Novel
with Strong Romantic Elements**

Welcome to Deadwood—the Ann Charles version. The world I have created is a blend of present day and past, of fiction and non-fiction. What's real and what isn't is for you to determine as the series develops, the characters evolve, and I write the stories line by line. I will tell you one thing about the series—it's going to run on for quite a while, and Violet Parker will have to hang on and persevere through the crazy adventures I have planned for her. Poor, poor Violet. It's a good thing she has a lot of gumption to keep her going!

Short Stories from Ann's
Deadwood Mystery Series

The Deadwood Shorts collection includes short stories featuring the characters of the Deadwood Mystery series. Each tale not only explains more of Violet's history, but also gives a little history of the other characters you know and love from the series. Rather than filling the main novels in the series with these short side stories, I've put them into a growing Deadwood Shorts collection for more reading fun.

The Jackrabbit Junction Mystery Series

Bestseller in Women Sleuth Mystery and Romantic Suspense

Welcome to the Dancing Winnebagos RV Park. Down here in Jackrabbit Junction, Arizona, Claire Morgan and her rabble-rousing sisters are really good at getting into trouble—BIG trouble (the land your butt in jail kind of trouble). This rowdy, laugh-aloud mystery series is packed with action, suspense, adventure, and relationship snafus. Full of colorful characters and twisted up plots, the stories of the Morgan sisters will keep you wondering what kind of a screwball mess they are going to land in next.

The Dig Site Mystery Series

Welcome to the jungle—the steamy Maya jungle that is, filled with ancient ruins, deadly secrets, and quirky characters. Quint Parker, renowned photojournalist (and lousy amateur detective), is in for a whirlwind of adventure and suspense as he and archaeologist Dr. Angelica Garcia get tangled up in mysteries from the past and present in exotic dig sites. Loaded with action and laughs, along with all sorts of steamy heat, these two will keep you sweating along with them as they do their best to make it out of the jungle alive in every book.

CPSIA information can be obtained
at www.ICGtesting.com
Printed in the USA
LVHW111951011220
673137LV00002B/164

9 781940 364537

7